PRAISE FOR MARETH GRIFFITH

REVIEWS FROM THE ORIGINAL PUBLICATION

Equal parts amusing and unnerving, COURT OF TWILIGHT is urban fantasy with a sci-fi kick, perfect for readers who are ready for a taste of something beyond angels, demons and shadow hunters.

— BOOKS BY SMITHIES

Court of Twilight's a pleasant story with some darker undertones; full of mystery and a modern-day take on the Fae world.

— KATE COE, SFF WORLD

Everything about this felt new and imaginative—the concept of the novel as a whole, the kind of threats faced by the characters, the concept of the fantastical elements. I never knew where it was going and I'm desperate for the sequel so that my questions can be answered.

— AMAZON REVIEW

THE YEAR KING

MARETH GRIFFITH

Originally Published in 2017 via Parvus Press as

Court of Twilight

The Year King

Copyright © 2017 by Mareth Griffith

Second edition copyright © 2018

Third edition copyright © 2020

Cover Art by Kaitlynn Jolley

Interior Design Elements by Jessica Lynn Henry

Paperback ISBN 978-1-7356505-0-0

eBook ISBN 978-1-73565051-7

Author photo courtesy UnCruise Adventures

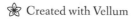 Created with Vellum

CHAPTER 1

The strange man was crouched among the flower boxes, sitting so still that Ivy didn't see him until she nearly stepped on him. Ivy stumbled back, nearly dropping her groceries, and stifled a surprised yell. The man blinked, as though the noise had startled him. He didn't say a word, staring owlishly at Ivy from underneath a long fringe of dark hair. Under the bangs, his face was dotted with shiny patches of skin that looked almost like burn marks, twisted and uncomfortable additions to the usual complement of features.

Strange people turning up on the front step was not something that usually happened in a place as gentrified as Howth. The man looked as though he ought to be sitting at a bus stop in Finglas in the wee hours of the morning, not in front of a row of townhouses in the middle of the afternoon. Still, there was no reason to think the fellow was creepy based on how he looked. Perhaps he was a friend of Mr. Abernathy's. Perhaps he was a meter reader from the gas company, though that still didn't explain what he was doing sitting among the flower boxes. Demi would pitch a fit if she knew.

"Um, hello?" Ivy said, taking a firmer hold on her purse.

The fellow blinked, glancing over his shoulder at the bare branches of the azaleas as though he thought Ivy might actually be talking to someone else.

"Could you possibly tell me; do you live here?" he asked. He spoke loudly and distinctly, as though he were addressing a particularly elderly pensioner, or someone who didn't speak English.

"Yes," Ivy said, trying not to look as though she were staring.

"In Number 42B, Thormanby Road?"

"That's me," Ivy confirmed, gesturing with her shopping bag to the townhouse behind her. Like every other house on the street, Number 42 was a trim two-storied townhouse, the abundance of doors and postboxes the most obvious sign that the house had been chopped into multiple apartments.

"Were you looking for someone?" Ivy asked. Maybe he was looking for Mr. Abernathy, in the adjoining flat. Or perhaps the red-haired widower the next house over. Aside from the number on the postbox, and the azaleas growing in the flower boxes, there was little to distinguish Number 42B from its nearest neighbors.

"Yes, and it isn't you," he said, sounding disappointed. He looked at the jumble of postboxes, then at Ivy, squinting shortsightedly at her. "Have we met before? It's far too early, but I could have sworn..."

The man trailed off, brushing at a bit of dirt that was clinging to his coat.

"Early for what?" Ivy asked, shifting the grocery bag to her other hip. For a moment, she wondered if he was another employee from the call center, because she *had* gotten off early today. On a usual workday, she wouldn't have been home until the streetlights were on.

But this hadn't been a usual workday, even before the strange man turned up in the front garden.

"Maths," the man said glumly. "Complicated ones. Well, that's that," he added, almost to himself. Pulling a small notebook out of his pocket, he flipped it open and crossed off something on the page. He slipped the notebook back into his coat and, without another word, headed toward the main road at the bottom of the hill.

Clearly not from the call center. Even Bonnie knew better than to hire someone for a sales job who couldn't provide a coherent answer to a simple question. When Ivy lived in Finglass, dealing with louts had been a depressingly regular occurrence; she hoped not to deal with them quite so regularly in Howth. Still, he seemed polite enough, if you didn't count the skulking in the bushes. And since whoever he was looking for didn't live here, apparently, that probably meant he wouldn't come back. Looking down the street to make sure he was gone, Ivy unlocked the door and stepped into the flat.

"I GOT YOUR APPLES," Ivy called, dropping her purse and bags on the chair by the coat rack as she knelt to unlace her boots.

"You're home early, aren't you?" Demi called from the back of the flat. It sounded like she was in the parlor. The sun lamps were on, their mustard-yellow glow visible from the hallway, mingling with the actual sunlight from the skylight at the top of the stairs.

Ivy took off her jacket, tossing it onto the coat rack between Demi's Bilberry and the encroaching vines from the nearby philodendron. A moment later, she dove back into her jacket pocket, pulling out a scrunched pay stub and slipping it into her purse. It was possibly going to be her last check for a while, and it wouldn't do to be misplacing it. She walked past the coat rack into the front parlor, sidestepping a tray of spotty-looking plants with tiny purple flowers, and collapsed into the depths of Demi's love seat.

"There was a man outside when I came in," said Ivy.

"Yes, someone rang the door a while ago," said Demi distractedly. She was standing in front of a long row of hanging baskets, tapping at a hygrometer with an annoyed look on her face, as though she suspected it of giving a false reading. Her hair was pulled into a thin braid, swinging between her shoulders like a pendulum as she peered at the dial. The sun lamps emphasized her lightly tanned skin, cocoa-colored and perfectly smooth, only a few shades lighter than her chestnut hair. Even dressed in sweatpants and a sweatshirt, Demi, as usual, looked stunning. She was one of those girls who managed to look pretty without putting any apparent effort toward her appearance. Only her nose, large and the tiniest bit crooked, saved her from being the sort of person who was too intimidatingly beautiful to immediately like. "Maybe around noon?"

If that was right, the fellow had been waiting in the flower boxes for nearly two hours.

"Did you answer the door?" Ivy asked, even though she already knew what Demi would say.

"You know I never bother with that," said Demi airily, which was true. It was one of the more infuriating things about having Demi as a flatmate: Ivy was forever answering the door, because Demi never bothered with it. This was only the first of

Demi's numerous strange and annoying habits. Though it didn't compare to the houseplants. The most annoying thing about Demi definitely had to be the houseplants. Most of them were here in the parlor: a half dozen hanging baskets over-flowing with flower-covered vines, several small palm trees in free-standing pots, as well as smaller leaf-filled pots dotting both end tables, the TV stand, and the top two rows of the book shelf. When the sun lamps were on, Demi's parlor looked like an exhibit room that had somehow escaped from the botany section of the Dublin Natural History Museum. The plants in the parlor weren't the end of it either. There were more plants in Demi's bedroom, as well as the philodendrons in the hall-way, and two trays of herbs growing on the kitchen windowsill.

"I don't think it was the same fellow," said Ivy. "That must have been hours ago; he couldn't have been waiting outside the whole time."

"Did he say what he wanted?" Demi asked, giving a final poke at the hygrometer and walking over to the tray of spotty-looking plants, still covered with stickers from the greenhouse in Dún Laoghaire. "Do you think these fuchsia would do alright in the downstairs bathroom? I put a full-spectrum bulb in there this morning; I'm just wondering about the humidity."

Ivy leaned across the love seat, peering at what she assumed were the fuchsia. The greenhouse's invoice was still sticking out of the side of their crate; Ivy pulled it out to get a better look at Demi's newest acquisitions.

"They match the shower curtain," Ivy offered with a shrug. At least the fuchsia weren't going to be living in *her* bathroom. Ivy's rooms were the only part of the house which remained, for the moment, mercifully plant-free.

She glanced at the invoice from the greenhouse as she set it back on the table next to the fuchsia. Or, at least, Ivy assumed it was an invoice. The back of the paper was covered with a glossy picture of what looked like a high-end block of condominiums, all towering stone buildings covered in turrets and gables. It looked like the sort of ritzy place that would come with a rooftop garden and its own on-site meditation studio.

Sweeping past the table, Demi picked up the invoice and scowled at it, making Ivy briefly wonder how much the flowers had cost. Still frowning, Demi set the invoice gently on top of the fuchsia as she picked up the tray.

"He just asked me if I lived here and then he left," Ivy added, unbuttoning the top button on her blouse. With the sun lamps on, it felt almost too warm to stay in the parlor. "Maybe he was with the census. He was saying something about maths —and he had these weird scars on his face."

Very abruptly, Demi fumbled with the fuchsia, scattering topsoil across the carpet as she hastily set the tray back on the table. She dropped to her knees, scooping up the dirt with her hands.

"Is that how they do it?" Demi asked after a moment. "Census people, you know. Just walk around and ask questions? Strange. You said you picked up the apples?"

"In the hall," said Ivy, and started to get up, but Demi shook her head, shooing her flatmate back into the love seat.

"I'll get them in a minute, I just want to get the fuchsia settled in first."

Second annoying trait about Demi—she was militantly vegan. Usually, Demi had boxes of organic whole foods delivered from some high-end produce shop in Grafton Street, but she frequently asked Ivy to pick up things from the grocery on her way home from work. Not that Ivy minded; the grocery wasn't very far. But Demi seemed to go to extraordinary lengths to avoid going there herself—or anywhere else where she might be expected to have to talk to people.

"Everything go alright at work?" Demi asked. "I hope you didn't get more crying ones today."

"Nothing bad on the phone," said Ivy carefully, thinking of the pay stub sitting in her purse. "But they sacked the lot of us today. Lost out on a contract, and they're outsourcing the whole thing to India. Laid off just about the whole department."

A call center job working atrocious hours ought to be the sort of position one was almost grateful to lose. But compared to the sticky counters and grease-stained wallpapers at Ivy's previous job at the Dream Cones takeaway, Eirecom's faux-leather desk chairs and ergonomic keyboards seemed appealingly sophisticated. The job itself, of course, was terrible—but the mere fact that she was working in a proper office lent the tiniest veneer of glamour over the daily monotony of her calls. As though Eirecom might be the first step toward the sort of job where her supervisors didn't depend on surreptitious glances at Ivy's nametag to remember who she was.

"I'd say I'm sorry," said Demi, brushing the dirt off her hands as she got to her feet. "But you're always going on about how you hate working there. Did you really want to spend eight hours a day doing something you don't like?"

Ivy sighed. This was beginning to sound like one of those inspirational self-help articles Ivy's mother was so fond of emailing her. Not that Ivy needed any self-help articles. People lose jobs all the time. These days, it was practically normal. Nothing to feel ashamed of in the slightest. Still, Ivy felt her face redden, and it wasn't entirely due to the sun lamps.

"I still need something to pay rent, though," Ivy pointed out.

"We're paid up here through the end of the month," said Demi with a shrug. "That's loads of time. I'm sure something will come along before that."

Privately, Ivy doubted that. Even in Dublin, there weren't

very many places that would be falling over themselves to hire a twenty-year-old ex-call-center employee. She'd been lucky to get on with Eirecom in the first place. Ivy didn't want to think about how long it might be until she found another job. She might be out of work for months, scraping together rent from the dole payments. Or moving back in with her Dad and step-mother in East Worring. Or living on the street and creeping about in other people's front gardens, like the strange man outside.

Ivy got up from the love seat, suddenly eager to get out of the jungle-like heat of the parlor. Maybe Demi was right, and something would come along soon. Then again, Ivy wasn't sure she should put much faith in job advice coming from someone who spent most days sitting in her sweatpants in front of her computer, or watching cooking shows on the telly, or obsessing over her houseplants.

"I've got the rent for this month," Ivy began hesitantly. "But next month, if I'm a little late with the check—"

"Really, Ivy," Demi interrupted, snatching the tag off the fuchsia's tray and tossing it into the rubbish bin. "That's weeks away. I wouldn't worry about it."

And with that, she picked up the tray of fuchsia and walked out of the parlor.

✦

Ivy woke the next morning to the sound of the front door slamming shut. Rolling over, she glanced at her alarm clock, momentarily panicking when she saw it was already past nine o'clock. Ivy had gotten one leg out of bed before she remembered she hadn't set her alarm, and her other leg out of bed before she remembered *why* she hadn't set her alarm. The call center was closed, and Ivy wouldn't be going to work there, today or ever again. She didn't quite know if she was happy about that or not.

Sighing, Ivy pushed her hair out of her face and grabbed a sweatshirt from the pile of dirty clothes at the foot of her bed. The crinkled envelope, with the abysmally small final paycheck, was still sitting on the desk where she'd dumped it out of her purse the previous night. Internet classifieds first, Ivy thought, pulling a sweatshirt over her head. Then she'd see if there were any likely job leads listed in the Dublin papers.

First, though, breakfast. Ivy came down the stairs, pulling her hair back into a quick, untidy bun. Demi's Bilberry coat was gone from the coat rack, but there were traces of water in the hall leading toward the parlor, as though someone had recently come through with wet shoes. Had Demi been in and out of the flat already? Or perhaps Mr. Kimball had finally come to fix the dripping pipe under the sink.

Ivy stepped around the wet spots, following the footprints down the hall.

"Mr. Kimball?" she called, as she stepped into the kitchen.

A strange man in a green coat was crouched by the dishwasher, peering into one of the lower cupboards, a bag of apples and two bulk sacks of chia seeds sitting at his feet. The fellow jumped, making Ivy startle as well. As he turned, the man tripped over the bags of chia seeds and caught himself on the side of the fridge, sending a shower of magnets, photographs, and bits of paper falling to the floor.

"Damn it," he muttered, wincing at the noise and looking nervously at Ivy, who was nervously looking right back. The man wasn't Mr. Kimball; Ivy tried to remember if the fellow might be one of his nephews.

"I'm terribly sorry," the man said, wiggling his fingers in a tiny wave. "I didn't know Demi had an, erm. . . ."

"A flatmate?" Ivy finished, coming a hesitant step further

into the room. The man, plastered against the refrigerator and still regarding Ivy with an unsettled look, seemed just as startled as she was. His hair was dark, longish and furiously uncombed; a black-and-white scarf hung loosely about his shoulders. Beneath the unbuttoned coat was a vibrantly blue paisley shirt, giving him the look of a fellow you might find loitering in the vinyl section of a downtown record store. "Yep, that's me. Did Mr. Kimball send you about the sink?"

The man shook his head, looking confused. "No, Demi, erm, sent me about the, um, aspidistra," he said hesitantly. "Worried it's ailing. Or, em, dying." He paused, as if he thought the plant's impending demise might be too delicate a subject to bring up in casual conversation. "She never... mentioned anything about it?"

Ivy hesitated, trying to remember if Demi had said anything about any of the plants doing poorly. Possibly—she fretted over them constantly, but Ivy didn't always follow her sometimes-lengthy explanations about fertilizer strength, relative humidity, or nutrient thermometers. And even if the aspidistras were dying, that still didn't explain why this fellow was standing in her kitchen.

"No, she didn't," said Ivy, crossing her arms. "You know Demi how, exactly?"

"Dublin Orchid-Growers' Association," he said, immediately looking more at ease. "I cultivated a prize-winning *Phalaenopsis bellina* a few years back."

Ivy relaxed slightly; if he really was a prize-winning orchid grower, it made sense that he and Demi knew each other. That still didn't explain what he was doing in her flat, but probably it meant he wasn't some random housebreaker. Also, Ivy didn't think random housebreakers would use Latin plant names in conversation.

Apologetically, the man began gathering up the magnets

and papers that had fallen off the fridge. "Said I could let myself in," he explained, hurriedly slapping magnets on the corners of one of the fallen photos—a snapshot of Ivy and her twin step-brothers at the stadium in Croke Park. "Would've rang the bell if I'd known anyone was home. I didn't mean to startle you."

Ivy narrowed her eyes; she'd been walking around upstairs for several minutes; the creaking floorboards should have been audible from every room on the ground floor. Maybe he'd thought the noise was coming from Mr. Abernathy's apartment.

"I'm supposed to be at the call center by now." Ivy caught herself; she wasn't supposed to be at the call center, this morning or ever again. "Usually, I mean. Just not today."

She felt her cheeks redden, and wished she hadn't brought up the call center at all. She was used to acquaintances giving her pitying looks when they found out she worked at one; when people found out she'd been fired from one, Ivy suspected the pitying looks would be worse. "The aspidistras are in the parlor," she added suspiciously. "And Demi's going to pitch a fit if her chia seeds end up on the wrong shelf."

"You know about the food, then," the man said brightly, picking up one of the bags of nuts, then squinting at the interior of the cupboard as though he were trying to remember which shelf to return it to.

That settled it. Whoever the man was, he clearly knew Demi—or at least, he clearly knew Demi had weird kitchen rules and was also obsessed with plants.

The man, squinting at the label on the sack of chia seeds, seemed harmless enough. Possibly even good-looking, if he ever bothered to comb his hair. If Demi had invited him to come by, Ivy supposed she ought to make an effort to be hospitable. Especially since Demi's interest in the health of her aspidistras apparently didn't extend to actually meeting the fellow who was doing her the favor of looking at them.

"Do you want some toast?" Ivy asked, walking over to the pantry and fishing around for a loaf of bread.

The man hastily replaced the sack of chia seeds on the shelf. "I thought you said you knew about the food," he said, looking suddenly and unaccountably nervous.

"Knew what about the food?" Ivy asked, setting the loaf of bread on the counter. "That she doesn't eat anything but nuts and lentils? All the stuff on her shelf is vegan, if that's what you're worried about. The pistachio mix in there isn't bad, if you're hungry."

He started to say something, then hesitated, as though he were debating something far more serious than pistachio mix. "Don't eat anything off that shelf," he said finally, a grim look on his face. "*Ever.* So, aspidistras." Bobbing his head nervously, he slipped past Ivy and out of the kitchen, his footsteps clattering down the hall toward the parlor.

Ivy grabbed two slices of bread and dropped them into the toaster, keeping an eye on the hallway where the orchid-grower had disappeared. A magnet shaped like a palm tree had rolled under the dishwasher; Ivy picked it up and stuck it back onto the fridge. Not only did this strange man know about the plant thing, he also knew about Demi's inexplicably odd kitchen rules. That wasn't the sort of thing likely to come up in a Dublin Orchid-Growers' Association meeting.

Maybe he was a boyfriend. Or an ex. If they'd shared a kitchen, that would explain why he knew about never cooking with her saucepans, or never borrowing anything from her shelves in the pantry.

Curious, Ivy pulled the toast out of the toaster before it was even half done, dropped it on a plate and quickly slathered it with jam. Taking a bite, she followed the orchid-grower into the parlor.

She found him staring pensively at one of the hanging pots, nose to nose with a cluster of star-shaped pink-and-white flowers peering from among a tangle of flattened leaves.

"Will it live?" Ivy asked, peering at the man across the pot. His nose had the same mildly crooked look as Demi's did, and his skin the same lightly tanned color, which Ivy had privately attributed to Demi spending too much time in the same room as her sun lamps. "The, what's it, the aspideria?"

"Aspidistra," he corrected, plastering a cheerful expression on his face, apparently with effort. "Of course it will. She's doing wonderfully with them. Shouldn't be worried at all. Hunzu," he added, apparently as an afterthought.

"What?"

"Hunzu," he repeated, louder and slower. "Didn't I say that already?"

"You did," said Ivy. "But I don't know what it means."

"It doesn't mean anything," said the man with a snort. "It's a name. My name, to be precise. Most of the time, Hunzu means me."

He said it like an owl, in two little hoots. Hoon-tzoo. Ivy found herself smiling at the fellow.

"Well, most of the time, Ivy means me," said Ivy, hoping he wasn't going to make any plant jokes.

"I suppose you'd be a distant relative of the notch-leaved Pelliona over there," Hunzu said, with a nod toward a spotty vine running up the side of the bookcase.

Inwardly, Ivy sighed, feeling her smile become the slightest bit fixed. She'd heard similar jokes far too often for her to find any of them amusing. When Ivy didn't laugh, he continued awkwardly. "How did you and Demi end up living together?"

"Craigslist," said Ivy with a shrug. "She was looking for a

roommate, and I'd been trying to get out of a flat in Finglas East for two months."

"Jumped on it right away, I suppose," said Hunzu noncommittally, bending over to examine the base of one of the potted palms.

"Not exactly," said Ivy. "She kept making excuses about not having it ready to show. I thought she'd gotten another tenant lined up, or maybe someone'd told her she ought to be charging a lot more for a place as nice as this."

"But she kept emailing you."

"Yeah," said Ivy, setting her empty plate on the end table next to a fuzzy-looking purple flower. "I didn't come to see it until almost three weeks after she listed it. But you can see, the whole place is gorgeous, and Demi's, well, once I got used to the whole plant thing. . . ."

"Yes," said Hunzu, and a mournful expression crossed his face, visible only for a moment before he turned back to the aspidistra, running his fingers along the edges of the pot.

Ivy watched him, wondering why it struck her as odd that Demi would have something as normal as a boyfriend. Even an awkward one who bragged about growing prize-winning orchids. Demi couldn't have spent her whole life just interacting with her flatmates and people on the Internet.

"You work in the City, I suppose?" Hunzu asked.

"Clontarf, actually," Ivy said, before catching herself. Turning away from the hanging basket, she went to the love seat, refolding the afghan thrown over the back. "Or, it used to be Clontarf."

"Used to be Clontarf?" Hunzu repeated, following her to the love seat and fixing Ivy with a critical look.

"I'm, um, between jobs at the moment," said Ivy with as much dignity as she could muster. It was just her luck—a nice fellow drops by the flat, and within five minutes she'd managed to bring up the fact that she'd been laid off. Biting her lip, Ivy looked around the parlor, trying to remember something interesting about one of the plants that might be enough to redirect the conversation.

"Recently?" Hunzu asked, looking far more concerned than Ivy would've expected from someone she'd only just met.

Glumly, Ivy nodded. She felt herself blushing, and suddenly wished they were still talking about plants. Or chia seeds. Or even making jokes about her name. She shouldn't feel embarrassed, Ivy told herself. Layoffs could happen to anyone these days. Hunzu wasn't even *her* friend, he was Demi's, and it didn't matter what he thought about her being out of work.

"The place was terrible," she offered with a shrug. "I suppose that helps."

"How did it happen?" Hunzu pressed. His voice seemed neutral enough, but his expression was wavering somewhere between concern and outright horror.

"It's not like I was fired," said Ivy quickly. "Well, I *was*, but it happened to everyone. They're sending the whole thing to India. Call center," she added, seeing Hunzu's baffled look. "Sold funeral packages to Australia. So we had to talk about why they'd be buying a funeral package, without really *talking* about it. There's a script, so you don't have to think so much. But every so often, you get someone who—you know—really recently. Then *I'm* the one who wants to hang up the phone."

Ivy realized she was babbling, and hurriedly shut her mouth. Hunzu was still regarding her with a worried expression, a tiny sheen of sweat standing out on his forehead.

"All the work was over the phone?"

"Yeah, mostly," said Ivy, wondering why he was so interested. Most people, when the subject of Eirecom came up, were content to tell her that working there must be dreadful (it was), and then hurriedly change the subject.

"This is going to sound strange," Hunzu said, his fingers kneading at the edges of his scarf. "When you found out—was it a letter, or did someone actually talk to you? It's important," he added, wrapping his scarf even more tightly around his fingers.

Abruptly, Ivy had a very good idea for why Demi had asked Hunzu to come over, and then arranged to be gone herself, if this was an example of Hunzu's ideas of casual and charming small talk.

"They talked to everyone," Ivy said, gritting her teeth, and making no attempt to hide her irritation. "I told you, it wasn't just me."

Hunzu took a deep breath.

"Would you like to go out for a coffee?" he blurted out, immediately hunching his shoulders as though he regretted the offer as soon as he'd said it.

Ivy blinked, trying to reconcile the fact that she'd just been asked on a date with the fact that it was barely quarter past nine, she was still in her sweatpants, and she wasn't wearing a bra.

"Not like that," Hunzu added, backing toward the potted palms as though he thought he might need to take refuge behind them if Ivy took exception to the offer. "It's just—even if it *was* a horrible place, it can't be fun to be booted out like that. There's a good tea room near the harbor. We can cut through the park on the way there; I bet the primroses are still blooming."

He wanted to go out for coffee, which Ivy didn't much like drinking, and he probably wanted to talk about plants, which Ivy didn't care about in the slightest. Maybe he was just being friendly. Maybe he was only offering to be polite, and he'd secretly be relieved if Ivy turned him down. Maybe he'd only want to talk about Demi the whole time. Or orchids, or being laid off from her job; Ivy didn't know which would be worse.

She hesitated. He seemed a nice enough fellow, he was offering to buy her coffee, and it wasn't like Ivy had anything else to do this morning. Both Demi and her friend Deirdre had been telling Ivy for months she could do a lot better than Colin, the guitar-playing, patchouli-cigarette-smoking bloke Ivy had hit it off with at a Pink Floyd cover band concert the previous fall. Though Ivy wasn't certain that an orchid-breeding hipster with hair sticking out like the crest on a cockatiel was necessarily an improvement.

If he was trying to be friendly, Ivy supposed she ought to be diplomatic about turning him down.

"I have some errands to run in the City, today probably isn't—"

"Of course," Hunzu interrupted smoothly. He sounded relieved. Only asking to be polite, then; Ivy sternly told herself she wasn't disappointed in the slightest. He started to say something else, then hesitated.

"Look," he continued, nervously fingering the edge of his scarf. "What I ought to tell you is you'd be better off moving out of this place as soon as you can."

"You want me to move out?" asked Ivy, completely taken aback. Hunzu'd known her for all of ten minutes, and he thought he knew best about where she should be living? Or with whom? Maybe he thought Demi would be better off without a flatmate. Maybe he thought anyone who worked for a telemarketer was automatically a terrible, insensitive, and interrupting person.

More charitably, maybe he figured she couldn't afford the rent now that she'd lost her job. It still wasn't any of his business.

"Which I know you won't do," he added bobbing his head

apologetically. "I'm sorry, I know you think it's none of my business—"

"No, it isn't," said Ivy, glaring at him. This was *definitely* why Demi had asked him over and then arranged not to be home.

"And if you've managed this long, another week'll hardly matter. Just don't eat the food. And something's going to be looking for her," he continued. A worried expression fell over his face as he pulled the scarf away from his neck, dabbing at the line of sweat over his eyes. "It probably won't hurt you, but it's still best to stay out of its way."

Ivy remembered the strange man with the scarred face sitting among in the flower boxes and her angry objection died in her throat.

"Out of whose way?" Ivy asked.

"Ask your flatmate," said Hunzu. Abruptly, he tugged at his scarf again, pulling it from his neck and shoving it roughly into his pocket. "She'll know. Demi's more dangerous than you realize, and so's what's coming for her. Though to be fair, it's probably not interested in you."

"What's probably not interested in me ?" Ivy asked. Nothing Hunzu was saying was making any sense. Demi was a committed introvert with an obsession for houseplants; she was quite possibly the least dangerous person Ivy knew.

"We don't quite know what it is," Hunzu said quietly. Diving into his coat pocket, he came up with a bit of paper and a stubby pencil, and began scribbling something on the sheet. "But if you ever notice that people don't seem to—I mean, if things with Demi—"

"I'm sure Demi knows your number already," said Ivy, seeing what he was writing and scowling.

"It isn't for Demi," he said, gingerly holding out the paper. "It's for you. If you ever—Look, if things ever get weird—"

"Already there, thanks," Ivy snapped.

"Not with Demi," said Hunzu. "With everyone else."

He hesitated for a moment, holding the paper out at arm's reach. Even with his coat unbuttoned and the sun lamps off, the man's face was covered in sweat. As if whatever nonsense thing he was talking about, he really was afraid of it.

Which was enough to send the tiniest shiver of apprehension up the back of Ivy's neck.

"Please, just take it," he said.

Ivy took the paper from his outstretched fingers, and slipped it into her pocket without looking at it.

Immediately, Hunzu backed away from the potted palm, cutting wide—very wide—around Ivy, as he darted into the hall. Ivy followed, coming around the corner just in time to see him open the front door.

"And think about getting out of town next week," he called as he stepped out, pulling his scarf from his pocket and wrapping it firmly about his neck. "Morning of the twentieth. Whatever you do, don't be here."

With that, the door swung shut.

Ivy stood motionless in the hallway for a long moment, then dashed to the door and threw the deadbolt. The lock securely engaged, she stood on tip-toe and peered through the door's fish-eyed security lens. She saw the man hop off the end of the sidewalk, hunched into his coat, hands shoved firmly into his pockets. Three steps and he was beyond the lens' pinhole view. She watched for another moment, resisting the urge to double check the deadbolt. It was hard to ignore the feeling that any moment, something was going to slink back up the sidewalk toward the door. Maybe it would be Hunzu.

Maybe it would be the thing Hunzu was afraid of.

Which was silly. With a sigh, Ivy dropped back to the floor, resting her head against the door for a moment. Hunzu could believe whatever he wanted; that didn't mean any of it was actually true. Hunzu was gone, and Ivy didn't have to worry about anything he said because she wasn't going to see him again. Unless—had Demi left the flat unlocked this morning, or did he have a key? She'd have to ask Demi about it. Wasn't there something in the lease about not giving out copies of the door key? At least it would be an excuse for asking Demi who the heck Hunzu was.

Turning away from the door, Ivy walked back down the hall, feeling the edges of Hunzu's paper in the pocket of her sweatshirt. It would also be an excuse for asking Demi what he'd meant about February twentieth.

And what he'd meant about something looking for her. And about that something being dangerous.

CHAPTER 2

Sighing, Ivy went back into the parlor, and sat down on the love seat. The room felt cooler than usual with the sun lamps off, the air moist with the smell of topsoil and mulch.

She pulled Hunzu's paper out of her pocket and unfolded it. On it was Hunzu's name and a mobile number, scrawled across the front of a flyer for two-for-one drinks at someplace called the Wells Street Pub. With a sigh, Ivy tossed the paper onto the end table.

Probably, she ought to rip up the flyer and shove it in the bin, and not think any more about it. But she couldn't quite discount the way Hunzu looked when he'd talked about something coming for Demi. Something dangerous. And something bad that was going to happen on the twentieth. Next Wednesday, Ivy thought, bringing up the daily planner on her phone.

Maybe she ought to find somewhere else to be that day. Visit her mother, Ivy thought absently, even though she already knew one of them would find an excuse for her to not actually come. Invite herself over to Deirdre's for a girls' night. Or surprise her step-brothers Garrett and Evan with a day at the athletics museum at Croke Park. Get out of the house for a day. Just in case.

Or maybe, thought Ivy, staring at the spackle marks on the ceiling, she should spend less time paying attention to vague, nonsensical pronouncements issued by strangers. If she needed more of those in her life, she could always go listen to the street preachers in Temple Bar. There was always a chance Demi really was involved in something dangerous, and Hunzu, somehow, knew all about it. But Ivy didn't think that was terribly likely. If Ivy hadn't heard of anything odd going on with her own flatmate, she doubted Hunzu would have known either.

She'd talk to Demi about it tonight, Ivy decided, peeling herself off the love seat and walking into the kitchen. At the very least, Demi ought to know that a crazy orchid-grower apparently had keys to their flat. And Ivy could ask if anything in particular was going to happen on the twentieth. Probably Demi would just shrug and say she didn't know what Ivy was talking about.

Filling the electric kettle, Ivy turned it on and pulled a mug out of the cupboard. A few magnets were still scattered on the floor, along with a stray photo, crumpled under the pantry door. Ivy pulled it free, trying to smooth out the corners. It was a picture of Ivy and her mother—her actual mother, not Dad's second wife Shannon—sitting on the front steps of the house at Trail's Cross. She'd nearly thrown it out rather than bring it from her old flat in Finglas, because it was her mother's boyfriend who'd taken the picture, an unpleasant and shifty man Ivy had been taught to call Uncle Patrick. But it was one of only pictures Ivy had of herself and her mother, which was why Ivy kept it on the fridge.

The teakettle whistled, and Ivy poured the water into her mug, opening the fridge to get the carton of cream. Maybe she'd meet Deirdre for drinks later this week. Maybe she'd meet a boy who wasn't a complete nut. Maybe Demi had cleaned up the fertilizer pellets she spilled on the back stairs.

Drinks with Deirdre seemed a manageable scenario. Ivy wasn't holding her breath about any of the others.

❦

IVY SPENT the next several hours updating her depressingly short CV and listlessly job hunting on the internet. By supper, she had applied to two different call centers, emailed a woman about a job at a dreary-looking pub in Oxmarten, emailed another woman about a housekeeping job in North Dublin, and watched several dozen cat videos on YouTube.

Shortly after six o'clock, Ivy heard the front door open. She closed her laptop and went down the stairs. As usual, Ivy could tell Demi had come home simply by the amount of clothing piled in the hallway. Ivy's flatmate seemed to shed things in layers, and wasn't always terribly prompt about gathering them back up again. Her coat was dangling from the coat rack, but the hat and scarf (plaid and matching) were both on the floor along with her winter boots (black and wooly, topped with something that looked suspiciously like rabbit fur). Following the trail of clothing, Ivy walked into the parlor. Demi was standing next to the love seat, the edges of her expansive wing tattoo just visible under the sleeves of her t-shirt.

"Hey Demi," Ivy called, trailing off as Demi turned around;

she was holding Hunzu's note. Holding it, in this case, meant crushing it in one hand, pink nails digging into the cream-colored paper. The paper was fluttering the slightest bit, as though the hand that held it might have been shaking.

"Ivy, did you go out at all this morning?" Demi asked.

"Yes, well, there was this fellow, he said you asked him to look at the plants, and—"

"You *saw* him?" Demi asked incredulously, and Ivy wondered why Demi was taking it so badly. Not that this was the first time Demi overreacted to something Ivy thought was trivial. "Hunzu was *here*?"

Apparently, Demi hadn't known he was coming over, which immediately made Ivy wonder what else he'd been lying about. Clearly, he knew Demi; at least, he knew about her plant obsession and her cooking habits, so he hadn't just wandered into the flat by chance. Which meant he was what, exactly? An ex? A stalker?

"This morning," said Ivy, trying to explain. "He said you asked him to look at the aspidistra—"

"You *saw* him," Demi repeated, as though she didn't quite believe it. She turned to the row of hanging pots, glaring at the aspidistra as if it were somehow to blame for Hunzu's visit. "What did he tell you?" she asked, sounding worried and still not looking at Ivy.

"A lot of nonsense," said Ivy heatedly. "Something about someone looking for you, and next Wednesday and—"

Demi turned abruptly away from the aspidistra, stalking past Ivy and into the kitchen. Ivy followed her, watching as Demi wrenched open the knick-knack drawer and pulled out a box of matches. "Damn it," she muttered as she struck one, and jumped a little as the flame caught. Carefully, Demi brought the match up to the edge of the flyer. Ivy almost put a hand on her arm to stop her, and immediately thought better of it. The paper flared as Demi dropped it onto the countertop, watching with a stony look as it burned. When the paper was reduced to little more than ash, she licked her fingers and snuffed out the remaining embers. If the remnants were hot enough to hurt, Demi's face didn't show it.

"Is everything alright?" Ivy ventured, wondering whether she ought to simply go back upstairs. Whatever was bothering Demi, she didn't look like she particularly wanted to talk. "Did Hunzu, I mean, *is* there something coming for—"

"No," said Demi, folding her arms and pacing toward the other side of the kitchen. "Don't be silly. Of course not." A moment later she was crying.

Ivy came a few steps closer. With anyone else, Ivy might have dared to give her a hug, but this was Demi, and she had a Definite Thing about being touched. Instead, Ivy switched on the radio, turning the dial to an Irish-language station, letting the incomprehensible murmur put the slightest edge of white noise over the stillness of the flat. Absently, she straightened one of the photos on the fridge, of Ivy and her parents eating funnel cake at the Stradbally Fair when she was twelve, a few months before her mum and dad split up. She'd meant to buy a frame for it when she'd moved here from Finglas; six months later it was still on the fridge.

"Would you like some hot chocolate?" Ivy asked, even though she already knew what the answer would be.

"Just some water," Demi said, wiping her eyes on the hem of her shirt as she walked back into the parlor.

Ivy got two glasses from the cabinet, and filled them from the tap, looking at the flecks of ash on the counter. What was it Hunzu had said? *Demi's more dangerous than you realize, and so's what's coming for her.* And now she didn't even have his phone number if that dangerous something actually showed up. Not that Hunzu would be Ivy's first choice for dealing with any

unforeseen weirdness. The Gardaí, perhaps. Or her uncle
Gavin, who'd once held a seat on the Dublin City Council. Or
her other uncle Liam, who'd once spent eight months in prison
on a conspiracy charge related to the attempted bombing of an
ice cream truck in Derry.

Following Demi into the parlor, Ivy set the glasses on the
end table, and sat down on the love seat. Demi was standing in
front of the hanging baskets, her fuzzy orange afghan wrapped
tightly around her shoulders, despite the warmth of the room.
She peered at one of the hygrometers, squinting at it as though
looking for an excuse to find fault with the thing. After a brief
scrutiny, she pulled it out of its pot and tossed it into the
rubbish bin. Silently, Demi made a slow circuit of the parlor,
occasionally sticking a finger into the soil of one of the pots, or
stroking a leaf, before finally settling on the overstuffed chair by
the TV stand. She didn't so much as glance at Ivy, as though it
were completely by accident they were sitting together in the
same room.

Again, Ivy wondered whether she ought to slip back
upstairs, except she wasn't sure Demi's silent treatment was
intentional. And if Demi needed to talk about something—
there weren't very many people Demi talked to. Ivy supposed
that meant she ought to make an effort. Living together made
them friends, after a fashion; Ivy suspected Demi didn't have
many of those. Not in the world outside of her computer
screen, at least.

"I'm sorry," said Ivy again. "He said you'd asked him to
come by. And—"

"I didn't," Demi replied, cutting her off. "God knows where
he got a key from. And you don't need to apologize."

"If he's bothering you, you ought to get Sean Oate to take
care of it," said Ivy, hoping to lighten the mood. Sean Oate was
the whip-thin manager of a used car dealership near Dún

Laoghaire, who had the looks of someone who'd spent time in the military, or prison, or possibly both. He did all the maintenance on Demi's blue Volkswagen Rabbit, which she dropped off every two months to have the oil and filters changed. He was muscular enough Ivy guessed he could probably bench-press one of his own cars.

Demi almost laughed at the comment. "He won't be bothering me again," she said, biting her lip, and pulled the afghan more tightly around her shoulders.

"I still don't understand what he wanted," Ivy said in a low voice. "Is there something next week—"

"Let's see about that hot chocolate," said Demi, in an artificially bright voice. She dropped the afghan on the back of the chair and went into the kitchen.

"Would you like some?" she called.

"Yes, please," answered Ivy, resigned to the fact that Demi apparently didn't want to talk about Hunzu, or any of the unsettling things Hunzu had mentioned. She got up, following Demi into the kitchen. Ivy knew from experience that Demi would thoughtfully leave the chocolate powder and the open jug of soy milk sitting out on the counter when she was finished making her own drink. From the doorway, she watched Demi measure out exactly eight ounces of milk with two tablespoons of cocoa powder. She poured the powder into the milk as she stirred, the movement causing the wing tattoo on her shoulders to flicker up and down as though she were moments away from taking flight.

When Demi finished, Ivy got a second mug from the cabinet, and dumped in two heaping spoonfuls of cocoa powder and enough milk to fill the mug all the way to the top.

"How was today?" Demi asked, as Ivy set both mugs in the microwave. "Other than him, I mean. Must be a bit like being on holiday, not having to go to work."

"I suppose," said Ivy, privately thinking that it wasn't like being on holiday at all. "Sleeping in was nice, but I think I'll be happier once I know where my next paycheck is coming from."

"Loads of time for that," Demi said, dialing in two and half minutes on medium heat. Demi was one of those people who habitually changed the temperature settings depending on what she was cooking, like the microwave manuals suggested, but no one did. It was as though she'd learned to work one by actually reading the instructions.

"I sent in my CV for a job at a bar in Oxmarten," Ivy added. "And another call center in South Dublin, nearly in Sandyford."

"Another call center?" Demi asked, sounding aghast. "But you hated working for Eirecom! Don't tell me you're going to turn 'round and go back to another one?"

"It's a paycheck, isn't it?" said Ivy defensively. "And Eirecom's the only proper office job I've had. Ought to at least be worth an interview. I can manage working sales again, until something better comes along."

"But you already know you don't like it, so why spend any more time doing it?" Demi asked, stepping toward the window and rubbing hastily at her eyes. "I mean, there's always less than time you think. Isn't that what people always say? Don't waste time with things that don't matter."

Ivy sighed. It was no good being happy and fulfilled and following your passion if at the end of the day you couldn't put food on the table. But Demi, who didn't apparently work, probably didn't see it that way. She could afford to spend all day grubbing about with plants and aerators and hygrometers and not worry about more mundane problems like rent and paychecks and job markets. If Ivy confessed that Eirecom had been her best hope for working her way up the ladder to the sort of job that allowed for things like hobbies and disposable income, Demi would probably just laugh. Or else look sad, and earnest, and sympathetic, which would be worse.

"It's not like I want to be working at call centers forever," Ivy clarified. "Just until something else comes along. Like you said, I've got ages."

The microwave beeped and Demi hastily opened the door, setting Ivy's mug on the counter. Ivy took a sip; though she'd never been a great fan of soy milk until moving in with Demi, she'd grown to like it with cocoa. Demi picked up her own mug and blew across the top, even though Ivy was sure it was precisely the right temperature already. For a moment, the kitchen was quiet save for the low Gaelic lilting of the radio.

"What if you didn't, though?" asked Demi, very softly, staring into the depths of the mug. "If you didn't have ages and ages. It's silly," she added quickly, sloshing cocoa over the side of her mug as she hastily set it back on the counter. "One day ought to be the same as another, no matter how many days you have before or after. But it isn't."

Out of nowhere, Ivy remembered Hunzu saying *do think about getting out of town next week*. February twentieth was six days away. He'd sounded so certain that something was going to happen.

"You're sure you're alright?" Ivy asked.

Demi smiled, but it seemed a fragile expression, and not in keeping with the look in her eyes.

"Of course," Demi said, switching off the radio and picking up her mug again. "Thank you for the cocoa." She padded out of the kitchen, down the hall toward her room at the back of the flat.

The days weren't the same, thought Ivy as she sipped her cocoa. Maybe they'd been the same when she was a little girl, like the grinning twelve-year-old on the fridge, her chin covered in cinnamon and powdered sugar. When no bad things happened and nothing ever changed. Until something did. Like two months later, when Ivy's dad had moved out and taken Ivy with him. Until the week it had happened, she'd had no idea it was all going to end.

Maybe that was what Demi meant about not wasting time.

Turning off the light in the kitchen, Ivy, too, took her cocoa and disappeared upstairs.

THREE IN THE morning and the stereo was on. Demi was playing the Levellers. Loudly.

It was an hour of the night when Ivy had every expectation of being able to sleep, and she was briefly convinced that every single person in her life was acting like a selfish, inscrutable bastard. Dragging herself out of bed, Ivy threw open the door to her room, ready to tromp downstairs and remind Demi that the ten o'clock quiet hours had been her own bloody idea, so could she please be good enough to stick to them herself?

She stopped dead at the top of the stairs. Demi had the stereo on and she was dancing, right there in the parlor, amidst the jungle of plants along the far wall. The room was dark, the only light from the streetlamp on the corner, fitfully streaming through the gaps in the curtains. Demi was swaying back and forth, and the tattoo on her back look like it was going to flutter right off her skin. Ivy could see her mouthing the words along with the singer.

And she was holding something: a little doll that Ivy had never seen before. Nothing more than a children's toy, really. It was a little fairy in a blue dress; Ivy could see the wings fanning back and forth as Demi swayed to the music, holding it tightly with both hands. Her eyes glittered, brighter than they should have been in such dim light.

Very quietly, Ivy slipped back to her room. She laid down on the bed, wriggling under the duvet and bunching the pillows over her ears. Somewhere in the middle of the next track, the music cut off abruptly. By then, Ivy was already half-asleep. It did not take her long to nod off entirely.

CHAPTER 3

D emi's coat and scarf were still in a pile by the door, so Ivy didn't realize she was alone in the flat until she found the note, sitting on the kitchen counter under a half-eaten bag of granola. The ink was slightly smudged, as though something had been dripping on the paper.

Ivy,

I double-checked with Mr. Kimball, and the rent is all paid up through the end of the month. My share of the rent for March is in the envelope under the begonias. Do look after the plants for me, and make sure to turn on the sun lamps for at least six hours a day. I know it's rather a lot. You've been lovely about the kitchen and the shopping and everything. I promise this is the very last thing.

—*Demi*

PS: *Mr. Dillon with the Dublin Garden Society would probably take some of the tradescantias if they get to be too much.*

Beneath the note were three pages of plant care instructions. Ivy flipped through them, then turned back to the first page and read the note again. It didn't make any more sense on a second reading. Had Demi decided to go somewhere? The rent for March wasn't due for another two weeks, so why would Demi be worrying about it now?

Note in hand, Ivy went down the hall, peering into the parlor. The room was dark, and empty of everything but the ever-present greenery. She flicked on the overhead lights. The corner of an envelope was sticking out from below a round pot in the middle of the bookshelf. Pulling the envelope free, Ivy flipped it open, revealing a startling number of hundred-euro notes.

Was that how much Demi was paying for the flat each month? Carefully, Ivy counted the bills, coming up with a total that would have paid for three whole months at Ivy's previous flat in Finglas. She'd known the flat had to be expensive, she just hadn't known *how* expensive. No wonder Demi wanted to split some of the costs with a flatmate. Feeling strangely as though she'd been caught with her hand in the biscuit tin, Ivy slipped the notes back in the envelope and hurriedly shoved the whole thing back under the begonias. No one had ever trusted Ivy with this much money in her life. It all had to be some misunderstanding.

Ivy went back down the hallway, and tapped lightly on Demi's door. Hearing no response, she pushed it open slightly. "Demi?" she called as she peered into the room. Something moved among the leaves, and Ivy jumped, momentarily startled until she realized it was only her reflection.

The back room of the flat, which Demi had appropriated as a bedroom, had originally been some sort of conservatory. It still had a glassed-in back wall, though it was impossible to see out the window because of the amount of pots, vines, and greenery in front of it. Aside from the plants, there was a bed and a small bureau, and a spindly desk covered in receipts, seed packets, and empty mugs. A discarded sweatshirt and a green turtleneck sat in a heap on the floor next to the bed.

The room looked pretty much the same as it had the few previous times Ivy had been back here. It didn't look like Demi had gone anywhere—she obviously hadn't bothered to clean, or pack much.

Ivy looked at the note again as she stepped back into the hall. Assuming Demi really had gone somewhere, she'd left no indication of where, or when she'd be coming back. The bit about the rent was strange—it seemed to imply Demi was going to be away for a long time. More than two weeks, if she figured she wouldn't be around to pay next month's rent herself.

Slipping the note into her pocket, Ivy headed for the flat's back door. She unlocked the deadbolt and opened the door, the hinge complaining with a rusty screech. The concrete steps were cold through her socks as she dashed past the hawthorn trees, towards a moss-covered garage facing into the back alley. A quick glance through the window confirmed the garage was empty; Demi must have taken her Volkswagen. The only things left in the garage were a half-full jug of windshield-washer fluid, and a rusty collection of rakes and lawn implements that almost certainly pre-dated Demi's acquisition of the flat.

Walking back into the kitchen, Ivy dropped the note, and the depressingly long list of plant-care instructions, onto the counter. Opening the fridge, she scooped a few spoonfuls of yogurt into a bowl, and topped it off with a handful of granola.

It had to be a misunderstanding. Demi sometimes went days without ever leaving the flat. It was hard to imagine her leaving in the middle of the night for a spontaneous weeks-long vacation. Ivy scowled at the bowl of yogurt, remembering what Hunzu said about February 20th. Could that be why Demi left in such a hurry?

Bringing Demi's note and the bowl of yogurt to the table, Ivy flipped to the plant care instructions.

Orchids, Demi wrote. *400mL every Wednesday for the Phalaenopsis and the Dendrobium, 500mL on Fridays for the Walkerinter. Boil the water and then let it cool to room temperature—give it at least an hour. Five minutes after watering, dab away any excess moisture from the leaves. Add 40mL of PolyGro every two weeks.*

Ivy sighed. She was going to have to get online and do an image search even to figure out which plant was which.

She dropped the note on the side table and pulled out her phone. This was silly; she'd just call Demi and ask what was going on. Not that she was being nosy, exactly. It wasn't any of Ivy's business where Demi went. But if Demi expected Ivy to take over the care and feeding of her houseplants, or figure out which orchid was a Phalaenopsis and which was a Walkerinter, Ivy had a right to ask for how long.

And make sure Demi really was okay. Make sure that Hunzu's vague pronouncements really were nonsense.

Ivy dialed the number and put the phone to her ear. As the call went through, a faint, bright noise came jingling down the hallway. It took Ivy a moment to recognize what it was.

"Damn it," she muttered, lowering the phone and following the noise down the hall. The ringing cut off before she opened the door, but a quick rummage through the receipts and seed packets on Demi's desk soon turned it up. Demi hadn't taken her phone with her. It was sitting on the desk, still plugged into its charger.

Well, that settled it, Ivy thought. Demi wouldn't have gone off and left her phone on purpose. She'd probably be back for it as soon as she noticed it was missing.

Unless she couldn't come back for her phone. If she was already on a plane, or halfway down the M7, she might not be able to return for it. But she'd obviously left in a hurry, to forget her phone *and* not bother to write down where she was going, or for how long.

Speculatively, Ivy picked up Demi's phone, running her thumb over the screen to unlock it. Surprisingly, the phone booted up without any objections or password requests. Ivy looked at the home screen, biting her lip indecisively. Probably, she shouldn't be snooping around on Demi's mobile. But Hunzu had said that Ivy should call him if anything got weird, and Ivy was starting to wonder if this qualified. Perhaps his number would be in Demi's contacts.

She opened the contacts page and scrolled down the list. Surprisingly, there were less than thirty names in the contact fields. Not counting the ones labeled Johnstowne Garden Center or Leinster Wildflower Supply, Ivy's own name and Mr. Kimball, their landlord, were the only entries she recognized.

Closing the contact list, Ivy hesitated for a moment, then pulled up Demi's email, trying to ignore the sense that the anthurium on the desk was watching her with disapproval. Ivy crossed her fingers as the application loaded, hoping for something innocuous, like a flight confirmation, or a last-minute invitation for a girl's weekend in Cardiff. Some usual and normal reason for leaving the flat in the middle of the night—and as soon as Ivy found it, she'd turn off the phone and go back to minding her own business.

The email client's logo appeared at the top of the screen, followed by two rows of banner ads and a string of messages. There were only a dozen emails in the inbox, in sharp contrast to Ivy's own account, where messages tended to linger until the sheer amount became embarrassing and she deleted them all at once.

Ivy almost clicked on the first line—*Come Back Home?*—before realizing it was just one of the ads, annoyingly positioned at the very top of the list of emails.

Ignoring it, she scanned the message headings. A newsletter from the National Botanic Garden, two ads from a horticulture supply company, a flyer for deal on brake pad replacements, and another flyer for an art show at a gallery Ivy had never heard of. Ivy skipped over those, finding only one email that seemed to be from an actual acquaintance, a week-old invitation (to which Demi had apparently never replied) for drinks at someplace called Club Verdi.

And at the bottom of the list of emails... *Come back home?*

It was the same ad from before. And now there were three copies of it, all trailing down the side of Demi's inbox. *Come back home? King's Haven Estate. Where you truly belong.* Beside the text was a picture of a tall building with a turret, which looked suspiciously similar to the picture Ivy'd seen on the back of the fuchsia's invoice the day before. Setting Demi's phone on the desk, Ivy rummaged through the packets and papers, eventually finding the invoice for the fuchsia crumpled at the top of the rubbish bin.

Carefully, Ivy spread the invoice flat against the desk. Sure enough, it was the same picture, and the same few lines of text.

Curious, Ivy turned back to Demi's phone, opened a browser window, and typed in the web address of the Dublin Villager. The same ad popped up at the top of the page. Ivy tried another website.

Again, the same ad.

Ivy clicked on the ad, wondering what was in Demi's browsing history that made her such a popular target for this condo company, or whatever they were. Or why the people who placed the ad were so inordinately interested in having it seen by gardeners.

As the page loaded, Demi's screen slowly filled with a larger version of the photo, except this time it was obvious the picture wasn't a photograph at all, but some sort of concept art. It looked like the sort of thing investors pass out trying to get people to put up money for buildings that haven't been built yet.

The building, which Ivy assumed was King's Haven Estate, looked larger than the picture in the banner ad had suggested, several stories tall, and built from a warm, creamy-looking stone. A wooden door stood half-open in the center; a few yards in front of it was a skinny-looking metal contraption that looked somewhat like an avant-garde bird feeder. There were gables over the door and several of the windows. Three thick, cylindrical towers rose up from the front of the building. It looked vaguely as though someone had been told to build a block of flats, but decided to build a castle instead. Or perhaps this was what castles looked like when they were new, before they began crumbling to pieces.

Ivy scrolled further down the page, expecting to see a prospectus, or at least a paragraph or two of advertising jargon. Instead, there was only the same few phrases followed by a phone number with a Dublin area code. Ivy scrolled back up the page, clicking to make sure the picture itself wasn't some giant link she'd missed. Aside from the concept art and the few lines of text, there didn't seem to be anything else on the page.

It was a strange sort of ad, that didn't even say what it was they were selling. Unless the company assumed their potential customers already knew. Unless they were selling to a very niche audience. An audience of one, for example. Someone who bought from garden supply stores, and had a browser history full of orchid-care sites. Someone who might know exactly what the ad meant, as soon as she saw it.

Before she could think twice about it, Ivy clicked on the phone number. The number flashed up on Demi's call screen, immediately replaced by a name: Taye. The number from the ad was already in Demi's contacts list. Ivy stared at it for a long moment, then hurriedly put the phone to her ear.

Someone picked up on the second ring. "Carillon speaking," said the voice.

"Hi, um, I, well, I saw on your website that you were um—" Ivy took a deep breath and started over, hoping Demi's own number wasn't programmed into this Carillon person's phone. "I'm interested in looking at a prospectus for your development."

"You saw our website?" asked the voice, sounding surprised.

"Yes," said Ivy, scrambling to come up with a coherent reason to explain why she was calling. "But there wasn't very much information. I'm interested in, erm, the square footage, the, um, layout options, the location—"

"I'm terribly sorry," said the woman, who didn't sound sorry at all. "You must have found that by mistake. We're not currently opening our properties to investors. Though we appreciate your interest. I'd be happy to take your details so we might send you more information in due course."

Her voice sounded familiar, but Ivy couldn't place where she'd heard it before.

"But I was told quite specifically you were considering taking on a partner," said Ivy, trying to think of how Demi might reply to someone who'd told her no. She'd act arrogant, and entitled, and bitchy, and important. "A friend of mine specifically mentioned it was a promising investment, but if this is how you're going to treat potential partners—"

"Well," said the woman, who paused for a moment, and the line beeped several times. "If you happen to know one of our shareholders personally, we might be able to make an exception." If this Carillon person had sounded irritated before, now she was practically purring. "What did you say her name was?"

Her name. Ivy hadn't said it was a woman.

It could have been coincidence. But Ivy didn't think it was. "I didn't," said Ivy, and hung up the phone.

She dropped it on the desk, staring at it for several seconds as though she were afraid the woman would ring back. Though why that should feel so unsettling, Ivy wasn't entirely sure. If these King's Haven people found out who she was—a cash-strapped, recently-unemployed call center associate calling from a phone that wasn't even hers—they wouldn't be happy she'd been trying to impersonate a potential investor. Although it wasn't as though they were falling over themselves to talk with her. At least, not until she'd mentioned a friend. Ivy had the strangest feeling the woman on the phone had known it was Demi. Or the woman *wanted* it to be Demi.

Wanted it to be the person they'd been trying to contact through these strangely-targeted ads.

Ivy went back to the phone's web browser, brought up a search engine, and typed in *King's Haven Estate*. The first two results were for apartments somewhere in Derbyshire, followed by several pages featuring a gated community in Godfrey, Indiana. Halfway down the list was a heading that was beginning to grow familiar: *Come back home?* The web address below it looked odd. Ivy assumed the King's Haven's web address would have been some variation on the name of their project, but it actually looked like it was part of a larger website. Trove dot ie dash something something.

Ivy opened another browser window and typed Trove.ie into the address bar. Trove Security Consulting, read the header on the page as it loaded. Below it were smiling photos of office workers, bullet-pointed assurances of quality and confidentiality, interspersed with a few glowingly vague testimonials from past clients. Nothing about it looked anything like the King's Haven ad. At the bottom of the page was a mailing address in the Liberties area of Dublin, a toll-free number, and a local number that looked suspiciously familiar. Ivy switched back to the call history. The number she just dialed differed from Trove's main office line only by the last two digits.

Grabbing a pen, Ivy jotted the address and phone number onto the back of the greenhouse invoice, then pulled up Demi's contacts list. *Trove* was listed there, too, though the number was different from the one on their web page. Ivy hesitated with her finger over the call button.

Slowly, Ivy closed the browser windows she'd opened, and set Demi's phone back on the desk. Maybe the person behind the ads was trying to help Demi. Or maybe they were someone Demi was running away from. Maybe they were connected to whatever Hunzu said was going to happen on the twentieth.

Or maybe Demi had simply gone on holiday, exactly as her note implied, and Ivy was inventing conspiracy theories out of nothing more than a weird browsing history and a flyer from a greenhouse.

But Ivy couldn't quite dismiss the way Carillon's voice had

changed, as soon as Ivy mentioned knowing an investor. Eager, and fishing for a name.

Demi's contacts list, at least, proved there was a connection between her and the company in the Liberties. The address was near enough to the City Center. It would be easy to take the bus, and it wasn't as though Ivy had anything else she ought to be doing. Besides ringing the employment office, updating her CV, checking the classifieds, and applying to any job that might conceivably want to hire her.

Ivy had enough things to manage as it was. It was silly to think Demi couldn't take care of herself. But something about the whole situation felt too much like the headlines Ivy read in the Daily Star: *Woman Last Seen at Bray Head Car Park. Teen Walks Home from Rugby Practice, Never Seen Again.* Maybe Ivy didn't have time to wait around and see if Demi turned up.

More accurately, maybe Demi didn't have time. February twentieth was only six days away.

❧❧❧

SLIPPING the greenhouse invoice into her pocket, Ivy went upstairs, walking into her bathroom and pulling out her makeup case from the bottom drawer. She'd all but given up bothering with makeup at the call center, since most of the people Ivy talked to couldn't actually see her. But going makeup-free wouldn't do for what Ivy had in mind. She smeared on a layer of foundation, carefully adding a tiny bit of eye shadow and lipstick. She pinned her hair back, examined it closely in the mirror, and then pulled it loose again. Hadn't Deirdre said she looked older with her hair up? Ivy pinned it up again, shaking her head experimentally to make sure it was going to stay.

She pulled out a cream-colored blouse, only slightly wrinkled, pairing it with beige trousers that fit well enough to look tailored, even though they weren't. Her black pencil skirt might have been better, but it was cold out, and Ivy wasn't certain she owned any stockings that didn't have holes. To this Ivy added her good pair of winter boots, and the Vuitton handbag Deirdre bought from a street hawker in New York who swore it was the real thing. Next came a pearl necklace that her mother had sent for Ivy's nineteenth birthday as though, against all evidence, Victoria was under the impression her daughter had grown into some sort of debutante. Ivy sent her mother a photograph of her wearing the necklace shortly after she'd gotten it, and had barely worn it since.

Over the necklace, Ivy wound a wispy blue scarf around her shoulders, then took it off and replaced it with one that was thicker, and bright red. To top it all off, Ivy added one of Demi's coats, a burgundy-colored, thigh-length shearling with a houndstooth print on the inside. Ivy straightened her collar, and looked at the results in the mirror.

Her first thought was that she looked ridiculous. But Deirdre wore stuff like this every day, and nobody thought *she* looked ridiculous. If Deirdre were wearing all this, she'd probably look glamorous and posh. Ivy arched her eyebrows in the mirror, as though she knew a secret her reflection could only guess at. She'd simply have to trust she looked just as posh as Deirdre. At least, Ivy thought, she didn't look much like an unemployed ex-call-center associate. Hopefully, she looked like a potential real estate investor—the sort of person who could afford an expensive coat and a real Vuitton handbag. Someone who other people listened to, instead of someone who spent all day talking to people who'd frequently hang up only a few lines into Ivy's sales script.

That sort of person, Ivy thought, thinking of the dwindling

supply of money on her bank card, would probably have their own chauffeur. Or would at least take a cab.

Can't have everything, Ivy thought, pouting at her reflection. Surely one of the bus routes from the City Center headed out that way. Pulling up the bus timetables on her phone, Ivy grabbed her purse and headed down the stairs.

CHAPTER 4

In the end, Ivy took the bus to the south side of the river, and hailed a cab from there. The address was buried in the winding streets of the Liberties, farther from the City Center than Ivy expected. Ivy winced as she handed over fare. She was probably halfway to Meath by now, Ivy thought as she watched the driver pull away, apparently in a hurry to get back to a part of the city where he had a better expectation of picking up fares. Ivy briefly wondered if she ought to have asked him to wait, but the thought of him sitting there with the meter running was enough to convince her she was better off letting him leave. She could always call up another cab if she needed to. The closest bus stop wasn't terribly far away, either, though she'd probably be in for a long wait once she got there.

The taxi had dropped her off in front of an ornate metal

gate bordered by a thick hedge. From the street, the building behind it seemed quite large, something like an overgrown townhouse, though the hedge was tall enough that Ivy couldn't see how far back the property actually went. Distantly behind it, Ivy could just make out the tower of the old Saint James's Hospital.

Beside the metal gate, large enough it was obviously meant for cars, was a smaller one built to more human proportions. Ivy pushed it, sighing with relief when the door immediately swung open. It would have been just her luck if she'd come all the way out here only to find the place kept odd hours or was closed on Thursdays.

She stepped through the gate, nearly jumping as it shut behind her with a clang. Trying not to look rattled, she straightened her purse, lifted her chin to a haughtier angle, and started up the path to the door.

On the other side of the hedge, the place looked more like a formal garden than the outside had suggested. A narrow driveway led toward the front of the townhouse. Beside it was a cobbled footpath with a landscaped border, a few flowers still holding onto a handful of defiantly out-of-season petals. Ivy surprised herself by recognizing a begonia, a handful of winter primroses, and a few weather-beaten azaleas. The entire complex must take up the better part of the whole block, Ivy guessed. Perhaps that explained why their offices were so far out of town—renting this sort of space in the city center would have been prohibitively expensive. Especially considering that so much of the acreage appeared to be nothing but shrubbery.

The footpath lead Ivy to a covered porch with an imposing door, and a metal plaque which read simply *Trove*. Tightening her grip on her purse, Ivy knocked at the door.

A moment later, Ivy heard the tapping of footsteps approaching from inside.

"We mostly keep it unlocked, you know," called a voice from the other side of the door.

"Oh," the man added, as the door swung open.

He was wearing a periwinkle suit with a vibrant neon green tie, and Ivy's first thought was that she didn't know anyone even made business suits in that color. Or that anyone would have taste questionable enough to actually buy one if they did.

The man's eyes were wide, as though Ivy's presence on the front stoop was the last thing he had possibly expected.

"Is everything alright, ma'am?" the man inquired, speaking at an even greater volume than he had when he'd been calling through the door. Ivy stepped back, alarmed. He sounded polite enough, but he was also nearly shouting. For a moment she considered bolting back past the shrubbery and toward the bus station. It was the thought of the cab fare, as much as anything else, that kept her from darting away from the wide-eyed man with the too-loud voice and the too-garish clothing. Probably he just didn't realize how loud he was. Maybe he was hard of hearing. Perhaps also color-blind, judging by the eye-popping combination of the suit and tie. And it would all be a wasted effort if she ran off now without even asking about Demi.

"Perfectly fine," Ivy said, walking into the lobby, leaving the fellow to scurry out of her way as she brushed past. Behind her, Ivy could hear the man scrambling to close the door.

The room she'd entered was floor-to-ceiling white, giving it a blank, sterile feel reminiscent of a doctor's office. The walls were plaster, and entirely devoid of pictures; the floor made of something that looked like real marble, but probably wasn't. Two imposing doors (also painted white) led off to either side, and between them was a large wooden desk. Sitting on it was a laptop, several stacks of papers, a large receptionist's phone with several dozen buttons, and an imposing ceramic pot filled with something mauve, shrubby, and flowering. The man had pushed the laptop back from the desk as he got up; he'd been playing Angry Birds.

The man hurried past Ivy to the desk. Against the unrelenting white of the room, the suit and tie looked even more garish. Ivy wondered how on earth he'd gotten away with wearing that in an office. It wouldn't have been allowed at the call center, and Eirecom's clients couldn't even see the employees. Following Ivy's gaze, the man quickly flipped his laptop shut and began hastily pulling on a pair of large white gloves.

"I have an appointment with Ms. Murphy, please," said Ivy, picking a name out of the air.

"I'm sorry, miss," the man said, still nearly shouting as he hurriedly flipped through the stack of papers, seemingly unaware that half the stack was falling to the ground as he did so. He paused briefly to tug the sagging white gloves further up his wrists. "No one of that name working here at present. Terribly sorry," he added again.

He grabbed a piece of paper from the stack, eyes flicking back and forth over the print as his other hand tapped nervously on the desk. Ivy slid her phone from her purse, glancing at the screen as though to confirm the appointment.

"Are you quite certain?" she asked. "I set it all up with Carillon last week. Perhaps I've gotten the name wrong. It was regarding King's Haven."

The man's eyes went wide again, like they had when she'd first stepped through the door.

"Let me check, Miss," he said in something approaching a normal volume. He picked up the phone's bulky handset, pressing four buttons to dial a number—an internal line.

"Yes, there's a woman here," the man began, and Ivy didn't miss the very slightest emphasis on the word *woman*. Nor the startled yelp in reply from whoever it was he was speaking to. "Yes, exactly. No, wait a minute. She says she has an appointment with someone named Murphy regarding the Haven. Set it up with one of Carillon's people sometime last week." He paused for a moment, listening. "Yes, sir," he said, and hung up the phone.

"If you'll come with me please," he said. The man went to a door to the right of the desk, and ushered Ivy into what appeared to be a waiting room.

"Ambrose will be down shortly," he said, closing the door almost before he'd finished speaking.

From the other side of the door, Ivy heard boots clattering across the entryway as he returned to his desk. She wondered why the man seemed so nervous. It seemed like the fellow couldn't get Ivy out of the room fast enough. Maybe he thought Ivy was going to tell his boss he'd been playing Angry Birds.

The second room was as unrelentingly white as the first, with a thickly-carpeted floor, and the same bare plaster walls. To the left hung a heavy, floor-length curtain, also white. Across the room was a small table containing three potted cactuses and a large spider plant whose enthusiastic cascade of offshoots created a curtain of leaves that nearly reached the floor. Ivy hoped the preponderance of plants was an indication that Demi really did have some connection to the place. Or perhaps Ivy had randomly fallen in with the most horticulturally-obsessed security business in the whole of Ireland.

Half a dozen chairs were scattered about, all wooden and spindly and probably antiques. Ivy picked the one that looked the least torturous to sit in.

Even through the heavy curtains, she could feel a draft. Perhaps they were in the middle of redecorating; it would explain why there wasn't anything hanging on the walls. It reminded Ivy of a theatre stage where the props were all set but none of the actors had entered. As though any moment, someone might walk out in front of the brilliant white background and begin declaiming soliloquies.

She slipped her phone out of her purse, nervously flipping it open and closed, wondering whether she ought to text Trove's address to Deirdre. Weren't hitchhikers supposed to text a car's license number to a friend before they accepted a ride? Just in case they headed off somewhere and were never heard from again? Just like Demi had headed off somewhere and—

That was silly, and Ivy wasn't going to think about it. Demi was fine. All Ivy had to worry about was what to do when this Ambrose person realized Ivy had absolutely no good reason to be here.

She dropped her phone back into the purse, and stared at the cactuses, tapping her fingers lightly on the arms of the chair. The door opened and a man walked in. Ivy hurriedly stood up.

Ivy's first thought was that this must be another receptionist come to whisk her off to some other part of the building. He looked young—hardly any older than Ivy herself, if she had to guess. He was wearing a bright orange tie over a canary yellow suit, both lending a sickly hue to his brown skin. Apparently, the entire office had a thing for gaudy suits. It must be some sort of bizarre take on casual day.

The man narrowed his eyes, and Ivy immediately revised her estimate of the man's age upwards. Ivy didn't know many boys her age who'd be able to pull off a look as calculating as that.

"You said you spoke to Carillon over the phone," said the man, pulling a pair of white gloves out of his pocket and slipping them onto his hands.

Ivy supposed this must be Ambrose, and he apparently didn't believe in introductions.

"Yes," she said, her faux-Vuitton confidence withering immediately. "But—"

"And I'm certain she told you we're *not* taking any inquiries about—well, about the Haven or anything else," he said, sounding exasperated. "I'm terribly sorry to disappoint you, but—"

"I know the person you're trying to find," said Ivy in a rush. She'd come here to ask about Demi, and she'd better do it quickly, before this fellow got irritated enough to toss her out. The man stared at Ivy for a long moment, opened his mouth, then just as quickly closed it.

"I'm sorry, but you must be mistaken," he said finally. "Trove doesn't deal with missing persons. You'd be better off ringing the Gardaí. Or Solly in the office can give you the name of a suitable agency." He went to the door, hand on the knob as though he meant to escort Ivy out, but his free hand was fiddling with the clip on his tie. Almost as though he were nervous.

She *was* being tossed out. But Ambrose hadn't denied he was looking for something. Or someone.

Ivy took a deep breath. She knew what she'd seen on Demi's phone, the same words repeating themselves over and over. Someone wanted to get Demi's attention. Someone wanted Demi to see those ads.

"The person you're looking for," Ivy began awkwardly. "I'm trying to find her, too."

The man stopped fiddling with his tie, hands dropping to his sides. "Can you confirm, if you please, who this person might be?"

Ivy hesitated. *Something's going to be looking for her,*

Hunzu had said. *It probably won't hurt you, but it's still best to stay out of its way.*

Could Hunzu have meant the people at Trove—the people who had listed the ad? Was Trove the dangerous thing Hunzu had warned her about? Ambrose himself didn't look particularly dangerous. Irritated and nervous and inexplicably fluorescent, perhaps, but not dangerous.

If there was any way these people could help her find Demi, Ivy supposed she'd have to trust them with a name.

"Demi Gentian," Ivy said. "Although maybe you know her by another name. Brown hair, mid-thirties, big tattoo on her back. I moved in with her about six months ago."

Ambrose suddenly turned pale. "Please take a seat," he said, gesturing vaguely toward Ivy's chair, before dropping very abruptly into the opposite one. "I think you'd better start at the beginning."

Ivy didn't sit. "No, I think *you'd* better tell me how you know Demi in the first place," she insisted, coming a few steps forward. "I know she doesn't work here. She's never said anything about this place."

"She most certainly did work here," Ambrose snapped, jumping out of his chair and moving quickly behind it. "I was her supervisor. And if she didn't mention us, how'd you know to come down here? Pick us out of the phone book, did you?"

"No, I saw the ad," she repeated.

"Ad?" asked Ambrose, looking confused. "What ad?"

"The ones about coming back home to King's Haven," said Ivy, biting her lip as she looked at Ambrose. Despite the suit and tie, he looked far too young to be anybody's supervisor. Far too yellow to be anybody's supervisor, either.

"Ads about the Haven?" Ambrose repeated, sounding appalled. He stepped backwards, as though even with the chair between them he didn't want Ivy getting too close. "On the internet?"

"On your website," said Ivy. "Or, the Trove website. At least, it had a Trove web address."

"There's nothing like that on our site," said Ambrose confidently, resting his hands on the back of the chair he'd apparently chosen as a barricade.

"It was a Trove web address, and the phone number was yours, too," Ivy insisted.

She pulled the crumpled fuchsia invoice out of her pocket. "Does this look familiar?" she asked, holding it out to Ambrose.

He didn't take it, but leaned forward to squint at the paper. He was still keeping the chair firmly between them, as though he thought Ivy might be about to strangle him with his own tie. Slowly, Ambrose pulled out his phone, pushing a few buttons. The phone beeped; Ambrose scowled at it. He pulled off his gloves, shoved them impatiently into a pocket, and prodded the screen again. He peered at it for a long moment, frowning as though he wasn't happy about what he saw.

"Yes, I know the number," he said finally. "Who answered? Taye?"

Ivy shrugged. "She said her name was Carillon. I asked about the ad, but she didn't seem to know anything about it."

Making no reply, Ambrose shoved the phone back into his pocket. Slipping on the gloves, he turned his hands back and forth as though checking for a hole or a stain.

Biting her lip, Ivy folded the paper and stuffed it into her purse.

"My name's Ivy Gallagher," Ivy offered after a moment.

"Ivy," Ambrose repeated dully. "Of course you are."

If Ivy harbored any doubts that Ambrose actually knew her flatmate, this settled it. Apparently, everyone knew about Demi's thing for plants. Ivy felt the first glimmer of hope that she'd actually managed something worthwhile from her taxi ride down here. She'd found someone who actually knew her—a more difficult task than it sounded, given the way Demi kept to herself.

"Do you know where Demi is?" Ivy asked. "She left last night and didn't take her phone—"

Ambrose abruptly turned away, rubbing a gloved hand over his face as he crossed to the table with the cactus.

"You'd know better than I would," he said quietly. "I told you, I haven't seen Demi in over six months."

"I thought you said she worked here. Did she quit?"

"She left," said Ambrose shortly, staring at the table as though he might as well have been talking to the plants. His face looked even more sickly than it had before, but perhaps it was only the hideous reflection from his suit.

Maybe this wasn't the first time Demi had disappeared. She worked at Trove, and then one day she just . . . left. Like she left the flat on Thormanby Road last night. Ivy wondered if she'd just discovered another annoying thing about Demi. Weird thing number three. She leaves people, and never talks to them ever again. Surprisingly, Ivy felt a twist in her gut at the thought of her flatmate walking out of her life, leaving nothing but a note about orchids. It shouldn't matter. It wasn't like they were best friends. Ivy should probably feel relieved. If Demi had walked out on people before, then maybe she wasn't in danger, like Hunzu had implied. Maybe this was just what she did.

Except that Ivy still didn't know that for sure. And if Ambrose hadn't seen her in six months, he could hardly be expected to know how Demi was doing now, or where she'd gone.

Ambrose turned back from the cactuses. For a moment, Ivy thought he was going to say something, but he didn't. He only stared at Ivy with a confused, almost hopeful look. As though Ivy might somehow have the answers to *his* questions, instead of the other way around.

"When I first met her, she was living in a flat in Thormanby Road, over in Howth," Ivy said slowly. "I moved in with her back in September."

"Why?" Ambrose asked, looking perplexed.

"It was so much nicer than my old place and—"

"No, no, no," he interrupted, frowning. "Not why did you move in with her? Why did she want a, um, flatmate in the first place?"

"I don't know," said Ivy, throwing up her hands. "I thought at first she just needed the help with rent. Or she wanted someone around to do the shopping and answer the door. She doesn't like being around people much."

"She stayed away from other people?" Ambrose asked. "Other than you?"

Ivy shrugged. "I suppose so. She's kind of an introvert. She'd—well, she didn't go out much. Mostly she was either on her computer or looking after her plants. And Hunzu—"

"Hunzu?" Ambrose cut in, sounding appalled. "Demi was with *him*?"

"Yes," said Ivy, bewildered. "Yesterday."

Ambrose's expression turned cold as he bolted to the door leading back into the foyer. He'd gone as far as putting his hand to the doorknob—and paused. Just as quickly, he stalked back toward Ivy and pulled out his phone, punching at the screen.

"Do you know hi—" Ivy began to say; Ambrose shushed her with a look as he brought the phone up to his ear. Faintly, Ivy heard the phone ring once; then go directly to voicemail.

"This is Ambrose," he snapped. "I am giving you three minutes to get down to the entry room. I'll spend those three minutes thinking up various ways to ask you *what the hell has been going on.* The beginning of the list is thumbscrews. If you don't want the list growing any longer, or more imaginative, you better get down here."

He hung up the phone and shoved it back into his pocket, fingering his tie again as though it had suddenly grown too tight.

"You know Hunzu?" Ivy asked faintly. She didn't quite know how to take the mention of thumbscrews. If it was some sort of joke, Ivy thought it rather tasteless. But Ambrose sounded too angry for it to be any sort of joke at all.

"Of course," said Ambrose. He glanced back at Ivy, as though he'd only just remembered she was still in the room. The man's scowl vanished, replaced by a bland expression of equal parts amiability and boredom. Ivy was willing to bet it was every bit as fake as the Vuitton handbag on her shoulder.

"You've been a great help, Miss Gallagher," he continued smoothly. "I'll remind Demi to call you. When I see her next, that is. I'll have Solly ring you a cab, if you like, save you a walk in the cold."

He was still trying to toss her out. And now that she'd mentioned Hunzu, he suddenly didn't seem interested in where Demi had been for the past six months— or, more importantly, where she was now.

"Wait a minute," Ivy protested. "I'm not going anywhere until you tell me what's happened to Demi!"

"You shouldn't *care* what happens to Demi!" Ambrose burst out. He immediately covered his mouth with both white-gloved hands. "That must have sounded horrible," he continued in a softer voice. "But it's still true."

"Why would you think I don't care?" Ivy asked.

Before Ambrose could reply, Hunzu walked through the door.

Ambrose whirled about as though he'd momentarily

forgotten he'd sent for him. His eyes went wide, and at first Ivy thought the noise of the door had startled him. But a ramrod stiffness had crept into Ambrose's spine. Ivy couldn't tell if it was anger, or fear, or some mix of both.

"When did you last see Demi?" Ambrose demanded, almost before Hunzu had closed the door.

"I already told you—" Hunzu began, and then spotted Ivy. Hunzu broke off, glancing between her and Ambrose, an expression very like panic crossing his face. "Miss Gallagher,"

Hunzu started again, in the same too loud voice the receptionist had used.

Ivy cut him off.

"Demi left last night," Ivy snapped. "She didn't say where, just that she'd be away for a long time. You said something dangerous was coming for her. Is that why she's gone?"

"Well?" Ambrose asked darkly, when Hunzu didn't immediately respond.

"If she's left Howth," said Hunzu, taking a deep breath as though trying to collect himself. "I assume it's for the same reason she left here back in July."

"The Enemy," Ambrose murmured. Ivy could practically hear the capitalization, as well as the edge of desperation in his voice. "She still thinks she can escape it."

"Probably not," said Hunzu flippantly, almost as though he were taunting the other man. "She knows better than that. Probably just wanted to be around someone who could manage to look at her without going all teary-eyed."

Ivy thought Ambrose would hit him; he went for the man with his hand raised as though he was ready to do just that.

"Stop it," Ivy hissed, but neither of them answered. "What Enemy?"

Without thinking, she stepped forward and grabbed Ambrose's arm.

The moment her hands touched his sleeve, he jerked away as though he'd been stung. Ivy jumped back, suddenly convinced that she shouldn't have gotten into the middle of this and now *she* was the one Ambrose might take it out on. But Ambrose was still scooting backwards, staggering as he caught his foot against the table covered with plants. The table lurched sideways; he went to grab it and missed. The table, pots, and plants all crashed to the carpet in a series of terrific thumps.

For a moment, they all stared in silence at the heap of chipped pots, cactuses, and topsoil.

The door behind Hunzu swung open the barest few inches.

"Everything is quite in order, Solly," Ambrose announced loudly.

Hesitantly, the door swung shut with a click.

Ivy wondered whether she might be better off making her excuses and following the receptionist out. Get herself back outside the building and into the nearest cab. Except it seemed clear that whatever was going on with Demi, these two knew something about it. And it was much more serious than a last-minute holiday, or a forgotten phone.

"Rather uncalled for, I should think," said Ambrose, dropping to his knees next to the pile of dirt, and gingerly trying to assist one of the cactuses back into its mostly-undamaged pot. Ivy didn't know if he meant knocking the table over, or Hunzu's remark.

"Do you know where Demi's gone?" Ivy asked Hunzu quietly.

"Where she's gone now, you mean?" Hunzu replied, hands shoved deep into the pockets of his trousers. "Haven't the foggiest."

"I can make an educated guess. Are you going to help with this or not?" said Ambrose, and glared at Hunzu, who quickly dropped to his knees beside the other man, and began scooping handfuls of topsoil and spider plants back into a cracked flower-pot. "Not you," he added perfunctorily, as Ivy started to join them. "At least we know who else has an interest in finding her."

Hunzu lifted an eyebrow. Ambrose hesitated, then shot a hard look at Ivy.

"I'm *not* leaving until someone tells me what's going on," said Ivy firmly, before Ambrose could try to throw her out again.

Ambrose got to his feet, hoisting the toppled table upright, then set a more-or-less intact cactus on top of it. He stared at Ivy for a long moment, then glanced at Hunzu. "Perhaps we should find a more accommodating space for our guest," he said after a moment. "Order some refreshment?"

Before Ivy could even open her mouth to reply, Hunzu leapt to his feet, abandoning the spider plants, and visibly bristling.

"She already knows," said Hunzu grimly. "About the food."

Sighing, Ambrose ran a hand through his hair, leaving a streak of dirt across his forehead, looking almost sheepish.

Ivy had no idea why Hunzu had reacted so violently to what Ivy had thought was a reasonably polite offer, or why Ambrose looked embarrassed. Except that Hunzu had talked about food at the flat, too—something else Ivy hadn't under-stood, except that he clearly knew what it was like to share a kitchen with Demi.

"Listen," said Hunzu, sidling closer to Ivy as he lowered his voice. "If you want to leave, now would be the time. Go back to the foyer, smile at the fellow listening at the keyhole, and don't look back. Call a cab, and get yourself home."

"And Demi?" Ivy asked.

"Most likely, you won't see her again."

Again, that tiny twist in her belly. She tore her eyes away

from Hunzu and glanced back at Ambrose. The other man hadn't moved, standing with his arms folded and a carefully blank expression on his face. Both sleeves of his yellow suit were streaked with dirt, a matching smudge smeared across his cheek.

"But you know where she is," Ivy said. "You think she's gone to this King's Haven place."

Ambrose nodded.

"Is Demi in danger?" Ivy asked, and it sounded like a ridiculous, melodramatic question even as she said it.

"Of course she is," said Ambrose, and he didn't sound worried, or even upset. Mostly, he just sounded very tired.

"Can you help her?"

"No," said Ambrose.

"Yes," said Hunzu in the same moment.

The two of them exchanged a look that Ivy couldn't interpret. Ambrose looked away first.

"Like it or not, Demi's recruited an agent," Ambrose said, looking down at the pile of dirt, broken pottery, and what remained of the spider plant. "We may as well fill in the gaps. Only, Miss Gallagher? You do understand that associating with us carries a certain level of risk?"

Demi's more dangerous than you realize, Hunzu had told her. *So's what's coming for her. Though to be fair, it's probably not interested in you.* If Ivy got involved, that might change in a hurry. And Ivy suddenly thought of the man in the flower boxes with the scarred face.

"I understand," said Ivy, knowing at the same time that she didn't, not precisely. But Ivy couldn't just leave without trying to figure out what sort of trouble Demi was in, and whether Ivy could help.

Although Ivy hadn't quite given up on the idea that when

she did see Demi again, her flatmate would only sigh dramatically and say it was all a terrible misunderstanding.

"Lovely," said Ambrose, and went over to Hunzu, who was still standing by the door with his hands in his pockets. "I'll leave it to Hunzu to manage the explanations. Not here," he added, when Hunzu started to say something. "She's still not a registered agent."

Hunzu's eyebrows looked as though they were trying to crawl up his face and hide in his hair. "You do realize I haven't done this before?" he said faintly.

"I'm sure you'll manage," said Ambrose frostily.

"All right," said Hunzu, running his hands through his hair as though he were thinking. "There's a pub, on the west side of Saint Stephen's Green, halfway along Grantham Street. Be there at half past five."

"What happens at half past five?" Ivy asked, trying to decide if this was all just an excuse to get her to leave.

"I explain why Ambrose looks like a goldfinch, for one thing," said Hunzu, gesturing at the eye-popping suit. "I still think you're better off going back to Howth and forgetting about the whole business, mind."

"We'd best leave before Solly gets it in his head to check in again," said Ambrose, bending down to pick up a remnant bit of the spider plant. He looked at Ivy as though he were going to say something else, but only turned back to the table with a sigh.

Gathering her purse and coat from the back of the chair, Ivy nodded at Hunzu. Maybe meeting him in Grantham Street wasn't the safest option. But the safest option and the right option weren't always the same things.

"Half five it is, then," she said, with more confidence than she felt, and slipped out the door.

The man at the reception desk was still sitting in front of his computer, his inexplicable suit and tie looking even more garish against the bare plaster walls. Ivy ducked her head, trying not to look like she was staring. This was made easier by the fact that the man was very obviously staring at her, the light from the computer screen exaggerating the dim circles of his eyes.

Ivy wondered—why *was* Ambrose dressed like a goldfinch? And how could that have any possible connection to where Demi had gone?

Her boots tapping against the marble floor, Ivy opened the outer door, the chill air biting at her face as she walked across the porch and past the leafless azaleas. The great metal gate was standing open, as though a car had recently come through.

It was silly, thinking an obscure orchid-growing friend of Demi's and a man in a yellow suit could possibly be of any help to anyone. Ivy would probably be better off going home and calling the Gardaí.

Ivy wondered if anyone at Trove reported Demi missing when she'd left *them* last summer. How long had Demi's friends waited for her to call? If she went back to Thormanby Road now, she'd only be sitting with the plants, waiting for the phone to ring, and wondering what Hunzu might have told her if she'd gone.

CHAPTER 5

Since she didn't want to bother going all the way back to Howth, Ivy hailed the first cab she saw, getting a ride as far as Fhearchair Street. She spent most of the afternoon wandering around St Stephen's Arcade, on the assumption that even if she couldn't afford to buy anything, at least she was out of the cold, and there was always the chance one of the shops might have a *help wanted* sign. None of them did. Ivy spent the better part of an hour strolling through the boutiques, looking at handbags and scarves that cost the better part of a week's pay at Eirecom.

She walked out of the arcade at ten past five, looking forward to the prospect of a decent meal at whatever pub Hunzu had picked.

Even given the vague directions, Ivy could hardly mistake

the pub, mostly because Hunzu was standing in front of it, wrapped in his green corduroy coat with the collar turned up. He hadn't even been smoking, which was the only excuse Ivy could think of for why he'd been standing in the cold. He smiled at her, holding the door open and motioning her past with a little nod of his head. Almost like a gentleman, even though Ivy suspected he wasn't.

She could've spent the evening drinking wine at Deirdre's flat, Ivy thought as she walked through the door. She could've emailed her mum. Or gone back to Howth and called the Gardaí, or flirted with the cute guy at the chip shop in the harbor, or looked for more job ads on the internet. Instead, she was having drinks with a very strange orchid-growing man, who had something to do with why Demi had left in the first place.

If it turned out Demi had simply gone on holiday, Ivy was probably going to murder her when she got back.

Inside the pub, it seemed almost as dark as the street outside, making the place seem seedier than perhaps it deserved. Or maybe it was to keep anyone from looking too closely at the stains on the carpet, or the holes in the chair cushions. Along a long wooden bar, two bewhiskered men sat with half-drained pints, occasionally glancing at a silent TV that was broadcasting a Warriors game. Behind them sat a pinball machine with an *out of order* sign taped crookedly to the front. The rest of the pub was completely deserted.

Ivy slipped her hand into her purse, feeling for her phone. She wondered whether she ought to excuse herself to the Ladies' and text Deirdre the name of the pub. Just in case. Or excuse herself to the Ladies' and get back to the nearest DART station before Hunzu had time to realize she'd left. If Hunzu really did have something to do with Demi's disappearance, maybe Ivy ought to follow her flatmate's example—namely, get as far away as possible, as quickly as possible, and don't leave any phone numbers or forwarding address.

Ivy looked at Hunzu again, appraisingly. The man was shrugging out of his coat and draping it over one arm, looking curiously around the pub. Under the coat, he was wearing a dingy green sweatshirt with a stretched-out collar. Emblazoned on the front was the outline of a fern and the phrase "I'm Frond of You, Too."

Ivy left her phone in her purse. Hunzu didn't look anything like the toughs Ivy'd seen loitering around the pubs in Finglas. She also had a hard time imagining someone with a hobby best suited to a white-haired great-aunt actually being dangerous. When she'd first found him crouched in Demi's kitchen, he looked as startled by her as she was of him. He'd looked frightened of Ambrose, too—and he definitely looked frightened of the possibility of meeting Ivy and explaining what was going on. Someone that jumpy couldn't be dangerous.

Unless he had something to hide.

Ivy hesitated, slipping her hand back into her purse and feeling the smooth plastic surface of her phone's screen protector. A waiter stepped out from the curtained doorway that presumably lead to the kitchen, wearing an expression suggesting that whatever he was doing back there, he didn't relish the interruption.

"One, is it?" the waiter asked sourly. He had a large gold filling in place of one of his front teeth. It gleamed dully in the faint light over the bar.

Ivy glanced at Hunzu, who only looked at her, and raised his eyebrows. Turning back to the waiter, Hunzu lifted his hand in a tiny wave. The waiter didn't wave back.

This was silly. It wasn't as though Hunzu were an axe murderer. Didn't serial killers pretend to be normal in order to blend in? Blending in did not appear to be one of Hunzu's strong points. Unless he was secretly growing things in his flat that the Drugs Bureau would be interested in, Ivy didn't see how he could possibly be much of a danger to anyone.

"Two, actually," Ivy said to the waiter.

The waiter shrugged, steering them to a booth at the far corner of the pub. An unlit candle sat on the table beside a small vase of plastic tulips.

"Here'll do," he said, dropping two menus on the table with a thunk. Tucking his hands into the front of his apron, he slouched back toward the bar.

Ivy sighed, and slid into the booth. The menus were thick, bound together like fat leather books, which Ivy hoped might indicate a reasonable level of culinary sophistication. God knew the rest of the pub wasn't giving that impression. What-ever reasons Hunzu had for meeting here, Ivy was fairly certain it wasn't for the food.

"Have you ever seen the video of the gorilla in the basket-ball team?" Hunzu asked, laying his coat across the back of the seat and folding himself into the booth.

"The gorilla in the what?" Ivy asked, certain she'd heard him wrong.

"In the basketball team," Hunzu repeated, crossing his hands behind his head. "You should look it up online. It's a demonstration that shows how easy it is to hide things. There's this video of a basketball game. You play it, and it asks you to count how many passes one team is making, or how many times they intercept the ball. Anything, really. And because they're paying attention to something else, most people completely miss seeing a gorilla walk right through the middle of the players."

"A gorilla?" Ivy repeated, again certain she'd heard him wrong.

"Well, a gorilla *costume*," Hunzu added. "Not an actual

gorilla. Not just the costume, either, there's somebody wearing
it. But that's not the point. The point is—"

"That people tend to ignore things?" Ivy said, wondering
why on earth Hunzu was bringing this up. "That's not terribly
unusual."

"Of course people ignore things. But ignoring a gorilla in
the middle of a basketball game? That's rather a lot to ask. And
yet you people manage to do it all the time, and you never even
notice you're doing it until someone points it out."

"Okay," said Ivy slowly. "Back at the office, Ambrose said
something about—"

"You should probably order something," said Hunzu,
sliding one of the menus in her direction. "Or at least look at
the options. No telling when the waiter's going to be back." He
made no attempt to look at the other menu, and Ivy wondered
if he was trying to put off talking about Demi for as long as
possible.

"So why did you want to tell me about a gorilla?" Ivy asked,
looking at him over the top of the menu.

"It's a useful comparison," he said. "Do you remember
what the waiter said as we came in? Oh, look, here he comes.
I've heard good reports of the beef au jus."

The waiter came back to the booth, pulling a notebook and
pen from the pocket of a greasy-looking apron.

"Fancy a drink while you're waiting?" the man asked
curtly.

"No, I think we're ready," said Ivy, hungry enough that
she'd just as soon get her order in as soon as possible. She
scanned the menu, picking the first thing from the entrée
section that caught her eye. "A filet mignon, please. And a glass
of white wine."

Hunzu waved expansively across the table as the waiter
tucked his notepad back into the top of his apron. "And pint of

Abbey Westlateven. West-la-te-ven!" he repeated, enunciating each syllable as though he thought the man might be hard of hearing.

The waiter had already turned back to the bar. "Excuse me?" Ivy called. "Did you get that?"

"Filet mignon and a house white," he said.

"Pint of Westlateven!" Hunzu repeated again, even louder. "Ask him if he's gotten it, Ivy; he isn't writing it down."

"Was there anything else?" the waiter asked, giving Ivy a strange look.

"Did you get the pint of Westlateven?"

The waiter pulled the ticket out and scrawled something across the bottom. "And a pint of Westlateven," he added laconically. "You want to hold off on the food until your friend gets here?"

"No, you can go ahead and put the order in," said Ivy, shooting a quizzical look at Hunzu. "Unless you wanted anything?"

Hunzu was already shaking his head. "Just the beer," he said, slowly and distinctly.

The waiter was still staring at Ivy with a strange expression, his tongue flicking over the gold filling.

"I think that'll be all," said Ivy. The waiter, still looking annoyed, tucked his notebook into his apron and slouched back to the bar.

Ivy set the menus on the edge of the table, wondering guiltily whether Hunzu would be picking up the tab. She couldn't afford to eat at a place this expensive even before she'd lost her job. Out of nowhere, Ivy thought of the envelope under the begonias. The money, granted, had vastly increased the amount of cash Ivy had at her disposal, but if she still wanted to be able to pay the rent for March, she'd better not spend it on anything else.

Hunzu leaned against the booth, watching the waiter rummaging behind the bar with an amused look on his face.

"He's not deaf, you know," Ivy said, giving Hunzu a stern look. "Did you see that look he gave us? I think he thought you were being rude."

"I don't think he heard me the first time," said Hunzu mildly. "Or the second."

Ivy sighed. At least if Hunzu wasn't ordering food, that probably meant he didn't plan on staying long.

"So about what Ambrose—" Ivy started to ask.

"We'll get to that later," Hunzu said. "But I think a demonstration would make this a bit easier. Just give it a few minutes."

"What sort of a demonstration?" asked Ivy.

"The kind you wouldn't believe any other way," Hunzu said, giving her one of his toothy grins.

"You were the one who told me to come here," Ivy said impassively. "You could have arranged all sorts of things ahead of time and I wouldn't know about it. If you want to impress me, maybe start with actually telling me what's going on with Demi!"

Before Hunzu could reply, the waiter reappeared at Ivy's shoulder, dropping two coasters on the table. Giving Ivy an odd look, he set down her glass of wine and Hunzu's beer.

"If one of those is for your friend, I'll need to card him when he gets here," the waiter said, tucking the empty tray under his arm and retreating back to the bar.

Not only was he a lousy server, he was also apparently blind. Ivy picked up her glass and slid the beer toward Hunzu, who was grinning widely as he picked it up. He took a long swig, coating his upper lip with a thick mustache of froth.

"It's like I told Ambrose," said Hunzu, wiping at the foam with the back of his hand. "I've never had to explain this stuff before. I just grew up knowing it."

"Knowing what?" asked Ivy.

"And we aren't even done with the demonstration," Hunzu chided her. "First things first."

Ivy dropped her glass back on the coaster, hard enough to slosh a few drops over the rim. Ambrose had mentioned thumbscrews in the voicemail he'd left on Hunzu's phone; Ivy was beginning to sympathize with the man's strategy for getting a straight answer out of Hunzu. "Your demonstration, as you call it, apparently consists of drinking bad wine at a pub with lousy service. That's not even remotely like a demonstration."

"Then maybe you aren't paying attention," Hunzu replied. "You're missing the gorilla."

"There isn't any gorilla," said Ivy, exasperated. "There's just you, and me, and a really terrible pub. That isn't an explanation, it's a bad date."

Across the pub, one of the whiskery men was nudging his companion and muttering something. Both of them turned around on their barstools to stare at Ivy, only to look away as soon as Ivy glared at them. The pub was quiet, but Ivy hadn't thought she was being that loud. Or maybe they were the sort to stare at any girl who came in the door. At least she was sitting with a boy, so they probably wouldn't try to ask for her number. Possibly the only thing Hunzu'd been good for this entire evening.

"Not my fault if you don't notice things," said Hunzu, picking up the vinegar bottle off the table and twirling it as if he was bored. "I'll see if I can order a dessert next time the waiter comes back. Do you like trifle or should I just ask for an ice cream?"

"We are *not* doing dessert," said Ivy, in a softer voice. "I am *not* sitting around this pub all night waiting for something to happen. You've got half an hour. Or until I finish my steak.

Whichever comes first. And if nothing happens, you're paying for my dinner, *and* my cab ride home."

"Agreed," said Hunzu happily, dropping the vinegar bottle back onto the table.

"I'll warn you, the filet mignon was expensive."

Hunzu only wiggled his eyebrows.

Resigned to the fact that Hunzu wasn't going to say anything about Demi until he was good and ready, Ivy took a long sip of her wine and contemplated ordering another glass.

Hunzu, completely unaware of Ivy's growing annoyance, prattled on garrulously about the provenance of the beer he had ordered. This particular ale, Hunzu informed her, was produced by a specific order of Belgian monks, who only brewed a few casks a year. On the day the ale was decreed to be sufficiently aged, the monks rolled the casks outside the monastery and sold them to anyone who happened to be passing by. The monks never advertised in advance when this was going to happen, which made this particular ale not only the best beer ever brewed, but also one of the most difficult to obtain.

"You're not even going to try, are you?" Ivy dropped her glass onto the table, and threw the napkin down beside it. The waiter hadn't brought her steak, and it hadn't been thirty minutes, but suddenly it didn't seem worth the effort to stay.

"What?" asked Hunzu, looking alarmed.

"You aren't even going to pretend you have something to tell me about Demi, because that's not why I'm here, is it? You just decided to bring me down here so that you could show off, or chat me up or God knows what else, and do you know what? I'm *not* bloody interested."

Ivy grabbed her purse and slid out of the booth, ignoring Hunzu's hand-waving efforts at stopping her.

She shrugged into her coat as she went to the door,

wondering if her face looked as red as it felt. She'd been silly, was all. Silly to think that Hunzu would actually tell her anything. He'd shown up at the flat and everything had turned strange after that. Maybe Demi never would have left if Hunzu hadn't come there in the first place. Maybe Demi really was on holiday, and she'd ghosted Trove six months ago because Ambrose was a terrible boss, and the only reason Ivy was worried about her was because of Hunzu and his vague, dire warnings.

As Ivy passed the bar, the waiter came through the curtain, holding a tray with a plate containing what Ivy assumed was her filet mignon. The wilted sprig of parsley did nothing to improve the appearance of the charbroiled hunk of meat, and Ivy was suddenly even happier that she wasn't staying to eat it.

"He'll get it," said Ivy, glancing back at Hunzu, who was slouched next to the booth, watching Ivy over the top of his beer stein.

"Who, miss?"

The door to the pub swung open, and two girls stumbled over the threshold, their clumsiness indicating that this pub was not the first such establishment they had visited. As the first girl passed in front of the pinball machine, the neon glare illuminated her shirt just enough for Ivy to glimpse a truly hideous shade of mauve.

"The fellow I came in with," Ivy said. "He'll get it."

"I think *you'd* better get it, miss," said the waiter, who was apparently choosing to ignore his new customers in favor of skulking after Ivy. He dropped the tray on the bar with a thump, moving to stand between Ivy and the door. His gold front tooth glittered in the light from the pinball machine, as he crossed his arms, leering at her. Did he think she was trying to run off without paying for the bill?

"Just bring it to the table, okay?" Ivy told him, backing toward the pinball machine.

"You're finished eating," said the waiter abruptly, fixing Ivy with a hard look. "Now, you're going to pay up and get out. Isn't she, Fergus?"

A second man had slipped out of the curtained doorway, and was leaning over the side of the bar. He was wearing a baggy-looking track suit that didn't quite manage to hide his hulking biceps, or the eagle tattoo standing out on his neck like a bruise.

"I think she is," Fergus replied, hitching up the edge of his trousers as he sauntered toward the door. "I think she's going to pay whether she's got the money or not. Am I right?"

Shakily, Ivy slipped her bank card out of her purse and handed it to the waiter. He held it up to the light, bending the plastic back and forth. Ivy shot a nervous look at Hunzu, who was watching from the other end of the bar, an uneasy look on his face.

"You got some ID to go with this, sweetheart?" the waiter asked.

Wilting under the waiter's look, Ivy dove back into her wallet, passing over her PSC, waiting as the fellow leered first at the picture, then at Ivy, running a grimy fingernail over the photograph as though he suspected it might have been glued on.

Finally, he ran the card; Ivy scrawled her name on the receipt and bolted out the door.

HUNZU CAUGHT up with her before she'd even made it half a block. Somehow, he'd managed to walk out of the pub still holding onto his half-empty stein of beer. She rounded on him before he could start jabbering again, shoving a finger into his chest and ignoring his startled yelp.

"You are a right proper bastard," said Ivy heatedly, poking him again for emphasis. He could have at least said something to the waiter. He could have at least *tried* to be helpful and chivalrous, instead of letting Ivy deal with those wankers completely by herself. "Give me that."

Mutely, Hunzu handed over the beer stein, which Ivy drained in a few large gulps. She'd paid for it, after all. Given the total on the receipt she'd signed, it must be a ridiculously expensive beer.

"I agree, this discussion certainly merits more alcohol," Hunzu said, as though in response to an opinion Ivy hadn't voiced.

"What discussion?" Ivy asked, shoving the now-empty glass back at him and starting down the street. "The one where you actually tell me what's going on and why Demi's in trouble? Because that one hasn't happened yet."

"Maybe here," said Hunzu, as though Ivy hadn't said anything, nodding at a neon-lit restaurant across the street, with a pile of off-season patio furniture chained up in a jumble beside the door.

"Really?" said Ivy, stopping to glare at him. "Are we *really* going to do that again? I just got thrown out of a pub because that asshole thought I was going to run off without paying, and *you* could have said something! You really are a bastard. I don't even know what you're trying to do."

"Right now, I'm trying to be nice," said Hunzu, and this time his grin looked the tiniest bit sheepish.

"You're doing a horrible job," Ivy pointed out.

"Yes, well," Hunzu mumbled. "You still haven't had supper."

"I still haven't had an explanation, either," said Ivy, crossing her arms.

"Yes and I'm trying to give you both," Hunzu said fervently. "Just go in, and order the cheapest thing on the menu. I'll take it from there."

"Are you paying this time?" Ivy asked pointedly.

"Fine," said Hunzu, pulling out his wallet and handing Ivy a handful of notes.

Somewhat placated, Ivy crossed the street, ignoring Hunzu's protests about jaywalking (Honestly, would you even *consider* using the crosswalks, Ivy?) and pushed open the door of the second pub of the evening.

The second pub was busier, and had a notably cleaner atmosphere than the first. The walls were plastered with film posters from a number of forgettable-looking sci-fi movies with names like *Earth versus the Spider*, and *Invasion U.S.A.* There was a small crowd at the bar; at Hunzu's direction, Ivy ordered a glass of wine and retreated to a small booth at the very back of the pub, taking her seat underneath a poster of *Terror from the Year 5000*.

"Wait here," said Hunzu, and walked back to the bar. He slipped under the divider, squeezing past the barman, who was counting out something at the cash drawer, and opened the fridge. The waiter didn't so much as glance up from his register. Neither did any of the customers sitting at the bar. Hunzu strolled past the barman again, this time holding a bottle of wine and a frosted bottle of beer. Ducking under the divider, he snatched a beer stein from a stack behind the counter. A moment later he was back at their booth, dropping the collection of bottles onto the table with a clatter.

"It needs a corkscrew," Ivy said, nodding at the wine.

"Indeed it does," Hunzu agreed, and a moment later he was back behind the bar.

Apparently, the corkscrews were harder to find; Ivy watched Hunzu rifle through several drawers before he found what he was looking for. Neither the bartender nor any of the patrons at the bar so much as glanced his way. As though it was perfectly normal for a customer to be lifting free drinks from the bar, or scrounging around for a corkscrew. As though Hunzu wasn't actually there. Just like that bastard waiter back at the dingy pub. As though Hunzu wasn't there at all.

Hunzu slid back into the booth. Flipping open a small blade on the corkscrew, he began sawing at the foil on the bottle's neck.

Ivy reached over and pinched him.

Hunzu yelped, louder than she'd expected, and dropped the corkscrew. The wine bottle rattled for a moment; Ivy caught it before it could fall off the table.

"Don't *do* that," Hunzu hissed, pulling back his sleeve as though he expected to find a bruise. "You're a bloody terror; I don't know how Demi could stand it."

"Just checking," Ivy said with a shrug. She hadn't even pinched him very hard.

She pulled the remains of the foil off of the bottle, biting at her lip as she looked at Hunzu. She remembered Ambrose wearing that ridiculous yellow suit. She remembered the receptionist, standing in a bare white room with a neon jacket and tie. How the waiter had said *who, miss,* when Ivy told him Hunzu would pay the bill.

"Am I the only person here who can see you?"

"Yes," said Hunzu pleasantly. Smiling smugly, he cracked open his beer and took a long swig.

"Are you going to explain that?" Ivy asked, frowning. "Or are you just waiting for me to ask you how the hell that's possible?"

"I *am* waiting, actually," said Hunzu. "This part is more

fun than I'd expected. Give it here, you're murdering that poor cork."

"Fine," said Ivy, handing over the bottle. "How the hell is that possible?"

"How do *you* think it's possible?" Hunzu asked, as if he were genuinely curious.

"You paid that waiter to make a fuss at the other place," said Ivy. Admittedly, the waiter hadn't looked like a confederate. But wasn't that the point of having confederates, that you couldn't tell who they were? "And the bartender here knows you and doesn't care what you take. Maybe you're the owner; *I* wouldn't know. And you're doing all this because you want to, I don't know, convince me of something that's completely impossible."

"Is that *really* what you think?" Hunzu asked, sounding disappointed. He slid the cork out of the neck of the bottle, and topped up her glass. "Give it another go."

Ivy picked up the glass, swirling it the way she'd seen Demi do. Ivy vaguely remembered Demi telling her that you could tell something about the quality of the wine by the way it sloshed about in the glass. Her flatmate had also been horrified to learn that Ivy routinely drank wine out of a coffee mug. You're not getting the full experience, she said. If you're not drinking out of a glass that lets you appreciate the aroma, you might as well not be drinking at all. You're missing all the subtleties.

"What you said about the gorilla," she said finally. "People don't see you. You're in the room, and they *should* see you, but they don't. They just don't notice."

"Much closer to the mark," said Hunzu. "Now, would you have believed me had I not arranged a demonstration?"

"I'm not sure I believe you now," said Ivy.

"You haven't run out of the pub yet," Hunzu pointed out.

"Only because you still haven't said anything about Demi," said Ivy.

"I'm getting to that part," Hunzu said, taking another sip from his pint and looking uncomfortable.

"You've been saying that for the past half hour," Ivy said, folding her arms. "Assuming you're not just playing me on, I still don't see what this has to do with Demi."

"Yes, well." Hunzu propped his elbows on the table, resting his chin in his hands. "All right. But we'll have to backtrack for a moment. A long time ago, in a galaxy far, far away—"

"I think I've heard this one before," Ivy said.

"Do you want me to explain this or not? A long time ago, in a galaxy far, far away there was a group of, well . . . let's call them people. It'll be simpler that way. These people, or rather these immigrants—actually, they hadn't immigrated anywhere yet. They did later, but maybe that's getting ahead of myself—"

"You were doing better with *Star Wars*," Ivy interrupted again. It almost sounded like he was cribbing his story from one of the dozens of sci-fi movie posters blanketing the walls.

"*Star Wars* has the benefit of a well-defined plot," Hunzu said, looking up at the ceiling with a pensive look on his face. Ivy remembered what he'd said about never having to explain any of this before. "The point is, we're not from here. Weren't supposed to be here at all, from what I can tell. There'd been a war. Actually, several wars. Actually, war doesn't quite cover it, but that'll do for a start. Most of the records I've seen are redacted, and they still make for gruesome reading. Some time afterwards, Valiard was attacked."

"Valiard?" Ivy asked. Something about the name seemed familiar, though she couldn't place where she'd heard it before. "It used to be the immigrants' home," said Hunzu. "My home, too. I've never been there."

"I just thought I'd heard the name before." Maybe he *was* cribbing from an old sci-fi movie.

"I doubt it," said Hunzu, taking another swig of his beer. "The place might not even exist anymore. Might not have existed for a long time." He coughed as he set down the stein. "When the place started falling down about everyone's ears, most everyone who could left through a certain door. One side of the door was in Valiard, and the other side of the door was here in Ireland."

"Doors don't work that way," Ivy pointed out.

"This wasn't a commonplace door. And they didn't actually know the door went to Ireland. From what I've heard, Ireland was a mistake; they meant to go somewhere else. But either they couldn't make it work, or else they never realized the door had sent them to the wrong place until it was too late to change it. And they didn't figure out the Enemy had followed them until a couple of years later. Angevin was never very clear on the details. Anyway, the trows went through—"

"Trows?" Ivy asked. It was another word that seemed to tickle something at the back of her brain, like looking at a Latin phrase on a science test and knowing you studied it but not remembering what it meant. She could almost hear her mother's voice saying the word, which couldn't be right. Victoria mostly tended to talk about her cats.

"Yours truly," said Hunzu, taking another swig from his pint, which was already more than halfway empty. So was Ivy's own glass, now that she looked at it. "Are you going to keep interrupting me?"

"Probably. I mean, you're basically telling me you're a space alien."

"I'm not a space alien," said Hunzu, sounding aggrieved. "I told you, I'm a trow. Rhymes with throw." With his slight Irish lilt, the words sounded nearly identical.

"Trow," Ivy repeated. "I almost thought you were going to say fairy."

"I'm going to ignore that," said Hunzu, giving her a dour look over the top of his beer bottle. "Because I am an exceedingly open-minded and tolerant individual. But in the interest of teaching you proper manners, calling me a fairy is exactly as rude as calling anyone else by that term."

"Sorry," said Ivy. "I didn't mean *that*."

"So—not space aliens. Not fairies. Just different."

"Different meaning invisible?"

"Sort of," said Hunzu. "We needed to stay out of sight. Out of sight of *your* lot, mostly, as well as from the Enemy—the thing that followed us from Valiard. In the early days, there was actually quite a bit of contact between our immigrants and the people among whom they'd landed. There was trade, commerce, treaties, even the odd marriage, if you can believe the old records."

Hunzu stopped, running his hands through his hair, making it stand up at an even more erratic angle than usual. He took a deep breath, started to say something, then ran his hands over his face again.

"Hunzu?" Ivy asked.

"Give me a moment," he said. "I'm trying to figure out how to explain this." He was pulling at the neck of his sweatshirt, stretching it out even further than before. "Imagine a plague. Not terribly contagious, or even terribly virulent, compared to things like the Spanish flu, or the Black Death. The symptoms can take years to appear, and decades can pass before the plague kills. But once the disease is contracted, it's incurable.

"Now imagine the immigrants' neighbors were, all unknowing, carriers of this plague. Every neighbor they'd ever said hello to on the street. Every friend they'd ever shared a meal with, every exotic stranger they'd ever taken to their bed."

"Is that what's happened to Demi?" Ivy asked in a low voice. If Demi were dying, and knew it, would she have wanted to disappear? To walk away and keep it from spreading to anyone else?

"It isn't Demi," Hunzu said, looking fixedly at the empty bottle. "It's *you.*"

The wine in Ivy's stomach seemed to curdle in an instant.

"Hunzu, you're scaring me."

"You should be scared of it," he said heavily, still looking at the beer bottle. "Most of you hardly know enough to be afraid of it. For you, it's just the way things are. The defining feature of your entire life and you barely even question it. It's scarcely begun to touch you, but it's going to. You grow old."

"Growing old?" Ivy repeated, wrinkling her nose. For a moment, she'd thought he was talking about a real illness. Which old age wasn't; it was just what happened to people. "*That's* the big plague your trows wanted to avoid? Old age?"

"Yes," said Hunzu harshly. "It doesn't happen to us, if we're careful. And we're extremely keen on being careful. Though we don't manage the disease so much as we manage the carriers. Do you remember what I said earlier about the gorilla?"

"You said it shows how easy it is to hide things in plain sight."

Hunzu leaned forward, running his thumb up and down the side of his pint glass. "What we did was become the gorilla. We're veiled—it's our way of becoming perceptually invisible. Humans simply don't see us. Or rather, they do, sometimes, but only if we stand out in some way, and there's nothing else competing for their attention. It limits contact. Safer that way."

"When you say veil, you mean like a kind of camouflage," Ivy ventured.

The trow nodded. "It's one of the only things we've brought over from Valiard that still actually works."

"That's why the waiter didn't see you," said Ivy. "Back in that awful pub. That's why he asked if I wanted a table for one. And why Solly and Ambrose were wearing those ridiculous clothes."

"Yes," said Hunzu with a nod. "The waiter only noticed me after you prompted him. That's one reason why I took you there. The place is ghastly, but it's deserted enough I can sometimes manage to order a drink. I wonder if the place is actually a front for some other establishment that also wishes to remain unnoticed."

"You took me to a restaurant that's a front for the mob?" asked Ivy, dropping her glass with a thunk.

"I'd keep your voice down," said Hunzu, glancing back at the bar and tugging on the neck of his shirt again. "Just because *I'm* effectively invisible here doesn't mean *you* are. And if you start looking like one of those crazy people talking to thin air on a park bench, you're probably going to get us tossed out again."

Ivy glanced nervously toward the bar. No one seemed to be looking at her. Still, she was suddenly glad she was sitting in one of the pub's darker corners. She supposed that, given what else Hunzu had said, the fact that the pub was probably a front shouldn't have felt so weird. It wasn't as though it was any weirder than anything else Hunzu had told her. And if she hadn't seen Hunzu scrambling behind the bar for a drink, or seen how the waiter acted at the first pub, she probably wouldn't have believed any of it.

"So, if all this is true," said Ivy quietly. "Which I am *not* admitting to, by the way, then how is it I can see you just fine?"

"I expect that would be Demi's influence," said Hunzu darkly. "You weren't just passing a gorilla in the street now and then—you were sharing a bloody house with one. You were around veils long enough that you began to see through them."

He picked up the bottle, apparently surprised to find it empty, and dropped it back on the table with a clatter.

"Demi's a—" Ivy took another nervous gulp of her wine. "Demi's like you. An invisible person."

"A trow," Hunzu corrected. "You spent too much time around her, and the veil just gave up, poor thing. Now, it can't keep you from seeing her. Or any of the rest of us, for that matter."

"So I can see fair—trows," Ivy corrected herself.

"Yes," said Hunzu. He picked up the bottle, peeling back the edges of the label with his thumb. "And that's a very bad sign. It means the veil isn't quite convinced you're human. Fortunately, it hasn't decided you're a trow yet, either."

"Why would it think I'm a trow?"

"Because it's a piece of junk that's nearly four hundred years old," Hunzu said, shrugging. "The veil was only meant to cloak a handful of trows for a few months at a time. Scout teams, mostly. Even then, the veil sometimes got confused. It thinks that a trow is a man, for instance. Or that a man is a trow. Or that either one is something else entirely."

Hunzu gave up fiddling with the bottle, staring at the movie poster behind Ivy's head.

"Supposing you ate our food, for instance," he continued, still not looking at her. "Or spent too much time in our company. Somewhere, deep in its rusting little brain, the veil might decide perhaps you weren't human anymore. Perhaps you were something else. And the veil, having come to this decision, would do what it was designed to do."

"It would keep me from seeing trows," said Ivy. "But you said it's already trying to do that."

"No, Ivy," Hunzu said heavily. "It would keep *humans* from seeing *you*."

"What do you mean, not see me?" Ivy asked, chilled by the stony look on Hunzu's face.

"You'd be the gorilla," he said simply. "The thing in the room no one can see. And it would be more than just waiters. It would be friends. People you care about. People you love."

What was it Hunzu said at the flat? *If things ever get weird. Not with Demi. With everyone else.*

"But the veil doesn't do that, right?" Ivy protested. "You just said it doesn't work on me. I'm not invisible."

"Not at the moment," he agreed. "But if you continue to spend time around us—if you continually force the veil to consider and reconsider what you are—then someday the veil may make a mistake. It's happened before."

"Well, why can't you just reprogram it? If the veil makes a mistake, just tell it I'm human!"

"It's not as simple as that," said Hunzu, crossing his arms over the table. "This thing is *old*. It's suffered through every sort of patch, repair, and jury-rig imaginable. There are only seven trows alive today who have even seen the original manual. And even if we did know how to reprogram the veil, it just isn't worth the risk."

"I'd take the risk," said Ivy.

I didn't mean a risk to *you*," said Hunzu. "I meant a risk to *us*. What do you think would happen if the veil failed?"

"We'd see you," said Ivy flatly.

"We couldn't hide," said Hunzu, equally firm. "If we aren't hidden, we aren't safe. End of story."

Ivy dropped her glass back onto the table, suddenly very certain her last drink had been a very bad idea. And maybe the one before that, too.

"This is what you were warning me about," she said, closing her eyes and trying not to think of her family. Of not seeing Dad and Shannon again. Or her step-brothers, Garrett and Evan. Not seeing her mum. Or worse, seeing them and watching their eyes slide across empty space. Just like the waiter had done when Hunzu had tried to order a drink.

"Excuse me, please," said Ivy, getting up from the table and bolting to the women's loo, pleased that at least she wasn't staggering. She pushed open the door, locking it behind her and leaning against the wall, which was probably crawling with all sorts of germs Ivy didn't want to think about. She took a deep breath, trying not to gag on the mildew smell faintly intermingling with the loo's citrus-scented air freshener.

Demi was a fairy. Or a trow, or whatever Hunzu said they were called. Demi was a fairy, and she was also Ivy's flatmate.

And no one but Ivy could see her, and that probably explained a few things about Demi's online shopping habits. And they'd lived together for six months, every moment of which Demi had been at risk of contracting some sort of weird human plague. And Ivy had been at risk of becoming permanently invisible.

And Demi hadn't said a word. At least *she'd* known what she was getting into. What had she been thinking? *I'll just invite a random girl to live in my flat and answer the door and water the plants, and hope she doesn't accidentally turn invisible.*

Why would Demi have done that?

Ivy flipped open her phone, as though she might still be expecting a message from Demi. The text alert light was blinking; Ivy's heart sped up for a moment until she saw it was from her mother.

Sent U a video of Suraklin playing w/the socks Im knitting. 2 Cute! Call soon?

Was Suraklin the calico one? Or was that Oriole? There were at least six of them in her mother's house; Ivy didn't always remember which cat was which. Ivy was convinced her mother only kept so many cats because their antics covered up all of the other strange noises the house at Trail's Cross produced. Victoria still claimed her house wasn't haunted. Ivy, who remembered what the house had been like when she was still living there as a child, disagreed.

Ivy's complete disinterest in her mother's cats didn't stop Victoria from emailing Ivy videos of them several times a week. Why her mother would think Ivy would be so interested in her cats, Ivy wasn't entirely sure. She'd never even met the darn things. They'd probably just aggravate her allergies.

OK thx, Ivy texted back, and slipped the phone into her purse.

Even if Ivy did turn invisible someday, she'd always have her mother's cat emails to look forward to. Thank God for the internet.

Glancing in the mirror as she straightened her blouse, Ivy noticed her eyeliner was smudged; she'd never taken it off after going to the Trove offices that morning. Ivy scrubbed off as much of it as she could with a paper towel. She looked paler and plainer without it, which Ivy couldn't entirely blame on the bathroom's greenish fluorescent lighting. Sighing, Ivy tossed the paper towel in the trash.

So Dublin was apparently full of invisible, plant-loving fairies. And Ivy had been living with one for the past six months. Did that officially make Ivy's life weird? Probably.

Except that Ivy couldn't quite shake the notion that maybe now things would go back to being normal. Or at least *more* normal. Like everything would go back to making sense, now that Ivy knew what was really going on.

Or else things would just keep getting weirder. Ivy knew which option she was betting on.

BEFORE RETURNING TO THE TABLE, Ivy stopped by the bar long enough to order a plate of chips. She slid back into the booth across from Hunzu, who'd apparently taken the opportunity to liberate a second beer from the pub's fridge. He'd also peeled both labels off the bottles, weighting the scraps down with the salt and pepper shakers as though he were trying to get them to lie flat. Ivy shoved her glass of wine toward the center of the table, determined not to touch any more of the stuff until she'd at least eaten something.

Hunzu fixed Ivy with a concerned look as she slid back into the booth.

"Are you quite—"

"Perfectly fine," said Ivy, interrupting him. "Does Demi know about this?" she asked, although she could already guess what the answer would be.

"Of course," said Hunzu, sounding surprised. "She was certainly aware of the dangers. At least she told you enough to keep you away from her food. If she hadn't, you and I might have been having this conversation under very different circumstances." He crossed his arms on the table, leaning against it as though he were suddenly very tired.

"Demi wouldn't have poisoned me, if that's what you're implying."

"Not intentionally," Hunzu agreed. "But try to think back to your fairy stories. You may remember there are a few common injunctions. Persephone, for example."

Ivy remembered reading the story out of an old illustrated copy of Bullfinch's *Mythology* that had once sat in her mother's bedroom. "She ate the seeds from a pomegranate, and she was trapped in—"

Hunzu, looking over her shoulder, lifted a finger to shush her. A moment later, a waitress wearing an apron covered in

Lord of the Rings pin badges appeared with a heaping plate of chips.

"Thanks," said Ivy as the waitress set the plate on the table. Hunzu, on the other side of the booth, sat as still as a statue, as though he'd be more invisible if he didn't move. Ivy wondered if that were actually true. There had to be some sort of threshold for what people would and wouldn't pay attention to. It couldn't all come down to outrageous ties and canary-yellow suits.

"Actually," Ivy said loudly, before the waitress could leave. "These are for my friend in the green coat. Just there," she added, nodding at the other side of the booth.

"Oh, sorry," said the waitress, sounding confused. She looked curiously at the other side of the booth. Her eyes narrowed, and Ivy was certain she'd spotted him.

"Right," said the waitress, and pushed the plate of chips over to Hunzu, still sitting motionless. Only his eyebrows, intensely furrowed, indicated his disapproval of Ivy's attempts to get round whatever it was that made him invisible.

The waitress turned back to Ivy, any hint of confusion gone from her expression. "Don't steal too many before he gets back, eh?" she said perkily, and laughed.

Watching the waitress retreating back to the bar, Ivy sighed. Hunzu hurriedly shoved the plate of chips back across the table to Ivy.

"Satisfied?" he asked glumly. "You'd better not make a habit of doing that, mind. People *can* see through the veil, in the right circumstances, but it isn't a good thing for anyone when that happens."

"Fine," said Ivy, grabbing the vinegar bottle and shaking it over her plate. "You want any of these?"

"No," said Hunzu, throwing up his hands. "I can't eat your

food, and you can't eat ours, either. Never eat trow food. Too much, and the veil starts working the other way."

"That's why Demi said she was a vegan," Ivy said, picking up a handful of chips. "It explained why she couldn't eat normal food. So, if there are all these rules, why did she move in with me in the first place? It sounds like she would have been a lot safer on her own."

We *both* would have been safer, was Ivy's unspoken thought. What if Demi hadn't labeled her lentil loaf one day, or left a plate of cookies sitting out on the table? If it had happened, would Ivy have noticed right away? How many days of sitting at her cubicle would it have taken before she noticed that no one in the office was saying hello back?

"That's something you'll have to ask Demi," said Hunzu flatly. "So no food, and no touching. That's where these come in."

He pulled a small package from the pocket of his coat and slid it across the table. It was a pair of white gloves, sealed in plastic as though they'd recently come from a costume shop.

"Wear them whenever you're around one of us," he continued. "There's nothing special about these ones; anything that keeps your hands covered will work. It's more for politeness than anything else. As you and your flatmate have already demonstrated, humans aren't so contagious that just touching one spreads the infection. Usually. It's in your own interest to minimize contact as well, to avoid confusing the veil. No shaking hands. No touching. That way, trows stay healthy, and humans stay visible. Are you with me so far?"

Ivy nodded, swallowing hard. No touching, and no food. It didn't sound terribly hard. This was just more of Demi's weird rules. Ivy had already managed six months of that without anything going wrong. Except that the consequences of breaking one of those rules were more dire than Ivy ever could have guessed.

"Do you think you can live with that? Think about it, Ivy," Hunzu added, cutting her off before she could answer.

"I can," said Ivy in a rush. "I mean, I'll try. I mean, well—" Ivy ripped open the plastic packaging, wiped the last of the vinegar off her fingers, and slipped the gloves over her hands.

"Yes," she said, turning her hands back and forth, checking the fit. They were large, and sagging at the knuckles, but they'd do for the moment. Ivy could always find something better back at the flat.

"Well done," said Hunzu, so softly that Ivy barely heard him. "Now for the practice round." He pulled his phone out of his pocket, and began typing.

"What are you doing?"

"Texting," said Hunzu, as though it was obvious. "Don't forget, you've managed to get Ambrose mixed up in all this, too. He's probably quite curious, actually. He and Demi were —close."

"Curious?" Ivy asked. "About what?"

"About why Demi would voluntarily live in a leper colony," Hunzu said bluntly. "Understand, most of us live in Dublin, but we don't live *with* you. We live *around* you. The practicalities of getting past the veil long enough to even speak to a human are difficult enough, let alone the chance you might contract an incurable disease."

Hunzu's phone let out a chirp; the trow glanced at the screen. "He's on his way."

"If it's so difficult for you to talk to humans, then how do you have a mobile?" Ivy asked. "How would you even be able to set up a contract?"

"The internet," said Hunzu, as though the answer was obvious. "The veil was meant to dissuade physical contact only. It doesn't do a thing for phones or webcams. Used to be, we managed everything by post. Nowadays, we do nearly all of our business with your lot online."

"Okay," said Ivy. If someone had told her she'd be meeting a real-life fairy, and Hunzu's objections aside, it seemed clear that's what they were, she'd never have pictured him using a mobile. Or texting.

"We should probably go outside," said Hunzu, draining his bottle, and gathering up his soggy collection of beer labels from underneath the condiment jars.

"Are you planning on paying for any of this?" Ivy asked pointedly, looking at the collection of bottles he'd swiped from the bar.

"No," he said. "Are you?"

Sighing, Ivy dug out her wallet and dropped the rest of Hunzu's banknotes on the table, before following the invisible man out of the pub.

CHAPTER 6

O utside, Hunzu walked to the curb, buttoning his
coat as he glanced down the street.
    "Ambrose will be along in a minute," the trow
said, scuffing at the pavement with the edge of his boot.
"There's no mistaking his car."

There wasn't. Something long, boxy, and black turned
down the street, pulling up to the curb in front of them. The
car's emergency blinkers came on and a slender figure hopped
out of the driver's seat, walking quickly around to the side of
the car and opening the door. Even though Ivy couldn't tell for
sure in the dim light, Ivy didn't think the woman was a trow.
She was taller than any of the trows Ivy had seen, and her hair
was the wrong color.

The woman opened the door and stood back, giving Ivy

and Hunzu a bland look that was either professional disinterest, or complete and utter boredom.

Hunzu leaned fractionally closer to Ivy. "This would be the part where you get inside," he said.

Ivy's eyes went wide. "With him? Aren't you coming?" Ambrose, she remembered, had offered to give Ivy food back at the Trove offices. And Hunzu had stopped him from doing it. Stopped him from doing it *then*, Ivy amended. No telling if Ambrose might still be considering poisoning her—though at least now Ivy knew enough to avoid eating anything by mistake. "He wanted to meet you, alone, and he wanted me to explain the ground rules before he got near you again. Agreeing was the only way I could get him to leave off with the thumb-screws," Hunzu murmured, ducking his head as though he couldn't quite look her in the eye. "I did warn you, you know."

Leaning closer, the trow prodded her encouragingly between the shoulder blades.

Ivy hesitated. There was a taxi stand only two blocks over; with the money under the begonias, she'd have enough to cover the fare all the way back to Howth, if the driver would agree to let her run inside and fetch it. She wouldn't have to worry about them catching up with her at the DART station, or some deserted bus stop. But Hunzu already knew where she lived.

And if she did get back to Howth, she'd never find out what had happened to Demi. She couldn't simply call the Gardaí and leave it up to them. If Demi was invisible, the police would never be able to find her. If anyone was going to help Demi out of whatever trouble she was in, it had to be someone who could actually see her. Which meant Ivy . . . or Hunzu . . . or Ambrose.

With a nervous glance at Hunzu, Ivy slowly stepped off the sidewalk. She wondered if she ought to text the license plate to Deirdre, but it was too dark to see what it was. Besides, it would only make Deirdre worried, and she'd probably be calling Ivy asking what was going on. Ivy didn't have the slightest idea what she could say that Deirdre would actually believe.

Slowly, Ivy stepped up and into the darkened interior of the car, grabbing at a handle above the door and swinging herself inside. She landed in a heap on a leather bench seat at the rear of the passenger compartment. The inside of the car looked larger than it should have been, almost like a limousine. Behind her, the door slammed shut. Ivy blinked, waiting impatiently for her eyes to adjust to the darkened interior.

Ambrose was sitting across from her, his face dimly illuminated by the glow of the phone in his hand. He'd exchanged the canary yellow suit for something far more beige and usual; the orange tie hung messily from his collar, as if he'd loosened it but hadn't bothered to actually take it off. He was giving Ivy the sort of look one might give an insect crawling up the wrong side of one's window.

Ivy raised her hands, placing them carefully on her lap so the man could see her gloves. Ambrose's hands were covered as well, not the white gloves he'd worn at the office, but a set of leather ones more suited to the chill weather outside. It felt almost too warm inside the car for him to be wearing them; Ivy could feel a hot breeze from the heating vent blowing against the back of her neck.

Ambrose nodded, as though answering a question Ivy hadn't actually asked. He reached over to a panel beside him, pressing a button and speaking into the intercom next to his head.

"A tour of Trinity College, if you would," he said. Ivy hadn't noticed it before, but Ambrose had the same lilt to his voice as Hunzu did, the slightest trace of a Gaelic-speaking accent.

The car slowly pulled away from the curb. From inside the

cab, the sound of the engine was nearly inaudible, and the tinted windows made it difficult to see outside. At least Trinity College was still in the city center. Unless Trinity College was some sort of code for *let's kill her and dump her body in the river.* Ivy tried very hard to convince herself that if Hunzu really thought Ambrose would hurt her, he would have told her to run. Unless he hadn't been kidding about the thumbscrews. . . . Except if Ambrose meant to kill her, he wouldn't have bothered getting Hunzu to tell Ivy all about trows.

There had to be a reason he'd wanted her to know all that. Ivy just had to figure out what it was.

"Do you usually drive around with a chauffeur, or are you trying especially hard to impress me?" Ivy asked, gripping the straps of her purse.

"That is almost a rude question," said Ambrose evenly. "Hunzu assured me you had better manners than that."

"Indulge me."

"If Hunzu hasn't muddled up his explanations, the reason for a driver should be obvious," said the trow, lifting an eyebrow. "Think what a nuisance it would be if Dubliners started phoning the Gardaí with reports of a car that is apparently driving itself. I'm assuming Hunzu already told you a few of the basic rules?"

"Wear gloves," Ivy said, listing them on her fingers. "No touching. No food."

The trow's eyebrow twitched again; he keyed open his phone, jotting something on the screen with a stylus. "Hunzu's getting ahead of himself. The bit about the food isn't normally included in a briefing at this stage. Please be aware," Ambrose added, glancing up from his phone. "That should you use this knowledge to attempt to poison a trow, we will rip out your entrails and leave you hanging from a hawthorn tree."

If Ambrose were kidding, Ivy would have expected him to

smile. But he wasn't; he was still fiddling with his phone. She swallowed hard; Ivy had the notion that Ambrose wasn't making an idle threat so much as he was stating some sort of usual and codified punishment out of the Handbook of Ridiculously Gruesome Trow Justice.

Ivy licked her lips, and wondered whether getting into the car hadn't been a mistake after all. Or maybe the mistake was agreeing to meet Hunzu in the first place. She ought to have gone back to Howth, back when she thought there was nothing going on but a security firm with appalling taste in clothing, and her flatmate's last-minute holiday.

The Gardaí couldn't help Demi. And if Ivy managed to make a mess of things with Ambrose, the Gardaí couldn't help Ivy, either. Not against people the officers couldn't even see.

"I won't," said Ivy hurriedly. "I mean, Demi and I did alright—"

"Yes, Demi," Ambrose interrupted, closing his phone and slipping it into his pocket. "She was well, when you saw her last?"

Ivy nodded.

"She was—managing all right? Living with you?"

"I suppose so," said Ivy, glancing out the window at a passing silhouette that might have been the Trinity bell tower. "She was careful. I guess she had to be. She said she was vegan, so that mostly explained why she never ate real food. She had me around to answer the door, and sign for packages, and fetch things from the shops. She went out every once in awhile, but mostly she was home with the plants, or watching gardening shows on TV. I'm sorry, that makes her sound really boring."

"Demi was never that," said Ambrose, with the first hint of a smile Ivy had yet seen. As though Demi still meant something to him, even though he hadn't seen her for months. Demi had to mean something to him, if he was willing to talk to a germ-infested person to try and find her.

Ivy didn't know if that in any way made up for his suggestion to poison her back at Trove's offices.

"Why did you want to meet with me?" Ivy asked. "Also, why are we driving around Trinity College, and why didn't Hunzu come?" Ivy could hear the plaintive note in her voice even as she tried to quash it. There was no reason to thin Hunzu was any more trustworthy than Ambrose himself.

"You like him?" the trow said, and it was almost a snort. "You probably shouldn't. I certainly don't."

"He wasn't the one who tried to poison me this morning," said Ivy sweetly.

Quickly, Ambrose glanced at the divider between the cab and the driver's seat, as though to make sure it was closed, and Ivy remembered what Ambrose had said about food not being in the usual briefing. She wondered how much Ambrose's driver knew about who, or what, she was currently transporting.

"I wanted to see for myself who Demi selected as her agent," Ambrose said, ignoring Ivy's comment. "She's trained you up quite well, all things considered. We're driving around Trinity College because it has a lovely arboretum, and Hunzu isn't here because I don't care for him."

"He's involved, though," Ivy pointed out. "He's the one who found Demi in the first place. If he hadn't gotten involved, you still wouldn't know anything about where she's been for the past six months."

"I'm aware," said Ambrose, gritting his teeth.

And if Hunzu hadn't come by the flat, he wouldn't have told Ivy that Demi was in trouble, and Ivy would have thought Demi really had gone on holiday. And she never would have tried to check Demi's email, or found the strange web ad, or come down to the Trove offices, and she wouldn't currently be sitting in the back of a limo making small talk with an invisible man who like to make jokes about thumbscrews.

All of a sudden, Ivy had an overwhelming wish that Demi was sitting in the cab with her. Demi would have known whether to trust Ambrose, whether to get in his car, whether the sagging gloves on her hands would really do anything to protect her. But Demi wasn't here, and that was the entire problem.

And there wasn't anyone else . . . Or maybe there was. If Ambrose tried to do something else to make Ivy invisible, Hunzu might be able to talk Ambrose out of it, like he'd done back at the Trove offices.

"Then call up Hunzu," said Ivy. "If I'm involved in this, then so is he."

Ambrose looked at her again, and a muscle in his jaw twitched.

"Neither of you is involved in anything," he said.

"Really?" Ivy asked. "I don't think you would've come all the way down here if you didn't want something."

"What I have in mind could be done by any agent," Ambrose said.

"Then why am I the one sitting in the car?" Ivy repeated.

"All agents legitimately recruited have paper trails. It would either be you, or an agent who isn't on the active rolls, and contacting one would take time."

"An agent like your driver? A human who can see you?"

"Someone like Meredith, yes," said Ambrose with a quicknod.

"Well, if you want me, then call Hunzu. Package deal."

Whatever it was that Ambrose wanted, Hunzu might at least be able to tell her whether it was dangerous or not. Though Ivy had a hard time imagining what it was that

Ambrose wanted. He was invisible; probably that meant he could do whatever he liked. Go wherever he wanted; take whatever he wanted, just like Hunzu lifting free drinks at the bar.

"Fine," Ambrose grunted, pulling out his phone again. "He'd probably be bothering me about it tomorrow at any rate. I doubt he's gotten any further than the nearest pub."

He texted a brief message, then pressed the button on the intercom.

"Hatch Lane," he told the driver; the intercom squawked something unintelligible in reply.

For a moment, there was only the muted sound of the engine, and a low thrumming noise that might have been the radio leaking through from the driver's compartment.

"Why is Demi in trouble?" Ivy asked into the silence. "If she's really a trow, why'd she run away from your lot in the first place?"

Ambrose abruptly dropped his phone onto the armrest with a clatter.

"Demi's in trouble," said Ambrose softly. "Because she is the King of the trows."

"EXPLAIN THAT AGAIN," Ivy demanded, looking from Hunzu to Ambrose in confusion. "Demi can't be a—a *king*; that's impossible!" The car had circled back toward Saint Stephen's Green, picking up Hunzu, who, judging by the clinking noises as he'd hoisted himself into the back of the car, had liberated several more bottles of beer in the interim.

"Best of friends now, are we?" Hunzu had commented, pulling a frosted bottle out of his coat pocket. Ambrose had given him a look that could have chilled the glass all on its own. Ivy hardly noticed him clambering in, still trying to take in what Ambrose had said. These days, kings were something you heard about in historical dramas, or the sorts of magazines that mentioned royalty in the same breath as movie stars and soap operas. Kings were supposed to be people who attended ribbon-cuttings for hospitals, or opening ceremonies at Parliament, or trooped about on national holidays wearing a lot of ceremonial bric-a-brac. Kings weren't supposed to be hiding in a Dublin townhouse amongst a veritable forest of orchids.

"It's very possible, actually," said Hunzu, opening the bottle and taking a sip before setting it carefully into the car's cup holder. "Though to be fair, Demi hasn't been king for very long."

For all that Hunzu had complained about humans being a repository of infectious disease, Ivy noticed he chose to sit next to her rather than Ambrose. She wondered whether the scruffy-looking trow was more afraid of Ambrose than he was of Ivy's germs.

"Why would her being the— the *king*—be dangerous?" Ivy asked. "Is someone trying to take the throne? Does that even happen?"

"It doesn't," said Ambrose, with a look of grim amusement on his face. "In fact, you'd find few who'd be willing to exchange places with Demi in her current situation. She was chosen by lottery last March, and her reign ends on Wednesday."

"What happens on Wednesday?"

Ambrose didn't answer right away, staring through the dimmed glass as though there was something of terrible importance hidden behind it. "The Enemy kills her."

"Kills her?" Ivy repeated incredulously. She looked to Hunzu in confusion. "But you said that was all settled a long time ago. The Enemy was back in Valiard. You got away, right?"

"We tried to," Hunzu corrected, giving a half shrug. "Turns out, coming here wasn't far enough."

The pair of trows looked grim enough that somewhere in the pit of her stomach, Ivy knew they were deadly serious. She looked at Ambrose, who was still staring out the window, not meeting her eye.

"So you knew this thing was coming after her. You've known since March that she was going to—" Ivy stopped, biting off the last word as if she was back at the call center and had been caught going off-script. Even when she was selling funeral packages, she wasn't ever supposed to say that word out loud.

"Going to die?" Ambrose continued brusquely, turning back from the window, though his eyes still seemed to be focused on something far away. "That's how it's been since we first left Valiard. One a year, every year. There used to be an actual ruling family, but that ended back in the 1740s. Ever since, the succession's been decided by lottery. No king rules for more than a year."

"And Demi knew," Ivy said.

"Everyone knew," said Hunzu, as though he was surprised Ivy would even ask.

Demi knew that the Enemy, whatever that was, was coming for her. And so did everyone else. Ambrose knew, and Hunzu, and Solly, and who knew how many other invisible people. They'd known for almost a whole year.

It suddenly felt stiflingly warm in the car; Ivy pulled the scarf off her neck and dropped it on the seat beside her. Something was going to kill Demi. And they'd known for a whole year, and no one had done anything to stop it.

Maybe that was why Demi had left the Liberties in the first

place. She was tired of living with people who took it as a matter of course that she would be dead within months.

"Why does the Enemy want to kill her?" Ivy asked.

"It hates us," said Ambrose, cutting off Hunzu, who had begun to answer. "Revenge for Valiard, I suppose. It was supposed to be hard to get through Tess Aketra's door, and even harder to build a new door from scratch. It *must* hate us; I don't know why else it would even bother."

"That's not entirely the whole story," Hunzu said mildly. "And it can't be coming all the way from Valiard every time; if it did, there'd be backscatter. Other things would come through with it," he added, nodding at Ivy. "But they don't. Maybe the Valoi have a hand in why it still happens. Maybe the Valoi *are* why it still happens—"

"Yes, fine," said Ambrose, impatiently waving his fingers at Hunzu. "If this is going to turn into a discussion about religion, you might as well leave. I already know your opinions, and you know mine."

"Can't she abdicate?" Ivy interrupted, breaking off what sounded like an incipient argument. "Like the king of England did?"

"Officially, no," said Hunzu. "But her disappearance has prompted a certain amount of speculation on what the proper line of succession would be. Though it's the Enemy who makes the final decision, in any case."

"Haven't any of the previous kings ever tried to get away?" Ivy asked. "Or hide, or fight back?"

"Of course," said Ambrose, shrugging. "But it all tends to be rather ineffective. We can't touch it, let alone harm it, and the Enemy almost certainly has a way to track those who've been selected. We don't even know why it chooses to abide by the constraints of our lottery in the first place. It could kill anyone it wants, as far as we know, but somehow or other it chooses whoever *we* choose in the lottery. It could probably kill more than one of us a year, if it wanted, but it doesn't do that, either."

"Don't go making suggestions," Hunzu said in a tight voice, looking around the cab as though he suspected something else invisible had snuck inside with them.

"It won't be here for another six days," said Ambrose impatiently.

"You don't know that for sure," said Hunzu, still sounding nervous. "So stop giving it ideas."

Ambrose merely sighed, rubbing his gloved fingers across his temples as though warding off an incipient headache.

"Could you *not* appoint a king?" Ivy asked.

"That happened frequently in the last days of the original monarchy," replied Ambrose softly. "The throne was vacant as often as it was occupied. Someone always died anyway—if not the king, then *someone*. Should the Year King die before the end of their appointed year, the same rules of succession would apply."

"Probably," Hunzu added, taking another gulp of his beer. "As far as we know, the Enemy can take whoever it wants, whether they're technically the king or not. Maybe one of these years it'll stop being so predictable. Might make for a nice change."

"There's several hundred years of precedent to the contrary—"

"We don't know why it only takes the kings," said Hunzu, talking over him. "So we shouldn't assume—"

"Who would succeed Demi?" Ivy asked, raising her voice as the two men talked over each other. "If she weren't found, I mean?"

"Found by us, or found by it?" Hunzu asked. "Because—"

"She'd be succeeded by her consort," Ambrose interrupted,

so smoothly that Ivy almost didn't catch the sharp look Hunzu gave him.

Pulling his coat closer around his neck, although it was already quite warm in the car, Hunzu picked up the beer and took another long drink.

"So what's your plan for saving her?" Ivy asked into the silence.

"There isn't one," said Ambrose, his irritated expression vanishing rather like the shuttered windows of a house. Hunzu, for once, didn't contradict him, merely cradling his fingers mournfully around the neck of the bottle. "Hard to argue with a few centuries of precedent," Ambrose continued. "I'd just rather—that she wasn't entirely alone when—"

"You want to see her before it happens," Hunzu interrupted, still staring at the bottle. He pulled out a second bottle from his coat pocket, twisting off the cap as he passed it to Ambrose. Ambrose took it, favoring Hunzu with an almost imperceptible nod.

"So, there's no way for Demi to get out of this," said Ivy slowly. "If what you're telling me is actually true, then this Enemy is going to kill her no matter where she is, or what we do."

"That sums it up fairly well," replied Ambrose bleakly.

For a moment there was silence in the cab, broken only by the faint hum of tires on pavement. They were looping back around Trinity College, Ivy thought, as she caught a glimpse of the Graduates Memorial Building through the window, reduced to a silhouette of gables and chimneys. What had Demi been thinking, knowing something terrible was coming for her, and running away from the only people who might be able to help? Not, Ivy reflected, that it sounded like there was much the other trows could do. . . .

"Not necessarily true," said Hunzu, speaking mostly to the

bottle cradled in his hands. "There were a few kings that were never properly accounted for."

"Hunzu, don't," said Ambrose, but it sounded like a token protest.

"Never accounted for how?" asked Ivy.

"Kings that didn't die when they were supposed to," said Hunzu, eyeing Ambrose over the top of the bottle. "Or maybe kings that didn't die at all."

"Bad record-keeping," said Ambrose dismissively.

"Larch Carillon wasn't bad record-keeping," Hunzu replied, crossing his arms and sloshing a few drops of beer onto the upholstery. "And he was a lot more recent than some of the others."

"Larch who?" Ivy asked. It was another word that seemed familiar somehow. A larch was some sort of tree, wasn't it? Maybe it was one of the plants in the parlor back on Thormanby Road.

"I didn't ask you here so we could discuss your conspiracy theories," Ambrose snapped, cutting off Hunzu, who had opened his mouth to answer.

"Fine," Hunzu said, taking another gulp of his beer. "Facts, then. Demi left the Liberties back in July. Yesterday, I was delighted to learn she is in fact still alive, and she's been living in Howth this whole time."

"Why were you looking for her?" Ivy asked. "She was doing just fine until you showed up. Why didn't you just let her hide?"

"Because I didn't know if she was alive or dead!" Hunzu burst out.

He took a deep breath, rubbing a hand across his face before continuing in a softer voice. "I traced her through a greenhouse in Dún Laoghaire. There can't be that many people in Dublin who have a thing for Walkerinter orchids. That got me an address."

"So you broke into the flat," Ivy said, crossing her arms. "Demi left as soon as she found out."

"I suppose she didn't think I'd keep her secrets," said Hunzu, fiddling with the edges of the label of his now-empty bottle. "I guess Demi didn't think to worry about you."

Ivy leaned back in the seat, startled. Hunzu was the one that broke into the flat. Hunzu was the one who'd started this entire mess in the first place, when he'd come to Howth. But if Ivy hadn't told Demi about him dropping by, Demi never would have known he'd been there. And Demi would probably still be at the flat, watering her orchids and pretending that something terrible wasn't about to happen.

"We've also learned that someone has been attempting to locate Demi through the internet," said Ambrose. "Hence the ads on Demi's computer. I did a full search of the Trove web page this afternoon. The page is only accessible through the ad, or by typing in the web address directly. It was created, by the way, three weeks after Demi disappeared."

"So someone else was looking for Demi, too," Ivy said. "Maybe it was a friend of hers."

"Perhaps," said Ambrose dubiously. "No one else seems to know anything about it. Or no one's saying anything if they do."

"Do you think they actually found Demi?" Ivy asked. "Do you think that's where she's gone?"

"It's a possibility," said Hunzu slowly. "And if that's true, we know where she is."

"Where?" Ivy asked.

"The Haven," said Ambrose tightly. "Exactly what it said in the ad."

"I take it King's Haven isn't actually a housing development."

"No," said Ambrose with a sniff. "King's Haven is a bit of a poetic license; Last Haven might be a better translation. It's one of our places."

"One of *Carillon's* places," Hunzu interrupted. "Most of us have better sense than living in the middle of a godforsaken potato field. The old Thane Carillon began building it the winter we came here," he added. "Parts of it are close to four hundred years old."

"Carillon," said Ivy, certain she'd heard the name before. "That's the person who answered the phone when I called."

"That would be the old Thane's daughter," said Ambrose.

Ivy took a deep breath and tried not to look stunned. She'd spoken on the phone with a person who was one generation removed from the Middle Ages.

"*That's* who's trying to find Demi?" asked Ivy. "She sounds like a pretty powerful person. Don't you think she might be safer where she is?"

"I'd like to make certain of that," said Ambrose, pulling his phone from his pocket and scrolling through something on the screen. "And unfortunately, I have no other way of contacting her."

"Can't you just go there and ask?"

Ambrose scowled. "Without a specific invitation, I wouldn't get any further than the door. Taye's careful of who she lets on the grounds. She's—"

"Paranoid," said Hunzu, not quite under his breath.

"Cautious," said Ambrose, giving Hunzu another look. "She has to be, given what else is in the house."

"But you think she might have taken in Demi?" Ivy asked. "Even with this thing that wants to kill her?"

"Curious, isn't it?" said Ambrose tightly. "That someone so concerned with security would willingly open her home to the Enemy's next victim? Perhaps Demi has friends in higher places than I realize. Or other bolt-holes, for that matter. Besides all that, Hunzu here is a member of her court, such as it is."

He leaned forward and clapped the trow hard on the shoulder. Hunzu swallowed, seeming to shrink further into the upholstery.

"Demi has a court?" Ivy asked. This seemed as strange as the idea that Demi could be a king.

"The *only* member of her court," Hunzu clarified weakly. "She never saw fit to pick anyone else before she vanished."

"But she did name you," said Ambrose, the glow from his phone lending a steely glow to his eyes. "I suppose that gives you the job of trying to keep her alive."

"Yes, I suppose it does," the trow agreed, though he didn't sound happy about it.

"So what are you going to do?" asked Ivy.

"You," said Ambrose. "Are going to pay a visit to King's Haven."

THERE WERE two things Ivy knew for certain about their plan. The first was that Ambrose disliked it just as much as Ivy did. The second was that none of them had been able come up with a better alternative. As the car looped around the city center, the three of them hashed out a sketchy outline of a what they needed to do.

There followed an awkward few minutes where Ambrose attempted to get Ivy's hem lengths and sizes, complicated by the fact that the only measuring device the trow had was his phone, which was only five inches long. It also didn't help that Ambrose was still very disinclined to actually touch Ivy, even though they were both wearing gloves. Not that Ivy could blame the trow for wanting to keep a healthy distance from her germs, but it still made things difficult.

She *could* blame Hunzu—he'd spent most of the time giggling and making a half-hearted effort to keep out of Ambrose's way.

Idly, Ivy wondered if whoever had written the story of the cobbler and the elves had any idea that elves were now resorting to smartphone apps to do their tailoring.

Writing down the last of Ivy's measurements, Ambrose pushed the intercom button, rattling off the address of the Thormanby Road flat. He'd begrudgingly offered to give Hunzu a lift as well, but the trow declined. Sooner than Ivy expected, the car was pulling up to the curb across from the townhouse, and the blonde-haired driver was opening the door.

"Tomorrow at seven," Ambrose called as Ivy climbed out of the car. The driver shut the door, nodding curtly at Hunzu, who had slipped out after Ivy. Moments later, the long black car rounded the corner, disappearing back toward Carrickbrack Road.

After the car had vanished, Hunzu dropped in a heap on the edge of the barren azalea planter, looking as though he were finally feeling the effects of the impressive number of drinks he had consumed.

"You ought to go to bed," he muttered. "If Ambrose says he'll see you at seven, count on him being at least ten minutes early. Since I'm *not* going to be meeting anyone at seven in the morning, I'm going to continue my evening's entertainments somewhere a little more populated. I'd wish you good luck tomorrow, but that would imply you needed it."

"Then don't wish me luck," said Ivy, looking up at the darkened windows of her flat. "Wish it for Demi. It sounds like she needs it most of all."

Hunzu grunted something that might have been agreement, fishing out of his pocket the beer labels he'd peeled off the bottles back at the pub. Tearing them, he scattered the quartered pieces across the pavement like confetti.

"Long live the King," he said.

Ivy watched the wrinkled bits of paper fall to the ground. "Do you think she will?" Ivy asked. That was the problem that seemed to hang about Ambrose's plan: even if Ivy found Demi, it didn't sound like there was anything they could do to help. Demi was still the king, and the Enemy was still coming for her.

"Always a chance," said Hunzu dully. "Granted, there's several centuries of precedent to the contrary. The strange years are probably exactly what Ambrose says they are—bad record-keeping. But there's always a chance things will change."

"Maybe not soon enough for Demi," Ivy said, looking up into the leafless branches of the oak tree across the street.

"Maybe not," the trow admitted. "But the alternative, my dear, is that the Enemy kills all of us, sooner or later. One by one. And we'll have a whole year to know it's coming."

Ivy wondered what she would do if someone told her she would die within the year. Probably she'd try to be a nicer step-sister to Garrett and Evan. Write her mother more often. Always eat dessert. And never waste another second of her life at the call center.

"When you were talking to Ambrose, it almost sounded like—"

"Like what?" Hunzu asked, looking sharply at Ivy.

"Like you had hope," she finished.

The trow sighed, leaning back against the bare branches of the azalea.

"One thing we learned from Valiard," he said. "Is that some things are meant to happen and you simply can't change them. Fixed events, and they're not always good things. Just remember," he continued, running a hand over his face as he pulled himself up from the planter. "Even if things go horribly wrong tomorrow, you still won't have changed the ultimate outcome. *That* is quite beyond any of us. And now, if you'll excuse me, I am off to frequent a pub even more disagreeable than the one I took you to. You should be pleased I'm not asking you along."

The trow bowed low, and to Ivy's complete surprise, took her gloved hand in his own and kissed the air above it, his lips hovering fractionally over her wrist.

"Good night," said Hunzu formally, and turned, sauntering down the street toward the harbor.

Lingering near the flower boxes, Ivy watched the disappearing figure until he was nearly at the bottom of the hill before she finally turned away and went inside.

CHAPTER 7

At ten to seven the next morning, Ivy was answering the door in sweatpants and t-shirt. It wasn't due to a hangover, or at least, not entirely. Based on what Ambrose had told her, there wasn't much point in getting dressed ahead of time.

"It's very green," was Ambrose's only comment as Ivy showed him into the flat. He was wearing a navy business suit with a green pinstriped tie, and was weighed down with a half dozen shopping bags. Stepping neatly around the wisteria trellis, Ambrose dropped the bags in a heap on the love seat.

Catching sight of Demi's afghan, thrown over the back of the love seat, Ambrose went very still. He reached out as though he were going to pick it up, before suddenly pulling his hand back as though he'd thought better of it. Ivy wondered whether it was something Demi had brought with her when she'd left the Liberties, or wherever it was she used to live.

The trow turned away from the afghan, and Ivy dropped her gaze, afraid Ambrose would think she'd been staring. Awkwardly, she pulled at a bundle of tissue paper spilling out of the top of one of the larger bags.

"Your gloves, please," Ambrose said softly.

Ivy pulled her bare hand back with a start. She'd completely forgotten she ought to be wearing them.

"Sorry," she murmured. Embarrassed, she dashed upstairs.

Back in her room, Ivy dug through the pile of clothes she'd dumped on the floor last night, eventually finding the gloves half-caught in the shirtsleeves of her blouse. She hurried back downstairs, tugging the gloves on as she went. She'd half-expected some sort of lecture from Ambrose on the topic of manners, or hygiene, or not being so much of a plague-ridden disease vector, but the trow merely pulled a skirt out of one of the bags, smoothing the wrinkles before laying it gently on the footstool.

"This is all for me?" Ivy asked doubtfully.

"You'll need to look the part," said Ambrose. "Your attempt yesterday was—admirable, but I think we can improve substantially."

"If you say so," said Ivy, lifting a corner of the skirt, running the fabric between her gloved fingers.

From another bag, Ambrose pulled two items that had more lace on them than on anything Ivy had seen in her life.

"Start with these, and we'll try a slip to match."

It became apparent that Ambrose was completely indifferent to Ivy's shyness about undressing in front of a stranger. Ivy supposed that she could run upstairs to the bedroom and change, but walking out in nothing but a bra and undies was hardly any better. And, Ivy supposed that if Ambrose could expose himself to Ivy's human germs, or whatever they were, then Ivy shouldn't make a fuss about having to change clothes. It was still awkward, and Ivy was certain she was blushing.

"Do you know the Cinderella story?" Ivy asked as she pulled the sweatshirt over her head. "The one where the girl wants to go to the ball and there's this—"

"We've all seen the Disney movies," Ambrose interrupted testily. "And if you say one word about fairy godmothers, the thing I'll turn into a pumpkin will not be the coach."

"Okay," said Ivy nervously, half-wondering if Ambrose could really do it. Probably he was just bluffing. Demi had never done anything that looked like magic. Except maybe growing orchids in a drafty Dublin townhouse in winter.

A quarter of an hour later, Ivy was twirling in front of the full length mirror in Demi's bathroom, feeling about ten years older and a few hundred quid more expensive. The outfit Ambrose had chosen was a teal pencil skirt and a matching jacket, an ivory shirt, and a pair of black leather boots. Ambrose disdainfully replaced Ivy's faux Vuitton bag with one he claimed was actually the real thing. He appraised the selection of coats hanging on the coat rack by the front door, eventually selecting one that actually belonged to Demi, an anonymous-looking navy-blue Bilberry so dark it almost looked black. It had a hood, and a fuzzy inner liner; Ivy hoped it turned out to be as warm as it looked.

Another of Ambrose's bags contained what looked like the entire Marks and Spencer cosmetics counter. The trow had apparently assumed Ivy would do her own makeup, but when Ivy admitted that she had never actually gone very far beyond eyeliner and a swab of foundation over the occasional zit, Ambrose merely followed her into the downstairs bathroom with a sigh and went to work. He applied the foundation standing a full arm's length away, but as he made his way through the various bottles and compacts, he gradually came a few steps closer. Apparently, his absorption in the task was enough to distract him from the fact that he was standing inches away from the carrier of a fatal disease.

Eventually, Ivy decided to risk a question she'd been pondering for most of the morning.

"Why did you want to poison me yesterday?" she asked.

"This would be easier if you weren't talking," muttered the trow, grabbing a cotton pad and rubbing at something at the corner of Ivy's mouth.

"You can talk," Ivy pointed out.

For a moment, Ambrose didn't say anything, continuing to trace something along the edges of Ivy's upper lip.

"Demi obviously found you more useful on your side of the veil, rather than ours," the trow said, picking up a feathery-looking brush and dabbing it into a tin of powder. "I've rarely had reason to question her judgment."

Which wasn't actually an answer, or an apology, but it was probably as close to either as Ivy was going to get.

"Take a look," he added, nodding toward the mirror as he snapped the makeup case closed.

The effect was rather dramatic. Ivy's skin had gone from mildly blotchy to a uniform cream, which made the added color on her lips and eyelids more noticeable. Garrett would prob-ably have told her she looked like a princess. Maybe Ambrose really *was* some sort of fairytale godmother. Or a fairy Godfa-ther, Ivy thought as she eyed the trow's reflection in the mirror. Complete with horse's heads and everything else.

Ambrose didn't give Ivy long to look herself over before h steered her back into the parlor, where he unlocked his brief-case and began leading Ivy through a harrowingly long list of prospectuses, contracts, and addenda.

"Remember," he reminded her. "You don't need to actually

understand it. You only have to act like you do. Like with poor Solly yesterday. Carillon's people won't have any idea who you are, or what it's about, so the Roinn—my office—gets a call to sort it out."

"Right," said Ivy, knitting her hands together to try and keep from wrinkling her skirts or messing up her hair. If the plan was that the trows at Haven would call Ambrose because they didn't know what Ivy was doing there, maybe it wouldn't matter if Ivy herself didn't know what she was doing there, either. "I still think I look too young to be a, an—"

"An escrow agent," sad Ambrose succinctly. "And you won't look young to them unless you act that way. To us, you look normal. The humans that look different are the ones who look, well—"

"Old," Ivy finished.

"It's unusual for us," said Ambrose, biting at his lip and looking uncomfortable. "Seeing someone's appearance change over time. Still, we manage, don't we?"

It sounded as though Ambrose thought watching a human age over the course of a few decades was more unpleasant to the trow than to the human in question.

"Now, was there anything you wanted to go over again?" the trow asked.

"I think I'm all set," said Ivy, trying to sound more confident than she felt. How real escrow agents managed to keep all these contracts and legal terms straight, she had no idea. Maybe the sheer amount of paperwork would keep anyone at the Haven from looking too closely at any one document. Ivy certainly hoped so; it seemed the only way she could possibly imagine pulling off Ambrose's scheme.

"Then I hope it's enough to ensure an adequate performance," said Ambrose, gathering up the papers and shoving them back into the briefcase. For a moment, Ivy wondered whether he might say something a little more comforting, like *you'll do splendidly* or *I'm sure this will work like a charm.* Then again, perhaps Ambrose's lukewarm sendoff was the best he could manage, under the circumstances.

"All right," said Ivy, mustering a smile. "See you in a few hours."

A moment later, Ambrose slipped out the door.

Ivy went back to the love seat, nearly dropping onto it in a heap before she remembered the skirt. Wouldn't do to be wrinkling it. She picked up the briefcase and fiddled with the latches for a moment. It would be at least another hour until she could call for the taxi. Carefully smoothing her skirt, Ivy sat down gingerly, pulled the briefcase across her lap, and opened it. At least wading through the contracts Ambrose left would help to pass the time.

⚜

NOT QUITE TWO HOURS LATER, Ivy was getting out of a cab in front of a large, weather-beaten garage in a warehouse district somewhere far enough to the west of Dublin that the cabbie had actually turned on his GPS to find the address. Even so, he'd still driven past it three times, making Ivy briefly wonder whether the trows' veil worked on buildings as well as people. Still, the building matched Ambrose's description: white with a double-wide blue checkered garage door with *Scotty's Auto Body* stenciled across the windows. Judging by the quantity of weeds growing up through the asphalt, the repair shop hadn't been open in years.

Ivy paid the driver and got out of the cab, clutching her briefcase. She went to the little office next to the garage, opened the door and stepped into the dim room. A small space heater was humming away in a corner, the only sign that the place was even marginally in use. A few dilapidated chairs stood along one wall, opposite a small desk and a bookshelf full of jumbled plastic binders. The air was heavy with the smell of diesel and mildew. Looking back through the dusty window, Ivy saw the tail lights of the cab disappearing down the street.

Pulling her coat more tightly around her shoulders, Ivy walked to the connecting door leading from the office to the attached garage. She opened it and stepped through, hearing a rustling noise that reminded her depressingly of mice. A dim flicker of daylight shone through the dust-caked windows, more than enough light to illuminate a bulky green Land Cruiser with a large trailer sitting in the middle of the cavernous garage.

The trailer was long, and painted the same dark green as the car, with a narrow row of tinted windows running along the top. It was attached to the car by the hitch and a thick length of chain, as well as a bundle of electrical cords that Ivy assumed connected to the trailer's brake lights. Slowly, she walked around to the rear of the trailer. The top half of the door was more tinted glass, and Ivy could see nothing but a dim reflection of her own face.

"Hello," she called softly.

The trailer jostled on its axles as something inside shifted and snuffled throatily at the edges of the door.

"Just checking," she told it.

Ivy went back to the Land Cruiser, opening the driver's door and tossing her briefcase into the passenger seat. The key was under the mat, right where Ambrose had said it would be. She put it in the ignition and turned it. The dashboard lit up with a bewildering number of buttons and knobs, which looked to be connected to the car's climate control and entertainment systems. There were two small screens on the dashboard: one that seemed to be part of the on-board navigation system, and a smaller one mounted opposite the passenger seat. On the screen, a dark, leggy shape swayed from side to side, perking up at the sound of the car's engine—a live feed from inside the trailer. The screen was also showing the date and time, along with a temperature reading of 16 degrees Celsius. Ivy assumed that was the temperature inside the trailer, as the Land Cruiser's cab felt significantly colder. She turned up the heater, and tapped the seek button on the entertainment console, stopping it when the radio hit on a station playing Snow Patrol.

Leaving the engine running, Ivy hopped out of the cab and pulled on the rope dangling in front of the garage door.

Wheezing and squealing, the door opened. Ivy dashed back into the Land Cruiser and put the car in gear. Cautiously, she pulled out into the deserted street, carefully watching the side-view mirrors as the trailer rolled out of the garage.

SEVERAL HOURS LATER, Ivy was pulling into a turning circle at the end of the long driveway outside the house indicated on Ambrose's map. She'd turned off the M7 nearly an hour ago, following Ambrose's directions onto smaller and smaller county roads, winding her way further into the hinterlands of County Clare. The place didn't look much like an ancient fairy dwelling. Ivy had been imagining something that could have inspired *In the Hall of the Mountain King*—an angular, jagged-looking castle with ravens perched on the rafters. Or a crumbled ruin sitting in a circle of toadstools and standing stones.

Not that there was any question that this was the right house. For one thing, it looked too much like the ad on Demi's phone. Three high turrets towered over the drive, and a shrubby-looking garden nestled at the base of the cream-colored stone walls. Beyond the house, Ivy could make out a few outbuildings, one of which was probably Taye Carillon's stables. Or rather, the stables of Ms. Owen T. Carillon IV, which was the name listed on the contract sitting in Ivy's briefcase.

Ivy pulled the car up to the gate, noting with some pleasure that between the car and the trailer, she'd managed to block the entire entrance. If the whole idea of her visit was that Ivy was meant to be conspicuous and problematic, she supposed she was off to a good start. Setting the hand brake, Ivy hopped out of the car, gathering her briefcase and smoothing her skirt. She pulled a pair of gloves from her pocket, slipping them quickly over her hands. They were black, and more suited to the cold weather than the ones Hunzu had given her. Ivy hoped it was cold enough that it wouldn't look strange for her to be wearing them. No need to be letting on she knew more about trows than she was supposed to.

Escrow agent, Ivy told herself, walking around to the back of the Land Cruiser. Even though the car wasn't moving, the trailer continued to sway impatiently on its axles. Ivy peered through the tinted glass, seeing only the vague outline of a long nose sniffing along the edge of the window. A delicate snort came from the air vents, followed by a sharp clatter of hooves. The trailer shifted again.

"Good boy," Ivy said, and wished she had an apple or two to give it, but Ambrose had warned her not to give it anything to eat prior to the car ride. Presumably, the trows here would be looking after it soon. If they were half as good with horses as they were at horticulture, Ivy was sure the creature was in good hands.

"Wish me luck," she told the horse, unlocking her briefcase and pulling out half a dozen papers at random.

It's just like at the call center, Ivy thought. Squaring her shoulders, she fixed a look of impatience and displeasure on her face, and strode to the door. Just another cold call. Ivy tried not to think of how many of her sales leads responded to her opening pitch by simply hanging up on her.

She was almost expecting a gate, like at the Trove building in Dublin, but there was only a small clump of immaculately pruned shrubbery, with a funny-looking metal contraption in front. Coming closer, Ivy saw it was a sundial, sitting on an ornate, wrought-iron pedestal in the center of the garden. Below it was an inscription.

*One hour alone is in thy hands—the NOW on which the shadow stand*s.

Or in other words, seize the day. Rather appropriate for a sundial.

She walked past the sundial and up to the porch, crossing beneath a pair of plasterwork vines climbing up the columns to either side. No touching, Ivy reminded herself, and no food. It couldn't be that hard to manage. Ambrose wouldn't have sent her here if he thought she'd end up invisible.

Immediately, Ivy wondered if that was true. Maybe Ambrose would have sent her anyway, or maybe he didn't care about Ivy's continued visibility one way or the other. Whatever was coming for Demi would be here in five days. That was probably considerably higher in Ambrose's priorities than whether or not Ivy would still be visible when she walked out of the house.

Taking a deep breath, Ivy rang the bell. She was expecting the chime of a doorbell, but the thing that was ringing sounded like an actual handbell, of the sort found in servant's corridors in historical dramas. The tinkling echoes had hardly faded away before Ivy rang it a second time.

The trick, Ambrose had said, was to not give them any time to make objections.

The chimes died away; Ivy counted to three, and rang the bell again.

The door was opened by a man was only slightly taller than Ivy herself. He had a familiar collection of features that Ivy was beginning to recognize as *trow*: a peculiar mix of dusky skin, slightly crooked noses and luxuriant brown hair. It reminded her of her step-mother Shannon's family reunions in Cork, seeing her step-brothers' dimples and cowlicks plastered liberally among most of the attending relations.

The man wore a blue-grey coat over a lavender shirt and his hair was cropped in a bowl cut that ended just below his ears. Ivy couldn't decide if the lavender shirt was supposed to make him more noticeable or was simply questionable personal taste. If it was, the shirt was considerably more subtle than the color palette they'd used in Dublin.

The trow began to wave her inside, then stopped, regarding Ivy with the same expression of confusion and dismay she'd seen on the face of the receptionist back in Dublin.

"May I help you, ma'am?" he said, speaking in an exaggeratedly loud sort of English that Ivy generally associated with British tourists vacationing abroad.

"I was told that there'd be someone to meet me at the road," Ivy said crisply, keeping her eyes on the papers in her hand. We still exist on paper, Ambrose had told her. Our names are still on census forms and television licenses. Pay attention to the paperwork, and it won't look quite so odd that you can talk to us. "Or would you rather unload him here in the drive? It would be so much easier if we could drive him straight through."

"Excuse me, madam?"

"Straight through to the stables. It would be much easier; don't you think? I'd like to get him settled in as soon as possible."

He hesitated.

She risked a glance up from her papers, narrowing her eyes

as she saw that the trow hadn't the faintest idea what she was talking about.

"I'm sorry, madam, but are you accompanying a guest?"

"Of course not!" Ivy spat out. "I'm seeing to the delivery of Clover Castilian, by Clover Caerphilly out of Larrimore's Dancer. The horse that a Missus . . ." Ivy glanced back at her papers. "Carillon . . . bought at auction last Thursday. I was assured that one of your grooms was going to meet us at the road. Now, is Ms. Carillon wishing to inspect the horse herself, or would you be able to sign for it?"

The trow, if it was possible, turned a shade paler than he already was. "If you'd be so good as to come inside, I'll ask," he said, bobbing his head as he stepped back.

He even spoke like someone out of a period drama. Nervously, Ivy wondered how old he was, and whether that might be exactly how people spoke at the time he learned English.

"Thank you," said Ivy brusquely. "And do be as quick as you can. I shouldn't like to leave him in the trailer any longer than necessary."

"Yes ma'am," the trow said, holding the door wide—very wide—for Ivy to step through. "Please come in."

Ivy supposed a real escrow agent would probably have insisted on waiting out in the cold with the horse, but the temptation to get a look inside the house was far too appealing. Besides which, the horse had already been in the trailer all morning; another five minutes was hardly going to matter.

Following the trow inside, Ivy caught herself looking suspiciously at the back of his head. Except for the bad haircut and the lavender shirt, he looked quite unremarkable, not anything like Ivy imagined a fairy would look like. Ivy glanced back at her papers, suddenly afraid that he might turn and catch her staring. But he merely crossed to the far end of the room, slipped through a tall wooden door and closed it firmly behind him.

The room Ivy was standing in reminded her of an expansive basement. The only window was a stained-glass transom over the front door, depicting a row of yellow flowers with a pair of red-eyed butterflies hovering above them. Ivy found it somewhat unsettling. Perhaps it was the way the butterfly's eyes seemed to glow, although Ivy knew that it was only an effect of the sun through the glass.

Ivy hoped he'd be back soon. The longer she stayed here, the better the odds that someone would figure out that her unexpected appearance wasn't simply a matter of misplaced paperwork. Ivy wanted to be well on her way back to Dublin before that happened.

Still juggling the briefcase and papers, she turned to get a better look at the room. The walls were made of the same creamy stone as the outside of the building, giving the impression that the entire house was made from one massively thick rock wall. Several cracks dotted the wall, about two feet long and not any wider than Ivy's hand. They looked almost like arrow slits, though Ivy had never seen any outside of a history book. Beside the closest slit was a small metal plaque, etched with a series of bewildering characters that didn't look like any alphabet Ivy had ever seen. Inside the room were a few small tables, two Tiffany lamps, and a few uncomfortable-looking wooden chairs. It wasn't a waiting room that exuded a great deal of welcome.

Ivy wondered what trows in this day and age would need to defend themselves from. It wasn't as though Vikings ransacked the coast anymore, or burned down monasteries. And even the best-designed castle in the world didn't sound like it would keep out someone like their Enemy.

The door swung open, and the trow in the lavender shirt was back, this time wearing a pair of starched white gloves.

"I'm afraid we're still attempting to sort out the papers," the trow said loudly. "But if you'd be so good as to give us a few minutes to—"

"I'm sorry," Ivy interrupted, in a tone that implied she wasn't sorry in the slightest. "I can't leave the horse without making an inspection, and I was assured one of your grooms would be on hand to unload it. Are you telling me they weren't even informed?"

"I'm certain he was, ma'am, but—"

"Then shouldn't you give him a ring?" Ivy asked, glancing at her watch. "I've already been waiting for nearly ten minutes."

"I am not in a position to accept the animal on Taye Carillon's behalf," replied the trow, with just the slightest edge of irritation to his voice. "Now if you would kindly—"

"I'm sorry, but you'll need to either accept the animal as we'd arranged, or refuse it and forfeit the deposit," Ivy said in the iciest tone she could muster. "Ms. Carillon was hardly the only bidder, and while I would hate to inconvenience a client, my first priority is the health of the animal. I don't suppose you're suggesting the horse remain in the trailer indefinitely, are you?"

"No, madam," said the trow nervously.

"Then if you aren't prepared to sign for him and allow the inspection, I won't take up any more of your time. Our office will be in touch later this week." As she spoke, Ivy opened her briefcase, and dropped the papers back inside, closing it with a snap.

Come on, she silently urged him as she walked purposefully toward the door. *Your boss's prize thoroughbred is going to disappear in about thirty seconds unless you do something about it.*

If the trows didn't take the horse, Ivy didn't want to think about who might get stuck minding the thing. That would be infinitely worse than babysitting Demi's orchids.

Ivy's hand was on the doorknob before the trow finally spoke up.

"I'll ask one of the grooms to meet you in the drive," he said nervously.

"Splendid," said Ivy, wondering at how naturally she was managing this haughty, irritated tone. She'd never been able to talk to clients at the call center like this. Back there, she'd either been reading from a script—or stammering an apology and hoping her floor manager wasn't listening in.

Ivy turned the doorknob and walked back outside, trying to shake the feeling that the butterflies in the transom were watching her as she left. She went back to the trailer, and took a quick peek through the window. Clover Castilian rubbed his nose against the door, as though he, too, were complaining that he usually didn't have to wait this long to get out.

Ivy wondered (not for the first time) how on earth Ambrose had managed to acquire a thoroughbred racehorse on twelve hours' notice. Probably it would be better if she didn't ask too many questions about that. It seemed unlikely he'd been stolen (at least, Ivy hoped it was unlikely). She assumed there would be more to stealing a racehorse than simply walking out without paying for it, like Hunzu had done at the pub.

Ivy heard the gate rattle, and turned around as two trows came through it. They both wore brown coats with large metal buckles, and spurs that glinted brightly at the heels of their boots. Covering their hands were the ever-present white gloves. As the pair approached, Ivy lowered the ramp on the back of the trailer and unlocked the door. Slipping the keys into her pocket, Ivy backed a few steps away from the trailer, nodding cordially at the grooms.

She was dearly hoping the grooms would take the initiative and get the horse out of the trailer themselves. Ivy didn't want to admit that she knew absolutely nothing about handling horses. If *she* tried to get Clover out of the trailer, the horse would probably rear, or kick, or take off running who knows where.

"I'm Silas," the first trow said, introducing himself with a little nod. He held his arms crossed in front of him, as though to ward off any possibility of a handshake. "Do you have the bill of sale?"

His speech reminded Ivy strongly of Hunzu when she'd first met him back in the flat—speaking a little too loudly and a little too slow.

Ivy hesitated. She hoped someone here had already called Ambrose. If they had, there wasn't anything else she needed to do but get a signature on the triplicate forms in her briefcase and get herself back to Dublin.

But what if they hadn't called Ambrose?

"Let's take care of the paperwork after I've seen the stables," she said.

Silas nodded and turned back to the trailer, which the second trow was already opening. The groom slipped inside, emerging a moment later with the horses' reins sitting loosely in his hands. Silas opened the trailer door wide, and Clover Castilian came trotting eagerly down the ramp.

The horse was silky brown in color, darkening to black along its legs, with a light, almost cinnamon-colored mane. Not knowing much about horses (aside from a *Misty of Chincoteague* phase that she'd rather not admit to), Ivy didn't quite know what to make of this one. Except that, like all of the other things Ambrose had given her, the horse looked gorgeous. And expensive. *Very* expensive. Ivy wondered exactly how much Carillon was supposed to have paid for it.

Clover Castilian stepped cautiously off the ramp, shaking his head as though he were unsure of the feel of asphalt under his hooves. The groom said something unintelligible, and took a firmer grip on the reins. Clover pawed at the ground nervously, but stopped as Silas stepped in front of the horse, making a clucking noise. While the groom held the horse still, Silas walked in a wide ring around the animal, the spurs on his boots jingling like coins. In the sunlight, the horse looked like a bronze sculpture that had recently been burnished.

"You wished to see the stables, ma'am?" Silas asked.

"Yes, please," said Ivy, trying not to look nervous about the prospect of walking further into Carillon's estate.

Silas went to the gates, while Ivy, the horse, and its handler fell into step behind him. Ivy was clutching her briefcase so hard her fingers were digging into the leather. Once she was through that gate, she couldn't just run back to the Land Cruiser if things went sour. And she couldn't expect Ambrose, or Demi, or anyone else to bail her out if things went wrong. Whatever happened, Ivy would have to manage on her own.

Silas pulled open the gate and motioned Ivy through. She stepped over the threshold, somehow feeling that she ought to duck, even though the door was more than tall enough to accommodate her. Behind her, the groom and Clover followed, and the door swung shut. Ivy heard the lock engage with a quiet snick.

The grounds behind the house were larger than they looked from the outside, surrounded by a low stone wall bordered by a thick hedge of barren branches. The path they were following turned away from the wall, sloping gently down the hill toward two low buildings a few hundred meters away. Farther off, Ivy could see a half dozen horses grazing at the bottom of the hill, and beyond them, a large copse of trees. As the path turned further away from the house, Ivy caught sight of a hedge-rimmed formal garden surrounding a small pond. A few ducks were circling its edges, swimming alongside something large and white that Ivy assumed was a swan.

Ivy heard a scuffling noise behind her, and turned just in time to see the groom settling himself on Clover's back. The trow hadn't even bothered with a saddle, merely throwing his own coat blanket-like over the horse's withers. The groom nodded to Ivy, and flicked the reins once, following it up with a quick jab of his spurs that set the horse cantering toward the stables. As the horse and rider passed them, the groom pulled a phone out of his pocket, switching the reins to his left hand as he typed with his right. Whoever this fellow was, he looked like he was ready to join the Lipizzaners. Or maybe run away with the rodeo.

Ivy deliberately kept her pace slow, studying the back of Silas' head as they continued down the hill. He looked familiar somehow. Nothing that Ivy could place, but something about his eyes, perhaps, or the way his brow wrinkled when he was examining the horse. Probably he looked familiar because he looked a bit like every other trow she'd met over the past two days. Now that she knew what to look for, there was no mistaking them for anything else.

Ahead of them, Clover and the groom disappeared through an arched doorway leading into one of the low-lying buildings. Ivy glanced behind her, feeling increasingly nervous the further she got from the Land Cruiser.

Nothing to worry about, she told herself. I'm only here delivering a hopefully-not-stolen horse to a very rich invisible person who might possibly have kidnapped my friend. Nothing to worry about at all. She'd just have a quick look around, get her damn forms signed, and get back in the car. Probably the whole trip had been pointless and Demi wasn't here at all. No way to tell from out here in the gardens. And why couldn't Ambrose have gotten something for her to deliver that could give her an excuse to be *inside* the house, like an antique bureau, or a Ming vase?

Silas disappeared under the arched doorway and Ivy followed, stepping into a long hallway, light flooding in from the half-doors on either side. The air smelled of hay and mulch.

Over the stall doors, the sleek heads of at least a dozen horses regarded her curiously. Partway down the hall, the groom dismounted, removing the coat from Clover's back and turning the horse into one of the stalls.

Ivy continued slowly down the hall, feeling the straw crunching underneath her boots. To her left, she passed what looked like a tack room—the pegboard walls were covered with a collection of saddles, halters, and bridles. Ivy glanced at the other side of the hall, which looked to be nothing more than an alcove jam packed with bales of straw.

Then a sheen of metal behind the straw caught Ivy's eye. It looked almost like a bumper, as though a car had been wedged into the storeroom and the straw stacked in front of it—almost but not quite obscuring it from view.

It was probably a farm truck, Ivy told herself. A farm truck that someone had decided to park in a barn and hide. But the bit of the car that Ivy could see didn't look like a farm truck. It looked suspiciously like the rear bumper of another car Ivy had seen recently. Demi's VW Rabbit.

"Ma'am," said Silas softly, and Ivy nearly jumped. She turned back to him, reminding herself the trow would think it perfectly normal that Ivy had momentarily forgotten he was there. She couldn't look like she'd been staring. If she looked too interested in the mostly-hidden car, Silas might wonder why.

"May I see his stall please?" Ivy said quickly, and started down the hall without waiting for Silas to answer. Behind her, she could hear the faint jingle of his spurs as he followed.

It had to be Demi's car. Why else would anyone have hidden it? If it was Demi's car, then it was the first evidence that Haven really was connected to Demi's disappearance. But had Demi come here herself ? Or had someone brought her here against her will?

"This will be Clover's here," said the groom, nodding to the box stall on his left as Ivy caught up with him. The stall was huge, nearly as large as the whole downstairs of Demi's flat, with a generous layer of straw on the floor, and a food trough mounted on the back wall that Clover was eagerly sniffing.

"Perfectly suitable," Ivy murmured, snapping open the clips on her briefcase, and rummaging through the papers. The bill of sale was in here somewhere, along with the rest of Ambrose's spurious paperwork. The groom would sign it, and she'd walk back to the Land Cruiser and drive away and she still wouldn't know anything at all. Apart from the fact that Demi *was* here.

Ivy spotted the bill of sale, pulled it out, and plucked a fountain pen from the side pocket of the briefcase.

At least when Ambrose came along later, *he'd* be able to take a proper look around.

But there was no guarantee Ambrose would tell her anything if he did. Ivy suddenly realized that she had no way to contact either of her trow confederates. Would Ambrose tell her if he found anything? Or would he just vanish, and tell himself it was for Ivy's own good? And on Wednesday, when the Enemy came, Ivy would still be sitting in an empty flat, waiting for a phone call.

If she didn't find Demi herself, today, she might not hear from Demi ever again.

Ivy needed to find a way into the house.

Silas had plucked a pen from somewhere in the depths of his coat, and was unscrewing the cap.

"Are you authorized to sign for Ms. Carillon?" Ivy interjected sweetly. "Because I'll need a notarized form if that's the case."

The trow's face fell.

A few minutes later, Silas and Ivy were walking back up the hill toward Haven.

⋘⋙

THEY ENTERED through a low door at the side of the house and turned down a narrow corridor. A breath of warm, musty air brushed past Ivy's face as she followed Silas into a small, brightly-lit courtyard. Large ceramic pots and raised planters took up most of the middle of the room, arranged around a small, tinkling fountain. The plants surrounding it were huge, leafy, and flowering. One particularly large palm was tall enough that its leaves were brushing the ceiling. A skylight bathed the room with more light than Ivy would have thought possible, given how dreary it was outside.

She followed Silas past the fountain and up a wide flight of stairs. Every few feet, the wall was marred by long, vertical breaks in the stone—more arrow slits. The only sound was the clatter of their boots on the stone steps, and the receding murmur of the fountain. There seemed to be no one else here other than Ivy and her guide. Either there weren't very many trows here to begin with, or else they'd all cleared out in advance of Ivy's arrival (and that of her scary human germs). Silas turned down a second passage, opening another door. The trow motioned Ivy in with a little nod of his head, then hurriedly shut the door behind her.

135

Resisting an urge to try the handle to make sure he hadn't locked her in, Ivy looked around the room. To her right was a large picture window; in front of it sat a small chair and a table with a garish collection of orchids sprawling out of small porcelain pots. Opposite the door stood a massive wooden desk with an empty leather chair behind it, and two thick tapestries of an intertwining knotwork pattern. Across from it hung an ostentatious gilt-framed painting of a dandified man sitting next to a large bowl of fruit. Above the door were two smaller transoms with the same weird butterfly design as in the foyer.

Twin beams of sunlight illuminated a long strip of dust motes hanging in the air. The room smelled strongly of wood polish. Gingerly, Ivy sat down in the chair next to the orchids, setting her briefcase at her feet. Away from the sounds of the fountain, the room seemed oppressively silent, as though something in the room were holding its breath.

Ivy wondered if Silas had gone to tell Carillon she was here. She pulled her briefcase onto her lap and clicked open the latches. As long as she was waiting, she might as well go over the particulars of the supposed contract one more time, just in case Carillon asked her any questions. The bill of sale was sitting on top; Ivy picked it up, trying to smooth out a few creases from where she'd hurriedly shoved it into the folder back in the stable.

Someone stood up from the empty chair.

Ivy jumped, the briefcase falling to the floor in a shower of paper. She glanced at the door, still closed, and looked quickly back at the desk. There was a woman standing behind it who hadn't been there before.

Not a woman, Ivy corrected herself. A trow.

The trow was tall, and a moment later Ivy was correcting herself, because she was no taller than any other trow Ivy had ever encountered, which was to say, barely any higher than Ivy herself.

"Your name is Ivy Gallagher," she said. "You reside in the Howth neighborhood of Dublin, and you were most recently employed by Eirecom, a now-defunct telephone sales business." Ivy recognized the voice from her call to the phone number listed on the King's Haven ad. Taye Carillon was wearing a white shirt with a high collar, and a row of tiny buttons running from mid-chest all the way up her neck. A similar row of buttons ran up the sleeves from wrist to elbow, disappearing into a dark, slitted tunic that looked like it could have come from the BBC's costume department. Her hair was brown, nearly the same shade as Ivy's own, and pulled into a tight French braid.

"You seem very well informed," said Ivy, trying not to look startled.

"I *am* very well informed," Taye Carillon corrected her.

"And who do I have the pleasure of speaking with?"

"You should say, rather, to whom do I have the pleasure of speaking?" said the trow carelessly. "I am, as you might be aware, the head of this small enterprise. You may call me Ms. Carillon."

According to Ambrose, Carillon was the daughter of one of the trows who'd originally come from Valiard, back in sixteen whatever-it-was. Ivy wondered how many generations of her own family it would take in order to find an ancestor who was born in the same year. Or even in the same century.

"Very pleased to meet you," said Ivy, and although she daren't risk shaking hands, she bent one leg in a sort of curtsy.

Carillon seemed to smile at that. At least, one corner of her mouth twitched, the way a cat's might, upon sighting a particularly plump-looking bird. Ivy shivered at that, feeling as though the collar on her new blouse had become just the slightest bit tighter.

"Please excuse me," Ivy said, dropping to her knees and gathering up the papers that had scattered on the floor. "I didn't see you."

"Indeed," said Carillon, and again Ivy had the sense that she amused the trow. Of course Ivy hadn't seen her. Carillon must be used to that. Assuming that Hunzu and Ambrose hadn't been telling her a pack of lies when they'd told her about veils. "I understand I have purchased a horse," said the trow casually. "I confess, the transaction must have slipped my mind. But as my groom assures me the animal appears to be a good addition to the stable, I shall chalk it up to a happy accident."

Ivy swallowed hard, ducking her head to shove the last of the papers into his binder. Hopefully the racehorse itself was valuable enough to serve as a somewhat unorthodox letter of introduction. It had to be a good sign that Taste was talking with her, instead of immediately tossing her out of the building.

If she'd just let Silas sign the damned paper, she'd probably be halfway back to the M7 by now. And she still wouldn't know anything about where Demi was. And if anyone knew here whether Demi was on the estate, it would probably be Taye Carillon herself.

"Do you have his stud papers, by any chance?" Carillon asked.

Ivy ruffled through the papers, pulled them out and started to hand them over, before catching herself and dropping them on the desk. Carillon wasn't wearing gloves: the first trow Ivy had come across who neglected the precaution.

Carillon picked up the papers, scanning through them for several minutes, raising her eyebrow at one point as though in surprise. Ivy waited in silence, straightening the rest of the scattered paperwork, hoping whatever Ambrose had given her would stand up to scrutiny. Aside from the slight rustle as Carillon flipped through the pages, the room was completely silent. Almost as though the room itself were waiting for something to happen. Like a creepy flock of butterflies flying in through the arrow slits, or the painted man in the gilded picture turning his head to wink. Which was nonsense, but Ivy still couldn't dispel the feeling.

"An impressive pedigree," Carillon said finally, dropping the papers into a drawer in her desk. "I'll look forward to seeing the creature in person. I understand you are in need of a signature?"

The supposed reason Ivy'd come up here; she'd almost forgotten it. Ivy dove back into her briefcase for the form, riffling through the papers. She thought she'd kept the blasted contract on the top of the pile, but it had all gotten jumbled after she'd spilled it on the floor.

"Haven't misplaced it, I trust?" Carillon asked, walking around the desk.

"No, here it is," she said, relieved. It had been at the top the whole time; Ivy wondered why she hadn't seen it in the first place.

She turned to drop the paper onto the desk, only to find Taye Carillon already at her shoulder. The trow took the contract, moving a letter opener and a few fountain pens to one side as she spread the papers across the desk. Her eyes flicked back and forth over the print as she scanned the top page, then the carbon copies underneath. Taking a deep breath, Ivy stepped backwards, remembering Hunzu's warnings about physical contact. If any of that were true, Carillon ought to be staying further away. She wasn't. Conversely, that made Ivy even more eager to keep a healthy distance between them.

"I prefer to approach these sorts of transactions with an

abundance of caution," Carillon said, gathering the papers back into a bundle. "Far better for one's long-term prospects. Would you be so kind?"

She was asking for a pen, Ivy realized. Slowly, Ivy pulled the fountain pen out of her briefcase, unsure whether to put it on the table, or place it in the trow's outstretched hand.

Carillon didn't wait for her to decide, but plucked the pen straight from Ivy's fingers. Turning back to the paper, she signed her name, then set the pen on the table for Ivy to sign it in turn. Cautiously, Ivy stepped forward, picked up the pen and bent over the contract. Carillon was standing so close that Ivy's sleeve was nearly brushing the side of the trow's tunic, and this was much closer that Ivy ever wanted to come to some alien creature who could make her permanently invisible just through mere proximity. Ivy signed her name as quickly as she could, slipping the pen into her briefcase as she stepped back from the desk.

Carillon was still looking at Ivy curiously.

"There seems to be a bit of straw in your hair," the trow observed. "If you'll allow me—"

"Please don't touch me," Ivy said quickly, backing up almost to the wall.

"Very well," said Carillon, dropping her hand. She gathered up the paper, slipping behind her massive desk. The trow tore off the top page of the contract, dropped it onto the desk, then tucked the carbon copies into a drawer.

"You appear to be new to the escrow agency," said Carillon, still shuffling through the open drawer as though she was looking for something. "In fact, the receptionist there had never heard of you. But it's apparent you've been working for some other agency for quite some time."

The trow stood up from the desk, turning back to Ivy. She was pulling on a pair of starched, white gloves.

Ivy felt her heart drop into her stomach. Carillon had been testing her. She wanted to know if Ivy knew enough to be afraid of close contact. And Ivy had just given away that she knew more than she ought to.

Which meant it wasn't going to be as simple as just getting her form signed and walking away.

"I work for quite a few people, Ms. Carillon," Ivy said, picking up the signed contract, slipping it into her briefcase, and closing it. "I shouldn't take up any more of your time."

"I believe you know the one I'm referring to," the trow continued, crossing her arms, running her fingers up and down the tiny buttons on her sleeves. "You're very good, you know. Almost as good as the Lewes girl was. Someone's obviously gone to quite a bit of trouble with you. I think we both know who that is."

At first Ivy thought she meant the horse and the trailer and the Land Cruiser; God knew Ivy had no idea how Ambrose had managed it all. But almost immediately, she realized Carillon meant something else. Ivy could *see* trows, could talk to them—at least, she could once she realized there was actually one in the room. *She's trained you up quite well,* Ambrose had told her.

Taye Carillon thought that she'd been 'trained up', as Ambrose had put it. And, in a sense, Ivy supposed she had.

Ivy took a deep breath. It was just like going off-script at the call center; she'd done that plenty of times. Here, there were no pre-written answers to fall back on; she'd have to muddle through on her own. Carillon already knew Ivy wasn't who she was pretending to be. She didn't think clinging to the illusion of being an escrow agent would get her anywhere with the trow.

It seemed much longer than three days since Ivy had last sat in her cubicle, an invisible voice reading someone else's words off a computer screen.

"I'm looking for a friend of mine," Ivy said. Carillon raised an eyebrow as though inviting Ivy to continue. "A friend who likes plants a lot more than she likes people. I used to run errands for her and I haven't seen her in several days. If she were in trouble, perhaps she would have gone to some of her acquaintances. People who were in a position to help her. People who had a certain degree of influence."

Carillon smiled, as though she were pleased that they'd finally gotten to the heart of the matter. "You've been running errands for Demi Gentian," she said quietly.

"Have you seen her?" Ivy asked bluntly. "Is she here?"

"Your associate has a great number of bolt holes, Ms. Gallagher," she said, ignoring the question as she glanced toward the gilt-framed portrait on the wall. "More than either of us know about, I suspect. Wherever Ms. Gentian has gone, I trust she's there of her own volition. Your friend would be a difficult one to coerce."

Even if Carillon wouldn't admit to it, Demi was almost certainly in the house, or had been very recently. The car in the stable proved as much. But whether Demi was here of her own free will, as Carillon claimed, wasn't something Ivy was prepared to accept just on the trow's word.

For the second time that morning, Ivy decided to do something Ambrose probably wouldn't approve of.

"I occasionally take on new clients," Ivy said, slipping a sheet of paper out of the briefcase, and jotting her mobile number on the back. "Just something to keep in mind. And I would be very interested in hearing from Demi again, if you should happen to see her."

She placed the paper on the table, since she wasn't going to risk handing it to the trow, with or without gloves. Carillon picked it up, cocking her head as she looked at it, then opened a drawer and slid the paper inside. Every motion seemed slower than it ought to be, as if she had all the time in the world. Which she probably did. Ages and ages to do nothing but read fine print, if what Hunzu had told her about their lifespans was true. No wonder the trows seemed to be so successful at whatever it was they actually did.

"The horse you've brought is a great indicator of your interest in Ms. Gentian," said Carillon finally. "In return, I shall tell you something of equal value. Regrettably, Ms. Gentian shall be leaving us soon. Her whereabouts until then are no one's concern but her own, and I doubt she'll be requiring your services. I suggest you think of this hiatus as an opportunity to reconsider your involvement in our business."

"I'm aware of the risks, Ms. Carillon," Ivy said.

Carillon didn't reply, merely walking around the desk toward the little table with the orchids, staring out the window into the garden behind the house. Ivy could distantly see a figure on horseback in one of the fields, and wondered whether it was Clover.

"Tell me," said Carillon. "What do you think of the painting?"

Surprised by the question, Ivy went to the portrait, looking at it carefully. It looked unusually modern for a place that included arrow slits and tapestries among its decorations. If you could call the Twenties modern, Ivy added, looking at the bow tie pinned haphazardly to the man's collar and the pince nez tucked into his pocket. The man in the painting had picked up an apple from an overflowing bowl of fruit, and was polishing it on his sleeve. The painter, strangely, hadn't quite captured his face, although the piece was obviously meant to be a portrait. The figure was too much in profile, showing only a rounded, flattish nose, broad cheekbones, and a head of brown hair, slicked back into what was probably a fashionable style for the time.

If Carillon was content to wear clothing that went out of style sometime in the Middle Ages, then the man in the painting looked like someone who fully embraced the costume of the period. Or perhaps that was simply how the artist had chosen to portray him—distracted by an apple and not even bothering to look straight at his observer. (In Taye's portrait, if there was one, Ivy was certain she'd be staring the observer full in the face. And it would probably be one of those creepy ones where the eyes follow you around the room.)

"It looks like he wandered into a still life by mistake," Ivy said. "It's very good," she added, not wanting Carillon to think she was criticizing it.

The trow snorted, a brittle sound that might have been a laugh.

"My son, Larch," Carillon said, still looking out the window. "He wandered into very many things by mistake, I should imagine. One of those mistakes took him from me." She turned back to the desk, folding her arms across her chest. "Before deciding on a course of action, Ms. Gallagher, it is always worth considering whether an imprudent move would cause pain to those we cherish most highly."

"Is business with you an imprudent move?"

"You would do better to ask that of my associates."

"Such as Ms. Gentian?" Ivy asked.

"Among others," sad Carillon calmly. "You would trust her opinion, then?"

"Yes," said Ivy, feeling like it was the first thing she'd said all day that wasn't partly a lie.

The trow reached for a small button at the corner of her desk. A moment later Ivy heard a bell chime somewhere down the corridor.

"Silas will show you out," said the trow, making another

little bow, which Ivy hastily returned. "It has been an enlightening discussion. For both parties, I hope."

It was on the tip of Ivy's tongue to say *Not as enlightening as I'd hoped it would be.* She still hadn't gotten a straight answer from Carillon about whether Demi was in the house or not— or if Demi wasn't here, why a car that looked suspiciously like her Rabbit was hidden out in the stables. But Ivy thought she'd pressed matters with Carillon as far as she could— certainly much farther than Ambrose's original plan had entailed.

Where was Ambrose, anyway? Still driving in from Dublin? If one of Carillon's people had called him, he should be on his way by now. Without the horse trailer, Ambrose—or his driver—would have made much better time than Ivy had done in an unfamiliar car and towing a trailer besides.

The door opened, and a second trow stepped silently into the room. It wasn't Silas, though he wore a similar coat, with light blue shirt underneath. A long fringe of hair hung across his eyes, giving his face an almost feminine look. Ivy stiffened, trying to hide her reaction, as she caught a glimpse of the line of puckered scars dotting his cheeks.

"Angevin, please take our guest to the foyer," Carillon said to him. "And ring one of the grooms to have her vehicle brought around to the gate."

Had the Land Cruiser been moved? Interesting, considering Ivy still had the keys. She looked back at Carillon in surprise, but the trow had a phone in her hand and was typing something on it. Not quite the Middle Ages after all. Biting her lip, Ivy followed Angevin out of the study.

This was the man from Demi's front garden, three days ago, the man who'd sat among the flower boxes, hiding among the dead azaleas. Apparently, Carillon hadn't only been relying on the web ad to track down Demi. She wondered how Angevin had known to look for Demi in Thormanby Road.

Ivy followed him walked back through the corridor and down the stairs, the sun from the skylight a fleeting warmth against the back of Ivy's neck. Here, the little arrow slits had polished metal inserts, twisted in what was quickly becoming a familiar shape. There were butterflies all over the place. And all of them looked creepy as hell. Sinister and scary and not quite what they were supposed to be, just like the face of the man ahead of her.

Ivy wondered what had happened to his face. . . .

Angevin stopped on the stairs and turned back to her, flipping his long bangs back from his forehead. The scars across his cheeks stood out, unsettling, pale, and rough. Ivy blushed as she realized he'd caught her staring.

"It never did hurt," he said, almost kindly. "Even right afterwards."

Ivy nodded, embarrassed, her face feeling flushed. "So, what are the butterflies all about?" she asked, more to change the subject than because she really wanted to know.

"Valoi," he said at once, clasping his hands beneath his chin. For a moment, Ivy thought he was introducing himself. "Your lot would call them changelings. No one knows what they really look like, so they're usually portrayed as butterflies."

"The red eyes make them look a little weird," she remarked.

"That's intentional," replied the trow. Unlike Silas, Angevin was actually speaking to her at a normal volume—apparently Carillon wasn't the only one who had figured out that Ivy could see and hear them just fine. "Think about it: a caterpillar builds a cocoon, but what comes out of the cocoon isn't a caterpillar anymore. Makes you wonder what the other caterpillars must think about that."

Ivy didn't think caterpillars would have the brains to give it much consideration at all, but it might be rude to point this out. And, because she was almost certain Angevin knew her address anyway, she added. "I think you were at my house a few days ago. Looking for a friend of mine, Demi Gentian."

"Demi Gentian!" repeated Angevin brightly, snapping his fingers. "Year King, 1784."

"No," said Ivy slowly. "I think that must have been someone else." Demi's grandmother, maybe. Certainly not Demi herself. "But why were you looking for her?"

"Was I looking for her?" the trow asked vaguely.

"Yes," Ivy insisted. "Thormanby Road. You asked me if I lived there. That's where we met—"

"We *did* meet before," said Angevin happily. His smile was slightly lopsided, as though the burned skin on his face didn't stretch equally on both sides of his mouth. "But it wasn't Howth," he added vaguely, as though he wasn't entirely sure. "The first time, it wasn't Howth."

The grin slipped away from his face rather suddenly. He turned away, and skipped down the last of the stairs. Ivy sighed as she followed; he'd made just as little sense back at Thormanby Road.

She caught up to him in the middle of the tiny courtyard garden; he was running his fingers gently over the petals of an amaryllis. And then, because Ivy didn't know when she would be able to ask it, or to whom: "Do all of you have a thing for houseplants?"

Angevin shrugged, turning away from the pot and starting down another hallway.

"There weren't very many of them, where we came from before."

"Amaryllises?" Ivy asked.

"Plants," Angevin corrected. He stopped at a door and opened it. "Wait here. They said they'd come straight away with your car," he added, but he looked confused as he said it, rubbing at his temples as though he might be on the verge of a headache.

Ivy walked past him and into a small sitting room, looking around curiously as Angevin closed the door behind her. More tapestries were hanging from the walls, and a handful of rickety-looking chairs clustered around a small table.

On the table sat a glass of water and a small plate of scones, curls of steam still rising from the flaking, golden-brown crust.

CHAPTER 8

I t took Ivy a moment to understand what she was looking at. A plate of food. In a trow house. Set out for Ivy to eat.

Don't eat anything off that shelf, Hunzu had said, the morning at the flat. Ivy remembered how he'd nearly backed out of the kitchen when she'd brought out a loaf of bread. She remembered Hunzu's warnings last night at the pub. *You'd be the gorilla—the thing in the room no one can see.*

Ivy had already taken a step toward the scones before she realized. She stopped, eyes darting around the room, wondering if someone was watching. Cameras, perhaps, or an empty chair that suddenly wouldn't be empty anymore?

The room suddenly felt too hot and too cold all at once. Had Angevin locked the door? Ivy hadn't heard anything;

rattling the handle might look suspicious. Best to act as if she hadn't noticed anything at all.

Ivy picked one of the tapestries at random—a bouquet of red flowers with yet another butterfly hovering over the petals—and went to it, plastering a tiny smile on her face, as though something about the design had caught her attention. Ivy stared at it as though it was the most important thing in the world, hoping her feigned interest in the tapestry might cover her sudden halt when she'd spotted the scones.

Could the scones simply be an oversight by the house's staff? She wasn't about to bet on it.

Unless there was nothing wrong with the food at all. Unless Hunzu lied about everything, and he really had paid off those men in the bar. If he lied, then Ivy was being an idiot and believing things that couldn't possibly be true.

What did she know about Haven, really?

A man from a security company had asked her to deliver a horse, for a large sum of money Ivy suspected had never been paid to anyone. She'd met this man through a fellow who'd broken into Demi's apartment. And Demi had vanished right after he'd appeared.

And the gloves. Taye Carillon hadn't worn any—at least, not at first. Angevin hadn't worn any at all, now that Ivy thought about it. And now there was a plate of food sitting on the table.

This isn't in the usual briefing, Ambrose had complained. Were most humans never told about the dangers of eating trow food? The way Ambrose had checked the speaker in his car when Ivy brought it up, she was willing to bet his driver didn't know. Maybe Carillon assumed Ivy wouldn't know the scones were dangerous.

Unless this was another test. Carillon tried to brush the straw from Ivy's hair to see what she'd do. Did the trow expect her to throw the plate across the room, or grind the scones into the carpet?

Or were the scones here because Hunzu had lied about everything, and this was where it all fell apart?

Drops of sweat came away from her forehead as Ivy rubbed a gloved hand over her face. She pulled the gloves off her hands and shoved them into the coat pocket, then pushed the coat further off her shoulders. The room still felt intolerably warm. There weren't any trows. There weren't any veils, and eating a scone wasn't going to make Ivy invisible. There wasn't anything out of the ordinary, and everything unusual about the past few days could be explained by a terrific combination of strangers, liars, and con men. Nothing magical at all. All so that Ivy would deliver a goddamned horse, and not ask too many questions.

But if Hunzu was lying, why hadn't he come up with something more plausible? No one believed in fairies any more. And even the people who maybe *did* believe in fairies didn't believe in fairies like Hunzu. He texted, for God's sake, and talked about Belgian beer . . .

Even if Hunzu was lying about everything, Demi was still missing, and someone's VW Rabbit was still hidden in the stables. If she could just find Demi, Ivy was certain her flatmate could explain everything. Perhaps she'd tell Ivy she was an idiot for believing anything Hunzu said.

Maybe it would be better if Hunzu had lied. If everything he told her was just a story, then the Enemy was just a story, too. And the scones on the table weren't poison, and Ivy wasn't going to turn invisible, and Demi wouldn't be murdered in five days.

But she remembered Hunzu in the pub, plaintively repeating his order to the unseeing waiter. She remembered Carillon standing up from an empty chair.

Ivy glanced around the room, looking carefully at the wooden timbers along the ceiling, peering at the wrinkled edges of the tapestries. There was nothing so obvious as a camera, but anything could be miniaturized these days. All sorts of things could be hidden in the walls, or the stones, or sewn behind the crimson thread of the butterflies. Whatever Ivy did, best to assume she had an audience.

She set her briefcase on one of the chairs, and went to the plate of scones. They were small, neat, and triangular, not lumpy and crumbling like the ones Ivy's step-mother made. Plump sultanas and swirls of cinnamon decorated the tops. They didn't smell like poison, but of hot bread and spices.

Ivy picked up one of the scones, breaking off a crumbling handful and dropping the rest back onto the plate. With the bit of scone still warm in her hand, she wandered to the far wall, stepping close to another wall hanging as though she were examining it. The design showed a leggy wolfhound with a spiked, crown-like collar fastened tightly about its neck. The dog looked as though it were trying to claw its way out of the tapestry, head tilted back, muzzle open in a silent howl.

Leaning closer to the tapestry, Ivy raised the bit of scone to her mouth. She squeezed it into a handful of crumbs, hurriedly slipping them into her pocket. Chewing on air, Ivy let her eyes wander over the tapestry. After a moment, she turned away, retrieved her briefcase, and dropped into the nearest chair.

Fine, Ivy thought, opening the briefcase and leafing through the papers at random. Let Carillon think she'd managed whatever it was she wanted.

In a way, the food was perversely comforting—if Carillon wanted to poison Ivy, that probably meant she was planning on letting Ivy leave. The scones seemed a wasted effort otherwise. Assuming that Hunzu was telling the truth and the scones really would make her invisible. Otherwise, Ivy had just made a crumbly mess in her coat pocket for no good reason. Maybe Hunzu was lying about everything.

But that still didn't mean Ivy wanted to eat the scones.

She'd give them ten minutes, Ivy decided. If no one had come back for her by then, she'd try the door and find her own way back to the Land Cruiser. If someone asked, she could always say she was looking for the toilet.

Not quite five minutes later, the lights flickered. It was so brief that Ivy might not have noticed but for the momentary squeal of an alarm, shrieking once and fading away almost immediately.

Slowly, Ivy slipped the papers back into the briefcase and got to her feet. In the wake of the alarm, the house seemed even quieter than it had before. Ivy listened, hearing a faint clatter that might have been the sound of running feet. The noise was gone before Ivy could properly decide if she'd heard anything at all.

Maybe she ought to forget about waiting for her hosts and just go back to the Land Cruiser herself. The front door couldn't be more than a few dozen yards away at most. Further down the hallway and somewhere to the right. Gripping her briefcase, Ivy went to the door. She grabbed the handle and turned it, half-expecting it to rattle uselessly against a deadbolt. But the knob turned silently and easily. Ivy pushed the door open and stepped through.

The corridor was dim, illuminated by one faint emergency light at far end of the hall. A green stained-glass window glowed eerily at the other end, lending a sickly gleam to the polished floors. The air smelled thickly of wood polish. Ivy wrinkled her nose as she closed the door carefully behind her.

Along the corridor was a series of wood-paneled doors, interspersed with heavy, rug-like wall hangings. There was no sign of anyone else in the corridor, or indeed, in the entire house. As though the inhabitants of Haven had become noise-less as well as invisible.

Something had happened, if the lights weren't working. Ivy had no idea what that might be. Maybe a tripped breaker. Maybe the alarm was some sort of fire alarm or carbon monoxide detector, and everyone else had already left the house and they'd all forgotten Ivy was still inside. Maybe Carillon was watching through a camera and it was all another test.

Whatever it was, Ivy was increasingly certain that she ought to get out of the house before anything else dangerous or unsettling happened. She'd done what Ambrose asked. She'd come here, and looked in the stables, and the house, and hadn't found a thing. Unless Ivy planned on searching the house top-to-bottom for Demi, it was past time Ivy left.

The main entrance ought to be just down the hall. Past the emergency light, around the corner, and out the door. Easy.

Feeling to make sure the Land Cruiser's keys were still in her pocket, Ivy started down the hallway, trying to keep her footsteps as quiet as possible. No need to draw attention to the fact that she was sneaking out of the estate.

A few more steps to the end of the corridor. Ivy walked quietly, listening for any sign that someone was waiting around the corner. If she were really prepared for this sort of creeping about, she would have brought a makeup compact that doubled as a periscope, or a ballpoint that was secretly a camera so she could look around corners. . . .

Ahead of her came the sound of a door being thrown open. Ivy froze, pressing herself against the wall. The door didn't sound very close, but now there were footsteps, and she couldn't tell which way they were going.

"Even if she did eat it, I still don't think it's a good idea," said a voice Ivy didn't recognize. The words carried clearly down the hallway, and a feeling like ice crawled up Ivy's neck. Her last quiet hope that the scones were an oversight vanished. They had to be talking about her, and the food on the table in the other room. Someone had left it there, on purpose. Someone had tried to poison her deliberately.

The footsteps were definitely coming closer.

Moving on instinct, Ivy grabbed the handle of the nearest door and turned it. The door, unexpectedly heavy, slid open on soundless hinges. As Ivy slipped inside, her briefcase caught on the edge of the doorframe. She winced at the noise, trying to hide behind the door even as she pushed it closed. It slid into place with the quietest of thumps.

Ivy stood motionless, letting her eyes adjust, because the room she'd entered was even dimmer than the corridor.

At first, Ivy thought she'd taken refuge inside a closet. The room was small, and the air full of a mildew-thick dampness, overlaid with something acrid and chemical. There were no windows. The only light came from the edges of the door she'd just shut—and a tiny yellow glow coming from unexpectedly far away.

Ivy realized what she had taken for a closet was actually the top of a set of stairs, uneven and made of stone, descending further into the house.

She bit her lip, glancing from the stairs back to the door. Could there be another exit from a lower level? Haven was built on a hill, it wasn't impossible that there might be a lower floor that still had a ground-level exit.

She turned back to the door, pressing her ear to the jamb. The metal crosspiece felt cold against her cheek. The smell of wood polish was nearly overpowering, all vinegar and lemon. She listened hard for several moments. And heard nothing at all.

Of course, the door Ivy was leaning against seemed enormously thick, and the walls were stone. There might be a tap dance routine going on in the hallway, and Ivy wouldn't be able to hear.

Below the door handle was a sturdy, modern-looking deadbolt, and a small card reader, both bolted not-so-subtly onto the timbers beside the doorframe. Two lengths of metal conduit ran from the panel down to the floor, like electrical wires in a badly remodeled house.

Why was there a lock on the *inside* of a door? Ivy hadn't seen anything else like this, even on the front door of the house. What was Carillon keeping down here?

Probably nothing, because despite the presence of the deadbolt and the keycard, the door wasn't actually locked. Or maybe there was an exterior door down here, and the deadbolt would allow people into the cellar without letting them into the main part of the house.

Speculatively, Ivy looked back down the stairs. It wouldn't take more than a moment to tiptoe down the stairs and look. Just to make sure it was only a musty basement, or an old furnace room, or a wine cellar, or something equally historic, useless, and without exits.

She started down, one cautious footstep at a time. With one hand, Ivy gripped her briefcase, feeling her way along the stone wall with the other. The air began to turn cold, making Ivy thankful she was still wearing Demi's coat. The sweat along the back of her neck felt suddenly chill.

Maybe the deadbolt wasn't for an exterior door. Maybe it was so that Carillon could keep people in the house and not let them leave. People like Ivy, for example.

Or people like Demi. Ambrose had assumed that if Demi was here, she'd come by choice. What if that wasn't true?

The ceiling became lower as Ivy approached the first turn in the stairway. As she passed beneath it, Ivy ran her fingers over the rough stone arch. The stones felt cool and rough, the same as the walls and what she could see of the floor. Ahead of her the faint light grew brighter, a glimmer of something around the next turning in the stairwell.

A breath of warm air shot past Ivy's face. She startled, pulling her hand back. The air felt hot, carrying with it a crackling scent of ozone and ash. It reminded Ivy of the furnace at her Dad's house, reluctantly coaxed to life on the first cool day in the fall—belching out singed dust and stale air for the first few days it was on.

The momentary impression of heat was gone in an instant, leaving behind the scent of damp stone and wood polish. The air in the corridor seemed even colder in its wake, the stairway ahead suddenly more cave-like.

The light ahead flickered, like the motion of a candle. Or like something walking in front of the beam.

Ivy froze.

"Demi?" she called in a strangled whisper. Nothing moved. But Ivy had the strangest feeling that something at the bottom of the stairs was listening. And that Ivy never should have gotten its attention by speaking aloud.

The sweat on Ivy's forehead felt like ice. Even if there was a back door, even if Demi was only a few yards away, Ivy was suddenly convinced she didn't want to go any further down the stairs looking for either one. Because something else was down there. Something that hid in cellars, and was kept behind locked doors.

Not daring to turn her back, Ivy slowly put her hand on the wall and stepped backwards, creeping her way up the stairs. She strained her eyes for another flicker in the light, but saw nothing.

Probably because there wasn't anything to see. It was only a drafty old basement, and there was probably nothing down there but dodgy electrical wiring, and a humongous old furnace that hadn't had its filters cleaned in ages. Ivy was just wasting time, poking about in cellars and scaring herself for no good reason.

There were far too many things in this house to legitimately worry about, without conjuring up make-believe monsters besides.

She was nearly back to the top of the stairs when there came a muffled click, and the lights came on.

Startled, Ivy looked first to the top of the stairs, then behind her, certain she'd see someone with their hand on a switch, ready to ask her what the hell she was doing here. But the stairwell was deserted.

If the lights were back on here, they were probably back on in the rest of the house, too. Taking a deep breath, Ivy hurried up the rest of the stairs.

Reaching the door, Ivy grabbed the handle and turned it. The handle turned, but the door didn't move an inch.

She wiggled the handle, turning it with increasing force, first one way, then the other. Setting her briefcase on the floor, Ivy pulled at the knob with both hands, fighting the goose-pimple panic creeping along the back of her neck.

The door wasn't budging.

Someone had thrown the deadbolt, or locked it from the outside. Ivy was locked in. Locked in with whatever it was that may or may not be waiting at the bottom of the stairs.

Ivy ran her hands across her face, pushing back the loose strands escaping from her braid, and tried to think. She ran her hands over the doorframe, hoping she might have overlooked some catch or bolt. But there was only the deadbolt she'd seen earlier, now slotted firmly across both the door and the frame. Beside the door handle, the keypad was now sporting a bright red light at the bottom corner. As though it was expecting a fingerprint, or a key card. As though it needed one before it would consider letting Ivy back out.

It must be some sort of fail-safe. When the power was out, the doors defaulted to being open, to prevent anyone from being trapped in case of a fire or a blown fuse. But now the lights were back on, and so were the door locks. She couldn't get out without a key card, or a proper fingerprint, or whatever else the keypad wanted.

Ivy was locked in.

Locked in with whatever else was down here in the basement of an ancient mansion built by fairies.

Diving into her coat pocket, Ivy pulled out her phone. The screen lit up at her touch; she didn't even need to unlock it to see the no service icon where the signal bars usually were. It wasn't even giving her the option to make an emergency call.

Even if she did have service, who exactly would she call? Her father? The Gardaí? What would happen if Carillon decided to feed them scones, too?

Ivy slid her phone back into her pocket and slumped against the door. She couldn't call anyone, and she wasn't getting out the way she got in. She could hammer on the door, Ivy supposed. Someone would hear her eventually. Or get suspicious when the Land Cruiser and its trailer were still sitting in the drive long after Ivy ought to have left with them.

But that would mean Ivy would have to explain why she was in here in the first place. To a trow who had already caught her in a lie, and had tried to have her poisoned besides.

Ivy had gotten herself down here, it was going to be up to her to get herself out.

That left the stairs. Picking up the briefcase, Ivy went to the top step and peered down. The stairway looked just as uneven as it had felt underfoot, rough-cut stone, touched with dark spots that looked like water damage. Across the ceiling ran a fat length of conduit, with small light bulbs sticking from sockets at intervals, bare but for a protective wire cage. The stairway looked considerably less cave-like beneath their unrelenting light.

She started down. The bulbs above her head were buzzing, the sound rising and falling every few feet. The walls and ceiling were covered with water marks, bits of rusted conduit, and gouges in the stone. It almost looked like the basement at Clarence Monaghan Day School, full of narrow hallways, gurgling boilers, and rows and rows of padlocked cages filled with outdated reference materials, old encyclopedias, and dust-covered course books that had been cut from the required reading lists decades ago.

Ivy reached the first turn in the stairway, resisting the urge to duck her head as the ceiling dropped. The bare bulbs seemed to multiply her shadow into a legion of silhouettes, all darting backwards and forwards against the walls as she walked on.

If there was still a light coming from the bottom of the stairs, she couldn't see it against the glare from the bulbs along the ceiling.

Another breath of hot air rushed past Ivy's face, followed by a searing whiff of ozone, gone almost before she had time to wrinkle her nose. It smelled hot, like the engine on Colin's shoddy Peugeot, the temperature needle flirting with the red after twenty minutes on the highway.

Just the furnace, Ivy told herself.

But if the furnace was down here, that didn't explain why it got colder the further Ivy went. She thought of the gloves in her pocket, but didn't stop to put them on.

The stairs ended at a stone-flagged landing, with a narrow archway leading into a further room. The stones forming the arch were nearly hidden behind a layer of chipped concrete

and metal brackets, as though the arch had required considerable reinforcement over the centuries since it was built.

Pressing herself against the stone wall, Ivy stopped just shy
of the arch and listened. She heard nothing but the low, insistent buzzing of the lights.

The faint light from before had to have been coming from
here. Which meant the thing that had walked in front of the
light was down here, too. Very slowly, Ivy peered around the
arch.

Before her was a vault-like room, much larger than Ivy was
expecting. The walls and ceiling were stone, supported at irreg-
ular intervals with more steel brackets and patches of concrete.
Numerous lengths of conduit snaked along the walls and the
ceiling, many of them dotted with more bare bulbs. All the
various lights seemed to populate the room thickly with
shadows.

There was no sign of the thing Ivy had half-thought she'd
seen.

At the far end of the room was a row of long cases, metal
below and glass above, looking like they might have come from
a jewelry store or a museum. The light reflected brightly off the
glass; Ivy couldn't see what was inside. The long cases
reminded her of something; she couldn't quite remember what.
Behind the cases and considerably closer to them was another
archway. It looked identical to the one Ivy was standing beside.
Perhaps it lead to another stairway, and a door that wasn't
bolted shut.

The glass cases looked very small in the empty silence of
the huge vault. Cautiously, Ivy stepped into the room, fingers
of dust rising up from the floor as she went.

She had taken three steps before she remembered that
Carillon's office had also looked empty at first.

Ivy stopped short, and took a deep breath. The cold was

back with a vengeance; she almost expected to see her breath hanging in the air like a frosted cloud. Very carefully, Ivy looked around the room, peering into the corners and shadows. She only saw her various twinned silhouettes twitching as she turned her head, tiny whirlpools of dust spinning at her feet. Nothing else.

Maybe because there was nothing else there. Maybe because something here was hiding. Or locked in, or hurt, or frightened.

"Demi?" Ivy whispered.

The word scattered across the room, returning in whispers and echoes. The silence did nothing to reassure Ivy that the room was as empty as it seemed.

She took a shallow breath, feeling her fingers digging into the handle of the briefcase. Suppose there was something in the room that didn't want Ivy's attention. Like Carillon, sitting in her empty chair.

How did one go about seeing through the veil? Ivy could do it, or so everyone kept telling her. But she didn't know how she pulled it off. Was it a matter of paying attention to the right things? The little tells and whispers you weren't supposed to notice? Or was it a matter of seeing what you expected to see? You see a person when you already know someone's there. You see an empty room when you think you're alone.

Ivy closed her eyes and took a deep breath, as though she were about to dive underwater.

There is someone else in the room, she told herself. He is standing in plain view. He isn't moving. He looks a little bit like Demi, and a little bit like Hunzu, and a little bit like Ambrose.

She waited, eyes closed, until she could see his features come together in her head. Until she could imagine him standing in the very thickest part of the shadows, watching her the same way she imagined herself watching him.

All at once, the temperature seemed to plummet even further, cold enough that Ivy was certain her breath would be steaming as she breathed. His breath would be steaming, too.

Very suddenly, Ivy was certain this entire idea had been a terrible one. She shouldn't have fled from the voices, shouldn't have come down the stairs, shouldn't have walked into the vault, and shouldn't have closed her eyes. Because this wasn't an empty room. There was someone here, mingling with the shadows and the stone, and Ivy's very life depended on *not* seeing him, because that's how you save yourself from the monsters.

You stay under the covers. You shut your eyes and never, ever look. . . .

Still keeping her eyes closed, Ivy reached behind her with her free hand. She could still get out of here without seeing it, if she just kept her eyes shut. Shuffling backwards, Ivy felt for the edge of the archway—

An acrid tongue of hot air brushed past Ivy's face and she jumped, her eyes flying open.

And there was nothing. Only the glass cases, the conduit, and the stone. An empty room that didn't seem empty at all.

Standing in the middle of the room, Ivy felt suddenly exposed. If she ran back up the stairs, the only thing she would find was a dead end and a locked door. She could run now, but that wouldn't help her get out. And running was no guarantee that the thing that wasn't here wouldn't follow.

She could hammer on the door, scream and kick at it until someone heard and let her out. But that would only be trading the thing she couldn't see for the suspect mercies of the trows upstairs. Ivy already had a good idea of what Carillon might decide to do with her. Poison and thumbscrews were only the start of the list.

Whereas the thing down here might not even be real.

The door on the other side of the room could lead to a way out. She just had to cross an empty room and look. There was nothing to be afraid of.

And, if there *wasn't* nothing, perhaps if Ivy refused to see it, it would be kind enough to return the favor. . . .

Keeping her eyes fixed on the floor, she hurried toward the row of glass cases. She didn't know what she was more afraid of —that something was down here and she wouldn't see it. Or that something was down here and she *would*.

As Ivy approached, she abruptly realized what the glass cases reminded her of. They weren't display cases. They didn't look like jewelry counters. They looked like caskets. As though under the glass would be something straight out of a fairy tale— a cold form stretched across the crisp satin lining, motionless and demanding a kiss. Something sleeping, or worse than sleeping.

Ivy could see hinges on the far side of the glass, as though the entire top of the case was actually a lid. The lids all had padlocks, heavy combination dials. Ivy remembered the deadbolt at the top of the stairs. Were the locks to keep something out? Or to keep something in?

Hardly daring to breathe, Ivy stepped closer to the glass. She craned her head, trying to see what was inside it while she was still far enough away to run, should something throw itself upwards, battering against the glass. . . .

They looked like feathers at first. A flock of half-furled wings reached upwards toward the glass, caught motionless between one wing beat and another. Lights reflected off the inside of the glass, blue and electric. Then Ivy saw the gleam of metal, and the pieces fell together.

They were all machines, nestled together inside the glass cases. The surfaces were glossy and metallic, glimmering with hints of color: rust, or tarnish, or circuitry, or something else altogether. The iridescence refused any attempt to pin the surface down to one single color. What Ivy had mistaken for wings looked like some sort of delicate heat sink, thin slabs of metal arching upwards, feather-like fingers splayed out like a fan.

They weren't all the same size, or even the same shape. A few of them looked like they had been taken apart, or partially destroyed, their heat sinks stumpy, or bent, or missing altogether. A few of them were glowing, hints of blue emanating from among the rust and verdigris. One, the largest Ivy could see, had a lightly glowing grey square along its front. It reminded Ivy slightly of a telly, when the screen was on but it wasn't actually showing anything. All of them were sitting on a padded grey surface, almost like foam, with insets carved to match their contours and curves.

Not a corpse under glass. Not a body. A collection of machines. But why were they down here, locked in Carillon's basement and kept under glass?

Paranoid, Hunzu had said. And Ambrose replied, she has to be. Given what else is in the house.

Was this what Ambrose had meant? The *what else* that Carillon was so careful about? Ivy stepped closer to the casket, looking speculatively at the things inside.

From behind her came the sound of footsteps, loud and hurrying. Without thinking, Ivy darted to the other side of the casket and dropped to the floor behind it, puffs of dust rising where her hands touched the floor.

The footsteps came closer, echoing broadly as they strode through the arch and into the vault, heading directly to the caskets. Ivy huddled closer to the case; the metal panel vibrated as Ivy leaned against it. She nearly pulled away in fright before realizing it must some sort of fan. The insides of the cases were probably temperature controlled.

The footsteps stopped; Ivy heard a whisper of fabric as the figure bent down. Something tapped against the glass; the padlock rattled on its hasp. In the silence of the vault, the sound was loud as a gunshot.

If he was distracted by the padlock, maybe Ivy could make the closer arch without being seen. But only if he wasn't looking in that direction. On her hands and knees, Ivy leaned forward, daring a look toward the front of the case. And caught a flash of yellow, of a strangely familiar hue.

Furrowing her eyebrows, Ivy popped her head around the corner of the case.

CHAPTER 9

"Ambrose?" Ivy hissed in surprise.

The trow jumped, his phone, bag, and a keycard falling to the floor in a noisy clatter as he whirled around. The collar of his canary-yellow jacket shone through under a heavier, slate-grey coat. Both were unbuttoned, flapping loose. Despite the chill in the vault, Ambrose's face was covered in sweat.

"Dammit," he whispered fiercely, running a hand over his forehead as he scowled at Ivy. "What in hell are you doing down here?"

"Demi's in the house," Ivy said in a rush, picking herself off the floor. The helpless feeling of fright that had dogged her since she'd first come down the stairs seemed to lift in an instant. She wasn't alone anymore, and Ambrose could help her. He'd opened the lock to get here; he must have a key. "Her car's in the stables, and I met Taye Carillon, and she had a plate of scones, and then the power went out—"

"Do be quiet," Ambrose snapped, cutting her off. The trow's expression had quickly shifted from surprise to anger, a nest of wrinkles around his eyes marring the usually smooth lines of his face. He bent stiffly to pick up the card and the phone, leaving the satchel where he'd dropped it, and turned back to the glass case. "I haven't any time for this, and if they find you down here we'll both be in for it."

He pulled a slip of paper from his pocket, peering at a series of numbers scrawled across the front.

"Have you seen Demi?" Ivy pressed. "Her car's here; we were right about her coming to Haven."

"Yes, I've seen her," Ambrose snapped, bending over the case as he looked from the padlock back to the paper. "She's fine. As fine as can be expected under the circumstances," he amended, in a softer voice.

Fine except for being fated to die in less than a week. Demi must be terrified.

Ambrose, for his part, didn't look terribly happy, either. Ivy wondered if they'd quarreled, or if Ambrose was angry at Ivy for managing to get herself locked down here. Then again, Ivy had never seen Ambrose in anything remotely close to a pleasant mood. Perhaps being irritable was simply a permanent feature, like a receding hairline, or a bulbous nose.

Even if he was in a terrible mood, Ivy was still terrifically glad to see him. Ivy just hoped the trow was as eager to help Ivy out of Haven as he'd been to get her onto the estate in the first place.

"She's still better off than you'll be if Taye catches you down here," Ambrose added, shoving the paper into his pocket and angling the padlock so it caught the light, his gloved hands running lightly over the numbers. A spring inside chattered as Ambrose spun the dial, stopped it momentarily, then turned it the other way.

"Because of all this?" Ivy asked quietly, stepping closer to look into the casket Ambrose was opening. "Is it all from Valiard?"

"Certainly isn't from here," he murmured absently, still staring at the padlock in front of him. He stopped the dial again, and turned it to the final number. The padlock opened with a click. Glancing quickly over his shoulder, Ambrose hurriedly removed the lock from the lid of the case.

"You *do* have a key to get out, don't you?" Ivy asked, still speaking in a whisper. She still couldn't quite shake the feeling that something *else* was close enough to listen in. "The power went out a few minutes ago, and the doors— did you do something with the lights?"

"*I* didn't," said the trow testily, lifting the lid of the glass case with a grunt. "*You* did. Or they'll assume so, if they notice."

A blast of cold air poured from the casket as the trow opened it, and again, Ivy smelled ozone, acrid and hot. Ambrose's face, patchily lit from the bare bulbs overhead, looked suddenly fox-like, his expression keen and acquisitive.

He leaned awkwardly over the open casket, letting the corner of the lid rest on his shoulder.

The trow reached inside, his hand hovering indecisively over the jumble of iridescent metal and foil-like wings. Exhaling sharply, he grabbed one, barely larger than his own hand. Its heat sinks jutted from between Ambrose's clasped fingers like the wings of a captive bird.

As soon as his hand was clear of the case, Ambrose let the lid fall with a muted thump. He pulled open his coat with his free hand, and shoved the thing into an inside pocket.

Fumbling, he picked up the padlock, ran it through the hasp, and spun the dial.

He turned away from the case, nearly colliding with Ivy, who quickly backed out of his way. Ambrose pulled his coat more snugly over his shoulders, running his hands over the front as though checking for a bulge.

"What is it?" Ivy asked.

Ambrose looked at her sharply, his hand settling over the faint lump marring the lines of his coat. He paused, taking a slow breath before answering her.

"Something whose sentimental value far exceeds its actual utility," he said, picking up his satchel. "Come on. Time waits for no man, and so forth."

Ivy nodded, only too eager to follow him out of the vault. Though as she followed him back to the stairwell, she noticed he kept glancing over his shoulder. As though he, too, felt the weight of eyes staring from among the shadows and dust.

"Do try to keep up," he snapped, though Ivy was barely half a step behind. It seemed the trow was almost as eager to get out of the vault as she was. She hurried along as they passed under the arch and started up the stairs. But in her head, she was still pondering the strange metal shapes, sleeping in their caskets. If this was where all the things from Valiard were kept.

. . .

"The veil's here," said Ivy, and it wasn't a question. "The thing keeping everyone invisible. It's down here in one of those cases."

Ambrose came to a dead stop on the stairs.

"You are going to forget you ever asked me that," he said, his voice almost a growl. In the light from the bare bulbs, Ivy couldn't see his face, only the drops of sweat at his neck and the hard set of his jaw.

"Do I have to remind you *we are on the same side?*" Ivy

snapped, folding her arms as Ambrose turned round to look at her properly. Perhaps it was her imagination, but she thought he looked the tiniest bit abashed. "You're the reason I'm here in the first place. You and Demi," Ivy amended. "I don't care about anything else."

Curtly, the trow nodded. He opened his mouth as if to answer, then closed it without saying anything. He started back up the stairs, and Ivy fell into step behind.

The air felt warmer here, now that they were away from the vault, and Ivy pushed her coat further off her shoulders.

"It's one reason why we don't bring agents here much," said Ambrose, sounding almost conciliatory. Ivy wondered if he were talking to her now to make up for snapping at her before. "The thing works on an inverse square: its strength is inversely proportional to the square of the distance. This close, it can even affect agents who've worked with us for years. Doesn't really fall off until you're much closer to the antipode."

Somewhere in those cases was the thing that made Demi, and Ambrose, and God knew how many other trows invisible. The thing that would make Ivy invisible, if she'd actually eaten the scone.

Hunzu had talked about the veil having a manual, but Ivy had never quite pictured it as an actual machine. Certainly not one with heat sinks, and cracked screens, and needing padded interiors and temperature controls. It looked more like the sort of thing you'd find on a server farm at the Microsoft campus in South Dublin.

As they neared the top of the stairs, Ambrose slid a small keycard out of his pocket. Running his thumb over its edge, he nervously smoothed the front of his coat. Crossing to the door, he held the card up to the plate, licking his lips.

The keycard had a picture on it. Between the trow's fingers, only half the face was visible, and it wasn't Ambrose's.

A shiver crept up the back of Ivy's neck. Why would Ambrose be opening doors with a keycard that wasn't his?

The small red light on the side of the plate turned green, and Ivy heard a quiet click as the deadbolt slid back.

"Friend of yours?" Ivy asked, pointing at the card.

Ambrose snatched the card back from the plate, fumbling with it for a moment before shoving it back in his coat pocket.

"Hardly think it matters," he said archly. He was patting the front of his coat again, running his hands over the bulge in the fabric. "Whose picture's on the front. You lot can't even see if we match the card in the first place."

Except it *did* matter whose picture was on the front. It certainly mattered in a house like Haven. Ambrose said it himself, human agents didn't come here. If anyone was looking at the card, it would be other trows. They could match him to the picture just fine. Or if the picture was completely unnecessary, why would they include it on the card in the first place?

Ivy took a deep breath.

Ambrose was lying to her. The card wasn't his. He'd gotten the card from someone else, and he wasn't supposed to be down here, either.

He'd gotten into the vault using a stolen card, and he'd taken something out of it. And Ambrose never would have come to Haven if it hadn't been for Ivy. *He'd* been the one who suggested she come here. Now Ivy knew why. Maybe he'd come to find Demi, and maybe he hadn't. Maybe he didn't care about Demi at all. Maybe he was only interested in Demi because it gave him an excuse to get into the vault. To take whatever it was he'd stolen.

Everything she knew about Ambrose suddenly came back in a strange and unsettling new light. He'd suggested poisoning her, back in the Liberties. He hadn't wanted to talk at first, about who

Demi was, or why he wanted to find her. He'd stolen a keycard, and then stolen the wing-shaped device out of the casket. He'd said in the car that Carillon wouldn't normally admit him to the estate; perhaps Taye had a good reason for not wanting him here. Maybe he was a thief, and a liar, and Demi had left the Liberties all those months ago just to get away from *him*.

Now Ambrose had gotten what he wanted. Maybe that meant Ivy was a loose end. If Ivy never came home, who would think to look for her here? Demi wasn't at the flat. Ivy didn't have a job that would report her missing. It might be days before Dad thought to worry that she wasn't returning his calls.
. . .

It was a cascade of suppositions, and Ivy didn't know if any of them were true. Demi might know. If Ivy could ever actually find her.

Ambrose reached for the door handle, but Ivy went for it first, banking that even with his gloves, Ambrose still wouldn't want to touch her.

The trow pulled his hand back, his expression equal parts annoyance and confusion.

"You said Demi was here, right?" Ivy said, sliding between Ambrose and the door as she covered the doorknob with her hand. "I want to see her."

"There isn't time," Ambrose said, frowning hard. "You've already been here far too long. You need to get off the estate before anyone realizes you've been wandering about."

Which sounded like Ivy could still walk away. What did it matter if Ambrose was a thief, if she could still get in the Land Cruiser and drive away and never have to deal with any of this ever again? She'd said as much to Ambrose: I don't care about anything else.

Demi didn't have the option to walk away. Not after next

week. And Ivy only had Ambrose's word that Demi was here at all.

"I'm not going back to the car until I know she's okay," said Ivy, trying to keep her voice steady.

The keypad buzzed unhappily, and Ivy felt a slight shudder as the deadbolt slid back over the door. Sighing through his teeth, Ambrose pulled the card out of his pocket.

"You stole that card, and you stole that thing out of the case, and you used *me* to get here," Ivy hissed, covering the keypad with her briefcase. "You prove to me that Demi is really here and she's okay, or I'll be yelling up and down the hall about that thing you took. I'm betting that'll go at least as badly for you as it would for me."

Ivy had thought Ambrose looked angry before—now he looked furious. Two dark spots of color appeared on his cheeks as the rest of his face grew pale. He looked almost sickly under the bare bulb's stark light.

"Deal?" Ivy pressed.

For a long second, the trow didn't answer, as though he were trying to guess whether Ivy was bluffing. She almost expected Ambrose to try and rush past. He could leave and lock her in, and hide the thing he'd taken somewhere else in the house. He could tell Carillon he had no idea what she was talking about. It would be her word against his.

The trow swore, and began stripping the gloves off his hands.

"Alright," he said, his voice tight and furious. "As long as you realize Demi's going to be in just as much trouble as the rest of us if this goes badly. And it'll be *entirely* your fault if that happens."

Ivy merely folded her arms over the briefcase, trying to stifle an imminent feeling of guilt. She had only Ambrose's

word that any of this was true. The only thing she knew for
sure was what she'd seen him take, down in the vault.

"Even if we don't pass anyone in the hall, there are
cameras," Ambrose said, shoving the gloves in his pocket.
"They could be watching, even after we leave the house. So
pull your hood down, and tuck your hair back. And try not to
look quite so tall."

Ivy set the briefcase on the floor, pulling the hood of
Demi's coat over her head, and shoving her braid under her
shirt collar. The trow reached over and pulled the hood several
inches lower.

"Ambrose, I can't see," Ivy pointed out, pushing it back
from her face.

"So much the better," the trow snapped, jerking the hood
back over Ivy's eyes. "Right now, all you need to do is follow
me. Keep your head down, and don't say anything. Is that absolutely clear?"

"Alright," said Ivy, swallowing hard.

She picked up the briefcase; Ambrose shook his head.
"Leave it here," he said, nodding at the corner behind him.
"Nothing that could identify you. No gloves, and no briefcase.
Just keep your hands in your pockets."

Ivy nodded, stepping cautiously away from the door to set
the briefcase in the far corner of the room.

"Ready?" he asked. He didn't quite sound as if he were
ready himself.

Ivy nodded, the hood flopping over her eyes. If Ambrose
was going to be leading her any distance, she'd be lucky just to
manage not tripping over her own feet.

Taking a deep breath, Ambrose pressed the keycard to the
pad, then stuffed the card back into his pocket. Opening the
door, he glanced up and down the hallway before motioning Ivy

to follow. She slipped out behind him, her skirt brushing against the sides of his coat. With the hood pulled over her face, she could hardly see more than the bit of carpet immediately ahead.

The carpet switched abruptly to flagstones as Ambrose turned down another passage, Ivy staggering half-blind beside him. The room with the scones was somewhere behind her; besides that, Ivy had no idea where in the house she was.

Ahead of them, a door creaked; the sound brought Ambrose to an instant halt. Ivy half-lifted her head to look before she caught herself. She froze, keeping her face carefully turned to the floor. Please be Demi, she thought.

"Ambrose," a voice called out. With a start, Ivy recognized Silas's voice. With the hood still flopping over her eyes, Ivy cautiously tilted her head. She could see his boots only a few feet in front of them, the spurs still spattered with mud.

"We've started containment, but Carillon wants your opinion on this one. The girl might be a sport," Silas added with a trace of disgust. "She's not in any of the active files."

Ivy could feel her heart thudding in her chest, as fast as a bird's. Silas had to recognize her. He'd spoken to her half an hour ago and she was still wearing the same coat. He had to realize she wasn't a trow.

But that was why she wasn't wearing gloves, wasn't it? Trows didn't bother with gloves around other trows. Her face was hidden, and her coat had been Demi's to begin with.

Ivy wasn't invisible, but that didn't mean she couldn't blend in. Be exactly the thing Silas assumed he'd see. Perhaps it was time to make the deception a little more realistic.

Hoping desperately she hadn't misinterpreted Ambrose's relationship with her flatmate, Ivy reached for Ambrose's hand, her fingers clumsily entwining with his own. His very invisible, very contagious bare fingers.

Ambrose, to his credit, didn't jump. After the briefest hesitation, he placed his free hand on top of Ivy's, his fingers lightly touching the back of Ivy's wrist. The spurs on Silas' boots rustled as he shifted slightly.

"Please give us a few minutes, Silas," Ambrose said quietly.

"Of course, sir," the trow murmured.

"Come along, darling," Ambrose said, starting forward and pulling Ivy along beside him. Her fingers were still entwined with the trow's. Ambrose's hands were slick with sweat, and Ivy was sure hers were no better. She leaned closer to Ambrose, ducking her head against the lapels of his coat, trying to look as much like a distraught maybe-ex as she possibly could. She could feel something sharp digging into her ribs through Ambrose's coat, the fan-like spines of the thing he'd taken out of the vault.

Ivy couldn't see Silas' boots, but she hadn't heard a door close. Was he still standing in the hallway, watching them? Ivy tried not to think about what might happen if the groom discovered who—and what—Ambrose was smuggling out of the house. Maybe they'd keep Ivy locked up until she had to eat trow food to keep from starving. Maybe there were thumbscrews in the basement. Or maybe Carillon would just kill her. Or Ambrose.

Ambrose turned down another passage, pausing before a heavy wooden door.

"Heads together," he breathed. "Like we're talking."

Ivy leaned closer as Ambrose pushed open the door with his free hand. She kept the hood low over her face as the trow led her over the threshold, past a frost-covered arbor and into the yard. The setting sun was shining directly into her eyes, uncomfortably bright after the dimness of the house, and the frosty air nipped coldly against her cheeks. Beneath Ivy's boots, the ground changed from gravel to grass. Ivy didn't dare raise her hood, relying on Ambrose to make sure she didn't trip over a rose bush or a garden gnome. Or a real gnome, for that matter. God knows what was out here in Taye Carillon's personal parkland.

"Where are we—"

"Just keep heading toward the trees," said Ambrose. "They can still see us from the house."

Ivy kept waking, raising her head long enough to glimpse a distant grove of trees, clustered together like an orchard.

A long minute later, they crossed under the shadows of the trees, the sun vanishing behind a canopy of thin branches and withered leaves. Slowly, Ivy pushed her hood back, looking up through the intertwined mishmash of twigs and limbs. Though the trees were spaced out in the orderly rows of an orchard, they were growing so close to one another that the grove looked like one great canopy supported by a forest of trunks.

Ambrose instantly let go of Ivy's hand, rubbing his palms furiously on the sides of his trousers.

"Quite the stunt," he snapped, glaring at her.

"It got us out of there, didn't it?" Ivy retorted. She would have thought Ambrose might manage to be the slightest bit grateful that her trick had gotten them out of the house. Judging by the look on his face, he wasn't. Then again, maybe he had good reason to be upset. There were very good reasons why she and Ambrose shouldn't have been holding hands in the first place.

"I hope you didn't hurt yourself," Ivy added haltingly. "Touching me, I mean."

"Won't know for sure for another few years or so," Ambrose snapped, fishing his gloves out of his pocket and pulling them on with quick, angry jerks.

Ivy looked away, feeling her cheeks coloring with more than just cold. She hadn't meant to endanger him—but if Silas had found them out, the consequences would have probably been even worse. Growing old at some indeterminate future date didn't seem like a very horrific fate, compared to things like being gutted and hung from a hawthorn tree. Everyone in the world grew old, sooner or later. Why should trows be any different?

"As near as we can tell, any instance of direct contact raises the possibility of infection by something around three-tenths of one percent," Ambrose said with a sigh. "But it's not an exact science. And it should have gotten me hazard pay."

Unbuttoning her coat, Ivy reached into her own pockets, fishing about until she found her own gloves. "Is it the same for me?" Ivy asked. "The percentages? I mean, did holding hands—"

"Put you under the veil?" Ambrose finished. "Probably not. Takes a bit more than casual contact for the veil to make a mistake. Though you don't have a years-long wait, mind. The veil's quick about it, once it makes up its mind."

Ivy looked at her hands critically as she pulled on her gloves. The tips of her fingers were beginning to turn pale with cold; beyond that, her hands didn't look any different. She wondered if they would look any different if she were invisible. Which was silly; the trows she'd met all looked normal enough, and they were invisible already.

"Better odds than chancing the scones, then," said Ivy, glancing back toward the house. Looking up the hill, she could make out Haven's turrets, the windows reflecting the glow from the setting sun as if the whole inside of the building were aflame.

"If you didn't eat any, I don't see what you're complaining about," said Ambrose, looking up into the branches of the trees. "I'd say she let you off rather lightly. Carillon could have done a great deal more than simply leave a tray of scones on the table."

"She really thought I was a threat?" asked Ivy, incredulous. "Just because I could see her?"

"Her own son was taken out of that house," Ambrose said tightly. "A long time ago, but I can assure you, Taye hasn't forgotten. And the veil is *our* weapon—nearly the only one we have left. Don't think we don't know how to use it."

Ivy wondered if that son was the same one from the painting in Carillon's office. She wondered how long ago he'd died, and how old he'd been when it happened. If trows didn't age unless they came into contact with people, how did they die? From disease? Accidents? Did they simply keep going until something vital finally wore out? And if trows didn't age, how long would that take?

A breath of wind blew through the branches above Ivy's head as she buttoned her coat, rattling the remnant leaves that still clung to the canopy. It occurred to Ivy that if someone were looking for a convenient place to dispose of an inconvenient body, a deserted grove of trees in the middle of a massive estate might rank very high on that list.

Some of Ivy's trepidation must have shown in her face, because Ambrose sighed heavily, running his gloved hands through his hair.

"As you so forcefully mentioned earlier, we're on the same side. We're not monsters, you know," he added, looking aggrieved. "I would've thought after six months with Demi, you'd have figured that out."

Maybe they weren't monsters. But they were certainly dangerous. Even when they didn't mean to be, like holding hands with Ambrose. Even more so when they *did* mean to be, like with the scones.

"That was before I knew you had another reason for coming here," Ivy said, nodding at the lump under Ambrose's coat.

"I came here for Demi," Ambrose shot back. "Same as you. But I'm hardly going to turn down opportunities when they present themselves."

"Such as theft?" Ivy challenged. Ambrose merely sighed through his teeth, his hand resting across the slight lump on the front of his coat. "What is it, anyway?"

"Inoperable," Ambrose grunted, giving Ivy a slide-long look. "We know little enough about how the damned things actually work. And we'll never learn if they stay locked up in a basement."

Ivy noticed he hadn't actually told her what it was supposed to do if it did work. Was it another veil? A weapon? A sort of weird fairy computer?

"Carillon seems happy enough to keep them down there," Ivy pointed out.

Ambrose looked back over his shoulder, toward the barely visible turrets of the house.

"The last time a working device left the house was in 1941," he said, his voice sounding strangely hollow. "Helped with modeling the original designs of the code-breaking machines for the Tunny and Enigma ciphers. Once Bletchley Park had their own prototypes, someone in Flowers' department decided the forced conscription of one veiled trow would be far more useful to the war effort than any number of computational trinkets. Two people died and I—" Ambrose broke off suddenly, running a hand over his face. When he continued, it was in a much quieter voice. "And I supposed I haven't learned from that mistake.

"Come on," Ambrose added, heading deeper into the cluster of trees. "It's cold out here."

Ivy fell into step beside him, thinking. Bletchley Park had been the center of Allied code-breaking efforts during the second World War. Decrypting the Enigma cipher had been a key part Britain's eventual victory. If the trows had been involved in *that*, what other events had they chosen to intervene in?

Perhaps not many, if that was how Britain repaid whoever had tried to help them.

The tips of her fingers were tingling slightly. Ivy sternly told herself it was only from the cold. Certainly not because she'd just held hands with an invisibly infectious fairy. Though she noticed Ambrose was still rubbing his gloved hands against the sides of his coat as they walked.

Suddenly, Ivy felt her boot catch on something, and grabbed at Ambrose's arm to keep from falling over.

"Careful," he said, as Ivy disengaged herself from his coat sleeve. "There's quite a few of the damn things lying around."

The rock Ivy had tripped over was about the size of a cinderblock, rounded at the edges and nearly hidden by the grass growing up around it. *Galen 1687*, it read. Nothing else. A few feet away, Ivy spotted the corner of another stone peeking out from underneath a tree root. There seemed to be similar stones scattered every few feet, as though the orchard had grown up within some sort of dilapidated cobblestone hall.

Then it occurred to Ivy what the stones really were.

"It's a graveyard," said Ivy with a start. She was suddenly certain that walking any further into these trees would be a very bad idea.

"Not exactly," said Ambrose, shifting his bag to his other shoulder. "There aren't any bodies here. But yes, it's a place to remember the Year Kings. We shouldn't linger," he added, glancing over his shoulder. "They'll be missing you at the house soon, if they haven't already."

Uneasily, Ivy followed him deeper into the orchard. It was darker than she'd expected under the trees, their shadows interrupted by occasional shafts of light breaking through the canopy. As often as not, the light revealed more stones, or sinewy tree roots sprawled across the grass.

"The original idea was to have a tree for each king," Ambrose said quietly. "Eventually, there got to be too many for that to be practical. So now we just keep the same number of trees and put the new stones wherever they'll fit. Some of the first ones supposedly came from seeds out of Valiard, but those died out a long time ago. Now, they're all apple trees."

Standing on tip-toes, Ambrose reached into the branches, snagging something and pulling it free. Somehow, Ivy had expected it to be red, the sort of perfect, blood-colored fruit Snow White might think twice about eating. But the apple in the trow's hand was green and round and showed not the slightest sign of withering, even though the air was cold enough to sting Ivy's cheeks.

Even more surprisingly, Ambrose lifted the apple to his mouth and took a bite, chewing thoughtfully as he dropped the remainder into the pocket of his coat.

"You can eat them, too, if you're hungry," he said offhandedly. "It's not cooked, so it's quite safe."

Ivy looked up into the branches. She could see other apples, wide, rounded shapes among the branches, though it was fast becoming too dark to make out their color.

"It seems disrespectful somehow," said Ivy cautiously. "Messing with the Year Kings' trees, I mean."

"It'd be more disrespectful to let the apples fall and not eat them," said Ambrose with a snort. "Besides, these trees will be mine too, someday."

"I thought you said this place was just for the Year Kings," said Ivy.

"It is," said Ambrose, his mouth curling into a brittle sort of smile. "It's a matter of maths. One trow is selected each year.

Barring accidents, every one of us will someday stand for the succession. This is very nearly the only graveyard we need."

Ivy looked across the ground, at the intermingled tangle of roots and stone. The roots look almost like hands, she thought uneasily. Stretched out from the jumbled graves of countless murdered trows.

"Look—that one has *two* names," said Ivy, pointing at one of the stones.

"Bern and Tara," said Ambrose, bending over to squint at the stone. "1797. That was one of the unusual years. The Year King drank poison a few days before the end of his reign. So on the appointed day, the Enemy killed his consort instead. Since both of them died that year, someone decided both names should be on the stone. Though if I were Tara, I would have been irritated Bern didn't just wait," Ambrose added. "Here's another unusual one."

"Delia and Pollux," Ivy read. "1884. Was that another—I mean, did one of them—"

"Our sort have never taken well to confronting mortality," Ambrose said darkly. "And the Enemy—well, let's say that there are easier ways out of this world than the method it employs."

"Sounds like being a Year King's consort is kind of a risky job," said Ivy. She'd meant it to be a joke, but Ambrose didn't seem to find it amusing.

A moment later, Ivy belatedly realized why. "I'm sorry," she began. "I didn't mean—"

"Here's another strange one," Ambrose said loudly, turning toward a particularly gnarled-looking tree.

"Larch," Ivy read. She was certain she'd heard the name before; it took her a moment to remember where. "This is Carillon's son? Why isn't there a year on it?"

"It ought to say 1936," said Ambrose. "Or maybe it was

1938. He disappeared; Taye refused to put a year on it because no one could ever prove for certain that he'd died."

"This is the one," said Ivy excitedly. "One of the Year Kings who didn't die! The one Hunzu was talking about in the car!"

"No, this is a Year King who died, and we just don't know how it happened," Ambrose corrected. "The Enemy killed someone else that year; I think her name's a few stones over. Best proof you could ask for that Larch was already dead."

"Because if Larch was still alive," said Ivy haltingly. "The Enemy would have killed him, instead."

The faint hope growing in Ivy's chest was abruptly stifled. Maybe Larch hadn't been killed by the Enemy—but that didn't mean he'd survived his year, either.

"It always goes after the kings," said Ambrose bleakly, and Ivy wondered if he were thinking about Demi. "Unless, of course, they die some other way before their year's up. The best you can say about Larch is it might have been an accident."

"How did it happen?" asked Ivy, unwilling to let it drop. "How did he disappear?"

"You'd be better off asking Hunzu," Ambrose said dismissively. "He's the conspiracy theorist."

Out of the corner of Ivy's eye, something moved. She turned toward it, trying not to stumble over any more of the stones.

"There's someone there!" she hissed at Ambrose, trying to keep her voice down. "By the tree!"

"Which tree?" Ambrose snapped. "There's more than one, if you hadn't— Oh."

The woman might have looked like a statue if she hadn't been tapping her foot. Covered from head to toe in a long dark coat, she looked a little like the cast-iron figures of the Fates in Saint Stephen's Green. Her hair had been hastily braided; bits and pieces were falling out of the braid and gathering in tangles across her face. A large, bulky-looking satchel hung from her shoulder.

"Demi!" Ivy called, hurrying across the grove, trying not to stumble over any more stones.

"Hello, Demi," Ambrose echoed cautiously from behind her.

Demi uncrossed her arms as she stepped forward, and for a moment Ivy thought Demi might hug her. Then her flatmate stopped abruptly, looking at her hands as though she didn't know what to do with them. Hesitantly, Demi reached into her coat pocket, pulling out a pair of crisp, white gloves. Reality asserted itself in a rush. Demi wasn't human, and Ivy shouldn't be touching her at all.

"Hi," Ivy said, lifting her hand awkwardly in a tiny wave. Something flickered across Demi's face, like the hesitant beginnings of a smile.

"I'm so sorry," Demi murmured, so quietly Ivy could barely hear her. She broke off, rubbing her gloved hands across her face.

Some tight knot of worry in Ivy's stomach that she'd hardly been aware of untwisted itself. As though now that she'd finally found Demi, everything else that had gone wrong in the past few days would presently fix itself. Which wasn't true at all. The Enemy was still coming for Demi, Ivy still needed to get away from Haven without Carillon finding her in the company of a thief and trying to poison her again, and there was a three-tenths of one percent chance that Ivy was invisible already, because of holding hands with Ambrose.

"Demi—" Ambrose began.

Demi dropped her hands, instantly rounding on Ambrose.

"I don't know what possessed you to get Ivy involved in this," she said harshly. "You're an idiot, and now I'm cleaning up the mess. And that isn't going to work for Ivy," she added, glaring at the satchel Ambrose was carrying.

"The Lewes girl could use them," Ambrose said placidly, which earned a hard, disbelieving look from Demi that seemed to encompass both of them. Ambrose slipped the bag off his shoulder and dropped it onto the grass. "I'm betting Ivy can, too. Did you really think I wasn't going to be looking for you? Hunzu's been—"

"No, don't tell me," Demi interrupted, hands on her hips. "Let me guess. Hunzu has his theories, and you went along without even asking why he was so interested."

"I know exactly why he's interested," said Ambrose calmly. "He'll help you, if you let him. You've hardly given him any choice about it."

"Was he the one who told you where I'd gone?" Demi shot back.

"He didn't," Ivy interrupted firmly. "I did."

Demi turned back to her flatmate, eyes widening as though she'd momentarily forgotten Ivy was there. Her eyebrows met in a furrow over her nose, normally the sort of look she reserved for a misbehaving hygrometer, or the recalcitrant vacuum back in Thormanby Street.

"I told you in the note—" Demi began.

"There was nothing in the note!" Ivy burst out. "Not about where you were, or what was really happening, or anything! I didn't know what to do, and you weren't around to ask!"

Demi swallowed heavily, as she looked first to Ambrose, then back to Ivy. Two spots of color had crept into her cheeks; Ivy couldn't tell if she was angry or embarrassed.

"I should have told you," Demi said in a softer voice. "I shouldn't have just gone like that, but—"

"You just wish you'd thought up a better lie before you

left," Ivy snapped. "Because you sure weren't telling me what was really going on!"

"You wouldn't have believed me," said Demi shortly.

Ivy bit off an angry reply, because maybe Demi had a point. Ivy hadn't believed Hunzu at first, either.

"Maybe not the whole invisible fairy bit," Ivy conceded. "But if you'd told me you were in trouble, I would have believed that."

That was the crux of the matter. Demi'd been living with a death sentence for the entire time Ivy'd known her. And Ivy hadn't known. She ought to have figured out some of it for herself. She should have been able to put it together: that Demi hardly ever left the flat, never answered the door, never had friends stop by. Ivy ought to have seen that all those things together meant something, even if she never would have been able to guess what it was.

"You live in a different world, Ivy," Demi said, and all of a sudden, she sounded very tired. "Yours has enough of its own problems; you shouldn't be mixed up in our problems, too."

Demi hadn't been the one to do that. Ivy had managed most of that on her own. And as for the rest. . . .

"He took something out of the house," Ivy said suddenly. "Just now. Maybe that's why he wanted to come here in the first place."

Demi glanced at Ambrose sharply, the whites of her eyes round and gleaming in the dim light.

"For God's sake," Ambrose muttered, as he began unbuttoning his coat. "It's not even a live one."

Reaching into his pocket, he pulled out the winged device, opening his fingers as he held it out to Demi. In the dim light, it appeared little more than a strangely shaped paperweight.

Demi stared at the device with a mix of trepidation and interest.

"I was thinking the University College's nano imaging center, but I suppose that's up to you now," Ambrose said. Very slowly, he took one of Demi's hands in his own, turned it palm up, and pressed the device between her fingers. "Or take it back to Taye, if you like. I'm sure your host would be tremendously grateful for the opportunity to get me thrown out of my own department."

"Tempted," Demi snapped. Slowly, her fingers closed over the metal body. As Ambrose began to pull away, she hurriedly grabbed for his wrist. Smoothly, Ambrose stepped closer, bringing Demi's free hand gently to his lips.

Very abruptly, something in Demi seemed to relax, as though some continuous calculation of distance had suddenly silenced itself. With a feeling like vertigo, Ivy realized this was the first time she'd ever seen her flatmate with one of her own kind. Demi's shoulders were shaking; there was a hitch in her breath as though she were trying very hard not to cry.

"I love you—" Ambrose began, and Demi immediately pulled her hand away.

"Don't start," she snapped. Demi shoved the device into her satchel, fiddling with the bag until the new addition was firmly ensconced at the very bottom. Or maybe the fiddling was just an excuse to not look at Ambrose. When Demi lifted her head, her eyes were wet. "I'm dead, Ambrose, give or take a few days. You'd be better off leaving and letting it happen."

"I won't do that," Ambrose said simply. "I love you, and you can't change that. Death can't change that, and the Enemy can't change it, either."

He took Demi's hand again, gently but insistently. He pressed a kiss to her gloved fingers, and he didn't stop there.

Embarrassed, Ivy turned away, suddenly and intensely aware that she shouldn't be here. Not in County Clare, not in the Year Kings' apple grove, and not overhearing this conversation between her flatmate and her flatmate's boyfriend. In Dublin, it had felt like the trows were the ones who didn't belong, either creeping about unnoticed, or desperately fluorescent when they were trying to talk to someone. Now, Ivy was suddenly the one skulking around the edges of something she wasn't a part of, and shouldn't be overhearing.

"It felt like you were dead," Ambrose murmured quietly. "Some days, I was afraid that was true."

"Why would you be afraid I was dead?" asked Demi, her voice sounding thick. "It wasn't *your* life that was—"

Whatever else Demi might have said was interrupted by an insistent, jangling chime. Ivy turned back as Ambrose, looking supremely irritated, pulled his phone out of his pocket. The light from the screen cast an eerie glow on his face; his expression darkened as he scanned the screen.

"We're out of time, I'm afraid—seems Carillon has discovered a certain escrow agent has gone missing," said Ambrose sweetly. "The house is going to be in an uproar. I'll try and delay the torches and pitchforks for as long as possible."

"What are they going to do if they find us?" Ivy asked, glancing nervously through the trees. She couldn't see the house—even the trees themselves were becoming little more than silhouettes in the fading light. Even Demi's thick winter coat wasn't quite enough to block out the cold.

"If Carillon thought you might be useful, she'd lock you up until she was certain you were under the veil. It's what I'd do," Demi added, shrugging at Ivy's horrified look. "See what your new friends have gotten you into?"

"You were the one who posted an ad for a flatmate," Ivy pointed out.

Demi might have flushed at that, but it was too dark to properly see.

"Hunzu can meet you both at the river," said Ambrose, texting a reply. "And Demi—"

Ambrose's phone beeped again; the trow glanced at the screen and winced.

"Just go, Ambrose," Demi said shortly, picking up Ambrose's satchel as she turned away, curtly waving for Ivy to follow.

"You're making this harder than it ought to be," Ambrose called after her.

"No," said Demi, still walking away. "No, I'm really not."

Ivy stared after her flatmate for a long moment.

"I'm sorry," she said to Ambrose in a rush, turning away before he could reply, hurrying to catch up with Demi before she vanished under the trees. What she was apologizing for, Ivy didn't quite know. Perhaps for going into the house when she shouldn't have, or agreeing to deliver the horse in the first place. Or maybe it was because Demi was going to die, and Ivy still didn't have any idea how to change that.

Behind her, Ivy heard Ambrose murmuring something into his phone, his voice growing fainter as Ivy followed her flatmate deeper into the grove.

The spaces between the trees weren't wide enough to walk side by side, forcing Ivy half a step behind as she followed. All she could see of Demi's face were the ragged edges of her flyaway braid. Ivy wondered if Demi intended to walk the entire length of Carillon's estate in awkward silence. Maybe that would be easier, especially since Ivy had no idea what she ought to say. But the Enemy was coming in five days. Ivy didn't know when they'd get another chance to talk.

"You never told me a thing, you know," Ivy said quietly. "Not for the whole six months we've lived together. Not about the Enemy, or the food, or anything!"

"I didn't want to talk about it," said Demi, turning back

toward Ivy suddenly enough to set her coat swirling around her ankles. "Any of it. I took precautions—"

"What if I'd eaten your quinoa?" Ivy snapped, feeling a prickle of anger between her shoulder blades. Because to Demi, it didn't matter if Ivy knew the truth or not. It didn't matter that she'd been lying by omission for the entire time Ivy'd known her. "What if—"

"I'm sorry," Demi cut in, giving Ivy a sidelong look. It was too dark to see her expression, but something in her voice gave Ivy the awful feeling that Demi might be about to cry. "You deserved to know what you were getting into."

Immediately, Ivy felt her cheeks turn hot. Demi was going to be murdered in five days, and Ivy couldn't manage to talk to her without snapping. But it still mattered, what Demi hadn't told her. Living together was dangerous for both of them—but Demi wasn't the one who needed to worry about the long-term consequences.

"Yes, I did," said Ivy, crossing her arms. "But not just about the food and things. I'm good for more than signing for packages. I could have helped you." And added, before she could think better of it. "If you're safer at the flat, I don't mind. Living with you. If it would help."

Biting her lip, Ivy pushed away the implications of that offer—if Demi was in the flat on Wednesday, the Enemy would be there, too. Hunzu had warned her to stay away from Demi when the Enemy came.

But Demi was only shaking her head, pushing her hair back from her face as she started walking again. Ivy fell in a half step behind her.

"I suppose Ambrose never told you why Hunzu wanted to find me," Demi said.

"They were worried," said Ivy, pulling her coat more closely around her shoulders. "I was, too, and you'd only been gone a day. Ambrose and Hunzu have been looking for you for months!"

"Hunzu wasn't worried about *me*," Demi said harshly. "He was just afraid I'd died ahead of schedule. The Enemy always takes someone."

Ivy remembered the stones Ambrose had shown her. Bern drank poison, and the Enemy came for Tara, instead. *Hunzu here is a member of her court*, Ambrose said, back in the limo. *I suppose that gives you the job of trying to keep her alive.*

"Hunzu's your consort," Ivy said, and the cold air seemed to prickle even more fiercely along the nape of her neck. "He's the one you named to your court before you left. The only one you named to your court."

"He's the only one I needed to name," said Demi in a low voice. "And it's not a court, Ivy. It hasn't been a real court for centuries—it's a list of people in line to be murdered. That's all we are. Kings of the twilight, dwindling away in a place we don't belong, skulking behind our veils until the Enemy finally exterminates us all."

"So why name a consort at all?" Ivy asked.

For a long moment, there was only the muted sound of their footsteps over the ground.

"I knew when I left the Liberties, I'd be on my own," Demi said, and her voice was shaking. "There wouldn't be anyone to help me. No one could see me, or hear me. I couldn't talk to anyone unless it was through a screen. Anything could have happened after I left. I couldn't bear to think of Ambrose being the next one the Enemy would take."

"Then why leave in the first place?" Ivy asked. "You would have been a lot safer if you'd stayed. People would have helped you."

"No, they wouldn't," Demi said, pushing her hair back from her face. "Sometimes I think the only thing we know how to do any more is hide. We're very good at hiding from your sort, hiding from the things we know are coming. No one can hide from the Enemy, but I thought I could try. Leave the Liberties, go someplace no one could find me—not you lot, and not my people, either. It was all I could do. It's silly—it's not them that'll kill me."

"They made you the king, didn't they?" said Ivy darkly.

"It had to be somebody," said Demi, rubbing at her eyes. "Even in the years we didn't elect a king, the Enemy always killed someone and there was no telling who it would be. I almost think it'd be better that way—never quite knowing."

Demi was silent for a long minute, her breath clouding the air in tiny puffs of frost.

"Ever since the lottery, everyone looked at me like they knew I was going to die. Even Ambrose. Like it was all he saw when he looked at me. Like it was all he could think about. But after I left the Liberties, it was different. I wasn't the only one. You're going to die, too. And so is Mr. Abernathy, and Sean Oate and every single person in Dublin, and you all act like that's okay! I don't understand it. You're brave, or crazy, or deluded, and I don't know how you manage."

Maybe this was why Demi never told her who she really was. What she was really hiding from. She didn't want Ivy to know because she was trying as hard as she could to forget it herself. She ran away and buried herself in a place where nothing could remind her she was different. Nothing could remind her she was doomed.

"Maybe it's hope," said Ivy quietly.

"Deluded, then," Demi sniffed, rubbing the edge of her cloak across her face. "It's pretty much the same thing."

It was too dark for Ivy to see the stones, though the rough-hewn edges were still catching at Ivy's boots at regular intervals. She wondered how many there were—and how many

were engraved with more than one name. Ivy wondered
suddenly whether Demi's parents might be here, but it seemed
too personal a question. Besides which, Demi's parents probably weren't even dead. They were probably alive, and worried,
and missing her—just like everyone else.

"The thing that's—" Ivy stopped. "The thing Ambrose was
talking about. The Enemy." Demi's shoulders quivered, but Ivy
pressed on. "What is it? Doesn't it have a name?"

"We don't know," said Demi in a brittle voice. "If it does,
it's never bothered to tell us."

"But what *is* it?" Ivy pressed. "Is it a trow, or what?"

"It looks like a trow," said Demi after a moment, tucking
her hands into the sleeves of her coat. "Like a trow out of the
old world. But it isn't. At least, we don't think it is. We can't talk
to it; we can't touch it. We can't kill it. I'll try, though," she
added, almost to herself. "If it comes to that, I'll try."

Demi slowed, and dimly Ivy could see they were
approaching the end of the trees. Ahead, the grove gave way to
a large meadow. It was too dark to see to the edge of it, but Ivy
remembered how expansive Carillon's estate had looked from
the road. Surely they weren't planning on walking the whole
distance.

"You'd better drink this," said Demi in a steadier voice,
pulling a small bottle out of Ambrose's bag.

"What is it?" Ivy asked, taking the bottle and unscrewing
the lid.

"Just water. Dehydration's a very common side effect. I
don't suppose you were ever a runner?"

"I dropped out of cross-country because of shin splints,"
said Ivy, looking across the expanse of grass with trepidation.
Was that Demi's plan for getting off the estate—running the
whole way back to the M7? "Besides, we're miles from

anywhere. Won't they see us if we try to cross the meadow? They have horses, if you didn't notice."

"The horses won't be a problem," said Demi. "At least, not if Ambrose is right about this."

Silently, Demi opened Ambrose's satchel, pulling out a pair of riding boots, followed by a thick blanket and a tangle of leather straps. She passed the blanket to Ivy, and began straightening the bundle of leather.

"That looks like Clover's bridle," said Ivy, recognizing a familiar clasp in the tangle of straps.

"Did your contract say anything about Clover's tack, specifically?"

"I don't think so."

"Then it's not actually stealing if Carillon doesn't get it back."

Satisfied with the bridle, Demi laid it on the ground and pulled off her gloves, tucking one into the other, and slipping them both into Ambrose's bag. She bent over, undoing the laces on her boots.

"You *do* know I don't know how to ride a horse?" Ivy asked nervously.

"If this works like Ambrose thinks it will, you won't need to," Demi assured her, slipping into the taller riding boots and tightening the buckles. Ivy caught a glimmer of something glinting at the heels, sharp and pointed like spurs. "Otherwise, you might be learning in a hurry. You'd better take your boots off if you don't want them torn up. And my coat, if you don't mind."

Ivy had almost forgotten the coat she'd taken was actually Demi's. Setting the blanket on the grass, Ivy shrugged out of her coat, took another gulp from the bottle, and started undoing her laces.

Dropping her own shoes into Ambrose's bag, Demi picked

up something that looked like another part of the bridle. The loop twisted strangely between her fingers, gleaming brighter than the darkened orchard would seem to allow. Demi cracked her knuckles, holding the bridle loosely in both hands.

"This is the part you won't like very much," she said. And before Ivy could stop her, Demi placed the glittering bridle on Ivy's forehead, her bare fingers twisting hard into Ivy's hair.

The branches of the apple trees began to spin. A moment later, the whole world went dark.

CHAPTER 10

Ivy was cold, and everything around her smelled of grass. She scrambled to her knees, fumbling against a blanket, woolen and scratchy and damp with sweat. Ivy pushed it away from her face, nearly gagging at the musty stench of it, only to pull it closer as the winter air nipped at her sweat-slick skin. Pulled it closer again as the blanket touched bare skin, far too much of it. Ivy began to wonder whether she was naked, a question with some urgency, as there seemed to be someone else close by, panting and sweating beside her. His boots were only a few inches from her face, the spurs stained and dripping. There was a coppery taste in Ivy's mouth and she ought to— what exactly? Kick him. Ivy staggered upright, pulling the blanket closer, momentarily confused as to why she couldn't kick with her hands. It would have been much easier than clambering all the way to her feet.

The man with the spurs was doubled over, an easy target, hands on his knees as if he'd been running.

Ivy tried to kick him and nearly fell, as if standing on two legs had suddenly become as difficult as balancing on a rickety ladder. She made a grab for the front of the man's coat and missed, just managing to catch herself before she fell face-first into the dirt. Something sharp was digging into her hip. She touched it and it hurt, her skin sticky like a half-scabbed wound.

"Easy," gasped the man with the spurs, tucking the blanket back across her shoulders. Gloved fingers brushed Ivy's arm, and she abruptly remembered what she wanted to do with her hands. Ivy hit him hard in the face, watching with satisfaction as he tumbled backwards into the hawthorns.

"Bloody hell," groaned Hunzu, one gloved hand pressed to his nose. Slowly, the trow pulled himself out of the tangle of thorns, wincing as the branches caught at his sleeves.

It was strange—the hawthorn looked almost like the one in the back garden at Thormanby Road. And there was the chipped birdbath next to the gate, and the tin-roofed garage where Demi kept her VW. Slowly, the various pieces of the garden began to fit themselves together, the yard haphazardly sketched in the yellowish light of the streetlamp three houses away. The rusted railing by the back steps, the rubbish bin with the dented lid, the empty bird feeder hanging outside Mr. Abernathy's back window.

It was her own back garden in the middle of the night, and Ivy didn't quite know how she'd gotten there. Or why Hunzu was with her, or what had happened to her clothes.

Hunzu was beside her again, making encouraging noises, slightly muffled from the woolen hat he'd pressed against his nose. Gamely, Ivy tried to get to her feet, knowing it was likely an impossible goal. This time, she didn't even make it as far as her knees. She coughed, and her mouth hurt. She tried to say something, and that hurt more.

Ivy reached over her shoulder and grabbed the edge of the blanket, tucking it more firmly across her chest. She could crawl. The back steps would be a bitch, but she could get herself inside. Eventually.

"Just hold still," Hunzu mumbled around the hat, and she felt his gloved hands on her shoulders.

"Leave me alone," she rasped, wishing she could shout at him, but her throat hurt too much. Ivy wondered whether she'd been shouting before. That might explain why her throat hurt. So did her legs, now that she thought about it.

Hunzu cursed under his breath; she heard the frosted grass crunching under his boots, the creak of the back stairs, and the squeak of the rusty door hinge Mr. Kimball had been meaning to grease. He was leaving her, and some wild thing in Ivy's heart sped up as though she were running.

Ivy remembered Hunzu walking away once before, leaving her stamping and tugging ineffectually against a loop of rope thrown over a tree branch. But she couldn't quite place when it was. Not when he came to Howth. Not at the pubs in Grantham Street, either. When had that happened?

A moment later, Hunzu was back. "Hold still, and don't scream," he said, listing the instructions on his fingers. "Probably best if we don't wake the neighbors."

With that, he scooped up Ivy and the blanket in one awkward bundle, staggering under the weight. Ivy tried to push him away, immediately grabbing his coat as he nearly tripped over the bottom stair. She didn't want him touching her, but if the alternative was being dropped into the hawthorns, Ivy supposed she could allow it.

Somehow, Hunzu made it up the stairs without falling, fumbling with the knob for a moment before it turned. He staggered inside as the door slammed shut behind them, cutting out the last of the yellow streetlight, and the coat rack fell over with a clatter. The trow cursed. Hunzu managed a few steps down the hall, turning into the conservatory, staggering the few steps into Demi's room without falling.

The trow made it as far as the bed before dropping her. She bit back a yell, because she didn't want to give him the satisfaction, and because she knew it would just hurt her throat more.

She'd been screaming before; Ivy was almost certain. And she was almost certain she'd gotten a kick in the stomach for her trouble.

Hunzu was back a moment later (Did he leave? When was that?), pressing a glass of water into her hands. He'd apparently found Demi's stereo; Ivy could hear an Electric Light Orchestra song drifting back through the flat.

"Drink it," said Hunzu, helping her raise the glass to her lips. "Dehydration's a very common side effect."

Ivy gulped at the water, soothingly cool against her raw throat. Perhaps Hunzu could tell her what happened; he always had the most fantastic explanations for things. Like when he told her he was a gorilla. Only that wasn't right; he was invisible like a gorilla. Except gorillas weren't invisible. Ivy knew she'd understood it at the time, but now the relevant details were all slipping through her fingers.

"What did—" Ivy started to say.

Hunzu shushed her, dropping into Demi's desk chair and propping his boots up on the edge of the bed. He'd filled a plastic bag with ice and was dabbing it gingerly against his nose. A trickle of blood ran sluggishly down the side of his face and Ivy wondered vaguely whether Demi was going to complain about the stains on her duvet. His boots were covered in mud, crusty and flaking along the leather, wet and glistening on the spurs. The glimmer of the spurs matched the streetlamp reflection in the trow's eyes. It was too dark to see anything else of Hunzu's face, except that he was still looking at her.

Ivy was suddenly certain it wasn't mud congealing on his spurs.

"Get out," Ivy rasped. "Now."

Hunzu slipped out of the room wordlessly, his boots tapping against the floorboards like hooves.

❧❦❧

SOMEONE WAS PACING, a rhythmic clatter of booted feet. Ivy wondered if she ought to get up and tell Demi off for making so much noise. Probably too much trouble. And it was Demi's bedroom, Ivy thought absently; probably that meant Demi could do whatever she liked. Strangely, the person pacing across Demi's room wasn't Demi herself, but Hunzu, prowling back and forth in the tiny space between the wardrobe and the desk. Aside from the sound of his footsteps, the flat seemed utterly silent, quiet enough that Ivy could hear the faint rustling of the tradescantia leaves as they brushed against the sides of Hunzu's jacket. He was still dabbing at his nose with the half-melted bag of ice, now wrapped in one of the tea towels from the kitchen. A dull, distant ache had settled into the muscles of her legs, though they didn't hurt as badly as Ivy was expecting. Perhaps, she thought dully, that was because she hadn't tried to stand up yet. Slowly, Ivy moved her jaw back and forth. It still hurt, as though she'd cut her lip. She pulled one hand out from under the duvet to feel for a mark.

Hunzu must have seen the motion, for he stopped, abruptly dropping into Demi's desk chair and flipping open one of her gardening magazines, scanning it with every appearance of

203

great attention. His absorption in the magazine might have been slightly more convincing were it not clearly too dark to read it.

For a strange moment, it seemed like everything in the room was balanced on a knife-edge, between the normal world on one side, and everything else on the other. As though it would only take the slightest motion to make everything fall one way or the other. As if all Ivy needed to do was pinch herself awake, and it would be the sort of night where the headaches all came out of wine bottles. The sort of night where she'd be quite happy to come home with a pretty-looking boy, and never mind if they'd only just met. Like the night she'd met Colin, when he'd walked up and paid for her cover charge at Copper Face Jacks and she stayed out with him until four in the morning, coming home on wobbly legs, falling into bed with mascara on her face and glitter in her hair.

But this wasn't that sort of night, and Hunzu wasn't that sort of boy. Very little about him was normal, or safe, and nothing about him was human. Ivy knew better, and it was silly to pretend differently.

She wondered why Hunzu had bothered staying. He'd gotten her home; she would have thought he'd have left by now. She wondered why he hadn't. And wondered what he'd done to get Ivy home, a question she found herself strangely reluctant to think about.

Ivy was home, and that was what mattered. Maybe it would be better if she didn't think too much about how it was she'd gotten here.

"Were you ever really Demi's boyfriend?" Ivy asked.

Hunzu continued to stare at the magazine for long enough Ivy wondered if he was pretending he hadn't heard the question. If he wasn't going to talk, it felt very tempting to simply roll over and go back to sleep, and trust that whatever had happened to leave cuts on her lips and bruises on her legs, it would all make better sense in the morning.

"I thought I might be," he said after a moment. A furrowed line crept across the length of his forehead, as though he was recalling something he hadn't thought about in some considerable time. "An indiscretion, you might call it. A dangerous one, as it turned out."

"But that doesn't mean anything unless—"

"Unless she dies before Wednesday?" he interrupted, flipping the magazine closed. "So you've figured out I've spent the last six months being Ambrose's insurance, in case something happened to her? Hardly matters now. They'll hold a new lottery in March, and we'll have a new king. After Wednesday, everything resets."

After Wednesday. After Demi was dead. And Hunzu was talking about it like it was certain to happen. "But Demi's trying to hide, she said—"

"We've tried that!" Hunzu said, dropping the bag of ice into a sodden heap on the desk. "We've tried everything! We've tried running, we've tried fighting, we've tried hiding, we've tried doing nothing at all and it still keeps killing us. One a year; every year, for centuries. So why does it still bother? Why does it still care?"

"When you came here before," Ivy said, pushing herself up against the pillows. "You weren't trying to help Demi. You just wanted to make sure she was still alive, so the Enemy would kill her instead of you!"

"Precisely," said Hunzu tightly.

"That's horrible!"

"That's life," Hunzu countered, sweeping the gardening magazine into the desk drawer with an impatient wave of his hand. "Or rather, that's death. And clearly, Demi doesn't want a consort who's willing to die for her. But like I said, it won't matter after Wednesday."

A tight, brittle smile flickered briefly over Hunzu's face. Almost as though he was pleased. Looking forward to Demi dying, to no longer being one heartbeat away from being the Enemy's victim himself.

"But there were some kings that lived," Ivy protested. Something wet was running down the side of her face; all her talking had broken open the scab at the corners of her mouth. Ivy grabbed the edge of the blanket, roughly dabbing at her chin. "Like Carillon's son, the one who disappeared—"

"They died," Hunzu said flatly. "The old kings died, and so did Larch Carillon, somehow or other. History just hasn't recorded the particulars of how it happened. And if I won't help Demi try and beat those odds, she only has herself to blame, doesn't she?"

A crooked grin spread across his face, made sinister by the dark circles under his eyes. Hunzu hadn't come to Howth to help Demi. He just wanted to make sure she wasn't already dead. Wanted to make sure the Enemy was still coming for her, instead of him.

"Demi's only trying to—"

"To what?" the trow countered. "To live? Aren't I trying to do the same thing? It isn't right, just to pick someone and—"

"And kill them?" Ivy spat out. "Isn't that what your lottery is all about?"

"And screw them over, and vanish, and everyone wonders if she's already dead!" His voice cracked, and he turned away abruptly, stripping the gloves from his hands and burying his fingers in his hair. "So she could do what she wanted and never worry about anyone she cared about. So she could *die* if she wanted, and nobody important gets hurt. She's going to burn, Ivy, and I'll be happy to watch."

A moment later he was pacing, his spurs jingling like bells, red and flaking and stained.

"That's cruel."

"Yes, she is," he replied distractedly, but Ivy was still watching his spurs.

"I didn't mean Demi," Ivy spat out.

"You hate me, Ivy?" the trow said, stopping his pacing and staring at Ivy, his eyes fever-bright in the darkness. "Want me dead? Just walk up to Demi and pull the trigger. It's that simple."

"Get out," said Ivy.

Hunzu turned toward her, a stricken look on his face, as though he'd only just realized what he'd said.

"I didn't mean—I only meant—she didn't have any right—"

"Get out," Ivy repeated, louder. "I don't *ever* want to see you again."

He closed his mouth without saying anything.

Slowly, Hunzu picked up his bag of ice. "Clever girl," he murmured as he walked out of the room.

But the hoofbeat echo of his boots in the hallway lingered in Ivy's dreams for a long time after.

A FEW HOURS LATER, Ivy awoke from a dream of running.

The plants in Demi's bedroom were the first thing she saw, and for a moment it seemed entirely natural that she was waking up in someone else's bed, with leaves and stems and green things everywhere. Then Ivy saw the reflection of her face in the window.

For the slightest moment, it looked like the face of a stranger. The face of someone she wasn't expecting, and would look past without a second thought.

A light was shining in the hallway outside, although Demi's bedroom was still dark. Ivy reached for the bedside light, wincing as the muscles in her arms protested. The light came on with a click and the room was suddenly far too bright. Ivy buried her head in the pillows, blinking furiously. The spots in her vision promised she was in for one heck of a headache.

After a moment, Ivy gingerly opened her eyes. Sitting on the table next to the lamp were three bottles of Gatorade, and two small pill containers. One was the Midol Ivy kept in her bathroom vanity; the other was a bottle of Vicodin made out to Mr. Carmichael in the next townhouse over. Apparently, these were Hunzu's slightly felonious attempts at first aid.

Ivy pushed back the blankets, incidentally discovering she still wasn't wearing a stitch of clothing. She unscrewed one of the Gatorade bottles, the cap pressing uncomfortably against a purplish mark on the base of her thumb. Both her hands were covered with bruises. They reminded her of the time Garrett had broken his toe playing rugby—half his foot had turned dark and lumpy, everything puffed up twice as big as it should have been. A quick check revealed that Ivy's feet were in a similar state. She was still partially wrapped in the tattered wool blanket. Both the blanket and the sheets below it were stained brown in several places; a few of the stains were still fresh enough to feel damp.

Ivy eventually traced the blood to a cluster of scrapes along her hips, a starburst of thin lines, only a few of which were deep enough to actually bleed.

Out of nowhere, Ivy thought of the groom Silas, his crop rapping sharply across Clover's withers, his spurs biting into the horse's flanks.

She drained half the Gatorade in a few gulps. Ivy rubbed at her mouth; her fingers came away sticky with flakes of dried blood. Experimentally, Ivy opened her mouth wider, stopping when she felt the prickle of a scab pulling at the corner of her lip. She took another sip of Gatorade, picked up the Midol and started to open it, then looked at the bottle of Vicodin. She opened the prescription bottle, shook two pills into her hand, and swallowed them with the rest of the Gatorade.

Ivy slept again, and dreamed of running.

⁂

HOURS LATER, and the sun had peeked over the gables of the townhouse on the other side of the little alley, and the light was shining straight through the windows. Ivy rubbed at her eyes, glancing at Demi's bedside clock, which was telling her it was just past eleven-thirty.

On the desk, Ivy spotted the coat she'd borrowed from Demi, neatly folded beside the tradescantia. She slipped out from under the scratchy blanket, the muscles in her thighs tight and aching as she limped across the room. Ivy picked up the coat and threw it on, zipping it all the way to her chin. The coat felt lop-sided; something weighed it down on the left side. Ivy reached into the left-hand pocket, finding her wallet and her mobile. She stuffed the wallet back into the coat, and keyed open her phone. The screen merely flashed a few seconds of a low battery alert, then went dark.

Sighing, Ivy shoved it back into her pocket alongside the wallet. It was just her luck that it would die; the thing didn't usually lose its charge overnight. She'd just have to plug it back in upstairs.

Ivy gathered up the pill bottles and shoved them into the other pocket. As she stepped around the bed, the leaves of the tradescantias brushed fawningly at the edges of her coat. Guiltily, Ivy pushed the leaves away. She hadn't done a thing for the plants in two days.

Not that any of it mattered, because Demi wasn't going to see any of them ever again. Probably that meant Ivy could do whatever she wanted with the damn things. Grabbing the two remaining bottles of Gatorade, Ivy slipped out of the room and limped up the stairs, wondering if it was too soon to take another pill.

Back in her own bedroom, Ivy dropped the Gatorade on the bed, dug her mobile out of the pocket, and plugged it into the charger. Unzipping the coat, she draped it over the back of her chair, and retreated to the bathroom. As she closed the door, Ivy heard the phone emitting a cacophony of bright, perky text alerts and missed call chimes. Briefly, Ivy considered checking to see who had called, but the thought of hopping into the shower was too tempting. Whoever had called, they could stand to wait until Ivy was clean.

It was only when the water began to turn cold that Ivy realized how long she'd been standing under the shower head, blankly staring at the honeycomb design on the tile walls. Shutting off the taps, Ivy stepped out into the shower, beginning to shiver as she toweled herself off.

Stepping out of the bathroom, she grabbed a sweatshirt from the bureau and pulled it over her head. As she limped past the window, Ivy caught a glimpse of the back garden. Something in the yard looked out of place. She stopped, leaning on the sill as she craned her head. The rubbish bins had fallen over, but that wasn't it. There was something else. Something about the grass. It was dimpled in places, even though Ivy remembered the whole yard being flat and fertilized and even.

It had to be moles. Or hedgehogs. Something little, innocuous, and inconsequential. But something about the yard had changed, and it didn't feel little, or innocuous, or inconsequential.

And Ivy would worry about it unless she went out and checked.

Gingerly, Ivy pulled on a pair of trousers, slid her bruised feet into her sneakers, minced down the stairs and into the back hallway.

Someone had stood the coat rack back up. One of its wooden pegs had been reduced to a splintered stump, only half as long as the other pegs. Had that happened last night? No, it had been like that before; Demi just kept the broken peg facing the wall. Probably it was the same thing with the back garden. It had always looked dimpled, and Ivy was just now noticing.

Opening the door, Ivy stepped outside, the cold air immediately seeping through her clothes.

The gate leading into the alley stood ajar; one of the rubbish bags was already ripped open where the rooks had been fishing for scraps. Ivy made a belated move to rescue the bins; she only made it halfway down the stairs before she noticed the grass.

Ivy was wrong; the yard hadn't been like this before.

She came a few steps into the grass, bending over to peer at the nearest mark as though closer inspection might change what it looked like. She ran her fingers over the furrow, tracing the curved outline as she smoothed the grass back into place, not quite letting herself think about exactly what she was touching.

A long-ago image came to mind, of sitting on the bright red sofa with her mother, watching a polo match on the telly. Dozens of women in posh dresses and fantastic hats, all running about turning over the divots at the half-time.

Demi should have been there, Ivy thought out of nowhere. I know she'd have just the dress.

Shakily, Ivy turned back to the house, leaning on the railing as she climbed the stairs to the back door.

Behind her, the back garden was covered with the crescent-moon divots of hoof prints.

⚜

BACK INSIDE, Ivy walked into the kitchen, and opened the fridge. Demi's name jumped out from a half dozen labeled Tupperware lids. Biting at her lip, Ivy closed the door. She'd need to throw all of it out soon. And anything else that wasn't in a verifiably unopened box. Now that Ivy knew about the food, she wasn't about to chance eating anything she wasn't absolutely certain was safe.

Turning the kettle on, Ivy grabbed a cup of pot noodles from the pantry and set it on the counter. She automatically reached into her pocket for her mobile, only to remember it was still plugged into the charger upstairs.

Might as well start with the newspaper classifieds, Ivy thought. Some distant part of her was surprised that she still bothered to worry about things as normal and mundane as job ads. Maybe because Ivy didn't much want to think about the things that weren't normal and mundane. Like the hoof prints in the back garden. Or that Ivy hadn't been wearing any clothes when she came home last night. Or that Demi was never coming back, because the Enemy would kill her in four days.

Opening the front door, the first thing Ivy noticed was that the *Irish Times* was much thicker than the Saturday editions usually were. The paper was wrapped up in a plastic sleeve, several sheets of glossy advertisements sticking out from among the newsprint.

As she bent to pick it up, Ivy spotted another newspaper—or what was left of one—sitting behind the flower boxes. It hadn't been wrapped in a sleeve, and it looked completely soaked. Ivy stepped off the sidewalk to rescue it, glancing at the illegible headline dripping across a blurry photo of Dublin's old, windowless Parliament House. Drying it out would be hopeless; she'd have to chuck it straight in the bin. Gingerly tucking the ruined newspaper under her arm, Ivy slid the glossy Saturday paper out of its plastic sleeve.

It wasn't the Saturday paper. Comics and ads, telly schedules and magazines fell out of the sleeve in a cascade of paper, far too much for a Saturday edition. The *Irish Times* had delivered the Sunday paper a day ahead of time. Which was absurd; they wouldn't even have the papers printed that early.

Ivy felt a sudden cold that had nothing to do with the chill air. The *Times* wouldn't deliver early. Which meant today was Sunday. Ivy had gone to Haven on Friday morning. And somehow, she'd lost an entire day coming back.

She dropped both papers and turned back to the flower boxes, frantically pulling aside the azalea branches as though an entire week's worth of missing days might have secreted themselves in bundles of newsprint behind the bushes.

Ivy didn't just not remember how she'd gotten home last night—she didn't remember anything from an entire day.

There wasn't anything else under the flower boxes. Returning to the porch, Ivy grabbed the paper, flipping it over until she could see the date over the main headline. Sunday the seventeenth.

Which meant the Enemy wasn't coming in four days. It was coming in three.

Tucking both papers under her arm, Ivy went back to the door, trying to conjure up any remnant memory of what had happened the previous day. She'd been running, Ivy was sure of that. But where she'd been running to—or what she'd been running from—she didn't have the faintest idea.

In the hallway, the kettle was shrieking. Following the noise back to the kitchen, Ivy switched it off, setting the newspapers and the torn plastic sleeve on the counter. Could she simply have slept that long? Even accounting for the Vicodin, Ivy didn't think so. Though that didn't necessarily rule out other drugs. And she hadn't been wearing any clothes when Hunzu brought her back. . . .

Ivy peeled the lid back from the cup of pot noodles, and picked up the kettle, slowly pouring the water into the plastic cup.

She watched the water, turned bright yellow by the cheese powder, inch up the sides of the cup, and thought of the labeled Tupperware sitting in the fridge. And the bags of chia seeds on Demi's shelf under the silverware drawer. She remembered the feeling of the scone in the parlor at Haven, the warm crumbs crumpling under her fingers as she squeezed it.

Was this what it felt like to become invisible? She'd held hands with Ambrose yesterday. She'd touched Carillon's scones. And God knew what might have happened between leaving Haven and arriving here.

For the past six months, Ivy had been skirting, all unknowing, around the edges of the trows' hidden world. Had she gone far enough in, that this was where the real world fell apart?

Ivy fumbled with the kettle, jumping back as the steaming water spilled across the counter. Shakily, she set the kettle down, looking for a tea towel to clean up the mess. The cold from outside seemed to have followed her into the kitchen, raising prickles and goosebumps along the back of her neck.

Was this what it was like to be the gorilla? The thing no one saw? Other people stopped noticing you—but what if you stopped noticing things, too? Things like days of your life. Things like where you'd been, or how you'd gotten home.

The whole idea was nonsense. The veil didn't affect trows that way. Demi was plenty weird, but she'd never struck Ivy as being literally crazy.

Then again, trows were supposed to be under the veil. Ivy wasn't. Maybe it affected her differently. Because whatever had happened to Ivy getting back from Haven, she ought to have remembered it. Even if it was something that couldn't logically have happened.

If Ivy was under the veil, there was an easy way to check.

Ivy tore back up the stairs, as fast as her complaining legs would allow, and grabbed Demi's coat from the back of her chair. Throwing it on, she stuck her hand in the pocket to check that her wallet was still there. Unexpectedly, she felt crumbs, and pulled her hand back with a jerk. Going to her desk, Ivy turned out the pocket, furiously shaking out the remnants of Carillon's scone in a messy cascade over the waste bin.

Her wallet dropped into the bin with the crumbs, along with a few dirt-covered tissues and a folded bit of paper. She reached into the bin and snagged her wallet, shoving it back into her coat as she hurried out of the room and down the stairs.

The nearest shop was three blocks away—a greasy chippie near the harbor all but deserted in the off-season. Ivy headed down the hill as fast as her limping gait would allow, keeping her hood up and her eyes on the sidewalk. Passersby wouldn't be a fair test; sometimes they said hello back, and sometimes they didn't. The cashier at the chip shop was supposed to pay attention to customers. She just needed to order something, and she'd know.

Ivy turned onto the main road, following it another block toward the harbor, and pushed open the door to the chip shop. A bell rang over the door as Ivy stepped through, unzipping her coat in the warm air. The shop smelled strongly of grease and fish. Even though it was nearing the end of lunch hour, there were two people in line in front of Ivy—a girl in a yellow rain-coat, and a man carrying on a conversation either with his Blue-tooth headset, or with someone no one else could see.

Taking her place in line, Ivy looked at the back of the man's head, glancing between him, the girl, and the man at the counter, and trying not to be alarmed that no one was making eye contact. The cashier handed the girl in the yellow raincoat her change; the man with the Bluetooth headset broke off his conversation long enough to bark out an order and hand over his cash card. He signed the receipt and moved further down the counter to wait for his order.

"Haddock and peas, please," Ivy said loudly, as she came up to the counter. And then nervously, as the cashier entered something into the till, "Did you get that?"

"Haddock and peas," the cashier repeated laconically. Ivy let out a breath she didn't realize she was holding. Then belatedly, as the cashier continued to stare, she shoved a handful of notes across the counter.

"Thank you very much," she added. The cashier looked up, flicking his hair out of his eyes as he gave Ivy her change. Ivy shoved the coins back into her wallet, and dropped into the nearest of the chippie's uncomfortable plastic chairs. Her legs felt wobbly, like the vertigo feeling of leaning too far over the railing of a bridge.

The cashier had seen her, and talked to her, and he'd gotten her order right. Even with other people in the room. So Ivy wasn't invisible. Or at least, she wasn't invisible yet.

Which meant everything was fine. Even if Ivy didn't remember what happened yesterday. Even if the Enemy was coming, and Demi and Ambrose and everyone thought it was hopeless. Ivy wasn't invisible, and that was as good a starting point as any. Ivy took a deep breath. Everything was fine.

"Haddock and peas," the cashier called. Leaning on the table, Ivy got up and grabbed her order. She started to take it back to the table, but suddenly, the thought of spending any more time sitting in the hard plastic chairs under the yellowish fluorescent lights was more than Ivy could stomach. Grabbing a handful of vinegar packets from the dispenser near the rubbish bins, Ivy fled the shop.

BACK AT THE FLAT, she flung her coat onto the coat rack and went into the kitchen. Grabbing a fork from the drawer, Ivy set the takeaway bag next to the lukewarm cup of pot noodles and peeled back the grease-soaked paper. The fish was crispy; the peas looked like mush. Ivy sprinkled the fish liberally with several of the vinegar packets, then stabbed at the filet.

Chewing, Ivy pulled her phone out of her coat pocket.

Two missed calls and four text messages. She pulled the first one up—a reminder that her mobile bill was due in two days. The second was from her mother, another YouTube clip of cats. This one, judging from the picture on the link, appeared to involve kittens wearing football jerseys.

Had 2 share, it really brightened my day, Victoria wrote. Ivy sighed, texting back a quick thanks without opening the video. You'd never catch Shannon sending something like that to Garrett or Evan. But all Victoria ever seemed to talk about were her cats, along with occasional complaints about her coding job. Ivy didn't see there was much to complain about, since the job was all work-from-home, which meant her mom could wear whatever she wanted, and make herself a cup of tea whenever she fancied, instead of confining herself to the seven-minute breaks and draconian dress codes they insisted on at the call center.

The third and fourth texts were from Deirdre: *wht do U think of the flat??? 75/week. At least tell me its cute?*

For a moment, Ivy thought Deirdre meant the flat at Thormanby Road, and had no idea why Deirdre would be asking such a thing. She scrolled down to Deirdre's second text, which was a string of a half dozen photos of a flat Ivy didn't recognize. A wood-floored living room with a lumpy black couch and flat screen TV. A kitchen with a small oven, and a large, looming hood vent. A bathroom with mismatched tile and a shower curtain covered in cartoonish-looking orange fish. A small, airy-looking bedroom with a large picture window. Ivy scrolled to the end of the photos, at a loss as to why Deirdre had sent them in the first place. Was Deirdre moving? Ivy hadn't heard anything about that. She'd just signed a new lease on her current place only a few months back.

Ivy flipped back to the voicemails. There were two messages; Ivy recognized Deirdre's number, followed by an unfamiliar number with a Dublin area code.

She pulled up Deirdre's message first.

"Hey Ivy, the news about Eirecom was in the papers," Deirdre's voice squealed through the phone. Wherever she'd called from, it sounded noisy in the background, as though she were shouting. "Don't know whether to say I'm sorry they're shuttered or not. Look, I'm over at Trish's; her friend Lauren's flatmate's moving out and she's looking for someone, and I don't know how you managed the commute from Howth, but if you land a job in the City it'll be a bloody nuisance, and this one's in Dartry and she's not hardly asking anything for it. I know you'll probably want to stay put, but I'll text you the photos, and just think about it?"

The background noise grew suddenly louder, as though Deirdre had put down the phone, but then Deirdre was talking again. "There aren't any houseplants—I asked," she added, and the message ended.

So that explained the photos, Ivy thought. Which was very nice of Deirdre, except Ivy already had a flat. Yes, it was almost an hour on the DART to get anywhere south of the river, but

the place was lovely. Big skylights, beautiful wood paneling—
and a flatmate who was going to be murdered by some sort of
alien serial killer in three days.

Ivy's phone gave a muted beep, and began playing the
second message.

"Roberta here," grunted an unfamiliar voice. "Got your
CV; the weekend girl's pulled a runner and now I've got four
shifts to fill. Come in tomorrow at three, it's the deadest shift of
the week, we'll see how you do. Eleven fifty an hour. We're
opposite the park in Oxmarten—the Blue Parrot. And don't
even think about showing up if you can't pass a drug test," she
added, and the message ended abruptly.

Ivy lowered the phone, picking up her fork and stabbing
the haddock, trying to remember where she'd sent the CV to,
and when. If Roberta left the message yesterday then she
wanted Ivy at work this afternoon. It was a shame, really, it
paid nearly two more per hour than the call center, but she
couldn't just drop everything and run down there because she
had to—

Ivy stopped, her fork halfway to her mouth.

Had to save her flatmate from an alien monster that had
been killing people for hundreds of years?

The Enemy was coming in three days, and Ivy couldn't
change that. Even Ambrose admitted he didn't know how to
help Demi. Even Demi had had only one idea for how to
escape—she'd disappeared. Except that Hunzu had found her,
and Ivy had blabbed about him coming by the flat, and screwed
that all up.

Though to hear the other trows talk about it, the Enemy
probably would have found her anyway. And in three days
something terrible would happen, and Ivy didn't want to be
anywhere near it when it did.

What could Ivy do in the meantime? What could possibly

happen in three days that would help? Demi still didn't have her phone, and Ivy certainly wasn't calling Carillon. Without a car, she had no way to get back to County Clare. If she did go, there was no telling if Carillon would ever let her leave. Or whether Ivy would still be visible if she did.

Ivy set her fork back on the plate, the bite of vinegar-soaked haddock untouched. The Enemy wasn't the only terrible thing in the trows' world. Ivy had been avoiding terrible things on a somewhat regular basis for the past six months. She hadn't eaten any of Demi's food—not even the vegan chocolate cake she'd made back in December; Ivy remembered drooling longingly over it during the week it sat in the fridge. Deirdre could have stopped by the flat when Demi was there, and might have called the psych ward when Ivy tried to introduce the two of them. The waiter at the terrible pub could have done more than overcharge Ivy for a horrible meal she hadn't actually eaten. Ambrose could have decided to poison her back at the Liberties, and Hunzu might not have stopped him. She'd held hands with a trow and hadn't turned invisible. She hadn't eaten the scones. All disasters, and somehow, she'd managed to muddle her way through.

Almost muddle through. Almost.

Whatever happened getting back from County Clare, that she couldn't properly remember. Whatever happened that meant her legs hurt when she walked up stairs.

She'd managed so far. But her luck was going to run out soon. Wednesday, to be precise. Demi was going to die, and Ivy couldn't stop it.

How long could Ivy live in a flat that would soon belong to a dead girl? In three days Demi would be gone, and Ivy would be alone in a flat in Howth with forty-seven houseplants, no job, and no hope of paying the rent beyond the month Demi already left. So many things could have gone wrong in the past few days. *She* could have been the one that couldn't sign for packages, the one that never left the flat.

The maths, the pen and paper part of the equation, were very clear. The money under the begonias would more than cover a security deposit and first month's rent at the flat with the cartoon-fish shower curtain, or any of a hundred flats like it all over the city. Eleven fifty was more than what Eirecom paid, and even if the pub turned out to be terrible, the paycheck would give Ivy time to find something else, without taking the dole, or having to move back in with her dad and step-brothers.

And beyond the maths? The things that were bigger than security deposits or pay stubs? She couldn't do anything for Demi. Staying in the flat wouldn't help her. Taking care of the houseplants wouldn't, either. Demi wouldn't even know. She probably wouldn't care, either, what Ivy did, or where she was living, or why. Nothing would make the slightest bit of difference, and it was silly to keep believing otherwise. She'd tried, and the only thing she'd gotten were bruises on her hands and feet, and the half-moon divots in the back garden. Maybe it was time to stop trying to take care of Demi, and start trying to take care of herself, instead.

Mechanically, Ivy picked up the fork, chewing on the now-cold haddock as she texted with her other hand. It was an hour to the city center on the DART; if she wanted to be at the Blue Parrot at three, she had less than an hour before she needed to leave.

Hey Deirdre, she texted. *Flat IS cute. Send me her number?*

AT TEN TO three that afternoon, Ivy was crossing the street opposite a small, weed-choked park somewhere in the west end of Oxmarten. Despite being reasonably near the city center, the

Blue Parrot was so buried in the warren of streets north of the river that it was still a long walk to the nearest DART station. Another dose of painkillers, and Ivy was managing to walk with only a slight limp. Her hands were tucked firmly into her coat. Ivy had, defiantly, left her gloves hanging on the coat rack when she'd left, for all that it was cold out, and likely to be even colder after dark.

The Blue Parrot faced the east side of the tiny park, the pub's sign—a large, piratical-looking bird holding a beer stein in its talons —nestled next to a tiny takeaway with a dilapidated sign advertising Chicken Tikka Masala and Parrot Burgers. Ivy pushed open the door, immediately stepping into a dim, high-ceilinged room smelling strongly of curry and stale beer. The telly over the bar was muted, broadcasting a replay of the United/Rangers match from the week before. In the far corner, a jukebox sat at an angle, as though it were in the process of falling through the floorboards and into the basement below. As Ivy looked at it, the jukebox began, with a great amount of whirring and chuffing, to shuffle through its reams of CDs, then abruptly fell silent.

Ivy slowly walked in, letting the heavy door swing shut behind her. A long wooden bar took up nearly the entire left wall of the room, with an equally long row of liquor bottles sitting behind it. The rest of the bar was decorated with spindly, stained wooden tables sitting below dust-covered Tiffany lamps. A handful of patrons were drinking in silent groups of ones and twos. One set of swinging doors led toward the loos, another to what looked like a small office. Behind the bar, a skinny boy was crouched over the sink, scrubbing at a pile of dishes. A long, floppy mohawk covered half his face, his hair swishing back and forth as he scrubbed at the pint glass. He didn't look up as Ivy came up to the bar.

"Hello," said Ivy, loudly, and the boy straightened,

brushing his hair out of the way, and leaving a small streak of soap on his forehead.

"Want something, luv?" he asked cheerfully, setting the pint glass onto a drying rack. "Or are you one of the ones Roberta called?"

Apparently, he'd already picked out that Ivy didn't look like their usual clientele. "Yes, someone called and said there were shifts open, but she didn't leave a number, just said to come down—"

"Yeah, she does that," said the boy unconcernedly. Setting the pint glass onto a drying rack, he slipped out from behind the bar. "Name's Will, by the way. I do weekends and Tuesdays."

"I'm Ivy," she replied, belatedly thinking she ought to shake hands, but he was already walking past her, to a pair of swinging doors at the back of the room.

"Roberta," the boy hollered. "One of 'em showed!"

From behind the doors, Ivy heard the screech of a chair behind pushed back. A moment later, the doors swung open and a large woman in a patch-covered denim jacket walked out. She had short grey hair, pink mascara, and vibrantly painted-on eyebrows.

"Which one are you?" Roberta asked, looking Ivy up and down.

"I'm Ivy Gallagher; you left a message yesterday about a job here—"

"Right, the call center girl," said Roberta, looking as though she'd hoped Ivy would have turned out to be someone else. "Well, if nobody else shows up by quarter past, you can take the shift. Don't cock it up tonight, and you can have three evenings a week to start. Will can show you what needs done— s'all very easy. If the till's short, it'll come out of your wages.

Very easy," she repeated, and disappeared back behind the swinging door.

"Right," Ivy mumbled to the closing door, and glanced at Will, who was unconcernedly drying a beer stein with a ragged-looking towel.

"She's always like that, pretty much," said Will affably.

"I tried to call to let her know I was coming," said Ivy, ducking under the bar divider to join Will behind the sink. "But the line just rang and rang—"

"Roberta doesn't believe in interviews," said Will, bobbing his head, and sending his mohawk cascading over his eyes. "Figures it saves time to just call three or four of the folks that sent in CVs, and then see who actually shows. She was hoping for this one girl who waitressed at Cavenaugh's last summer." Will set down the rag and the pint glass as he looked at the clock. "But if she hasn't turned up by now, I suppose the job's yours. You can put your bag under the counter there, and I'll show you how to ring through a sale."

"Great," said Ivy, trying to sound as though the prospect of working at the Blue Parrot was still as thrilling as she'd thought it was before she'd walked through the door. It was a paycheck, she reminded herself. And she wouldn't be reading off a script, or repeating the same desultory conversation dozens of times a day.

And, Ivy reminded herself, she wouldn't have to worry about turning invisible if she ate the wrong food or shook hands with the wrong person.

"All right," said Will, leading Ivy to a dust-covered computer terminal with a flickering screen. "Credit cards are through the reader there, cash through the till. Tabs are lined up there next to the Glengoolie Blue, and nothing on credit unless it's one of our regulars."

"Who *are* our regulars?" Ivy asked, looking around the all but deserted pub.

"They come in weeknights, mostly," said Will. "But there's a few in now. The fellow with the blue overcoat? Foreman for the remodel they're doing at the Stonegate building. Name's Owen, drinks Smithwicks. He comes in here to use the Wi-Fi mostly, but his whole crew will be in here drinking after work some nights. And the bald fellow by the window? Works for one of those historical houses somewhere up the road, and he always orders the house whiskey." Will nodded toward a sticky-looking bottle of Powers Gold Label sitting next to the ice well. "Then there's the whole crew from Haunted Dublin."

"Haunted Dublin?" Ivy asked nervously.

"Haunted Dublin Tours," Will said, his mohawk flopping again as he nodded. "Across the street—the one with the fake bats on top. The whole staff's in here all the time, 'cause Roberta gives 'em half-price drafts. Don't know why; she must have a thing for boys in frilly shirts."

"This place isn't haunted, is it?" Ivy asked, looking nervously around the pub. She didn't much like the idea of sharing the pub with anything that rattled, moaned, or shrieked. Mysterious footsteps, or strangely moving objects reminded Ivy too much of what it had been like at her mother's house at Trail's Cross. If it turned out the pub was haunted, she desperately hoped the ghosts were of shy and retiring dispositions.

"I don't know," said Will, leaning against the side of the bar and looking thoughtful. "Things move around sometimes. I came in one morning and the taps key was sitting right there on the counter when I knew I put it away the night before. And the fellow that cleans on weekends swore he saw a man in a black coat standing next to the jukebox."

Ivy looked skeptically at the jukebox. As though sensing

the attention, it wheezed loudly and began playing the opening notes of *Strange Magic*.

Her life, Ivy thought, would have been a lot simpler if she'd turned out to be completely insensible to ghosts, trows, fairies, brownies, or whatever other strange and unnatural creatures might inhabit Dublin. If there were ghosts in the Blue Parrot, Ivy hoped they were invisible—to her as well as to everyone else—and that they had the good sense to stay that way. The last thing Ivy wanted was to discover there were other odd things living in Dublin besides trows.

"If you really want to know about the ghosts, you ought to talk to Killian when he comes by," Will was saying. "He knows stories about most every building in Oxmarten."

"Right," said Ivy, thinking the last thing she wanted to do was listen to stories that would leave her frightened of every dark alley or eerie-looking tenement on the street. The walk back to the DART station was long enough without worrying about chance encounters with the spirits of the restless dead.

Halfway through the second verse, the jukebox spluttered into silence, leaving the whole pub quiet, apart from the hum of the keg chiller. In the back corner, the man with the open laptop took a final swig from his pint glass, dropping it back on the table.

"Another of the same, Owen?" Will called across to him.

The man nodded, and Will turned back to Ivy, rubbing his hands together, as though he was ridiculously pleased by the prospect of even a minor task on such a slow afternoon.

"Right, so if you open the cupboard behind you, there's the pint glasses. Now let me show you the best way to pour one so the foam doesn't go everywhere."

Ivy DIDN'T GET BACK to the flat at Thormanby Street until
nearly two in the morning, and that was only because she'd
rushed to the DART station after closing to make certain she
caught the 1:10 train. She'd locked up the taps, learned how to
tally out the register, how to switch out an empty keg for a full
one, and how to punch in and out with the Blue Parrot's finicky
time clock. She'd served whiskey sours to a noisy contingent of
Bohemian Football Club fans, and innumerable pints of half-
priced Guinness to the Haunted Dublin guides, a garrulous
crowd of velveteen-covered blokes, most of whom seemed to be
students at Dublin's various drama schools. She'd dozed on the
ride back from the city center, stumbling sleepily up the hill
from the Howth station with her hands shoved into her pockets
and her hat pulled down over her ears.

She wasn't a call center girl anymore, Ivy thought, reaching
into in her bag for the door key. She didn't work in an office,
and in another few days, she might not be living in Howth.
Three text messages had been enough to set up an appointment
with Deirdre's friend to look at the flat in Dartry. Ivy planned
on bringing enough cash from the envelope under the begonias
to cover the deposit, if it turned out she liked the place.
Lauren's previous flatmate had already moved out; if Ivy liked
the flat, she could be moved in by the end of the week. Before
Wednesday, even. Which was silly, because Ivy wasn't the one
with a deadline. Wednesday shouldn't mean anything to her,
and the flat in Howth was paid up for another week and a half.

But after Wednesday, Ivy would be living with a dead girl.
Even if Ivy never saw or heard from Demi ever again,
Wednesday changed things, and it didn't seem right to stay.

One thing Ivy was certain of—whoever Ivy lived with next
had better be completely and absolutely normal in all possible
respects. Normal friends, normal jobs. No weird hobbies, and
no strange kitchen rules.

MARETH GRIFFITH

Ivy pushed open the door to the flat and closed it behind her, turning the lock and throwing the deadbolt. She pulled off her coat and draped it over the coat rack, then bent over and began tugging at the laces of her boots. Her bag slid off her shoulder and hit the floor with a clatter. Ivy winced, instinctively wondering whether she might have woken someone. She hadn't. Demi wasn't here, and Mr. Abernathy could barely hear anything when he wasn't wearing his hearing aids. Still, it was hard to resist the urge to mince about in silence, as if the very fact that it was two in the morning meant that she ought to be quiet, even though Ivy was the only one in the flat.

The knots on her boots weren't coming loose, and it was too dark in the hall to see how they ought to untie. Picking up her bag, Ivy tiptoed down the hall to the parlor, and dropped into the love seat. She hadn't thought to close the drapes before she'd left, and the light from the streetlamp outside was enough to outline the parlor, giving a jungle-like look to the bookshelves and tables. She hadn't so much as watered any of the plants since Demi left. Thinking of her flatmate's detailed instructions, Ivy winced. It was too dark to see, but Ivy was certain some of the plants were wilting and sagging, ready to collapse into an accusatory pile of dead leaves and topsoil. Ivy suppressed an instinctive frisson of guilt that Demi would be disappointed when she found out Ivy hadn't been keeping up with them.

Which was silly. Demi wouldn't know—because she wasn't going to be alive long enough to find out. But it seemed a little cold-hearted to give up on the poor things before Demi was even. . . .

Ivy didn't finish that thought. There wasn't anything she could do. She could be the world's most perfect and conscientious plant-sitter, and it still wouldn't do Demi any good.

The laces finally gave way; Ivy slipped her foot out of her

left boot, and turned her attention to the right one. There was nothing she could do for Demi. There was nothing anyone could do.

Leaving her boots on the parlor floor, Ivy limped up the stairs to her room.

The rubbish bin was still sitting in the middle of the floor. Ivy shoved it back under the desk with her foot, seeing the little crumbs of scone amongst a few crumpled tissues. Sitting among the tissues was a larger sheet of paper, folded in half, and Ivy suddenly remembered pulling it out of her coat pocket along with the remnants of Taye Carillon's scone. Gingerly, Ivy reached into the rubbish bin and snagged the edge of the paper. She unfolded it, and immediately recognized Demi's handwriting. The letter looked as if it had been written hastily, with little regard for spelling and none whatsoever for penmanship.

Dear Ivy,

Make sure to drink ALL the Gatorade—your legs will probably be a little wobbly for the next few days. I thought about coming back to Howth with you, but I can't see how it will help. Ambrose and Hunzu have agreed to stay with me here. Hunzu says you might come back to see me, but he might only be saying it to cheer me up. It's terribly selfish, but I want to see you again. There's so little to look forward to now. I'll talk to Taye—I believe I can guarantee your safety. These days people will promise me anything, it seems.

—Demi

Ivy read the letter again, and folded it up. A moment later, she unfolded it, bending the paper back and forth as she read it a second time.

She dropped the note on her bed, leaning backwards

against the pillows, feeling the edge of the duvet rubbing against her cheek.

Demi wanted to see her again. For what, exactly? Her funeral? Her wake? A few days of drinks and carousing before the Enemy carried her away? Or sitting up with her all night and crying? Hours and hours of waiting. Like waiting for news in a doctor's office, except you already know what he's going to say.

She shouldn't go, and it was horrible of Demi to even ask. It was dangerous, and she shouldn't be involved. She shouldn't ever have gone to Haven in the first place. Ivy would just be putting herself at risk again, and all for a few days of not eating proper food, and trying not to touch people. And even if she did go, there wasn't a thing she could do to stop what was going to happen.

Ivy balled up the letter into a crumpled heap, tossing it toward the rubbish bin. It hit the edge of the desk and rolled off into the corner. Getting out of bed to throw it away properly suddenly seemed like far too much bother. Not when she had to be in Dartry in just over nine hours. Blearily, Ivy changed into her pajamas, leaving her clothes in a heap on the floor as she dropped, exhausted, into bed.

THE FOLLOWING NIGHT, Ivy was back at the Blue Parrot, stacking pint glasses on the tiny drying rack, and wondering how long it would take her to move all her stuff out of Demi's flat. There were only four other people in the whole pub—five, if you counted Roberta, somewhere in the back office chewing on peanut shells and rummaging through paperwork. The fellow from the Historical Trust was still nursing his latest whiskey; four pints of half-priced beer had gone to a group of lads whose frilly cuffs and button-covered vests marked them as Haunted Dublin guides on their dinner break. One of them, who introduced himself as Killian, had left his fellows to chat flirtatiously with Ivy for half an hour before bolting out to run his second tour.

Ivy wasn't sure if he was actually interested, or merely angling for free drinks. He seemed nice enough, if you didn't look too closely at his costume, which involved massive quantities of frippery and velveteen. She couldn't understand how he managed to be comfortable walking around in the cold wearing trousers that only came down to his knees. It had to be below freezing outside; the crawler bar on the muted TV had mentioned snow up in the Wicklow Hills.

Most of the customers had trickled out hours ago. Maybe they'd heard the weather forecast, too. Ivy had spent the last forty minutes wiping down the rows of liquor bottles, and morosely watching the clock. Only another half hour until the end of the shift. If the till balanced properly the first time she counted it, and if she hurried, Ivy reckoned she could just make the second-to-last train. Otherwise, she either had to walk ten minutes in the other direction to the bus stop, or go to the DART station anyway and hope the first train was late. Or wait in the cold for another forty minutes for the very last train of the evening.

The flat in Dartry was on the bus line, only a ten minute ride from the main station if she caught an express. If nothing else, moving flats was going to considerably simplify Ivy's evening commutes.

Deirdre's friend's flat turned out to be a ground-floor brownstone on the south side of the river, rented by a medical transcriptionist with bad acne and a droolingly affectionate bulldog named Grinch. Lauren had shaken hands without wearing gloves and there was normal food in the fridge (Ivy had checked). Everything seemed very usual and boring. These days, those seemed to be Ivy's only inflexible standards in flat-mates. Ivy had signed the lease and paid her deposit on the spot, telling herself it was a completely logical, rational, and adult decision. It wasn't like she was running away.

Or maybe she was, Ivy thought, as the jukebox roused itself and began playing the first few bars of Aerosmith's *Dream On*. Maybe running away was exactly what she was doing, because it was the only thing she could do. Hadn't Demi tried running away herself ? Maybe the only logical solution when faced with ancient murderers and contagious fairies was to get as far away from all of it as possible. But Ivy still had a queer feeling in her stomach when she thought of walking out of the flat in Howth, and leaving everything of Demi's sitting there to collect dust.

Ivy ran her fingers over the surface of the bar. It felt sticky, despite the fact that Ivy had just wiped it down not ten minutes earlier. The whole surface seemed so saturated with the stale remnants of spilled beer that Ivy didn't think it would ever be possible to remove all of it.

Very abruptly, the jukebox made a clunking noise, and Steven Tyler's wailing falsetto immediately fell silent. Besides the muted hum of the refrigerators, there was hardly a sound in the whole place. As if the whole of Oxmarten were holding its breath, waiting for something to happen, or for someone to walk through the door. Someone like Colin. Or Hunzu. Or maybe Ivy's old boss from the call center.

Which was silly, because none of them knew she worked here. Ivy didn't know whether that made it more or less likely that one of them would turn up.

Picking up a rag from the sink, Ivy dunked it briefly under the faucet and began scrubbing at the bar again, even though she suspected it would be just as sticky after she'd finished.

The bell over the door rang, and Ivy looked up to see a man

in a long, dirty coat stamping his feet and rubbing at his hands as though they were chilled. His ears, sticking out like pot handles from underneath his woolen cap, were cherry-red with cold. Little wonder, Ivy thought, rinsing the rag and wringing it out over the sink. It could be snowing outside already.

Ivy draped the wet rag over the side of the sink, grabbing a clean rag to dry off a handful of still-damp pint glasses sitting in the drying rack.

Meanwhile, the old man had shrugged out of his coat and dropped heavily into a booth in the far corner. Propping his boots on the edge of the table, he leaned against the back of the booth, settling the woolen hat unconcernedly over his eyes.

The fellow hadn't even ordered a drink. Didn't look like he was going to, either. And if Roberta caught him asleep with his mucky boots on the table, she'd probably pitch a fit.

Nervously, Ivy glanced between the man in the booth and the swinging doors leading to Roberta's office. She probably ought to get Roberta and let her deal with it. Except that Ivy had the distinct feeling Roberta wouldn't think twice about tossing the old man out, no matter that it was freezing outside. Maybe he was a street person. He probably wouldn't be sleeping in the booth unless he didn't have anywhere else to go.

Ivy shoved the last of the beer steins back in the fridge, considering. If he'd just take his feet off the table, she'd give him a glass of soda water and tell Roberta he'd ordered a G&T, if she asked. If he didn't smell, Ivy amended, slipping out from behind the bar and edging cautiously toward his table. If he did smell, she'd fetch Roberta, and she could decide what to do about him.

"Would you mind not putting your feet there?" Ivy asked.

The head jerked backwards, nearly dislodging the hat, and Ivy wondered if the man had already nodded off in the two minutes he'd been sitting there. He'd probably been drinking somewhere else, she thought. Possibly several somewhere elses.

"I said, would you mind—"

"I heard you the first time," said the man archly, setting his boots back onto the floor. "No need to get nattered about it, Ivy Gallagher."

He pushed his hat back, exposing a high, wrinkled forehead dotted with liver spots. His grinning teeth resembled a ragged fence of yellow clapboards.

"Uncle Patrick," said Ivy in surprise, which meant it was too late to say, Sorry, Ivy who?

"The very same," said the fellow happily. The clapboard grin grew even wider; Ivy immediately wished she'd left off the *Uncle* part. Patrick wasn't actually her uncle; he wasn't any sort of relation at all. Ivy supposed she ought to be happy her mother hadn't insisted on Ivy calling him anything worse.

But now that she'd called him Uncle, Ivy supposed that meant she had to be polite.

Only for five minutes, though. Ten at the most. They were closing in half an hour, and she'd have every right to ask him to leave.

"How are you?" asked Ivy, plastering a politely interested sort of smile on her face, hoping he wasn't going to start rattling on about lumbago or rheumatism. He looked even more decrepit than the last time she'd seen him, wrinkling like a papier mâché doll that had been left out in the rain.

"I might as well be asking you the same question," said Patrick with an accusatory snort. "Are you even old enough to drink? I thought you were working at the ice cream place over by the University?"

He meant Dream Cones, Ivy's first job after she'd left school, and she hadn't worked there in nearly a year.

"Tips are better here," said Ivy, shrugging.

Patrick looked over the nearly deserted bar, one caterpillar eyebrow twitching, his lips pursing over the yellow teeth.

"And yes, I'm old enough, I'm nineteen—"

"Nineteen," Patrick interrupted quickly, as if he'd just remembered. "Yes, indeed. Still living with Peter and Shannon, then?"

"No," said Ivy, unable to keep a glimmer of pride out of her voice. "I have my own place up north."

She'd almost said Howth, and as much as Ivy would have loved to see Patrick's expression if she said she lived there, it would probably just bring up questions about how Ivy could afford it on the wages she earned at a pub. Plus, she had a nervous feeling that she'd rather Patrick not know where she lived. Ivy wasn't entirely sure which she was more afraid of— that he'd show up on her doorstep looking for a place to sleep, or that he'd show up on her doorstep with some ridiculous present (like the Nancy Drew mystery set he'd sent when Ivy turned sixteen), and want to be all friendly and familial.

Patrick had been friendly when Ivy was younger; at the time, she hadn't understood why. He'd tousled her hair, and asked about school, and read her agonizingly boring essays about nesting habits of chaffinches or the mineral resources of Zaire, or whatever else St. Louise's Junior School had assigned for homework. Ivy had basked in the attention until shortly before her parents had split up. Then, even at twelve years old, it had been surprisingly easy to see Patrick's attention for what it was—another way for Patrick to be appealing to Ivy's mother.

"Your own place?" Patrick repeated nonsensically, his mouth opening and closing like a fish. "Isn't that lovely?"

"Yeah," said Ivy, nodding faintly. Things had been just as awkward every time she'd met Patrick since her parents' divorce. Almost as though Patrick had forgotten how to do anything but ask silly questions and then repeat back Ivy's own answers.

"Look," said Ivy, before he could say anything else. "You'd better buy a drink if you want to stay. And not on credit either. I mean, it's Roberta's place and she sets the rules," Ivy added, wondering if she'd been too blunt. "We'll be closing up in half an hour."

"Yes, of course," said Patrick, kneading the woolen hat between his fingers. "Just stopping in for a nightcap. Pint of bitter, if you could."

"Right," said Ivy, escaping back to the bar to pour his drink. Gathering his damp coat from the booth, Patrick followed Ivy to the bar. He gingerly installed himself on the swiveling chair at the far end, the one hardly anyone sat in because it was jammed up against the ridiculously ornate chair rail. Spreading his coat on the empty chair beside him, Patrick accepted the pint with a grin and produced a wilted handful of notes in return, smoothing them between his fingers as he slid them across the bar. Ivy rang up his bill and handed him the change, retreating back to the beer fridge while Patrick laboriously sorted through the coins. Eventually, he dropped a handful into the plastic tip jar and returned the rest to his pocket.

Ivy wondered, rather uncharitably, if he mightn't be developing some sort of premature senility. Maybe not even premature, she thought, looking at the folds of skin dangling from his neck like an ill-fitting scarf. He'd puzzled over the coins as if he didn't quite know what they were.

For it being a Monday night, Ivy found a surprisingly large number of things that urgently needed doing, most of them located at the very opposite end of the bar from Patrick. Once or twice, Patrick opened his mouth as though he was about to say something, but each time he only gulped more of his bitter. He was down to the dregs in less than ten minutes. That suited

Ivy just fine. It was close enough to last call that maybe she could get away with not giving him another one.

Patrick didn't ask, merely sliding the empty glass across the bar. Picking up his coat, he shook it, and folded it carefully across one arm.

"Look after yourself, Ivy," he called, embarrassingly loud, congenially slapping the Dublin Trust fellow on the arm as he went by. Just shy of the door, Patrick doffed his hat, a humiliatingly lengthy process beginning at his temples and ending some scant inches above the carpet. He replaced it on his head with a flourish as the Dublin Trust fellow, looking the same chalky color as the wallpaper, stumbled off his barstool and made straight for the men's loo. "And call your mother. She worries."

And with that, Uncle Patrick slipped out the door without even bothering to put on his coat, for all that it was still bitterly cold out.

CHAPTER 11

The next morning, Ivy was sitting in the hall in her sweatpants, taping closed the top of the sixth box she'd managed to pack that morning. She'd airily texted her father that all her things would fit in his Nissan in one trip; seeing the pile of boxes stacking up in the hall, Ivy was beginning to wonder whether that was physically possible. She'd have to come back with his car again sometime next week.

It was probably silly, rushing about trying to move in two days, but Ivy couldn't picture herself casually watching telly or fixing tea, not after what was going to happen tomorrow. The flat already felt too quiet. It wasn't the quiet of an empty room, either, but a quiet that reminded her keenly of the vault underneath Haven. The quiet of a room where something Ivy couldn't see was patiently holding its breath.

Maybe something was. Tomorrow was Wednesday, and the Enemy was coming, and Ivy couldn't quite dismiss the notion that the Enemy might come here. Which was silly—the Enemy always went after the kings, and it never failed to find them. That was Demi's problem in the first place.

But Ivy still caught herself checking behind the potted palms, or under the sink, or in the back of the pantry. Almost as though she were expecting to see someone looking back. Like Hunzu, or maybe Demi, coming back to hide in Thormanby Road after all. Or the man with the scarred face, sitting quietly among the dining room chairs the way he'd sat among the flower boxes.

Conveniently, some of Ivy's things were still packed up from when she'd first moved into the flat back in September. One box was still taped up from when she'd moved out of her dad and step-mother's house, over a year ago. Largish and heavy, it was sitting at the top of the stairs, dust bunnies and bits of flaking drywall clinging to the tape.

Setting aside the roll of packing tape, Ivy looked at the dust covered box. Ivy had no idea what was inside, except it couldn't be very important, or she would have missed it by now. Probably it was full of school year-books, or piles of the cat-themed greeting cards that her mother sent on every conceivable holiday. Maybe it held the course books from Ivy's last year in Clarence Monaghan Day School. Ivy remembered boxing them up, but she didn't remember what she'd actually done with them. They were probably still sitting somewhere in her Dad's house, waiting until such time as Ivy's step-brothers grew old enough to be pestered into reading the contents.

Maybe she should just leave the box behind, Ivy thought glumly. It wasn't as though leaving an extra box or two was going to matter—not when Mr. Kimball was going to have to deal with all of Demi's things as well.

Ivy would leave the plant-care instructions with Mr. Kimball when she turned in her key, and *he* could figure out what to do with it all. He was probably keeping Demi's security deposit—that would more than pay for a few fellows to come and haul it all away. Or maybe Ivy should ring the greenhouse in Dún Laoghaire, and see if they could possibly be persuaded to take any of the houseplants back.

The one thing Ivy refused to do was feel bad about not bringing them with her to Dartry. They were only plants, after all. It wasn't like she was abandoning a flat full of puppies and kittens.

Maybe she'd take *one*, Ivy amended. Just one, and only if it would fit in the car. Not something that needed special fertilizer, or wanted its pot rotated or its soil churned up. Something little, and pretty, and low-maintenance, that Ivy could throw into the car and take with her, and maybe not feel so guilty about walking out of the flat, and locking the door behind her and never looking at any of the other damned things ever again.

Which was, if you thought about it, pretty much what Demi herself had done when she'd left.

Glaring at the mystery box, Ivy picked it up and carried it down to join the growing pile in the parlor. Setting the box at the foot of the love seat, Ivy went into the kitchen and poured herself a glass of water. She still had her saucepans to pack, and a handful of spice jars. Plus the pictures on the fridge. Maybe this move would be the one where she finally bothered to put them in frames.

Idly, Ivy pushed the magnets to one side as she took the photos down from the fridge. Garrett and Evan, looking suspiciously respectable in their most recent school pictures. Deirdre in the middle of Temple Bar, waving a glittery

Carnival mask over her head. Garrett and Evan on Christmas morning, slouched in a beaming, pajama-clad pile of wrapping paper, Legos, and Ninja Turtles. Ivy herself, wearing a tasseled, American-style mortarboard at her graduation from Clarence Monaghan.

She smoothed the photo against the kitchen counter, trying to flatten out the corners where they'd curled against the magnets. The Ivy in the picture was grinning, the tassel from her mortarboard falling over her eyes. Dad and Shannon were standing on either side, arms around Ivy's shoulders. Garrett was slouched a few feet away, looking bored, so it must have been Evan who was taking the picture. He hadn't zoomed in very far; Ivy's family looked nearly lost in the crowd milling about the gymnasium. The subjects of the photograph were noticeable mostly because they were the only ones actually looking at the camera.

Almost the only ones.

The strange woman was standing a few feet behind Ivy, and looked enough like Victoria that she had to be some sort of relative. A third cousin or a great-aunt: some vague connection Ivy must have met and promptly forgotten about. Ivy's father had come up with an inexcusably long list of relatives to whom Ivy was required to send graduation announcements. Dutifully, Ivy mailed them out, annoyed that what in most schools would have been settled with a firm handshake and a mailed copy of the Leaving Certificate, in Clarence Monaghan required an odd gown, an even odder hat, and the entirety of a Saturday afternoon. To Ivy's surprise, a few of her invited relations had actually bothered to come.

Ivy hadn't remembered meeting this woman, whoever she was. Which was odd, because Ivy would almost certainly have remembered someone who so closely resembled her own mother. Especially since Ivy's mother hadn't come to Ivy's graduation. Not that Ivy had expected her to. But it would have been nice, if Victoria decided to show up to a family event for a change.

Ivy stopped, her hand hovering over the strangely familiar face in the photograph. Victoria hadn't come. But there was someone in the photo who looked eerily like her, that Ivy didn't remember meeting at the time.

We still show up on film, Hunzu had said. The veil doesn't do a thing for phones or webcams.

An invisible person could be standing right in the same room, and normal people couldn't see them. But cameras could.

Ivy shoved the graduation photo to the bottom of the pile of pictures, scattering magnets as she snatched the whole stack off the counter. She hurried back to the parlor, prying up the cardboard flaps of the closest box. The tape came loose; Ivy bent back the flap, and shoved the photos inside.

The idea was nonsense. Just because magic and evil and monsters existed in Demi's life didn't mean they existed in Ivy's.

Victoria had never come to Ivy's graduation. That was just how things were. Victoria sent letters, and emailed cat videos, and never came in person. Not for birthdays, or holidays, or anything else; it was all greeting cards instead. Cards and emails and phone calls, every single time.

We do most of our business with you lot over the internet, Hunzu had said.

It was simply a coincidence. It had to be someone else. Picking up the roll of packing tape, Ivy wrestled the open flap back into place, sealing it shut.

Ivy's mother wasn't invisible. And she wasn't a trow, either. The whole idea was just as silly as fairy serial killers skulking behind the potted palms, or hiding in the pantry. Victoria had never come to Ivy's graduation, so it couldn't have been her in the photograph. It was silly to think otherwise.

There was a simple way to check. It would only take a minute, and then Ivy could be sure it was all a coincidence.

Dropping the roll of tape, Ivy dashed up to her room and slid her laptop out of its bag. She turned it on, trying to ignore the feeling that something inside the taped-up box in the parlor was listening as she waited for her computer to boot up.

She clicked through several folders until she found the file she wanted, buried in a collection of bootleg videos of a Glasgow guitarist Deirdre thought was hot. The home video Dad had recorded of Ivy's graduation.

If the mystery woman had come to Ivy's graduation, there was a chance she'd be somewhere in the film. Probably she didn't look anything like Ivy's mother, and the photo had simply caught her at a funny angle.

Ivy opened the file and pressed play.

Peter had started recording ridiculously early in the ceremony, while the graduates were still trying to sort themselves into a line. Ivy skipped forward, seeing herself straightening the tassel on her cap as the line formed, the camera reluctantly panning to the podium where Headmaster Creel was huffing and clearing his throat.

Impatiently, Ivy jumped forward again, hearing the headmaster's speech as a jumble of disconnected words. *Crowning achievement, warmly thanking the members of, culmination of years* . . . Peter had kept the camera erratically focused on the headmaster, the frame tilting from one side to the other as though he'd been shuffling his feet while he was filming.

Ivy skipped forward again, past the speeches and the cheering and the interminable line of students marching across the stage, past the stilted handshakes and the awkward moments where the graduates paused with their certificates for the official photographer to take pictures. Finally, the last student stepped down from the stage, and the camera tilted wildly as the crowd of spectators began to rise from their seats. Ivy caught a dizzying glimpse of herself, tassel bouncing as she skipped toward the camera, her Leaving Cert tucked tightly under one arm.

Someone else was coming toward the camera as well, with the same greying hair as in the photograph. She was exactly the same height as Ivy, and walking a few yards behind. The woman followed Ivy for a few hurried paces before stepping aside. Briefly lost in a jumble of people, she reappeared, scampering to catch up only to be cut off by someone else.

The screen went black as the video ended. Ivy backed the video up and played it again, starting from when the last student crossed the stage.

The video didn't show her face very clearly, only a blurred suggestion of dark eyes and grey hair, so there was no way to tell exactly who it was. Probably it wasn't a relation at all, just someone in the crowd who happened to be walking in the same direction as Ivy. The illusion might have been convincing at first, but there were too many things that were off. For one thing, Ivy remembered her mother being much taller. And the hair was all wrong; Victoria had always kept it short, and frequent visits to the hairdresser on Bridge Street assured it was immaculately curled. Which meant the resemblance was only a weird coincidence and didn't mean anything at all.

That didn't stop Ivy from rewinding the video and watching it a third time. And a fourth.

The video only caught the woman for a handful of seconds, but in that time, she stepped out of the way of no less than four people. None of them stepped aside, or paused, or even nodded to her. As though she were somehow exempt from the normal give and take of crowds and gatherings. But strangely, the woman almost seemed to anticipate this. She walked as skittish as a colt, darting to one side, then stopping short, turning and walking again. As though she already knew they wouldn't get out of her way. As though she knew they couldn't see her.

The crowd might not have seen her, but the camera did.

And through the camera, Ivy saw her, too.

Demi hadn't been the first, and it hadn't started with the man in the flower boxes. The strange things had been dogging Ivy's steps for longer that. Longer than Ivy wanted to think about. And somehow, somewhere—one of the strange things had gotten to Ivy's mother.

This was why she never came. Not to graduations, or Christmases, or birthdays. Because she knew no one could see her. Or else she hadn't stayed away. Maybe Ivy's mother had been there, every time. And Ivy hadn't seen her. Had looked straight past her own mother, like she wasn't there at all.

Ivy shut the computer and threw open her desk drawer, looking blankly at the bare interior before remembering she'd already packed her address book. She ran down the stairs and tore into the stack of boxes, ripping open the carefully-taped lids until she found the little black notebook. She flipped it open to an address in North Dublin, the address that Ivy had carefully copied onto the letters she'd sent from the time she was twelve years old. Victoria Gallagher, 18447 Calgary Road, Trail's Cross, North Dublin. Ivy was already phoning for a cab before she even made it out of the flat.

❧❦❧

AT FIRST, Ivy thought she must have gotten the address wrong, because the woman who opened the door was much smaller than Ivy remembered. But the woman simply said, "Oh," covering her mouth with her hands. She still wore a wedding band on her finger; above it were two eyes the same color as Ivy's own.

"Mum?" Ivy asked in a small voice.

"Hello, sweetheart," said Victoria, with a smile entirely at odds with the way her voice was shaking. "I'd hoped you might turn up."

"Hi Mum," Ivy said around the growing lump in her throat, managing that much before dissolving into tears.

❧❀❧

"I PUT LEMON IN IT," Victoria said earnestly, setting two cups of tea on the kitchen table. She squeezed her daughter's shoulder as she went back to the kitchen, her fingers digging in a little too deeply, hanging on a little too long.

The house looked different, smaller than Ivy remembered, with a new sofa in the parlor, and different pictures hanging on the walls. Sasquatch, the yellow cat who'd been Ivy's as a girl, was long gone; a large Abyssinian whose name Ivy couldn't quite remember perched regally at the top of the bookcase.

Victoria came past, setting a dish full of sugar cubes onto the table. It wouldn't be only the cats that had changed. Victoria must have cut her hair again. It looked shorter, and perhaps thinner, and there was a hint of a stoop to her mother's shoulders that Ivy had never seen before. Seven years of little differences, all piling up at once.

Ivy smiled and picked up the teacup—and stopped a moment before the tea touched her lips.

Had *Demi* ever drunk tea? Had she ever drunk any tea *Ivy* had made?

Which was nonsense. Did Ivy really think her own mother was going to poison her?

Silently wishing she could ignore her suspicions, Ivy set the mug back on the table, untouched. Would Victoria know what was safe and what wasn't? If she was under the veil by accident, would she even know what had happened? If she had eaten the wrong food, held hands with the wrong person, spent time with someone she'd dismissed as an eccentric, or a shut-in.

. . .

Uneasily, Ivy realized she wasn't sure she wanted to know what had happened. If something had gone wrong when she'd lived with Demi, is *this* what it would have been like afterwards? Living alone with too many cats? Never seeing her Dad or step-mother again? Going to Garret and Evan's graduation, and knowing they would never spot her in the crowd?

"Are you a trow?" Ivy asked.

"A what?" Victoria asked, cocking her head birdlike at the word as she settled into the chair opposite Ivy.

"An invisible person," said Ivy haltingly. "Only . . . Sometimes I don't think they're people at all."

"They're not," said Victoria shortly. "And yes, you can drink the tea."

Ivy hastily picked up the cup and drank, embarrassed her mother could still read her so easily. So Victoria knew. Whatever happened, someone had told her that much. About food that was really poison, and people who looked like people until you realized that no one else noticed them at all.

With a flick of its tail, the Abyssinian dropped to the floor and vanished into the kitchen. A smaller calico, emerging cautiously from behind the sofa, followed it. Oriole was the calico, and wasn't the Abyssinian named after some children's book character?

"Has Patrick been talking to you?" Victoria asked after a moment.

"No," Ivy snorted, surprised, and *no* was the right answer, because ten minutes of awkward small talk at Ivy's new job didn't count. It wasn't as if Ivy meant to run into him. "Why would he?"

"No reason," her mother said quickly. "It just sounds like someone's been telling you stories." She stood, straightening a cookbook on the shelf next to the door. "I'm sorry; I'm not being a very good host. Let's try this again. How have you been, luv?"

"Good," said Ivy, nodding automatically, resisting the urge to say *it's all there in the emails*. Because, of course, it wasn't. Not anything of substance. Nothing about Hunzu, or Demi, or waking up in your own back garden and not knowing how you got there.

It was much easier to edit out those sorts of things when she was only communicating via email and texts. Her mother probably didn't even know she'd been let go from the call center—let alone everything that happened since.

"It's been—it's been okay," Ivy continued, struggling for how to summarize the last seven days. Or maybe the last seven years. "I'm working at a pub now, just off a little park in Oxmarten. The curry chips at the shop next door are to die for, and the tour guides for Haunted Dublin came in last night and were telling each other stories that would curl your hair. And I'm moving to a new place soon, in Dartry. It's close to the bus line, and she has a dog, and this big clawfoot bathtub . . ." Ivy heard herself rambling and shut her mouth. It was just like writing another email. All cat videos *and I saw the prettiest little bird today*. Nothing of substance.

No sense tiptoeing around it. There was a reason it had only been texts and emails. And Ivy ought to know what it was. Who it was. Because someone had done this to her mother, the same thing Demi and Hunzu and Ambrose had almost done to her.

Ivy took a deep breath, and jumped right in. "How did it happen?" Ivy asked.

"Sounds like you know enough to make a guess," said Victoria, looking pointedly at Ivy's cup of tea as she sat down.

"I don't want to guess," said Ivy, crossing her arms over the table. Dizzyingly, Ivy remembered crossing her arms in just such a way as a girl, as if simply being in the house had turned her back into the Ivy of seven years ago: younger, more petulant, blissfully unaware her family wouldn't be a family for very much longer. "Something happened after Dad and I left. I don't care if it's trows, or space aliens, or a voodoo curse, I want to know what happened."

Victoria looked down at the table, her hands clenching around the handle of the teacup, a gleam in the corner of her eye that made Ivy suddenly afraid her mother was about to start crying.

Ivy picked up the cup of tea and took a sip, an excuse to look anywhere but at her mum's face. And nearly spilt the entire cup because very suddenly, Ivy realized she had it wrong. Not what had happened to her mother—that was clear enough, but *when* it happened. . . .

"It wasn't after Dad left," Ivy said in a low voice. "When Dad left—that was why."

For the longest moment, Ivy's mother merely stared out the window, both hands gripping the tea cup. It felt curiously difficult to breathe, as though the very air were thicker than it ought to be. As though there were a trick to breathing it that Ivy hadn't yet mastered.

The Abyssinian cat slunk back across the kitchen floor, winding its tail around the legs of Victoria's chair.

"He would have left anyway," Victoria said finally, reaching down to pet the cat. "Even if none of it had happened. I'd hoped you would have been a bit older, is all."

That was what made everything else come apart. That was what sent Ivy across Dublin in a cab, surrounded by bags and suitcases, to join her father in a shabby bedsit in the south side of town. That was why Ivy only had a mother through letters and emails.

Because Demi hadn't been the first trow to waltz into Ivy's life and risk trapping her under twilight shadow of the veil. There'd been someone else, and they'd gotten to Ivy's mother first.

With a sickening feeling, Ivy wondered how many people had been taken in just such a way. She remembered seeing homeless people sleeping rough in the DART stations, huddled in nests of overcoats and blankets, lurking in the doorways at Temple Bar long after the buses stopped running. Most people walked right by as if they couldn't see them. Maybe most people couldn't.

"People . . . couldn't see you," Ivy said hesitantly.

Victoria did blink then, rubbing at her eyes with one tea-stained finger. The calico cat glided back into the room, glancing suspiciously at Ivy before jumping into a chair at the far end of the table.

"*You* could, sometimes," she said, still looking toward the window; she might as well have been addressing the cat. "Sometimes it seemed like you could see me better than anyone else. Certainly better than Peter could. He knew I was slipping out of his life and neither of us understood why. It was different with you. Sometimes you'd sit at the table and chatter about your day like I was right there with you. Other times you wouldn't seem to hear me. Like you'd forgotten I was in the house. Shouting for me up the staircase, even when I was right there with you."

"Who was it?" Ivy asked stonily, though of course, there was really only one person it could possibly be. Ivy remembered how he'd propped his feet up on the table as though he had every right to do it, and fumbled through his change as though he'd forgotten how to handle money.

"I knew from the start Patrick wasn't like other people," Ivy's mother said, turning to straighten the cookbooks on the shelf, which were already standing at perfect attention. "I suppose when I was younger I took him for a fairy. I met him in a pub in Portrush, a few years before I married your father. It was around the corner from the shop I worked at; some nights I'd stop there for a drink. One evening, I walked in and there he was, asking me to join him. He told me later he'd been buying me bad ale for nearly two weeks before I noticed. People would step around him in the street without knowing why. He'd steal any trinket he fancied, just because he could, or maybe because he knew it shocked me. I'd never met anyone like him before. We spent a few weeks together before the weather turned, and he headed off south. Back to fairyland, I told him. Never expected to see him after that. But the next summer, there he was back again."

Ivy remembered how he'd looked at the Blue Parrot, old and wrinkly and feeble, like trows weren't supposed to look. If Victoria had run afoul of the terrible border between the trow's world and the real one, at least the same thing had happened to Patrick. Something horrible happened to Victoria, it was only fair something horrible happen to Patrick, too.

"Did he ever tell you why he was invisible?" Ivy asked.

"He said all sorts of nonsense," said Victoria with a snort. "Very charming, but nonsense all the same. Some days he claimed to be a fairy. Some days, a space alien. Some days he told me his people were refugees from some big war in the future. He never seemed to want to talk about it—not seriously, it was always jokes and yarns with him."

"Lies, you mean," said Ivy, crossing her arms again. Her mother might say jokes, but how could you joke about something like what he'd done to Victoria? "Did he tell you he could turn you invisible? Or did he lie about that, too?"

"He didn't lie," Ivy's mother said flatly, though she was rubbing at her eyes in a way that made Ivy very afraid she was going to start crying again. "Not about the important things."

Leaving the cookbooks, Victoria sat back at the table, and gave Ivy a tentative smile, and something in Ivy's stomach clenched, because she'd forgotten that look, the way her mother smiled when she really meant it, and it was different from the way she smiled in photographs.

"Ivy," she continued earnestly. "It was a long time ago; it doesn't matter. Can't we talk about something else just now? Did you like your Christmas presents? How are Garrett and Evan doing in school?"

Ivy swallowed a lump at her throat, guiltily thinking of all the things there were to catch up on. Seven years of Christmases, and birthdays, and everything else. For a moment, Ivy was tempted to forget all about poisonous food and invisible people, and do nothing but sit in the kitchen, and drink tea with her mother for the first time in too many years. Patrick didn't matter; he was old and unimportant and if looks were anything to go by, he'd be dead soon anyway.

Just like Demi would be dead soon, some voice in the back of Ivy's head whispered. Another terrible thing that Ivy couldn't change. It was entirely out of her hands, and she couldn't fix any of it.

But maybe she could fix things with her mother. Or at least make a start.

"The Christmas presents were lovely," said Ivy, thinking back to whatever it was she'd unwrapped three months ago. "You sent a green sweater, didn't you? And a book on horses— no, that was the year before. . . ."

"No, you're right," said Victoria, waving Ivy into silence. "I

haven't been a mother in a very long time, and I'm out of practice at it. Of course you ought to know. Patrick—"

"I don't care about Patrick," Ivy interrupted heatedly. She
wasn't going to sit here and listen to her mother defend him, not
when what Patrick had actually done was even more horrible
than Ivy had always supposed.

"It wasn't how you think," Victoria said, sounding tired.
"He came for one of his visits a few weeks after your father left.
I don't know what he thought he'd do—get down on one knee
and make it official, or just mess about for a few weeks and be
off again. He found me cutting coupons out of the Sunday
paper to buy groceries, because my job had let me go, and the
woman at the dole office—I'd tried to get the papers filed in
person. You can imagine how that went. As soon as I saw him, I
knew. Not the particulars—but I knew what had happened.
And Patrick knew it, too.

"Patrick explained how things were going to be. He was the
one who suggested sending you to Peter; he didn't know what
the—the *veil*—might do to you if you were living with me. You
could already see through it at times. Patrick said that wasn't a
good sign."

"That's why you sent me to live with Dad?" Ivy asked,
aghast. Not only had Patrick broken up her parents' marriage
and ruined her mother's life, he'd also been the one to decide
that she live with her father. Patrick wasn't family; he shouldn't
have the right to decide things like that. "Because *Patrick*
thought it was a good idea?"

"Well, he certainly knew more about it than I did," Victoria
pointed out. "He thought it might be dangerous if you ever
learned to see through the veil. You could become invisible, too.
I knew Peter would take good care of you. Besides, how do you
think it would have worked, sweetheart, living with a mother
no one else could see?

"Patrick helped me apply for the dole—through the mail, this time. He stayed long enough to make sure I wasn't going to starve, or be evicted, and that I knew enough to keep it from spreading to anyone else. He told me I was the first one he'd seen this happen to. Sometimes I think there must have been others, and he just didn't want to talk about them. There were a good many things we couldn't manage to talk about, there at the end. . . ."

The Abyssinian cat leapt from the windowsill, crossing the dining room in a few quick strides, and jumped into Victoria's lap. It circled once, stretching its forelegs as Victoria absently stroked its head.

"It was too early for Patrick to know much about the internet," she continued. "But when the Council put the lines in, I got a modem. Things got a bit better. I did online training for a coding job, and I've been able to work from here. The money's not bad, and the grocer delivers every week, and I've got the whole city to walk through. And the cats pretend they don't notice me, either, but I suppose they do. Or at least, they notice me as much as they notice ordinary people. . . ."

"I'm so sorry, mum," Ivy said in a whisper. "I didn't know."

"Nothing to be sorry about," said Victoria, though her voice shook as she said it. "I suppose I shouldn't ever have taken up with him in the first place; trouble does come of that sort of thing."

Ivy wondered whether she meant taking up with trows, or whether she meant taking up with one man when you were already married to another one.

"Your turn," said Victoria, tapping her fingers nervously on the edge of her saucer. "Are you sure Patrick hasn't been talking to you? Because, if you wanted—"

"Why would Patrick be talking to me?" Ivy asked, crossing her arms. She hadn't much liked Patrick before, when he'd only been some old boyfriend of her mother's. Now that Ivy knew what he'd done, she never wanted to speak to him again.

"Clearly, someone has," said Victoria, her eyebrows narrowing into a disapproving line. "Sounds like you already know all about it. I won't ask how you've gotten involved. God knows we've all made our mistakes. But you have to stay away from them, Ivy. It's dangerous, and you've no idea how hard it can be."

Victoria was talking as if Ivy *wanted* to get involved in something dangerous. She hadn't—she'd answered a Craigslist ad six months ago and everything else had just happened.

"I'm not involved in anything," Ivy protested, dropping her empty teacup into its saucer with a clatter. "It all started when I moved in with a really weird girl. By the time I found out *how* weird, she'd already left. And she's not coming back."

"Well, I hope that's the end of it!" Victoria said sharply.

"It is," said Ivy, biting out the words as if they were some sort of challenge. It was ending, in a far more permanent way than Victoria knew. "Someone's going to kill her tomorrow."

Victoria stopped with her hand on the head of the cat, both of them, for the moment, still as statues.

"It's still happening, then," said her mother in a tired voice. "He hoped it had all ended by now."

"What had all ended by now?" Ivy asked. "Did Patrick tell you about their Enemy?"

An entirely unwarranted sliver of hope fluttered to life somewhere in Ivy's chest. Maybe Patrick knew something about the Enemy. But even if he did, it would be the same things Ivy already knew. The Enemy killed the kings. It had always done so, and it was never going to stop.

"Sometimes," said Victoria nervously, gathering Ivy's empty cup and saucer, elbowing her own cup hard enough that it nearly overturned. "He talked about a lot of things, you know. Nonsense, all of it."

"Mum," Ivy said, reaching out to steady the cup. "What did he say about the Enemy?"

"I already told you, it was all a lot of nonsense." She shoved the cat off her lap; it dropped to the floor, giving Ivy a gimlet-eyed look as it stalked into the kitchen. "You don't need to be hearing his old stories."

If all it was is old stories, why didn't Victoria want to talk about it? She'd talked about Patrick, and the dole officer, and sending Ivy off with her father. The Enemy wasn't a threat to Ivy—if the Enemy couldn't turn Ivy invisible, then it was conceivably less dangerous to Ivy than trows were.

"Did he ever say anything about a Year King?" Ivy pressed.

"Ivy, really," she said, shaking her head as she picked up the stack of teacups and saucers. "It was a long time ago and—"

"What aren't you telling me?" Ivy asked, and it was coming back to her, how her mum and dad used to fight. How her mother would dance around all but the most direct of her father's questions.

"Nothing," Victoria snapped. She stood up, cradling the pile of dishes to her chest as she went into the kitchen. "Everything he said was nonsense and none of it matters anymore. I haven't seen him in years."

Ivy got up from the table, following her mother into the kitchen. She didn't want her first conversation with her mother in seven years to turn into an argument. She didn't want to push things until her own mother stopped ignoring her questions and started answering them with lies. But she didn't want Demi to die tomorrow, either. It was as though Victoria didn't realize that what she thought of as an old story still had deadly consequences for other people.

"Maybe it doesn't matter to you," said Ivy harshly. "But it

still matters to Demi. Patrick's Enemy has been killing trows for a long time. And he's going to kill Demi tomorrow, and if Patrick told you something, I want to know what it is."

"Please?" Ivy added, when her mother didn't immediately reply.

Victoria turned back from the pile of dishes, a frayed tea towel in her hands.

"Whatever you're involved in, stop it," said her mother sharply. "Not if it involves people like Patrick. Not another word, not another favor. It won't stop. Not until you're like them. Next best thing to invisible."

It had to be something important, or her mother wouldn't be making this much of a fuss about telling her. If the only thing Victoria knew was that the Enemy killed trows, why didn't she just come out and say it? There had to be something else. Like the things Ambrose called conspiracy theories. Kings that hadn't died when they were supposed to. Or kings like Larch. Kings that disappeared, and maybe hadn't died at all.

Or did Ivy only want that to be the case, because otherwise everything was hopeless? Not just for Demi, but for whoever they crowned next year, and the year after that. Until there were so many stones under the apples trees there'd hardly be room for the grass.

"All I'm asking is if he told you anything," Ivy protested. "About the Enemy, or where he came from, or why he kills people. Look, if I know, I—I can phone her," Ivy lied. "She has email, for God's sake, and if I can help her, maybe everything can go back to being normal."

Ivy regretted the words the moment she said them; things obviously hadn't been normal for Victoria for years. But her mother didn't seem to notice her slip.

"They aren't people, Ivy," her mother said, folding her arms. "You said it yourself, they aren't—"

"Look, maybe I don't know what Demi is," Ivy admitted. Demi might be a space alien or some weird contagious fairy, but she was also a frightened girl, who liked orchids, and old black-and-white movies, and drinking cocoa with soy milk. "But I know she doesn't deserve to be murdered tomorrow."

Victoria looked at the floor, draping the tea towel over the edge of the drying rack.

"He'd mention it sometimes," her mother said slowly. "The Enemy, I mean. I always thought he meant another fairy."

"It wasn't another trow," said Ivy, shaking her head. "At least, I don't think it was. They told me the Enemy was someone out of their old world—the place where the trows came from."

"Whatever it was, Patrick was running from it for a long time," said Victoria. "Long enough that the habit stuck, even after he'd stopped being afraid of whatever it was that was after him."

"Patrick was running from it?" Ivy asked, surprised. But Patrick shouldn't have been afraid of it. Everyone had been very clear on that point. It only came after the kings. No one else. So why would Patrick have been afraid? Why would he have thought the Enemy could come for him?

What if Hunzu had never found Demi, hidden away in Howth? Would her name have been carved on a stone? Presumed dead, even though no one knew for sure.

"Patrick wasn't his real name, was it?" Ivy asked, even though she already knew the answer, could feel the words hovering in the air.

"No, it wasn't," her mother said. "His given name was Larch."

The silver cat jumped onto the counter, retreating to the floor as Victoria quickly shooed him away. Ivy took a deep breath; feeling as though the world had abruptly changed around her. Larch hadn't been killed, and the Enemy wasn't infallible. The stories about the old kings surviving were more than conspiracy theories after all.

And if Demi could do whatever Larch had done, maybe she could survive her year, too.

"Wait here," Victoria said, abruptly turning away from the sink. "I'd better show you something."

Victoria returned, dropping a yellowed envelope onto the counter. The address was written in bold, looping cursive, in an ink that was beginning to fade into the envelope beneath it. *Taye Carillon,* Ivy read, followed by an address she'd seen on the GPS in her borrowed Land Cruiser four days ago. Larch's mother—Patrick's mother, Ivy realized with a start.

Ivy picked up the letter and saw that the envelope had already been slit open, the cut edges ragged and tattered.

"He doesn't deserve to have secrets," said Victoria in a flat voice. "Not from me. I hope there's something in there that will help your friend. But I don't know that there is."

"Thank you, mum," Ivy said, and stepped closer for a hug, momentarily taken aback when Victoria hastily stepped away, wrapping her arms around her own shoulders as though taken by a sudden chill.

Of course, Ivy realized dully. Victoria couldn't touch her for the same reason Demi couldn't. Too much time among invisible people, and the veil might decide Ivy was one of them.

"Just remember your promise," Victoria said, twisting her wedding ring around her finger as though she were nervous. "Don't go back to those people. Call her, sweetheart. I'm sure she'd appreciate a phone call."

"I'll call her," said Ivy, hoping she wasn't lying. Maybe someone at the Liberties would know how to contact her. Would Demi even be taking phone calls between now and tomorrow? If Ivy knew she was going to die in less than twenty-four hours, she doubted checking her voicemail would be a high priority.

But if there was something in the letter that could save Demi's life? For that, Ivy would head straight back to Haven, pound on their door and make such a ruckus they'd have no choice but to let her in and listen to her.

Ivy stood up from the table, slipping the letter into her coat pocket. She grabbed her purse and headed to the door, shadowed by Victoria and the Abyssinian cat.

"And tell your friend—tell her good luck," said Victoria, as Ivy neared the door. "I know Patrick hoped it wasn't still happening. He hoped the Enemy had given up."

"I'll tell her. And I'll be back in a few days," Ivy added, and saw a shadow lift from her mother's face, as though Victoria had been afraid to ask. Or afraid that her daughter would disappear for another seven years, like some enchanted maiden out of a fairy tale.

"I love you, sweetie," she said.

"I love you, too," said Ivy, and closed the door as the silver cat slipped out of the apartment at her heels, slinking across the garden before disappearing into the shrubbery at a run.

"THORMANBY ROAD," Ivy told the cabbie as she climbed into the back of the taxi. As the cab pulled away from the curb, Ivy took the letter out of her pocket, slipping a pair of thin sheets out of the yellowed envelope. For several minutes she read in silence, as the cab drove through the winding streets.

Some minutes later, Ivy dropped the paper onto her lap.

She tapped at the window. Wordlessly, the cabbie opened the slot dividing the front and back seats. Ivy could hear the faint drone of a Rangers game drifting in from the radio.

"I need to go to a different address," she said.

CHAPTER 12

I n March of the local year 1935, I was chosen by lottery
and precedent to assume the title and duties of the King of
the Trows in our two hundred forty-seventh year of exile.
*My title meant little; my duties negligible, aside from one—that I
was to die on the appointed day by the hand of our old and
inescapable Adversary. I remember very little of the first weeks
following my election. Or rather, I remember drinking to excess,
and perhaps the forgetfulness is excusable under the circumstances. I suppose other kings have better borne up to the
inescapable duty of our office, but I must admit I am not one of
them. Still, I managed as best I could; many a Year King could
say the same.*

*By the early weeks of 1936, I had said what goodbyes I could
manage, though I put off the two that promised to be most bitter.*

The first, to my darling Peregrine. The second, to my esteemed mother, whom I hope is still alive to receive this letter, a long-delayed missive from a long-absent son.

I have no words of apology adequate for my long silence, nor for the pain that my absence and presumed death has caused. I will not raise your hopes; if the woman to whom I have entrusted this letter does as I have asked, I will be dead by the time you read this. Take comfort, if you can, that the method of my passing was lengthier—and far pleasanter— than anything I could have imagined back in 1936.

Three days before the day on which I was to meet both my Adversary and my Maker, I awoke to find myself on the deck of a large ship. It was called Eritria, and it was headed to South America—though I only learned this much later. When I woke, I had no idea where I was, nor where the ship was bound, nor how I had gotten aboard. More to the point, I did not know what day it was. I spent an anxious week cowering in the depths of the freighter, waiting for a creature out of the nightmares of my people to appear before me in a wreath of fire and—

I shan't continue that description. I have witnessed the passing of the Year King on three occasions. If you, dear reader, have seen such an event, you already know what I feared. If you have been blessed with ignorance of the Adversary's methods, I shall not trouble you with a recitation of details.

The cargo included potatoes and apples, along with several dozen cattle and a shocking quantity of bootleg whisky. The foodstuffs, at least, spared me the unpleasant decision of either starving to death or sentencing myself to a slower death by poison. The crew was Portuguese, as I understood much later, and consequently even the little I could overhear concerning our destination made little sense to me. I left the ship at their first port of call. It was several weeks before I had a ready comprehension of where on the earth I had found myself, and

*several months before I had anything approaching an under-
standing of the local language. If nothing else, my first year
abroad gave me some comprehension of what it must have been
like for the first of our folk, finding themselves alone in a world
populated by beings with whom they could not readily
communicate.*

*I did not return to Ireland. I shan't defend the decision; I
merely tell you it is what I chose. Evading the Adversary once, I
had no wish to risk its fire a second time. I traveled through the
Americas; my movements somewhat curtailed during the second
outbreak of what my human neighbors quaintly referred to as a
Great War. The conflict was perhaps a too-convenient excuse
for not risking a crossing back to Europe.*

*It was during those years I discovered the first of many signs
that indicated that my reprieve from death was merely temporary. There are no reliable risk tables for the cumulative effects of
exposure as lengthy as I have now undergone, and I am in no
position to consult them even if there were. Perhaps the sheer
amount of time I have spent among those unlike myself would
have caught up with me no matter what precautions I took.*

*I mention, with the hope that Peregrine will forgive me, that
my life since our parting has not entirely been a lonely one. I
deliberately breached the veil's concealment on several occasions, with little thought for the risks I was laying on my
companions. I have made what redress I could; there may well
be others whom time and distance have rendered me unable to
find. The worst mistakes are always the ones that lie beyond
one's power to correct. . . .*

*This letter grows maudlin. Back to the question of my disap-
pearance and presumed death.*

*I am convinced that my waking up aboard a ship—crewed
by people who spoke no English, with a cargo of raw food and
bound for an isolated port as far from our own colony as it is*

possible to go—was no accident. It was no small undertaking to find an itinerary so perfectly suited for a kidnapping.

My kidnapper, it seems, saved my life. I don't know why my benefactor chose not to reveal himself to me, or enlist my aid. If you are laboring under the delusion that I might have resisted an attempt to escape the deed that would end my year of service, then you are doing me the great favor of overestimating both my courage and my dedication to my subjects. I would have been a willing partner in any scheme that might have preserved my life.

I don't believe merely removing me from Ireland was enough to spare me. Though I do not have the records at hand, I seem to recall that the Year Kings of 1727 through 1734 were killed at the colony near Bruges. So it seems probable that physical distance was not enough to hide me. Perhaps that I was so far from land at the time I should have been taken? Yet I can hardly believe that such a small thing as an ocean could confound an enemy who has proved itself capable of reaching across time itself. Or if water were a barrier, what would have stopped it from locating me the very moment I set foot on shore?

Had I any secret, some weapon or trickery that might overcome our old Adversary, the Valoi themselves would not have hindered me from bringing you word. To my regret, I offer neither answers nor solutions, merely the suppositions of a man with too many hours to ponder such things.

Conjecture: someone unknown to me saw it necessary to remove me from the society of trows. This seems unlikely, as it was well known that the Enemy would have done so (and on a far more permanent basis) only a handful of days later.

Conjecture: perhaps this unknown trow would have in some way benefited by the death of someone close to me, had I been killed before the expected date and the kingship fallen to another. In that case, murdering me outright would have been a much safer course than merely kidnapping me.

Conjecture: someone wished my death not take place at Haven, or in any other location where a fellow was likely to witness it. I can perhaps see Peregrine's hand in this; might you have thought an unseen demise easier for my mother to bear? In this case, my survival was entirely unintentional, and just as inexplicable as if I had never been taken from Ireland at all.

Conjecture: I was not killed by the Adversary because no one knew where I was—excepting, of course, the one who orchestrated my disappearance. Perhaps an unremarked murder does not strike the terror that the Enemy, it seems, is bent on maintaining.

The suspicious old trow in me must add a further conjecture. I was not killed on the appointed day, therefore the power of the Adversary to locate its chosen prey is not infallible. This raises the stink of collaboration. Postulate One: among my people, there is one who knows, or at least suspects, how it is the Adversary never fails to find the king on the appointed day. Postulate Two: that this traitor is known to me, and may have perceived himself to be acting in my interests.

Which leaves only one final conjecture: that the incidents of February of 1936 were merely accidents, and one is a fool to ascribe any meaning to them at all.

I returned at last to Ireland in the spring of 1988. The ravages of my affliction are all too apparent now; I have no wish for my kinsmen to see me in such a state. Leave that for the humans, among whom the slow decimation of time is no more than an everyday calamity, one which they accept with the ease of long familiarity.

Foreknowing is, and has been always, our curse. Not simply the horror of a foreseen death. Might the Adversary, too, die with everything else, when the gears of history grind the world around us to dust? Thin consolation indeed, for any of us unfortunate enough to survive into the beginning years of the Event.

Though I never sought them out, I believe I saw trows several times. Glimpses only—half-heard footsteps, half-imagined shadows. I cannot help but suspect that some may have been phantom visitations from a mind fast becoming as weak as its body.

To this day, I do not know whether the Enemy has continued its incursions into our adopted home, or whether it at last sated its vengeance upon Sabre, my immediate predecessor, the Year King of 1935. In my fondest hopes, the Adversary is vanished, no more than a bogeyman that mothers call upon to ensure their children come home in time for supper. I have no way of knowing whether my hope is true. Perhaps the Adversary, in my absence, sated its wrath upon another of my kindred, and has been continuing its bloody works every year since.

Forgive a King for being such a coward. A true King should never fear the people whom he serves. And yet I fear approaching my old haunts too closely, perhaps afraid of being recognized, perhaps for fear of breaking the unknown equilibrium that has kept me alive all these years. Perhaps, too, for fear of seeing nothing at all. I have learned, to my cost, that I am still trow enough to pull humans into our shadow world. I fear I may now be human enough to pass along the contagion of age to a trow. Were that to be true, the veil would undoubtedly bar me from those I might infect.

Peregrine, I have never regretted my unexpected life. I have often regretted not sharing it with you. I have been free at least, and happy at times, though the two are not nearly as synonymous as many would believe. I hope you also have been happy, through all the years that have separated us.

Mother, though I do not see you again in life, it is my hope that this letter will be brought to you, so that the knowledge of the strange reign of Larch Carillon might not die with me. I shall enter into silence very soon, and I hope it shall be as you once told me. That I shall go ahead to the halls of Valiard, and look with transformed eyes upon the home I have never seen. Until that day, I remain as I am—not quite one thing, and not quite another. I believe it has been enough.

Yours,

Larch Carillon

Year King, 1936

THE LETTER WAS STILL STICKING out of her purse as Ivy got out of the cab at the tiny, weed-choked park across from the Blue Parrot. Ivy had read through it twice more during the cab ride. The second and third reading hardly proved any more enlightening than the first.

Fact One: Larch survived. Fact Two: even *he* didn't know how or why. Fact Three: without knowing how or why, it would be nearly impossible for Demi to replicate his feat. Which lead to Fact Four, not contained in the letter, but depressingly apparent after what she'd seen in the apple grove: the Enemy hadn't killed Larch in 1936, but it *had* killed someone. If Demi did survive her year, it would almost certainly be at the expense of some other trow.

And even if Larch had tried to be as clear as possible in his would-be letter from beyond the grave, there was still a good bit of it that was incomprehensible, at least to Ivy. As though Larch thought there was something waiting in the future even worse than the Enemy's yearly murders.

Ivy turned off the sidewalk, her shoes splashing through the puddles as she cut across the park. The sky, grey and overcast, had finally started to drizzle. Ivy pulled the hood of her coat more tightly over her ears, and tucked the letter deeper into her purse.

There had to be something else. Something Larch hadn't put in the letter; maybe something he didn't realize was important. Something he'd guessed, or seen, or remembered. It would have been helpful if she'd known all this two days ago, Ivy thought morosely. Larch (Patrick; she was still getting used to the idea that they were the same person) had been in the Blue Parrot only last night; it was the first time Ivy had seen him in over a year.

Given the chilly reception Ivy had given him, Patrick wouldn't likely be returning to the pub any time soon. She ought to have pretended to be friendly and asked for his mobile number. Assuming he even owned a phone.

Maybe Ivy's mother knew how to contact him, even though Victoria claimed they hadn't spoken in years. But given how reluctant her mother had been to give Ivy the letter, Ivy didn't think she'd have any luck in persuading her mother to give her Patrick's address. She'd probably just be letting herself in for a lecture about staying away from trows.

Patrick had come to the Blue Parrot, which proved he came through Oxmarten at least occasionally. He'd said he stopped by for a nightcap. A quick drink on the way back from doing whatever invisible people do all day. Which apparently involved a lot of standing in the rain, judging by the state of his clothing. It had all been soaking wet, and he'd draped half of it over the barstools.

When he'd left, Patrick had gathered it up, and hadn't even bothered to put his coat back on. As though it wouldn't have been worth the trouble. Maybe he had a car parked nearby. Except that driving a car wasn't a very straightforward proposition for an invisible person. Even Ambrose had used a human driver. Patrick probably wasn't traveling by car, and a trow could hardly rely on calling a cab, or hailing a bus. The DART might be an option, but the closest station to the Blue

Parrot (as Ivy was well aware) was still a ten-minute walk away.

Wherever he'd gone, Patrick probably planned on walking to get there. And his destination was close enough that he hadn't bothered putting on his coat. Which narrowed down Patrick's home from the entirety of greater Dublin, to perhaps a six-square block radius of Oxmarten. Assuming he really had gone home, and not off to some other pub that adhered to a more flexible interpretation of closing hours. Even if Patrick did live near the Blue Parrot, Ivy couldn't exactly go knocking on doors asking if anyone had seen him. It would be like trying to find a ghost.

Which was, when you got right down to it, pretty much what Patrick was.

And Ivy happened to know a few people who specialized in finding them.

❧

THE "BACK AT 4 PM" sign was hanging from the door as Ivy came up to the Haunted Dublin kiosk, and Ivy quietly cursed. If the tour guides had already left for their dinner break, there was no telling where they might be. She wondered if she could get what she needed by looking at their brochure, or if their tour routes might be posted on the internet.

Their kiosk was hardly bigger than a garden shed, its plastic siding painted to look like wood, with fake bats perched above the door, wings spread and toothy mouths agape. While the kiosk's door was closed, the padlock wasn't across it. Giving an uneasy glance at the bats, Ivy knocked at the door.

"We're closed," shouted a voice from inside; Ivy immediately pushed the door open.

"I know," Ivy said. "I'm not here about a tour. I just—"

Killian and an Indian man in a frock coat turned toward the door and Ivy stifled a shriek, because blood was dripping from a hideous gash across Killian's throat. For a moment, she was possessed by the completely illogical assumption that the Enemy had struck at the wrong time, and had come for a completely different person.

Then she noticed Killian had a towel in one hand and a makeup compact in the other. A mirror was propped up on the reception desk, next to a tin of pancake makeup and a handful of red grease pencils.

"The lad who does Robert Emmet has an exam tomorrow," said Killian apologetically, dabbing at the red stain running down the side of his neck. "Needs a bit of a touch up between tours."

"Right," said Ivy, taking a deep breath and trying not to look like she'd just been startled half to death. If Killian's tours were anything as scary as walking in on his makeup sessions, Ivy never in her life wanted to go on one.

"Did you want to come along on the next one?" piped up the other guide, stroking a bristling black mustache that appeared to be attached with spirit gum. "We could do you a free ticket, seeing how Roberta's such a chum about the drinks. The name's Dennis, by the way."

"Ivy," she said, bobbing her head. "I can't come tonight— but I was hoping to talk to you about some of the buildings on your tour route. And maybe a few of the buildings that aren't." The man in the frock coat glanced at Killian, who shrugged, which made the gash across his throat ripple alarmingly, as if it were attempting a smile.

"My next bus tour isn't for another hour," Dennis said. "And you've got plenty of time before you need to show up for the Lord Norbury bit."

Killian turned back to the desk and pulled a length of

plastic wrap off of a roll. He looked skeptical. "I like to be there early; otherwise all that talking at Croppie's Acre just drags and drags. Besides," he said to Ivy. "It's really Ilse you'll want to talk to, she's the history buff. But she won't be in until the weekend."

"No, it needs to be tonight," said Ivy. "Just a quick drink, is all." She could see him wavering, and decided on a hefty dose of flattery. "I mean, there must be so much you know about the area. It must have taken heaps of time to learn the stories for all those tour stops."

"It did," said Killian devoutly, looking in the mirror as he carefully pressed the sheet of plastic wrap over the dripping red cut on his neck. "And there's loads of good bits most punters don't even care about. School project, is it? I suppose we've got time. We'll just nip over to the Parrot and—"

"No, it can't be the Parrot," said Ivy quickly. Her shift started in an hour; she'd never get away if Roberta spotted her.

Killian hesitated. Recklessly thinking of the envelope under the begonias, as well as the ever-dwindling number of hours before the Enemy's arrival, Ivy added. "We'll go over to the Alehouse, and I'll pay."

"Righto!" beamed the man in the frock coat, smiling widely enough that one end of his mustache pulled loose from his lip, dangling beneath his nose like a bristling caterpillar. Surprisingly, Ivy felt a matching grin stealing over her face.

Ivy wished, suddenly and fervently, that she had absolutely nothing else to worry about tonight besides drinks and ghost stories with a couple of good-looking boys.

A few minutes later, Dennis was locking up the kiosk behind them as Ivy and Killian (a plaid scarf draped concealingly over the stage makeup) headed down the street.

Before she'd gotten what she needed, Ivy ended up buying three hamburgers, two rounds of Guinness, and a plate of curry chips. The entire process (drinks, small talk, tangential stories, more drinks, boasts about tips, complaints about tourists, interspersed with the occasional bit of useful information) took long enough that Ivy had to excuse herself, coughing theatrically in the back alley behind the pub for several minutes before she felt sufficiently hoarse to call the Blue Parrot and tell Roberta she was sick. She hoped she was coughing loudly enough to cover the traffic noise, not to mention the electronic pinging from the gaming machine by the Alehouse's back door. Considering that Roberta took the news by cussing and then hanging up on her, maybe she'd heard the pinging after all.

Ivy quickly determined that many of the Haunted Dublin tour stops could be ruled out entirely. Croppie's Acre was only a big abandoned football pitch; she could hardly imagine Patrick spending any length of time there. The haunted houses on Hendrick Street had been demolished in the sixties, and Saint Mary's church was little more than a fallen-down pile of stones. If these spots were haunted by anything, it was more likely to be a ghost that didn't concern itself with things like heat, or indoor plumbing.

Fortunately for Ivy, Killian and Dennis were well aware of the reputation of certain buildings that weren't on the official tour, and were happy to regale Ivy with the specifics. As long as she paid for the beer, that is.

By the time Killian left for his tour appearance as the ghost of Robert Emmett, Ivy had a list of nine addresses, scribbled onto the back of a Haunted Dublin flyer, reputed to be visited by the spirits of the restless dead. The sort of places where footsteps echoed in empty rooms, spectral voices were heard whispering late at night, and lights turned off and on seemingly by themselves. The list included four private homes, two pubs, a solicitor's office, an old hotel, and a townhouse owned by the Dublin Historical Trust. Ivy had no idea Oxmarten contained such a concentration of haunted houses.

Shoving her half-empty beer stein across the table, Ivy tapped her pencil against the Haunted Dublin flyer, considering her route. The pubs would be easiest, and they'd be open late; logically, they'd be best left for last. Also, Ivy wasn't sure she could stomach drinking any more beer—though she could see herself wanting a shot or three of something stronger later on. Probably this whole thing was going to be pointless and awkward. Probably she'd called off work and pissed off her boss for no good reason. Probably she ought to take a cab to the Trove offices in the Liberties, shove Larch's letter through the mail flap, and forget about the entire thing.

Instead, she was going to knock on doors and ask random strangers if they thought there might be an invisible person living in their house.

That settled it, thought Ivy, glancing once more at the flyer before shoving it back into her purse. She was *definitely* saving the pubs for last, because there was no conceivable way this evening was going to end well. She was going to spend half the night running around Oxmarten in the rain. She was going to drink too much and then wake up tomorrow and move all of her earthly possessions halfway across Dublin in a compact car with a hangover. And try not to think about how Demi was about to be murdered.

Better get started then, she told herself, buttoning up her jacket as she slipped off the bar stool. At least running around Oxmarten all evening would keep her from thinking too hard about what was going to happen tomorrow.

THE SOLICITOR'S office was a complete bust. Ivy waited for nearly half an hour in a stuffy reception room which managed to feel both eerily drafty as well as stiflingly overheated. She asked the receptionist a couple of wide-eyed questions about the supposedly-haunted houses on nearby Hendrick Street, and stayed long enough to set up an appointment (which Ivy had no intention of keeping) to discuss her fictitious boyfriend's equally imaginary drugs-related court appearance the following month. Ivy didn't know if she sounded particularly believable, but at least the receptionist nodded in the right places and didn't throw her out. She supposed it helped that Colin really *had* been up on drugs charges once. (Once that Ivy knew about, at any rate.) And to think Deirdre always claimed that dating Colin would never do Ivy any good.

Unfortunately, the only creaks and groans in the solicitor's offices could almost certainly be chalked up to the draft; the receptionist hadn't wanted to gossip about haunted houses, and Ivy herself had seen nothing to indicate that Patrick had ever been there.

Also, Ivy could hardly imagine Patrick willingly spending time in someplace as tedious as a solicitor's office.

Reluctantly, Ivy crossed the address off the list.

The Historical Dublin townhouse was next, on the faint supposition that the place might still be open. If not, she'd probably be limited to peering through the windows, and hoping the neighbors didn't see her and phone the Gardaí.

Encouragingly, the townhouse was still lit up from the inside as Ivy turned up the sidewalk. The place was narrow, an anaemic-looking stone building brilliantly lit by a pair of security lights trained on the front wall. A sign at the gate proclaimed *A. R. Thripmorton Town Home—Tuesday– Saturday 11–6—Audio Tours Complimentary With Admission —Guided Tours By Arrangement*. As Ivy started up to the door, two Yorkshire terriers in the neighboring building yapped furiously in the front window.

Ivy opened the door, stepping cautiously into a large foyer covered in black and white tile, patterned and gleaming like a chess board. The ceiling was higher than she'd expected, with a wide stairway curving along the outside wall. To the left was a smaller hallway, blocked off by a velvet rope and a sign saying *Staff Only*.

In the middle of the room sat a spindly-looking reception desk; the flat-faced man sitting behind it was very obviously in the middle of counting out the cash in his register drawer. A tag reading *Hello My Name Is Elliot* dangled crookedly from his collar. He looked up at Ivy and scowled, a fistful of euro notes in each hand.

"We're closing," the docent grunted. "Come back tomorrow at eleven."

"But the sign says you're open for another ten minutes," said Ivy, pointing to the hours and fees sign at the front of the desk. "It's just something for school; I won't be more than a minute."

The docent sighed, looking mournfully at the handful of notes, and then shoved both piles of bills back into the drawer.

"Fourteen fifty," said the man glumly. "There's no student discounts, and I close up at six. And not a minute later, you hear me?" And the docent glanced up the stairs to the landing, biting nervously at his lip.

"Thank you," said Ivy, handing over her last twenty-euro note.

Slipping the change into her purse, Ivy hurried away from the desk, passed the sign for the restrooms and started up the stairs. She heard the clank of the register drawer behind her as the docent began re-counting the till.

Ivy hauled herself up to the first floor as quickly as her

aching legs would allow. She reached the landing, passing another sign announcing that a temporary exhibit on cufflinks and stick pins was currently on display on the second floor. Beyond the sign was a long wooden hallway leading further into the townhouse. Inside, the house looked much larger than its narrow frontage had suggested. Ivy wondered worriedly how long it was going to take to look through the entire place.

She started down the hall, the floorboards creaking and protesting at her every step. A series of pale, bewhiskered portraits looked out from the walls as she passed, interspersed with heavy, wooden doors, propped open with brick stops.

Ivy went through the first door she came to, peering over a set of velvet ropes into what looked like a music room. A lanky-looking upright piano sat next to a wooden music stand, rows of painted songbirds in flight along the wallpaper behind them. The windows, framed by dark, floor-length curtains, reflected the glossy black of the street outside. Beside them was a glass-fronted cabinet, a collection of ivory-colored plates and teacups jumbled inside. Nothing else.

She stepped back into the hallway, moving on to the next room. Beyond the velvet rope, a large wooden desk nestled between two rickety bookshelves bristling with musty-looking books and papers. A coat rack sat beside the door, with a top hat and greatcoat draped across it, as though some harried nine-teenth-century barrister had stepped out of the room only moments before.

The next room contained a pair of bristling taxidermied badgers, staring glassy-eyed from their perch atop a mantle, overseeing a row of glass cases filled with fob watches, hair pins, and letter openers. A ponderous grandfather clock was ticking away loudly in the corner. No sign of any ghost, and according to the clock, it was already after six. Ivy hoped the thing was running fast.

Stepping back into the hallway, Ivy saw something moving out of the corner of her eye. Turning toward it, she peered into the opposite room.

On the far side of the velvet ropes sat Uncle Patrick. He was sitting on a blue overstuffed chair near the back of the room, calmly polishing a flute with a dirty bit of cloth. In his scuffed white shirt and woolen vest, he almost looked like a living part of the exhibit. Blue veins stood out from the backs of his hands as he worked the cloth underneath the keys. The old man glanced up briefly as Ivy entered, continuing to run the cloth up and down the flute, studiously ignoring her.

Somehow, Ivy expected him to look different, now that she knew what he was. And what he'd done to her mother. But he looked the same as she remembered: an old man, a little too wrinkled, and a little too loud.

He didn't look like the sort of man who might ruin someone's life. He didn't look like a fairy, or a legendary king. He didn't look like the sort of person on whom Demi's life might depend. Sitting amongst the cabinets, filled with obscure and long-forgotten bric-a-brac, Patrick didn't look like much of anything at all.

"Hello Uncle Patrick," Ivy said.

The old man looked up again and nearly dropped the flute. Leaning hard on the carved arm of the chair, he got to his feet, clutching the flute to his chest. Wrinkles erupted across his face as the old man gave Ivy a nervous grin.

"Ivy, my dear," he said, a little too loudly. "That chair looked far too comfortable not to be sat in, don't you think? Best not tell the fellow downstairs, he'd be terribly annoyed." Patrick was hurriedly shoving the flute into a small case sitting on the dressing table beside him. Slamming the case shut, he crossed the room, stopping just on the far side of the velvet ropes. He glanced at Ivy, then the hallway beyond.

"They'll be closing up soon," he added, flicking the latch on the flute case back and forth. "You'd best be running along."

"Valiard," Ivy said, very distinctly.

Patrick stopped fiddling with his flute case; his face suddenly went very still.

"I haven't heard that name in a very long time," said Patrick in a low voice, his eyes flicking to the door behind Ivy. "Now if you'll excuse me—"

"We need to talk," said Ivy loudly. "Now—" A voice from the stair interrupted her.

"Miss, we're closing up," the docent shouted, his voice echoing up the stairs from the lobby.

Biting her lip, Ivy stepped back toward the hallway. She could hear the docent's footsteps slowly coming up the stairs.

Patrick merely folded his arms over the shabby flute case, his eyebrows meeting in a V along his liver-spotted forehead.

"You do understand," he said slowly. "What will happen if that fellow sees you talking to me?"

"Yes, I do," Ivy snapped, trying to keep her voice down. She remembered the waiter back at the horrible pub. The docent would see her talking to thin air, and probably think she was a nut. "If we can't talk here, then come with me outside. It's important!"

She could hear Elliot's footsteps coming closer. Any moment now the docent would walk past the door, and see Ivy talking to an empty room.

"Nothing about Valiard has been important in years," said Patrick.

"The Year King, then," Ivy hissed, and Patrick's face went suddenly pale. "You remember what day it is, don't you? You remember what happens tomorrow?"

"No," said Patrick, his face gone utterly still. His hands clenched tighter against the flaking leather of the flute case as he backed further away from the velvet rope cordoning off his half of the room. "Absolutely not!"

"But," Ivy began, and then stopped as the docent walked past the door. Ivy looked at him, then glanced away, fighting the notion that she'd just been caught doing something wrong. It wasn't as though *she* was the one standing on the wrong side of the ropes.

"There you are," said Elliot, sounding relieved. He rubbed his hands briskly against his trousers as he walked into the room. "Best be off now; we're closing up."

He didn't so much as glance at Patrick, standing stone-faced beside the dressing table. Not that Ivy actually expected him to notice the trow.

"Right," said Ivy, looking desperately between Patrick and the docent. Catching the trow's eye, she nodded suggestively toward the door. Patrick merely narrowed his eyes, minutely shaking his head.

Why wouldn't he just come with her and talk outside? He'd seemed willing enough to put it all down in the letter. And if Ivy didn't talk with him now, tonight, it would be too late for anything he said to matter. Not to Demi, at any rate.

"Miss?" Elliot asked, a distinct edge to his voice as he glanced at his watch.

Demi was going to die tomorrow, and Patrick wouldn't even talk to her. He was acting as though none of it mattered. He'd said Valiard wasn't important anymore; maybe this wasn't either. Maybe he didn't care that the Enemy was still killing people. Maybe he'd written his letter and sealed it up, and not given any of it a second thought since.

He didn't care about the Year King. And he didn't care about Ivy, either. Not enough to actually talk to her. He'd torn Ivy's mother away from the rest of the world, and then he'd sent

Ivy away from her, too. And now Patrick was just going to hide behind the velvet ropes, and not say a word.

And Ivy didn't dare say anything else with Elliot in the room.

"Right," Ivy repeated breathlessly, and she was surprised to notice that her voice was shaking. It wasn't only because of Patrick. Because here was where it all ended. Here was where everything stopped. She'd found what she'd wanted. She'd found living proof that it was possible to survive the Enemy. And he wouldn't even talk to her.

Out of nowhere, Ivy remembered fishing at Lough Leane, years ago. Patrick had stood beside her in the rain, a fat yellow maggot bloated and wriggling between his fingers. He impaled the worm on Ivy's fishhook when Ivy refused to bait the hook herself. Ivy remembered flinging the hook into the water as quickly as she could, so the maggot would drown and she wouldn't have to watch it squirming as it died.

He'd killed the only fish they caught that day, a bream, its fins translucent and thin, like the wings of a dragonfly. Patrick had slipped the hook from its lip, dashed its head against a rock and left it, stunned and dying, on the wet grass beside their picnic hamper. The bream twitched for several minutes after. Patrick hadn't looked at it, merely gathered up another maggot and stabbed it on his hook, while the dead bream shuddered and gasped.

Beyond the velvet ropes, Patrick's eyes were as glassy and distant as the eyes of the dying bream.

For a moment, there was only the ticking of the clock on the hallway, and a matching beat in Ivy's ears that might have been her own heart. Please, she mouthed, trying to catch his eye. Please don't leave, she added in the silence of her own head. Don't say it's hopeless. Don't say she'll die.

An expression almost like pain flickered across Patrick's

face before he turned away, limping the few steps to the dressing table. He set the battered flute case on the table and flipped up the latches, as though dismissing Ivy completely. As though the only thing he cared about was playing music that no one would ever listen to, and no one would ever hear.

Suddenly, Ivy was furious. Was this how it had been for Victoria? He just walked away whenever he wanted? How many other times had he turned his back? He'd walked away from his own people, hadn't he? Ran off to South America and never gave anything he left behind a second thought. Wrote a letter years after the fact, never to be read until he knew he'd be dead. Until he wasn't around to face any awkward questions, about how he'd survived when so many others hadn't.

He walked away from his own mother. Taye Carillon must have spent decades looking at a portrait, in place of a living son. He walked away from Victoria.

Ivy'd be damned if Patrick was going to walk away from her, too.

She took a deep breath and looked at Elliot, hovering in the doorway and regarding her with a sour expression. The room was devoid of any decent hiding spots; all spindly desks and tables. No bed to crawl under, no wardrobe to hide behind, and the curtains stopped a good foot before the floor. She tried to remember whether any of the other rooms had looked any better.

"Five minutes," Ivy said desperately, turning from Patrick to Elliot, unsure which of them she was actually asking.

"You've already had five minutes," said Elliot, coming further into the room and looking at his watch. "It's nearly ten past. Come back tomorrow, if you're so keen."

Tomorrow wouldn't matter—Demi would already be dead.

Shooting a dark look at Patrick's back, Ivy reluctantly took a few shuffling steps toward the hallway. Patrick might not be looking at her, but Ivy was sure he was still listening. Even if Ivy couldn't quite speak freely with Elliot in the room, Patrick could say all he wanted. Elliot probably wouldn't hear a word.

"You can talk about things, can't you?" Ivy asked, loudly and carefully. Her voice was still shaking but she tried to ignore it. "About things that happened in the past? Isn't that something you can do? Answer questions?"

Elliot let out a deep breath, the air whistling through his teeth. "Yes, but you'll have to come back later. When we're open," he added pointedly.

But of course, it wasn't really Elliot she was talking to.

"I'll answer questions," came Patrick's voice from behind her, low and gravelly. "But not about that."

Elliot didn't seem to hear the trow, merely furrowed his brow for a moment, rubbing at his forehead as he lead Ivy from the room.

"I've ended up with an old letter," Ivy said, loudly and distinctly. She glanced back in time to see Patrick's shoulders twitch. "Something I inherited from my mother. Would anyone here specialize in that sort of thing?"

She slid her hand into her purse, feeling for the edges of the paper.

"If it's family documents, the Museum of Country Life in Cork might be interested." Elliot said thoughtfully. "Our focus is on materials that have some connection to the Thripmorton family. Our archivist is here most weekdays, if you want to stop by."

Patrick unhooked one end of the velvet rope, stepped through, and replaced the hook on its stanchion, following them.

"I might have guessed Victoria would read it," he said. "But she had no business showing it to you. None of it is your concern."

"And what about tomorrow?" Ivy asked, glancing between the docent and the invisible man behind him. "What happens then?"

"Well, we open at eleven—" Elliot started to say.

"What always happens," Patrick said firmly. "It always has happened, and it always will happen, and I don't see why it's any business of yours."

"It didn't always happen, and you're proof," Ivy snapped, rounding on the trow, ignoring Elliot's surprised shout. She probably looked like a crazy person, but Ivy was suddenly too angry to care. "Tomorrow it's going to be someone I care about, and—and you won't even talk to me! You're just going to hide here and ignore all the bad things and pretend they don't matter! Just like you did with my mum!"

Patrick was standing stock-still, his flute case in his hands, a black look on his grizzled face.

"Miss, you need to leave," Elliot snapped, pulling his mobile out of his coat.

Patrick fixed Ivy with a nasty look. "You want to know about the Enemy?" he asked. "About Valiard? If you wish to discuss it, I'll be in the Egmont room."

"I can't stay here," Ivy snapped. Something else Patrick didn't care about—that Ivy was about to be thrown out of the townhouse by a docent who undoubtedly thought she was nuts.

"No, you can't," agreed Elliot fervently. The docent's phone was in his hand, his finger hovering over the screen as though he wasn't sure whether he ought to place the call. Whoever it was—the Gardaí, the Historical Dublin security company, the nearest mental hospital—Ivy was certain it wouldn't be anything good.

"Not my problem," said Larch sarcastically. "If you're truly intending to go up against the Enemy, dealing with a cut-rate historian ought to be no trouble at all. So figure it out."

The trow turned away, leaning on the dressing table as he stepped back over the velvet ropes.

This was ridiculous. She wasn't like Larch; Elliot could see her. She couldn't just walk about under people's noses and count on them not to notice. If she didn't leave, Elliot would just call the Gardaí. Larch could tramp about the townhouse all he wanted and Elliot wouldn't ever know. He could stay here, hidden away from everything, as if everything wrong in the world didn't matter.

That was one thing Ivy could change.

"You've heard this place is haunted, right?" Ivy said, glaring at the docent. "I think it's time you met the resident ghost."

Reaching across the velvet rope, she grabbed the front of Patrick's vest and pulled hard.

"Don't you dare," Elliot started to say, then everything happened at once.

Larch startled, pulling away from Ivy with a curse. His vest, wet and woolen, slipped through her fingers as the trow jumped back, wrinkled face transformed into a snarl. He tumbled into the dressing table's chair as Ivy's legs tangled in the velvet ropes. One of the stanchions fell to the floor with a clatter. Ivy caught herself; Larch didn't. As Larch stumbled, he grabbed for the chair; it screeched loudly across the wooden floor before smacking against the side of the dressing table with a thud.

The flute, tumbling out of its case, rolled softly across the floorboards before colliding with the fallen stanchion with a quiet ping.

"What the hell was that?" Elliot hissed, looking back and forth between Ivy, the flute, and the fallen chair. His eyes were wide.

"It's your ghost," snapped Ivy. "He's right there—just look!" Elliot looked, gripping the phone so tightly his knuckles were turning white, though Ivy had no idea what he was actually seeing.

Larch, glowering as he clambered to his feet, gave Ivy a dark look.

"You want answers so badly, then?" he asked, stepping over the velvet rope. With a smirk, he picked up the stanchion, setting it into place with a deliberate clang.

Elliot yelped.

"Bloody hell," the docent hissed. He grabbed Ivy's arm, his fingers digging hard into her sleeve. "Did you see that?"

"Of course I saw it," said Ivy, trying to tug loose. "Let go— I'm just trying to talk with him!"

"No, no, no," said Elliot, shaking his head as he half-dragged Ivy back toward the hallway. "We're not talking to it. You're one of those girls, aren't you? Like the girl from the Borley Rectory—you show up and all sorts of mad things happen!"

As they stumbled into the corridor; Elliot kicked wildly at the doorstop. The brick slid out of the way and the door slammed shut.

"He's not a poltergeist," Ivy shouted.

"I don't care," snapped Elliot, finally letting go of Ivy's sleeve. "Look, just leave. You just go, and we won't say any more about it. Fair enough?" He sounded anxious, as though whatever he'd seen in the sitting room had been enough to convince him he wanted nothing more to do with any of it.

At the far end of the hallway, a door flew open with a slam that sent the portraits rattling against the plaster walls. Both of them jumped; Ivy scanned the hallway for Larch. She only caught the slightest movement from beyond the door, a vague shadow stepping further into a darkened room. Elliot's face was white.

In the sudden silence, Ivy could hear the monotone ticking

of the grandfather clock in next room, and the squeak of Elliot's shoes against the floor as the docent took a hesitant step toward the stairs.

"Just let me talk to him," Ivy hissed. "Five minutes!"

Elliot licked his lips, eyes narrowing as he considered her request.

"I'm calling security," he said instead, and started to punch something into his phone.

With a quiet click, every light in the house went out.

Ivy jumped. Behind her, Elliot cursed and dropped his phone. Blindly, Ivy kicked toward the sound of the clatter, hoping Larch was behind the lights going out. Hoping, desperately, that the trow was giving her an opening. For what, Ivy didn't know, but she knew she didn't want Elliot completing that phone call. Her foot connected with something; she heard the phone skid across the floor, followed a second later by a splintering crash as it slammed into something at the far end of the hall. Elliot cursed again, but Ivy was already moving, running back toward the stairs.

Ivy dashed blindly through the first open door she came to, the floor changing from wood to carpet beneath her boots. Here, at least, her footsteps were muffled. The streetlight outside the window gave a hazy outline to the room: curtains, a bureau, a four-poster bed. Nothing else. Ivy stepped quickly over the velvet rope. The curtains were too lacy to hide behind; she'd only be backlit by the light from the window. The bed didn't look high enough off the floor to hide her, but Ivy bent down to check anyway. As she knelt, Ivy spotted a gleam of light from the other side of the bed. Coming closer, she spotted a tiny knob, and the outline of a door. She dashed toward it and grabbed the handle. It felt cold and rickety under her fingers.

"You have two minutes, you nutter!" shouted Elliot, his

voice echoing through the hallway. "If you don't leave, I'm calling the Gardaí!"

She turned the knob and threw open the door, wincing as the hinges creaked. Inside, Ivy saw an array of blinking lights, a mass of cables, and absolutely no room to hide. The heat from the electronics was a momentary warmth against her face; she could hear a fan whirring quietly above her head. For a dizzying moment, Ivy was forcibly reminded of the vault below Haven, the eerie bursts of hot air, the dust that rose up with each footstep.

Inside her purse, something chimed brightly. Ivy startled, diving for her phone and quickly silencing the text alert, then turning it off entirely. The tattered edges of Larch's letter brushed against her fingers as she slid the phone back into her purse. The last thing she needed was her mobile giving away her hiding place.

"Sixty seconds!" hollered Elliot, his voice echoing from somewhere down the hall.

Ivy shut the closet door, looking helplessly around the rest of the room.

"Damn it," she muttered under her breath. Probably Larch only offered to talk because he knew it was impossible for her to stay in the house. She couldn't hide like he did. The Gardaí would come and she'd be dragged out in handcuffs. All it would take was one squeaky floorboard or rusty hinge, and they'd know exactly where she was. . . .

Suddenly, Ivy knew how she was going to get Elliot to leave. She took off down the hallway at a run, the floorboards protesting loudly under her feet. The portraits along the walls blurred together as she passed them, a vague impression of pale, disapproving faces. She grabbed the banister at the top of the stairs and started down.

MARETH GRIFFITH

Another set of footsteps echoed behind her, far too quick to be Larch.

"That you?" Elliot called, his voice still echoing in the corridor above. "You'd better be shoving off !"

"I am," Ivy hollered behind her. All the better if Elliot knew exactly where she was—for now, at least. "I'm going! I just thought it wanted to talk."

In the dark, the last step blended with the floor below it; Ivy missed the step and fell, her knees slamming hard into the tiles. A shower of coins fell out of her purse; a tube of lip gloss rolled away into the dark. Ivy didn't stop to grab it, merely scrambling to her feet, legs momentarily tangled in the straps of her purse. She dashed past the hours and fees sign. Her footsteps against the tile were too loud to hear anything else.

Darting past the reception desk, Ivy raced to the front door and grabbed the handle, the knob ice-cold under her fingers. Turning it, she threw open the door; the hinges shrieked.

Winter air poured inside like a breached floodgate; the white tiles of the lobby shone in the sudden glow of the security light outside.

Blinking against the light, Ivy waited an infinitely long second—then slammed the door shut as hard as she could.

The noise echoed throughout the house, trailing off like a clap of thunder, as though the sound had rattled every painting in the place. Purple afterimages of the security light swam in Ivy's vision as she turned away, sliding her feet carefully over the tiles, shuffling as fast as she dared. She'd be across the lobby in a moment; surely there was somewhere in the back offices where she could hide—

A brighter afterimage gleamed in the corner of Ivy's eye. With a start, she realized it was a flashlight; Elliot was already at the top of the stairs.

Abandoning her hopes for the back hallway, Ivy threw

herself past the restroom sign and into the shadow of the stairs. She could hear the docent's footsteps above her. Ivy pressed herself as far into the corner as she could get, her fingers digging into the straps of her purse. The restroom's doorknob was digging into her hip, but she didn't dare try and open it. It would only take one out-of-place sound to give her away.

Of course, if Elliot swung his flashlight toward this side of the lobby, he'd see her in any case. She desperately hoped that Elliot hadn't already fixed whatever Larch had done with the lights.

Like the tolling of a clock, the docent's footsteps descended the stairs. His flashlight swung back and forth like a searchlight; the dropped coins from Ivy's purse glittered in the beam. As the docent crossed in front of the reception desk, Ivy burrowed her face deeper into her coat.

I'm not here, she thought furiously. I ran out and slammed the door behind me and all the weird things are over and you can go home.

Training his flashlight on the corner of the reception desk, the docent bent down and picked something small and cylindrical off the floor. Ivy's lip gloss.

"Nutter," he murmured fervently, and tossed the tube into the rubbish bin beside the desk.

Ivy let out a breath she hadn't realized she'd been holding. The weird things are over, she repeated to herself. You can go home.

She could almost envy him for that.

Turning back to the reception desk, Elliot picked up his coat. She heard a bright jingle of keys as the docent crossed to a small panel next to the door. As he opened the panel, the green glow of a keypad briefly illuminated his face. Elliot punched in a code; the keypad chirped contentedly in response.

He pulled a pair of mittens from his pocket. As Elliot began to pull them over his hands, the flashlight beam swung wildly. For one blinding instant, the light shone straight into her alcove. Ivy froze, spots in her vision, her heartbeat loud in her ears.

She blinked away the spots in time to see the front door swinging shut behind him. A moment later, the lock engaged with a quiet click.

Around her, the townhouse fell silent.

Very slowly, Ivy straightened up, rubbing her hip where the door knob had been digging into it. Cautiously, she came a few steps into the hall.

Nothing else moved. The lobby was dark except for the faint glow from the drapes in front of the windows and the steady green glow of the panel's keypad.

Ivy stopped short, considering the panel and biting her lip. It was probably connected to some sort of security system. Most likely, Elliot had armed it when he left. Maybe there were motion detectors, or infrared cameras. Maybe she'd already set off a silent alarm and the docent was going to be charging back through the door any second.

Then again, whatever security systems were in the house were apparently not an impediment to Larch's residence here. Ivy could hardly imagine the trow spending all night sitting in one spot for fear of setting off an alarm. If there were alarms, they were probably only on certain doors. Like the front door, for instance, or cabinets containing particularly valuable bric-a-brac.

Turning away from the glowing panel, she started up the stairs, leaning heavily on the handrail. The muscles in her legs were aching again, and her knees hurt too, stinging as though she'd scraped off a good bit of skin. She'd probably have no choice but to set off the alarm when she left, Ivy thought. Unless Larch happened to know how to disable the system.

Ivy just hoped that the Egmont Room wasn't one of the doors with an alarm wired to it.

⤜✦⤚

LARCH WASN'T in any of the rooms on the first floor. Ivy walked the length of the corridor, peering into every room she could find, without success. Aside from the muttered coughing of the furnace ducts, the townhouse seemed eerily silent. The Egmont Room, whatever that was, must be on the second floor. Following the sign advertising the cufflinks and stick pins, Ivy tackled the second set of stairs with two throbbing knees and a growing sense of irritation. By the time she limped into the Egmont Room—drawn by the faint flicker of candlelight visible from the hallway—she was angry enough to want to dash to pieces the next set of historic crockery she saw.

"All right," Ivy said as she stepped over the velvet rope and past a pair of spindly-looking chairs. "Are you through playing games?"

"I don't know," Larch shot back querulously. He was sitting in an overstuffed chair next to an expansive curio cabinet, his face illuminated by the faint glow of a phone sitting on his knee. The screen was cracked in several places; it looked suspiciously like the docent's mobile, the phone Ivy had kicked down the hall. "Are you finished mucking about with things that don't concern you?"

"No," Ivy replied bluntly, coming up to the edge of his chair and crossing her arms. He'd lit a handful of candles in a small candelabra, the flames dancing over a collection of tiny music boxes. In the flickering light, the figurines on the decorated lids almost seemed to move.

Larch frowned at her, raising an eyebrow.

"Look," Ivy said. "By this time tomorrow, a friend of mine's going to—" Ivy stopped, afraid to finish that thought, and she started again. "It's all going to be over one way or another, so why can't you just answer my questions?"

Absently, Larch set the phone on the cabinet beside him. "They're dangerous questions," he said, folding his arms. "If you really want to help, drop that letter you've acquired into the nearest post box, and don't give any of it a second thought."

"But isn't there something she could do?" Ivy asked, insistently. "The Year King—if she left on a ship, like you did?"

"If anyone reads that letter, they might try something of the sort for next year. For whoever they decide to kill next." Impatiently, Larch got up from the chair, leaning heavily on the arms, and limped over to the window. He opened the shutter, glaring at the deserted street outside with one hand on his hip. "They still hold the lottery in March, I suppose?"

"It's still the same," said Ivy quietly. "Nothing's changed."

Decades of people being murdered while Larch hid half a world away and pretended it must have stopped, never bothering to get in touch with anyone who might have told him differently.

"The waiting was the worst, you know," the old man said softly, closing the shutter as he turned away from the window. "Having a year to know it, and not able to do anything at all."

Ivy wondered if that really was the worst part. Probably the worst part was the actually dying part, which was the bit Larch had conveniently managed to skip.

Besides, Demi hadn't just waited. She'd gone to Howth, and made a little world for herself. A world where she could pretend the Enemy wasn't real. And she brought Ivy there—not so Ivy could open doors, or fetch groceries, or sign for packages. Demi wanted to someone in her world who didn't know Demi was going to die. Someone to pretend with. Someone who didn't know any of the bad things.

And now the Enemy was coming tomorrow and Demi couldn't pretend any more. For a moment, Ivy remembered how she'd looked standing in the fading light of the apple grove, eyes bright, her hair in tangles. Ivy rubbed her hands across her face, surprised when they came away wet, and wiped away the evidence against the side of her coat.

"I'm sorry," said Larch gruffly, his eyes bright in the candle-light as he glanced back at her. "Do you know the current king well?"

Ivy nodded. "We live together," she said, only realizing after she'd said it that it wasn't really true anymore. Tomorrow, Demi would be dead and Ivy would be moving to Dartry. To a place without houseplants, or invisible people, or poisonous vegan meatloaf. Without ghosts, or fairies, or magic. Not that Larch would care. He'd probably be just like Victoria, thinking it was better for Ivy to stay as far away from all of it as possible. He must have cared, once. Years afterwards, he'd still thought about the Enemy. Thought about it enough to put it all down in a letter, a half-century or more after it had happened.

Impulsively, she stepped closer, taking Larch's gloved hand in her own. The trow looked at her sharply, his hands cool and twig-like beneath the wool.

"Come with me to Haven tomorrow," said Ivy urgently. "You could meet Demi. You could give Carillon the letter your-self. Maybe it won't help, but at least—"

"Go back?" the trow barked, pulling his hands away and rubbing his gloves on the side of his trousers. "And meet your friend just before the Adversary kills her? See my mother, only to tell her I'll be dying again very shortly?"

"Then what should I do?" asked Ivy. Larch was living proof that it was possible to survive the Enemy. And now he was telling her it was hopeless, too. "They'll kill her tomorrow!"

"You can't do anything, so I'd recommend you stay away,"

Larch said, hobbling away from the window. "You can't help her, so you'd better start thinking about helping yourself. It might be for the best the Adversary is killing her; a girlfriend'll have you under the veil quicker than you can say hot cross buns."

"We aren't," said Ivy stiffly. The yellowed envelope crinkled as her fingers tightened around her purse strap. Impatiently, she shoved the bundle of paper further into her purse.

"Good," Larch said, addressing one of the painted ballerinas among the music boxes. "Best keep it that way. There isn't any way to right that kind of mistake."

Absently, he reached out to stroke the ballerina, woolen fingers brushing lightly against the figurine's painted head.

Ivy swallowed, fighting a strange tightness that had sprung up in her throat. She didn't know how she could face Demi tomorrow if she came to Haven empty-handed. How do you talk to a friend who might be dead in less than a day? It was too much, to talk about the weather, or the plants, and try and pretend that nothing was wrong. What do you say when it's the very last conversation ever?

After everything Ivy had tried, she hadn't managed anything beyond an old letter full of useless speculation. She'd done everything she could, and it turned out to be exactly as hopeless as everyone said. Ivy wondered if she could even get to Haven in time to see Demi, before it happened. The rural bus routes probably didn't go within ten miles of Haven. Car agencies didn't rent to nineteen-year-olds. And every single remaining euro in the envelope under the begonias still wouldn't be enough to cover a cab the whole way across Ireland.

"Look—you could still help," Ivy insisted. "You escaped the Enemy—just come and talk to her! Or if you've really been the Year King all this time, maybe—"

Ivy stopped, horrified at the thought even as it entered her head. Larch turned back from the curio cabinet, a bushy eyebrow crawling quizzically up his liver-spotted face.

"You're trying to talk me into attending, and then telling me I'll possibly be murdered if I show up," he said shortly. "Which is it?"

"I don't know," Ivy admitted. Would the Enemy even notice a former Year King? Or would it ignore Larch, the way the trows said it ignored everyone else? "But—"

"Finally a bit of sense," the old man said. "I know what'll happen and I'll spare myself the unpleasantness of telling you. You'll see for yourself soon enough, if you really are bent on going."

Ivy bit her lip as Larch hobbled back to the over-stuffed chair, resting one hand against the back of it. How would it happen, when the Enemy came? With a shudder, Ivy remembered the grinning cut on Killian's throat. Whatever happened tomorrow would be far worse than anything Killian could conjure up with makeup and spirit gum.

Larch turned back to the window, pulling back the shutter, then abruptly closing it again.

"Any other questions?" he asked irritably, still looking at the shutter. "Haven't done this in a while, have we? Spending time together."

"So all of a sudden you want to talk," Ivy said, crossing her arms. It was on the tip of her tongue to snap at him, to tell him the time together didn't count. Not when she had to escape a hopping-mad historian bent on calling the police just to get him to answer a question.

Except that it had been a long time since they'd talked, properly. Given what Ivy knew now, she'd be perfectly happy never talking to him ever again. Not after what he'd done to her mother.

MARETH GRIFFITH

But maybe it would be kinder if, just for now, Ivy pretended that wasn't true.

"The Enemy," she said instead. "Why does it still kill people? Why does it still care?"

Larch didn't answer right away, looking at the ballerina sitting on the top of the curio cabinet, the corner of his mouth turning up in a regretful sort of smile.

Out of nowhere, Ivy wondered how it was she'd been able to see him when she was a child.

"Perhaps it's revenge for Valiard. For coming here in the first place. For being here, but not being able to change what's going to happen," the trow said abruptly. Behind him, Ivy caught a momentary glimmer of blue from under the shutters, gone almost before she'd seen it properly. "Do you always concern yourself with such depressing things? What shall we talk about next— war, pestilence, or famine?"

Ivy didn't answer, still picturing that tiny flash of blue light. Abruptly, she went to the window, shouldering Larch out of the way as she threw back the shutter.

A Garda patrol car, its blue and white lights spinning, was pulled up to the curb in front of the townhouse.

"He *did* call the Gardaí," Ivy exclaimed, exasperation fighting with a sinking feeling in the pit of her stomach.

"He didn't, actually," replied Larch darkly. As Ivy turned to look at him, the trow nodded to the cracked phone sitting on the curio counter. "I did."

"Why the *hell* would you—"

"Seven years ago, I promised your mother I'd keep you away from exactly this sort of thing," he said, cutting her off. In the street below, two uniformed figures got out of the car and turned up the path to the house. Their shadows, thrown by the security lights, looked monstrous, long and thin and grasping. "Maybe a night in jail and a trespassing charge will be what it takes to convince you that meddling in their world is dangerous."

He hadn't really wanted to talk; he'd just been stalling for time. He'd rather see Ivy taken away from the house in handcuffs than actually talk to her. Ivy should have known it would be something like this. He'd never done anything good for Ivy's mother, why should he be any different with Ivy herself?

But she hadn't known, and she'd trusted him. Ivy wouldn't have expected the idea of Uncle Patrick betraying her to hurt, but it did.

Ivy grabbed the phone off the cabinet and slammed it hard against the window frame. She felt the screen shatter; the plastic shards of the back cover gleamed in the candlelight as they fell to the floor. It wasn't enough, so she did it again, harder. Something inside the case gave way with a jolt, and Ivy let go, letting the mangled bits fall to the floor. It still wasn't enough—but at least he wouldn't be using the phone again.

"I can see why Mum hates you," Ivy spat out, the most hurtful thing she could think of. She didn't wait to see if the barb hit home, but turned on her heel, dashing out of the Egmont room and heading for the stairs.

If the Gardaí found her here and hauled her off, she'd never see Demi again. And Demi would die thinking Ivy hadn't cared enough to come. Not to mention things like criminal records, or fines, or jail time.

Ivy would simply have to get out before they found her. There had to be another entrance, somewhere in the back.

Reaching the stairs, Ivy looked for an exit sign, trying to remember if she'd seen one earlier. Would the officers come inside, or would they simply poke around the bushes and check the locks? Maybe she should just hide somewhere and see if they drove off.

Of course, if he really wanted Ivy caught, Larch could

easily give them something to investigate—like throwing open the front door, for instance, or tossing a chair out a window. . . .

Approaching the lobby, Ivy slowed her steps. Faintly, she could hear dogs barking—the two Yorkies in the townhouse next door. A beam of light flickered at the edge of the curtains. The Gardaí could open the door at any moment, and Ivy would have nowhere to hide.

She stared across the lobby, wincing at the sound of her boots on the tile. Maybe they didn't have a key to get inside. Maybe they didn't know the code to disarm the security systems.

Of course, Ivy didn't know the code, either. If there were alarms on the doors, Ivy could very well set them off herself trying to leave.

Halfway across the darkened lobby, all the lights in the building came on.

Ivy froze, fighting the urge to bolt as a surprised murmur came from outside the front door, a raised voice, too muffled to make out the words. The door handle rattled, as though someone were jimmying a key.

So they were trying to get inside. Not that Ivy expected any differently, now that they'd seen the lights come on.

Hardly daring to breathe, Ivy tiptoed across the tiles, past the *Staff Only* sign and into the back hall, hoping it wasn't leading her to a dead end. Behind her, the front door rattled again. In the hallway, Ivy scrutinized the doors as she passed them, a succession of shuttered offices. Briefly, she considered flinging herself behind the nearest door and out of sight. But hiding wouldn't help if the Gardaí made a thorough search of the building—and she'd be effectively trapped in the office for as long as someone was on the ground floor. Better to find a back door and get out of here as quickly as possible.

At the end of the hallway, Ivy finally spotted a dusty exit

sign, sitting atop a dingy wooden door. The upper half was clouded glass, with flaking metal bars affixed to the outside, the glass nearly opaque with dirt. Above the antique-looking handle was a gleaming metal turnkey and a deadbolt of a considerably newer vintage. *Emergency Exit Alarm Will Sound* read a faded plastic sticker in the bottom corner of the window.

Peering at the edges of the door, Ivy spotted a wire running along the ceiling to a small, round sensor at the top of the door-jamb. Probably there was some clever way to disarm it, by cutting the wire or stabbing the sensor with a hairpin, but Ivy had no idea what that might be. It would almost certainly start howling the moment she opened the door.

The timing, however, was entirely up to Ivy.

She glanced back to the lobby—still bright, motionless, and empty. She couldn't see the blue and white lights of the Gardaí's cruiser anymore; the lights in the lobby were too over-powering.

Maybe they'd already left. Maybe they didn't have a key, or maybe they'd gotten a call about a shooting, or a burglary, or something far more urgent than a trespasser at some musty old museum.

Ivy wondered whether Larch was still upstairs, waiting to see her hauled off in the squad car. It didn't seem fair that Larch could set the Gardaí on Ivy for trespassing when he himself had apparently been living in the place for months. It would serve him right if Historical Dublin decided to install video cameras after tonight. Or motion sensors, or something else that meant he couldn't go on pretending to be nothing more than a ghost. Couldn't go on hiding amongst the relics and stick pins, exempt from everything that happened in the world. Because there were no such things as ghosts—not here, and maybe not anywhere. Only strange people, hiding in plain sight. That was all that was here in the townhouse, and the ghost that had haunted the house at Trail's Cross. . . Victoria had known what it was all along. She'd asked it in to live with her, and look what happened since. . . .

Maybe Elliot would be better off if he knew exactly what it was that shuffled through the corridors here, and rearranged the books.

In the lobby, the front door shuddered, and a growing crescent of light splayed across the tiles as the front door swung open.

Ivy didn't wait. She couldn't help the alarm. But she could pick the best moment to set it off.

She threw back the deadbolt, setting her shoulder against the door as she twisted the knob. The door groaned, the noise immediately muffled by the shrieking wail of an alarm. Behind her, a woman shouted in surprise, but Ivy was already through the door, not stopping to close it, nor look back. Blindly, she ran up a moss-covered stair, and through a rusted, half-open gate.

The gate opened into a narrow alley, the cobblestones slick and uneven beneath Ivy's boots. The alarm was still shrieking, the sound partially drowned out by the apoplectic barking of the dogs in the neighboring townhouse. Hopefully, the Gardaí would assume they'd triggered the alarm themselves when they opened the front door. Hopefully, they'd be busy enough trying to silence it that they wouldn't notice the unlocked back door. At least, not until Ivy was well clear.

At the mouth of the alley, Ivy slowed her steps long enough to look back, pulling her coat more tightly around her shoulders. The alarm was still shrieking, and lights were beginning to come on in the neighboring houses. No running footsteps had followed her, no shouts. No flashing lights, or the wailing sirens of a squad car in pursuit.

On the second floor of the Thripmorton Town Home, one window was open despite the chill in the air. The shutters were thrown back; the curtains moved restlessly in the wind. Larch's silhouette was just visible against the faint light behind him. As Ivy watched, the figure tentatively raised a hand. Ivy immediately turned away, shoving her hands in her pockets. Two steps past the mouth of the alley, and the townhouse was out of sight. The alarm lingered, the furious squalling slowly diminishing as Ivy walked away.

It wasn't his fault he couldn't help Demi, Ivy thought in a sudden burst of pity. And it wasn't his fault he didn't die back in 1936.

Though Ivy couldn't quite dismiss the thought that things would have been much better for Ivy's family if he had.

She turned into the street, passing a pub, a group of smokers huddled noisily under the awning, a few of them clutching their pints illicitly under their coats. It seemed inconceivable that it was still early enough for the pubs to be open; it felt like Ivy had spent half the night running around Oxmarten chasing ghosts.

Ivy slipped her hand into her purse, just long enough to feel for the edges of Larch's letter. Still there, for all the good it had done her. Useless speculations about the Enemy's murders, wrapped up with dire-sounding nonsense about the end of the world. Not likely he would have given her a straight answer, if she'd asked. It felt like yet another mystery she'd stumbled over, like the wing computers sleeping in their vault or the hoof prints in the back garden. Some other terrible thing that didn't belong in the real world, and that no one was bothering to tell her about. Something terrible that everyone knew about, but no one was trying to change.

She stopped at the edge of the awning, wishing, obscurely, that she smoked so that at least she'd have an excuse to stand still. Just for a minute or two. Just until she knew what to do next.

Because this was where it all ended. Ivy had spent the past week running all over Dublin and beyond, trying to save Demi from a catastrophe she'd only half-believed in at first. She'd discovered that fairies were real, and were far different than commonly supposed. She'd learned that fairies had enchanted her mother. She knew why she'd been sent to live with her father when she was twelve years old.

But that hadn't been what Ivy wanted to find out. Maybe there wasn't an answer, Ivy thought, looking through the window at the neon-lit faces inside the pub. Not just for Demi, but for all of them. The Enemy would come, this year and every year afterwards, and there was no way to stop it, and it was just as inescapable and meaningless as dying any other sort of way. Some people might even think it was fair—that dying like that, even if you had to know about it beforehand, was better than growing old.

But it wasn't fair, she thought, watching as a red-haired woman took a long swig of her pint, giggling silently at something her companion had said. Demi tried so hard to escape what was happening to her. Larch hadn't done a thing, and he'd been the one to survive.

Maybe it would be better if Demi didn't know about Larch at all. Maybe it would be kinder if she didn't go to her death knowing that someone, somehow, had helped Larch, but not her.

At least after tomorrow, it wouldn't be anyone Ivy knew.

They'd call another lottery and pick someone else and Ivy wouldn't have to care about their Year King, no matter who it was.

And Ivy thought of Hunzu, and bit her lip. If it was a lottery, it could be anyone. Even him. Though why that thought should be so troubling, Ivy wasn't sure.

Opening her purse, Ivy took out her gloves and started to

304

put them on. It was only when she saw her phone that she remembered she'd gotten a text. Slipping the phone out of her purse, she switched it on and pulled up the message.

I can't help over lunch hour if it'll take more than one trip. Left the Nissan in the back alley, put the keys in your mail slot. We'll swing by your new place tomorrow night and pick up the car. Remember, lift with your knees, not with your back. Love, Dad.

Suddenly, Ivy knew exactly how she was going to get to Haven.

CHAPTER 13

T he sky was just beginning to turn pink when Ivy finally pulled the Nissan into a gravel turnout next to a leafless hawthorn bush. Farther up the hill, she could just make out the corner of the tall metal gates marking the entrance to Haven's long driveway. Given how things had gone the last time she'd been here, Ivy didn't want to risk driving up to the front door, even if Demi had invited her to come. This turnout was probably the closest place to legally park the Nissan off the road; Ivy didn't want to risk some overzealous Garda towing her father's car.

Catching sight of herself in the rearview mirror, Ivy winced. Her eyes looked baggy and dark, her face even paler than normal. Her hair, fallen out of its braid hours ago, hung limply across her face. She'd only managed a few hours of sleep, in a bedroom made suddenly strange by the absence of most of Ivy's things, everything stripped down to bare furniture and boxes.

Pocketing her keys, Ivy slipped out of the driver's seat, crossing to the passenger side and opening the door. She pulled out her rucksack, looking critically at the plastic pot sitting behind it. The anthuriums seemed to have survived the trip without any obvious signs of distress. She'd propped up the pot with pillows; only the tiniest bit of dirt had spilled onto the upholstery. Ivy hoped the car ride hadn't been too taxing for the poor things; she'd kept the cabin blisteringly hot for the whole trip. Better get them inside as soon as possible, and hope that someone in Haven owned a heat lamp.

Bringing the anthuriums, their flowers garishly orange against the Nissan's sedate upholstery, seemed like a useless and maudlin gesture. Like bringing flowers to a funeral, the sort of thing one does when all practical options have been exhausted. Hopeless and pointless and futile.

Ivy pulled the anthuriums out of the car, set the pot on the Nissan's trunk, and locked the car. She slung the rucksack over her shoulder, and felt the apples digging uncomfortably into her back. She'd brought a whole sack, along with a bag of biscuits, two oatmeal packets and a squished bowl of instant noodles she'd found in the back of the pantry. Not that Ivy was planning on staying long, but it didn't hurt to be prepared. Also, Ivy didn't entirely trust that Taye Carillon wouldn't try to poison her again, no matter what Demi's note had said. Whatever understanding Demi had come to with Carillon regarding Ivy's presence on the estate, Ivy hoped it would still be in force after—after whatever was going to happen.

It felt terrible to even think about that.

But, some terribly practical corner of Ivy's mind pointed out, Demi wasn't the one who would have to worry about what happened afterwards. There wouldn't be an afterwards for her, but there would be for Ivy. She still had to worry about turning invisible, or what else might happen if Carillon decided she didn't want Ivy hanging about.

Which probably meant Ivy shouldn't have come at all. But she couldn't do that to Demi—not when being here was the only thing she could do. Even if being here wouldn't make the slightest bit of difference.

There was the letter, still sitting in the bottom of Ivy's purse. Larch hadn't wanted his mother to see it until after he was dead, but Larch's opinions had stopped carrying any weight with Ivy about the time the Garda squad car turned up at the Thripmorton Town Home. Ivy would have to decide what to do with it herself—after.

The entire idea of Demi dying seemed both oppressively close and inconceivably unreal.

Ivy readjusted the bag on her shoulder, then picked up the anthuriums, making sure she had a good grip on the pot.

Standing on tip-toe, Ivy could barely make out the tops of Haven's turrets, the creamy-looking stone turning pink as it caught the first rays of the sun. She squinted, but it was too far away to tell if there were any lights in the windows. Looking across the pasture, Ivy picked out the chess-piece shapes of horses grazing on the opposite hill. She wondered whether Clover was still there, or if Carillon had gotten rid of him. Beyond the field lay a cluster of leafless trees, the shadows of their branches reaching back toward the house like fingers. With a start, Ivy realized she must be looking at the Year King's apple grove.

It was just past six in the morning; Haven looked exactly as deserted as any house would at such an unsociable hour. Taye Carillon probably wouldn't be pleased to see Ivy at any hour, even if Demi had invited her to come.

What if it had all happened at midnight?

Technically, it had already been February twentieth for over six hours. How strictly did the Enemy adhere to its timetable? Would Demi know down to the second when it would happen?

Ivy looked toward the distant grove of trees. Even if Demi was in the house, Ivy didn't think it was likely she could just ring the bell and walk in. Given the trows' fastidiousness when it came to interacting with humans, there would probably be a lot of fuss before she'd be able to see Demi. And these next few hours were the last that Demi would ever—

Ivy didn't finish the thought. But there were trees in the grove, and Ivy thought suddenly of Demi's bedroom in Howth, the multitude of plants, and the way the leaves reflected in the glass. Somehow, Ivy didn't think Demi would want to spend her last few hours inside.

"You finally showed up," wheezed a voice from the other side of the hedge.

Ivy jumped, her rucksack slipping off her shoulder and banging hard into the anthurium's pot, as Larch limped around the corner of the Nissan.

He was panting, as though he'd come down the hill in a rush. His mud-splattered coat was wrapped about him like a robe, the woolen hat sitting crookedly on his liver-spotted head. Buckled over the coat was a flaking leather belt; tucked into the belt was a revolver that looked as if it might have been pilfered from one of the display cases back at the Thripmorton Town Home. Though tarnished, the metal gleamed as if it had been freshly oiled.

"No thanks to you," Ivy snapped, stepping back from the car, holding the flower pot in front of her like a shield. "You going to call the Gardaí again? Or just tell me to get back in my car like a good little girl?"

Larch's lip twitched, what might have been a grimace or a smile.

"Not the first time I've broken a promise to your mother," he said with a shrug, as though dismissing it as completely unimportant. "I wouldn't bother with the house, not a soul in the place. Are you sure this is where your friend said she'd be?"

"She was pretty specific," said Ivy. For a befuddling moment, Ivy wondered how Larch had even known how to find the place. But Larch was Taye Carillon's son. He'd lived here—maybe even grown up in this house.

Ivy shifted the flower pot to her other hip, telling herself she ought to be angry. She ought to clobber him with the anthurium's pot, or dump all the topsoil over his head, and storm off and never speak to him ever again.

Except none of that would help Demi. Perhaps the only thing Ivy could do now was not make a scene. Shouting and throwing things could wait until after, because Ivy had all the time in the world to be angry. Demi had hardly any time left at all.

And in some fragile corner of her heart, Ivy felt obscurely grateful that the old man was here. Even if Ivy had to walk down the hill, and talk to Demi, and see her crying and watch her die, at least Ivy didn't have to do it entirely alone. Even if the person had to be Uncle Patrick, maybe having Uncle Patrick beside her was better than having no one at all.

"I think Demi might have gone to the apple grove," Ivy said in a rush.

"Then we'd better hurry," said Larch, starting down the hill without waiting to see if Ivy would follow. "The Adversary seems to make a point of being punctual."

Ivy started after him, stopping briefly to untangle the anthurium, whose stems had gotten knotted with the straps on her backpack. By the time she caught up with Larch, he was already halfway across the meadow, walking quickly despite his limp.

"When?" Ivy asked, resting the anthurium's pot against her hip as she scampered to keep up with the old man's pace. "And why are you—"

"Soon," the old man wheezed. The revolver chinked brightly as it jostled against his hip.

"But why did you change your mind? You said—"

"You aren't supposed to be here, either," said Larch, interrupting her. "Don't worry, I won't tell your mother."

And the trow winked at her. Before Ivy could insist on a proper answer, they were underneath the apple trees, and it was all Ivy could do to keep up with Larch without tripping over any of the roots or stones.

But she wondered about the gun. The Enemy wasn't supposed to come after anyone but the king. Which, technically, Larch was.

"Look," Ivy shouted. "Over by the tree!"

"Where?" Larch asked.

Ivy tried to point with the anthurium, but only managed to spill dirt over the side of the pot. "Just there—there's someone in the grove."

The trow quickened his pace, Ivy falling further behind as she tried to rebalance the anthuriums' pot. Nearly tripping over the edge of a stone, she crashed through a tangle of low branches a few seconds after Larch.

Larch had gotten halfway across the small clearing before Ivy even came through the hedge, but the people in the clearing hadn't noticed. Or maybe they were doing that weird trow thing where they got really still around people they didn't want to notice them.

There were four of them in the clearing, which was little more than a stone bench set into a tiny gap among the surrounding trees. Demi was sitting on the bench, huddled next to a woman with tear-stained eyes. Ambrose and Hunzu were standing together, Hunzu's hand resting awkwardly on the taller man's shoulder. Ambrose was holding a small pocket-watch, nervously flipping it open and closed.

Demi sprang up from the bench and ran to Ivy, who barely had time to put down the anthuriums before Demi threw her arms wildly around Ivy's neck.

"You did come," Demi said, her hands dropping away from Ivy's shoulders, stepping back almost as quickly as she'd approached. "I'm sorry, I know it's too late to worry about me, but I still should have better manners."

"It's okay," said Ivy, dredging up a smile from some brittle place in her chest. "I found your note, and I didn't know if I should come, or if it would be safe, and my dad left his car. . . ." Ivy knew she was blathering like an idiot, but Demi was still standing there smiling, even though her eyes were wet as though she'd been crying, and her jeans were damp to the knees with dew.

"Anyway, I came," Ivy finished lamely. There suddenly seemed to be a hundred things she ought to tell her—that none of the houseplants had died, that she was moving out, why her mother had sent her to live with her Dad, that she'd found Larch Carillon's letter, and then found Larch Carillon himself. But suddenly, Ivy didn't have the words for any of it.

Maybe it was enough that she was here, Ivy thought. Maybe, when you got too close to the end, finding the exact right thing to say didn't matter so much. There wasn't any time left to go dredging up the perfect words.

Demi put a hand to her head, rearranging a small circle of metal perched awkwardly atop her braided hair. The circlet was jumble of silver and bronze crescents, entwined about an empty, blackened fitting that might once have held a gem. The

Year King's crown, Ivy thought suddenly; the circlet was far too shabby and tarnished to be anything else.

The crown slipped across Demi's face again; she pushed it back into place, patting it as though trying to get it to settle onto her hair.

Ambrose had come up to the bench and was talking quietly to the other woman, who was staring at Ivy with an expression equal parts surprise and disgust. She was wearing black, as though at a funeral. As though she were already in mourning. As Ambrose looked up, Ivy could see circles under his eyes, dark as a bruise.

All of them were mourning Demi, even though she was standing right there.

"It's okay," Ivy said to the trow woman, dropping her rucksack on the ground next to the anthurium and holding up her gloved hands. "I know the rules."

The woman glanced quickly at Demi, swallowed hard, and nodded. "Welcome, Ivy," she said shortly, sounding as though she was making only the barest effort to be polite.

Uneasily, Ivy nodded back and glanced to Hunzu, who was still standing under the apple tree with his hands shoved deep in his pockets. The trow gave her a tentative smile. Ivy felt an answering smile flicker hesitantly across her face.

"Demi, I want you to meet someone," Ivy said, and turned, only to find that Larch was standing some ways off. His face was half obscured by the shadows of the trees, and his hands were balled into fists at his side.

"Just for the record, the house probably wasn't empty at all," he said.

"Larch?" Ivy asked.

"It's alright, Ivy," he said, but he didn't sound alright at all. The old man turned back to the apple tree, his boot tracing the outline of one of the stones at the foot of it.

"Ivy," Ambrose said in a conciliatory tone, coming around the bench toward her. "This is probably not a good time." With obvious trepidation, the trow laid his hand lightly against the small of her back, as though he might escort her away.

"What do you mean it isn't a good time!" Ivy snapped. In less than a week, Ivy had found a Year King who'd been missing for seventy years, and no one seemed to care. Or even notice. "You said he could help!"

"You thought who could help?" Demi asked.

Ivy took a deep breath, glancing between Demi's hopeful face and the old man behind her, scuffing his boots at the base of the apple tree.

"The man you can't see," Ivy said.

Demi and the other woman exchanged a look that Ivy couldn't interpret, and the other woman began grappling for something in her coat pocket, something far too bulky to merely be gloves. Hunzu's head came up with a start, his eyes flicking intently across the grove.

"Ivy, there's no one here," Ambrose insisted.

"He's standing right there," Ivy said, pointing. "And he can't—you can't see them either, can you, Larch?"

"They're all here, aren't they?" asked the old man, sounding for once as frail as he looked. "Don't know who you'd be talking to otherwise."

"He can't be veiled, Ivy; veils don't work on trows," said Ambrose firmly.

"Well, we might not know if they did," Hunzu pointed out, staring intently in the direction Ivy had pointed as he crossed the clearing to join them.

"Ivy, are they here?" Larch rasped.

"Yes, they're here," Ivy told him, not sure how long she'd be able to continue having two different conversations between people who couldn't hear each other. "Four of them, at least."

"Who's here?" Ambrose asked. "Four of what?"

"Larch Carillon," Ivy said, nearly shouting. "The Year King of 1936."

There was a long silence, broken only by the sound of Larch's ragged breathing—he couldn't still be out of breath from walking down from the house, could he?

Ambrose turned to the trow woman, rather ineffectually trying to lower his voice. "Isabelle, could you please escort Ms. Gallagher up to the house?"

"Ambrose, for God's sake!" Ivy shouted. It was just like what happened at the townhouse. Elliot hadn't believed her, that there was someone else in the room, and Ambrose didn't believe her, either. Now they were going to shuffle her off somewhere, like what she said didn't matter. "Can I see your phone? Oh, never mind."

Ivy pulled her own mobile out of her pocket, flipping it open and pulling up the camera function. Pointing the phone at Larch, she snapped a picture, then handed the phone to Hunzu.

"Look," Ivy snapped. "He's right here!"

Hunzu looked at the screen, his head snapping up to the far side of the clearing, then back to the image on the phone.

"How do you enlarge this?" the trow asked, switching back to camera mode, the screen shifting as he panned the phone through the air. Demi stepped closer, her long braid brushing Hunzu's coat as she peered over his shoulder. Ivy heard Demi's sudden intake of breath as she saw the image in the screen.

Demi turned to the woman behind her. "Isabelle, get Taye Carillon. Get her down here now."

"Wait," said Hunzu sharply, tearing his gaze away from the camera phone and grabbing Isabelle by the arm. "This could be anyone."

Hunzu was looking at Larch, and he still didn't believe her.

"Hunzu, you can see him yourself," she snapped. "Stop being an idiot!"

The trow rounded on Ivy with a dark look. "Someone's going to die very soon," he said urgently. "And there's someone here that none of us can see! *Think*, Ivy."

"It isn't him," Ivy shot back, trying to ignore the little part of her that remembered the revolver, the glint of well-oiled metal at his waist. "He hasn't as much as seen another trow since he disappeared!"

"What are they saying, Ivy?" Larch asked, still looking about him as though he could make himself see the gathering of trows by force of will alone.

Hunzu flipped the phone back open, panning until he relocated Larch in the screen. Slowly, he took a step forward, holding out his left hand.

"Ivy, please tell me what on earth is—"

The old man broke off as Hunzu's fingers touched his face, making both of them jump. Hunzu pulled his hand back as if he'd been stung, then gritted his teeth and reached forward again.

This time, Larch caught Hunzu's hand; Ivy could see the muscles twitching under the old man's mottled skin as he gripped the trow's arm. Slowly, Larch raised Hunzu's hand to his own face. Hunzu turned pale, as though he were only keeping himself from pulling away by a substantial effort of will. Slowly, Hunzu lowered the phone, looking directly into the old man's rheumy, red-rimmed eyes.

"Hello, there," said Larch softly.

A strange buzzing seemed to flicker at the edges of Ivy's awareness, and Ivy wondered if this was the trow's veil—shaking the very air in its efforts to keep the two of them from seeing each other.

"He isn't a trow," Hunzu said finally, though he didn't

remove his hand. "Maybe he's a—a sport. Maybe he's—Look, I don't know what he is, and I don't think the veil does, either. But he shouldn't be here. This isn't any business of his."

Hunzu dropped his hand, and Larch stumbled backwards, a brittle sound escaping his lips that might have been a sob, or a laugh, or something else altogether. Hunzu let him go, watching the old man through the camera with a bleak expression on his face.

"Should we kill him?" Demi asked, her voice thready and tight.

Ivy turned to her flatmate, aghast.

Demi was peering over Hunzu's shoulder, staring dispassionately as the man on the screen wiped at his eyes with the backs of his gloved hands. More troubling, none of the others were objecting. As though they didn't care. As though they might consider killing Larch as casually as Ambrose had suggested poisoning Ivy, back at the Liberties.

"Of course not!" Ivy hissed.

"Is this the Enemy?" Demi asked, looking between Ambrose and Hunzu.

It couldn't be. Hunzu said the Enemy looked like a trow, but it couldn't be Uncle Patrick. With his blotched face and balding head, he hardly even looked like what he was. Patrick might be a liar, and a horrible person, but he wasn't a murderer. He couldn't have killed all those innocent people, through all those hundreds of years. . . .

"I don't know," said Hunzu, biting his lip. "If he is—"

"If he is, then it's very clear what happens next," said Ambrose tightly.

"He's not what you think," said Ivy, grabbing Ambrose's sleeve. "He's only here because I asked him to come!"

They weren't listening. The woman beside Ambrose—the one Demi had called Isabelle—was pulling something out of her pocket, the weak sunlight glancing off the metal of the barrel. She undid a lever at the top of the pistol, dropping a bullet into the firing chamber with an audible click.

Larch was only here because of Ivy—because Ivy tracked him down, and refused to leave, and waved his own letter in his face. Which meant if they killed him, it would be Ivy's fault he was dead.

"Stop it," Ivy shouted, throwing herself between Isabelle and Larch. "Demi, it isn't him! You're not even going to wait for the Enemy, are you? You're just going to become murderers yourselves!"

Now there were two Year Kings, and the Enemy that killed them would be here soon. Ivy didn't have the slightest idea what that meant. Maybe no one did. Would the Enemy recognize Larch as a victim that eluded it? Or would it ignore Larch, the same way it had done ever since he disappeared?

"She's right, Isabelle," said Demi, giving the woman a sharp look.

"Why?" Isabelle shot back, not raising the pistol, but not lowering it either. "We don't even know what it is—"

"He's the same thing I am," Demi said fiercely, something in her voice that sounded almost like pity, or perhaps like hope. "He's a Year King."

"Ivy, is he talking again?" Hunzu asked, glancing between Ivy and Ivy's phone, still in his hand.

Trying not to take her eyes off Isabelle, Ivy glanced back to Larch, who did seem to be mumbling something, so softly that Ivy could barely hear it.

"Is there a speaker on this thing?" Demi asked.

"Maybe in video mode," Hunzu replied, jabbing at the screen.

Brushing past Ivy, Larch took a few steps further into the clearing, muttering, and rubbing at his eyes as if he still thought it might help. Isabelle was craning her neck to see Hunzu's screen, her pistol still pointed at the ground.

Which was something of a relief until Ivy remembered that the Enemy, when he came, would have no such compunctions.

"I am the King of the trows," Larch whispered. He said it again, louder; the speaker on Ivy's phone echoed it a moment later. "I am the king of the trows. I am the king of the trows!"

"Ivy," said Hunzu, in the gentlest voice she'd ever heard him use. "This man isn't a trow."

"Then why can't anybody see him?" Ivy demanded. "He can turn people invisible—how could he do that if he isn't a trow? And how would he know about all *this*?" And Ivy pulled the yellowed letter from her coat.

Hunzu grabbed it, nearly dropping Ivy's phone as he opened the envelope, riffling through the sheets of paper. He scanned the first few lines intently, then shoved the pages roughly into his coat.

Then Hunzu did a strange thing. He stepped forward into the clearing, and dropped to one knee, clasping his fist over his heart. "Life to the King of the Trows!" he shouted.

Slowly, Ambrose sank to his knees beside him. "Life to the King of the Trows."

Demi knelt, followed a moment later by Isabelle. "Life to the King of the Trows," Demi said; the woman echoed it a moment later.

Ivy knelt as well. "Life to the King of the Trows!" she shouted.

Larch turned around, a stunned look on his face, and for a moment Ivy didn't know why.

He couldn't hear *them*. But he could hear her.

"They said it," he murmured, his eyes fever-bright.

Slowly, the old man drew himself up, straightening his collar and the tails of his coat.

"I am the King of the Trows," he shouted. "Protector of those in exile, defender against the scourges of time, willing agent of the Valoi and preserver of the memory of Valiard. I claim my right to the throne, and I shall defend it by word and deed, through all trials, and against all comers!"

Larch held out his hand, palm up, causing Ambrose, watching through the phone, to scurry backwards to get out of his way.

"If your friend is anything of a traditionalist, she'll have the crown," he said to Ivy. "I think I should rather like it back, if you please."

"He's asking for the crown," Ivy said, and Demi nodded. She rose to her feet, pulling the circlet off of her head, turning it about in her hands for a long moment.

Ivy made a move to take it, and Demi stopped her. "Where is he?" she asked.

Ivy pointed and slowly, Demi stepped forward, reaching out with her free hand, her eyes narrowed to slits. She touched Larch's arm, and the old man jumped. Demi's gaze sharpened, and she reached out with both hands, tugging off his woolen cap as she slipped the circlet onto his liver-spotted head. Larch seemed to stagger under the weight of it, reaching up to keep it from falling, or perhaps to see if it was really there at all.

He looked hardly anything like a king, in his mud-splattered tailcoat, with the shabby crown sitting crookedly over his ears. But there was something in his red rheumy eyes, bright and searching and determined. For the briefest moment, Ivy remembered an old portrait in her school books of the English King George V, hard eyes staring out from a wrinkled, bewhiskered face.

Was Larch the king now? And if he was, would the Enemy agree?

Demi hadn't stepped back, but was running her ungloved

fingers down the old man's neck and shoulders. She ran her hands along the seam of his coat, down the sleeves, grasping at his fingers. Larch was breathing hard again; they were close enough that Demi's braid was nearly touching his shoulder.

"Demi," Ambrose said in a tight voice. He was looking at his watch again, staring it as though if he gave it enough attention, he might slow the incessant creeping of the hands across the dial.

Demi jumped back, taking a hesitant step toward Ambrose before checking herself. She backed away from the bench, hands outstretched as though to warn away anyone from coming close. Her breath was loud in the sudden silence.

Ivy began to take a step forward; Hunzu stopped her, his hand heavy on her shoulder. He was still holding Ivy's phone, watching Larch through the screen as the old man adjusted his iron crown, and glanced at his watch.

Somewhere far up the hill, a horse whinnied, a long, raucous bellow that carried easily in the still morning air, and Ivy remembered the hoof prints in her back garden. The hard and unrelenting evidence of terrible and inexplicable things. Like the terrible and inexplicable thing about to happen here.

"How did you do it?" Hunzu asked into the air, a desperate intensity coloring his voice. "Ask him, Ivy! If he escaped the Enemy once, he can do it again. We can learn to do it every time. Larch! Larch, it doesn't have to be like this! Ivy, tell him!"

"Larch—" Ivy began.

"Is Peregrine here?" he asked, interrupting her.

Before she could stop herself, Ivy glanced at the tree at the corner of the clearing—no different from any of the others, save for the small stone at its foot. Somewhere in the grove, prematurely, was Larch's own. And somewhere among the others...

Peregrine had been dead for longer than Ivy had been alive.

Something else Larch had run from. Some other bad thing he didn't want to know.

Out of the corner of her eye, Ivy saw Hunzu shake his head. "She's—"

The word stuck in Ivy's throat. "She's not here," she said instead.

Larch nodded, but he was still staring across the clearing as though he were looking for her anyway. Or as if he knew he could see her better in his memory than he ever could with his eyes.

"Probably for the best," he said. "She was always rubbish with goodbyes."

"Larch!" Hunzu shouted again, as though he could breach the veil by volume alone. "Ambrose, get Carillon, maybe she'll talk to him—"

"Hunzu, there isn't time—"

But Larch was speaking again, tapping at his watch as though he suspected it wasn't giving the correct time.

"Are you listening?" he asked the air. "You like to watch sometimes, don't you?"

Ivy felt a shiver like ice along her spine. She didn't think Larch was talking to the trows. Or to her.

For the first time, Ivy felt a sick certainty that very soon, someone she cared about was going to die. And it was all happening right in front of her.

"Someone went to a great deal of trouble to spare me once," Larch continued, the speaker on Ivy's phone still echoing his words. "Will you do it again? What was it that stayed your hand? Was it a bargain? A collaborator? Who—"

There was a man standing in the shadow of the apple tree, hooded, and a light was in his hand.

He didn't appear. There was no sound, nor light, nor smoke. It was as though the figure had been standing among them for a very long time, and they had only just noticed he was there. The clothing he wore covered him darkly from head to toe, like a hooded jumpsuit, revealing only a face, plain and emotionless, turning to Larch, cocking his head almost like a bird—

Beside her, Ivy saw Isabelle raise her pistol.

"You," Larch hissed at the same moment, bringing up his revolver and sighting along the barrel.

He never completed the motion. Light was suddenly across his skin, and the revolver fell from his hands, gleaming with reflected fire. Ivy's hands went to her mouth, then she pressed her fists to her ears, because he'd started screaming. Even the rapid-fire shots from Isabelle's pistol couldn't quite drown out the sound.

The whole grove went hot, sickly and searing, like a lightning-split sky. In the middle, a white-hot column of flame that might have been mistaken for a bonfire, were it not for the outstretched hands.

He didn't scream for very long. The crackling of the fire lasted for some seconds afterwards.

Demi was beside her a moment later, holding onto Ivy and turning her face away, as though she might still hide her friend from the worst of it. But Ivy had already seen enough. She didn't know if the worst part was the look on Larch's face when the flames covered him, or the empty stillness on the Enemy's face as he'd done it. Behind her, Ivy could hear Ambrose quietly being sick. It wasn't until Ivy finally pulled away that she realized Demi was shaking, and might have thrown her arms around Ivy just to keep from falling over.

Hunzu was the only one who'd dared come any closer, standing as close to the pyre as the heat would allow.

"Why now?" shouted Hunzu in a loud voice, dancing back

and forth in a futile attempt to catch the Enemy's eye. "Why now, but not in 'thirty-six? What changed?"

The figure in black made no answer, merely inclined its head toward the dying flames. And Ivy must have blinked, for when she looked again, the man under the apple tree was gone. A moment later, the flames were gone as well, their yellow tongues smothered and dead. In the place where Larch had been standing, a bleak scorch mark had burnt through the grass and a few inches into the earth below. The wind was already beginning to scatter the thin pile of ash on top of it.

It's so very little, thought Ivy. She had the strangest thought that someone ought to hold onto the ash, gather it and bottle it up properly in an urn. Some little thing to remember him by. But no one moved, and the little pile of ashes was already growing smaller and smaller. Something gleamed from out of the pile; Ivy realized with a start that it was the crown.

The crown remained, but not the king who wore it. Ivy glanced at Demi, standing with her arms wrapped around herself as though she were shivering. Demi was still here. The Enemy had come, and it hadn't killed her. She'd won.

And so had Ivy—she'd tried to save Demi, and she'd done it.

The dwindling pile of ash didn't look like victory. It only looked like Ivy'd helped murder someone else instead.

Ivy walked a few steps toward the apple tree, giving a wide berth to the mark in the grass. The figure, the man with the light in his hand, would have been standing just *here*. There wasn't so much as a bent blade of grass to show that anything had ever been there. Only the chipped wood in the apple tree a few yards away, apparently the target of Isabelle's ineffectual bullets. There was only a smoldering scar on the grass, and a foul smell in the wind, to show that anything had happened here at all.

"I'm going up to the house," said Hunzu. His voice seemed

loud in the silence that had fallen over the clearing. "Carillon. Better if someone. . . Before she hears any rumors," he added, glancing uneasily at the pile of ash.

Rumors like Larch not dying in 1936. Rumors that he'd survived the Enemy once—only to be killed by it decades later.

Ambrose merely nodded, still looking pale. Demi, staring at the pile of ash, didn't seem to hear him at all.

For a moment, Ivy had the strangest thought that perhaps she ought to stop Hunzu from going. Perhaps it would be better not to say anything. Not to Carillon, or anyone else. Pretend Larch really had died in 1936. Would his mother want to know any differently?

Victoria won't want to know he's dead, Ivy told herself, wondering whether she wasn't simply giving herself an excuse not to mention any of this to her mother.

Hunzu pulled his hat from the pocket of his coat and jammed it low over his ears. The trow glanced at Demi, opened his mouth as though he were about to say something else, then just as quickly closed it again. He pulled the hat off and shoved it back into his pocket, as though he'd forgotten he'd just put it on. Slowly, he shuffled away from the clearing and the little pile of ash that none of them seemed able to look away from.

As he passed her, Ivy nearly took his hand, only snatching her fingers back at the very last second. For a moment, she'd forgotten what he was. She couldn't touch him. Not now and not ever. Even if maybe she wanted to.

Hunzu merely glanced sadly at her as he walked out of the clearing, biting at his lip as though he'd seen the gesture, and guessed at the impulse behind it. Though why that should make him look even more troubled than before, Ivy didn't know.

As Hunzu disappeared among the trees, Demi stepped forward, and knelt by the pile of ash. She prodded it cautiously with one finger, hooking the edge of the crown and pulling it free, apparently finding it cool enough to handle. She stood, pulling a handkerchief from her pocket, brushing the ash off the crown with a strangely detached look on her face.

Ivy came closer, as Demi tucked the handkerchief in her coat and turned the crown over in her hands, staring at the ruined diadem as though she were looking for something hidden in its depths.

"Whose is it now?" she asked. It had been Larch's, maybe for three minutes or maybe for seventy years.

"It doesn't belong to anyone," said Ambrose faintly, coming up beside them. "Not until next month. They'll call another lottery."

Demi looked at him, and for a moment, Ivy saw something hard in her eyes, the same thing she'd thought she'd seen in the painting of the old English king. And in Larch's, in the minutes before he burned.

"No, they won't," said Demi. Her hands, holding the crown, were shaking, but her voice was firm. "There won't be another lottery. It was mine before, and it's still mine now."

"But why—" Ivy started.

"Because this changes things!" Demi said fiercely.

Ambrose only looked between the blackened crown and the equally dark scorch make on the grass. "Someone else died instead of you—*this* time," Ambrose said bleakly. "How does that change anything?"

"I don't know," Demi said, her eyes beginning to tear up as she looked between Ambrose and Ivy. "Will you help me find out?"

"Yes," said Ivy, and wordlessly, Ambrose nodded, and threw his arms around Demi. All three of them were crying, and a flutter like wings was beating in Ivy's ears. Blinking hard, Ivy tried to smile anyway. Demi was alive, and that was reason enough to be happy. Demi was alive; that meant Ivy'd won. But even as she forced a grin across her face, Ivy couldn't quell the feeling, somewhere in the pit of her stomach, that she'd done no such thing. She hadn't won; she'd merely reset the counter. And Uncle Patrick had died so she could do it.

All so that somewhere, in whatever unknown place the Enemy had vanished to, its unfathomable countdown to murder could start all over again. In one year, the Enemy would be back to kill Demi.

Which meant Ivy had a whole year to find it and kill it first.

ACKNOWLEDGMENTS

Two works of real-world ethnography provided insight into the trows and their world: *Meeting the Other Crowd: The Fairy Stories of Hidden Ireland* by Eddie Lenihan and Carolyn Eve Green, and *Bury Me Standing: The Gypsies and Their Journey*, by Isabel Fonseca. The folk stories of Shetand were also a source of some of the trows' history and terminology—including the word 'trow' itself. Christopher Chabris and Daniel Simons' experiments on inattentional blindness (some of which Hunzu references in Chapter 5) provided a framework for how the trows' veil actually works. Anyone curious about real-world examples of ignoring gorillas may wish to read their book, *The Invisible Gorilla*, or visit their website *www.theinvisiblegorilla.com*.

Thanks to brave beta-readers Chloe Donaldson, Marion Glaser, Kaelyn Considine, and Jessica Ryles for their feedback and comments. Thanks to the Seward Writer's Circle for camaraderie and support. Thanks to Rachael Dugas of Talcott Notch Literary Services for her thoughtful critique of the opening chapter. Big thanks to Colin and Eric of Parvus Press, for believing in this book's potential, and for still wanting to work with me even when I told them I could only answer email one day a week. Also to Colin for suggesting what to do with Chapter 12. Thanks to John Adamus for insightful editorial help and suggestions. Thanks to Lovely Creatures Studio for the cover design for the first edition. This book is vastly improved thanks to all of your efforts.

Thanks to Dan, Mark, Penny and the Contemporary Youth Arts Company of Charleston, West Virginia for giving me my first glimpses at how good art comes into being. To Trish for sharing music. To Heather Gallagher and Killian Sump for their generous contributions to the Fictional Character Name Donation Program. To Scotty and the staff of the Wine Shop for desperately trying to bring me up to speed on pop culture every Christmas. To Ryan Collins of Paddler's Realm, for being a friend and mentor both on and off the water. To Captain Keith and the crew of the *Wilderness Discoverer,* for many shared adventures. To the Rathlin Island community, for a summer in the Kinramer Camping Barn.

To my extended family in West Virginia and Alaska—Gina, Donald, Emily, and my grandmother Mary; also Kate, Mike, Sarah, Jolie, Dan, Marion, Jesse, Everett and Violet, and Ben, Rebecca, Kristin and Tyler. Opal and Nova, you are probably the reason why Ivy has twin step-brothers. To the staff of Alaska Wildland Adventures and Kenai Fjords Glacier Lodge, for being my home for five years and because I *am* rubbish with goodbyes.

A final thanks to the staff and writing community of National Novel Writing Month. Without their arbitrary deadlines and enthusiastic support, this thing you are holding would have turned out very differently. Check them out—you, too, can accomplish more than you think you can.

Additional acknowledgements for the third edition: .

Thanks to Labyrinth Room beta readers Teresa, Mike, and Tim, for sticking with me and giving feedback. Everything I write is better because of folks who've taken the time to help, edit, and critique. To Alaskan coffee houses 13 Ravens and Resurrect Art, for everything you do for Seward's arts community, and for Seward in general. If you're in the area, stop by for a drink.

Thanks to Kaitlynn Jolley for bringing Ivy to life through the amazing cover design for this edition. Thanks to artist extraordinaire Jessica Lynn Henry for creating the lovely knotwork designs at the head of each chapter and at the section breaks. Thanks to the friends and fellow wordsmiths of the Alaska Writer's Guild, the Surrey International Writers' Conference, and 49 Writers.

Cheers to the crew of the *Safari Endeavor*, for three weeks of doing edits after hours in the ship's linen locker to meet my deadline for the original publication. To Liberty Miller for publishing advice. To Mary Robinette Kowal and Steven Salpeter for taking time out of a convention to give a complete stranger advice on rights reversion. To Rekka for assistance with contracts, and because a little bird told me you did a lot of de facto copyediting for the first edition with Parvus.

Last and always to Colin, for teaching me that reliability is really what matters most. Publishing business aside, you are the best close reader this book could have asked for. You still should have taken me up on my offer to change Ivy's boyfriend's name when you had the chance.

COMING SOON...

Dartry wasn't even a seedy neighborhood. Strange things were not supposed to happen here: that was precisely why Ivy had moved in. It was terribly impolite of the strange things to have followed her.

Ivy's adventures continue in *Changeling*.

Follow Mareth on Twitter, Amazon, or Goodreads for news about the sequel.

ABOUT THE AUTHOR

Mareth Griffith bounces between the Pacific Northwest coast and various warmer locations. She mostly lives in Seward, Alaska, and assures you winters there aren't as bad as you think.

When she's not writing, she works as a naturalist and wilderness guide, leading adventurous souls on epic quests to seek out glaciers, bears, and whales in the wilds of coastal Alaska. She's also lived and worked in Scotland, Mexico, New Zealand, and Northern Ireland—where her nearest neighbors included two thousand puffins and the ghost of a spectral black horse.

Originally from West Virginia, Mareth attended Smith College in Massachusetts, studying music and theatre. Mareth plays classical violin well and rhythm guitar badly.

You can follow Mareth on Twitter: @magpiemareth

THIS PAGE INTENTIONALLY LEFT BLANK AS PART
OF A VAST TROW CONSPIRACY...